AGGIE IN SPACE

R. C. Thom

Aggie In Space

Library of Congress registration number, effective Dec. 5, 2019
TXu 2-175-307

ISBN for Print 978-1-7321459-8-6
ISBN for E-book 978-1-7321498-9-3

Copy Editor: Lisa Cross
Cover art: Rachel C. Thompson
Book design: Gayle F. Hendricks
Line editing and proofreading: Pattie Giordani

For editing services contact Pattie Giordani
at pattiegiordani@gmail.com

Contact R.C. Thom at

humanrights4all@aol.com

RCThom.com

E-book price is $3.99

Print book is $12.95

Books by R.C.Thom

SOUL HARVEST
an Aggie Piper Novel
print ISBN 978-1-7321459-1-7
e-book ISBN 978-1-7321459-0-0

AGGIE IN ORBIT
an Aggie Piper Novel
print ISBN 978-1-7321459-1-7
e-book ISBN 978-1-7321459-0-0

DRAGON FIRE
print ISBN 978-1-7321459-2-4
e-book ISBN 978-1-7321459-3-1

STALKING KILGORE TROUT
print ISBN 978-1-7321459-4-8
e-book ISBN 978-1-7321459-5-5

Coming soon:
BOOK OF ANSWERS
ANTHOLOGY TWO

Previously in *Aggie in Orbit* ...

Aggie Piper, barely eighteen, managed to escape the Military Industrial Complex's attack on her and her alien mothership. Aggie must leave the solar system before the next attack, but there is a problem: Starship Mother won't leave without an Earthling crew and Aggie is obligated to provide them. Meanwhile, everything on Earth is changing for the worst and all of her alliances are shattered. Aggie must make hard choices to survive but first she needs get out of her own way.

PRELUDE

General Tommy Brinks entered his Pentagon office and dropped his case and newspaper on the desk. He had his metaphorical hands full, but it was more a juggling act. He had a dozen plans in motion. The highest authority, Majestic Twelve, thought he was their man. He wasn't. The Joint Chiefs of Staff thought he was under their control. Hardly. The CIA and NSA knew their place. Each entity that "used him" had their agendas but Brinks had his own ideas of how alien disclosure will play out. The others didn't know everything he had in mind. He'd make the war he wanted happen. Only he had balls enough. World hegemony was flatly necessary and long overdue but what the aliens required wasn't in his plan. Under his control, pooling resources, the aliens wouldn't stand a chance. Why rule the world alone when you can rule the galaxy? Congress was too weak, the former president too kind, the judges on too many payrolls and the people too stupid to know what was good for America and Earth.

The coup against President Jane Albright was still in play and the population hadn't figured out he was behind it … yet. The CIA did what he asked. *She's as good as dead.* Once operations discover where she is, she's finished. The front page headline in the New York Register said, *"President Albright, Traitor or Crook?"* The propaganda machine spun, but too slow for General Brinks.

Aggie Piper had her own gristmill. His attempts at shutting off the internet were overridden. He made a note to redouble internet propaganda. Piper's subversive blogs kept coming after the Navy trashed Haiti. The Navy blew up half the island with Piper and her mothership on it. But where was the wreckage? That was the first clue. Piper must be alive. Who else could commandeer the internet? Who else has access to advance alien technology? Poor dead Sanderson was worried about the UN, but Brinks didn't care about trade deals. Piper was the bigger problem. Her influence subverted his power. She had to die.

It was early morning inside the Pentagon. His secretary wasn't in the outer office yet, thus his inner office double doors were left open. The NSA tech man he was expecting rapped on the door's frame. Brinks waved him inside and started electronic countermeasures.

"This better be good news," Brinks said as the NSA rep shut the doors.

The man turned and stiffened. "Yes sir. It's confirmed. Al Branford, using a watch phone, called Aggie Piper last night." The man handed a transcript over. "Branford's call was picked up by an alien relay satellite. We traced it, there's a string of them. Piper is alive and we think the ship is orbiting Mars. Branford is still in Washington. Do we pick him up?"

"No, I have a better idea. What else. Any luck tracking down the blog server?"

"Not yet sir, but we're closing on Melisa Van Ness."

"Fine, dismissed."

The man made a quick exit. Once out of view Brinks picked up the phone. He had a direct line to Space Fleet Command. The duty officer in Guantanamo Bay picked up. The man in charge wasn't there. Brinks felt heat building under his collar.

"Tell Artie to outfit two ships for distance. Whatever it takes to get to Mars. I want it yesterday. Have him call when he gets his lazy ass out of bed."

Brinks hung up. It was time to address another loose end. The Chiefs won't like it, too bad. They think Branford and his research operations are still valuable, but Brinks got all he could out of Branford Industries. Piper's grandfather wasn't going to provide the star drive. Brinks didn't have the evidence until now. Branford won't do what's needed to take Piper's starship. He'd run a blockade. Bradford's recorded warning call to Piper proved that America's top defense contractor turned traitor.

General Brinks pressed the hot key for his CIA contact. "Move against Branford, do it now."

"We need time to set it up."

"Make it fast. This time don't screw up. Your move on Albright was half-assed." Brinks hung up and leaned back in his chair.

The internet was alive with debates about President Albright. Piper's alien equipment hacked that CIA operation and the Van Ness girl spilled it all over the net. The CIA's murder film wasn't done right, wasn't good enough. Too obviously faked. The President wasn't the shooter but how and why did Albright escape? How long before the people riot? It didn't matter. More reasons to use force against the population was good. Dictators in waiting must use force. Force sets the right tone. He made a note to have the media jack up anti-Albright propaganda.

"Keep it simple." Brinks reminded himself. First things first. With a hard push he might have Albright and Piper handled before attacking the alien's moon base. Brinks didn't believe in luck. Power was his only belief. Too many in power didn't know how to use it. He did.

"All for the good and glory of America."

That reminded him, he had an appointment with the explosives expert. Brinks took up his briefcase, marched forward and pushed his secretary out of the way as she arrived. She hit the deck. He exited without addressing her. Men of action make no apologies.

ONE

Aggie in Bed

Aggie woke up, she had to pee. She felt pissy and it had nothing to do with too much water before bed. Aggie waited all through high school, no boys, girls or drugs. She saved herself for college and now college wasn't going to happen. So, OK, finally after talking about it with Mel for two weeks they finally decided it was time to do it like real gown ups, barring that doing it with another girl might not technically be losing your virginity. Last night was it, go time, the big event and it was a total flop.

It was ink-dark in Aggie's room. Starship Mother had made her room exactly like her old home on the outskirts of Key West. Her bedroom was made from a shipping container that had washed up after a hurricane. Dad, he insisted every-one call him Po-boy, had attached that big metal box to the old bait and tackle shop in which her family were squatters. Back then she didn't know her estranged Grandpa Branford actually owned the place which was why the cops never came around and evicted them. It helped that the place was on the end of a dead-end road and surrounded by mangrove swamps and wild chickens. Mark's Marina was on the other side of Giger Avenue so at least she didn't have to go far for work.

The room was the same right down to the recycled oak pallet planks that Po-boy used to line her walls. As she lay there in bed, she smelled old oak. But Mother didn't get everything right. The smell of the sea and dead fish wasn't there. No rotting seaweed and chicken crap. No smell of Mom's pot or Dad's oily boat motor junk. No sounds of nature. No sound of boats firing up across the mudflats over at Bixby's. The only sound was Melisa snoring. You'd think a starship would sound like something.

It still pissed her off that Mother got inside her head and made this room right out of Aggie's own memories without asking. What right did a starship have to invade her brain like that? OK, Mother didn't mean any harm but it was still creepy. Praytis should have said something.

Mel stirred and snorted. *Dang, that girl sleeps like a truck driver.* Wide awake, Aggie swing her legs off the bed. Her feet hit the floor with a slap. She wasn't in the Keys anymore, no loose sand under her feet. The deck was smooth and cold and made from flat metal instead of painted plywood. There was always sand, sand got into everything everywhere. She never noticed it then but now it was just another thing missing from her life: *stupid sand.*

Aggie should have felt homesick but she was more just mad. Mad because they tried to kill her. Mad she can't ever go back home because the federal government would shoot her on sight. Mad that the propagandists on Earth made her look like the world's biggest butthead when *she* was the one who saved their stupid lives.

Aggie found the door no problem, the little galley kitchen was beyond and the light over the stove was on like always, but the bathroom door was now on the wall facing Mom's bedroom. Sky Flower's bedroom should have been on the other side but it wasn't. The other door, the kitchen's exit, now led into one of the ship's corridors and not the bait shack's old living room. But the bathroom looked the same. Ugly green tile and a toilet old enough to have been used by Hemmingway. After flushing Aggie wondered if it shoots out into Mars' atmosphere, where it'll become life in a billion years or if they'd be boiling pasta in it later? Maybe that's how the entire universe got seeded with humans. No, spaceships were good at recycling. Mom would approve.

Aggie tripped over Mel's boots but made it back into bed unharmed. Mel's Earthside bedroom was a mess, she never put anything away. Why should it be any different while orbiting Mars?

Grandpa had called last night. That meant the government knows where they are. Aggie had a big day ahead. She had to figure out how to get out of dodge before the sheriff came calling. Aggie closed her eyes and tried to sleep — she managed to doze off for a little while but as usual, her brain kelp spinning.

Aggie lay there half-asleep playing yesterday over in her head. Ship's time was coordinated with Key West time. One eye opened and read the alarm clock. It was 6 a.m. here and back home, home on Earth. Weird, no rooters waking her up as usual. What was weirder, she woke up early on her own without Mom making her get up. If this was adulthood, so far growing up was crap. *I'm due at work.* Aggie bolted upright. No, she didn't have to go to work, Mark's Maria was a million miles away. This isn't a dream. This is a real spaceship.

She swung her legs and sat on the bed's edge careful not to wake Melisa. *Maybe I still got to pee.* Aggie made to the bathroom and back while Mel snored. No reason to get up. Aggie laid back.

Aggie, Sanderson, Mel and Praytis were safe, kind of, not really. In the two weeks since they escaped Earth after the attack on them in Haiti, she knew this peace couldn't last especially since Grandpa called and told her to take off for real, as in, get out of the solar system and fast. What was that about? Did the military know where they were before he called? Sanderson practically guaranteed it. But Aggie wasn't ready to deal with it.

Starship Mother had to have an Earthling crew and won't take no for an answer. So, Mother was planted orbiting Mars and Aggie was on the hook for a crew. She didn't have any good ideas on how to get them. What made her feel crappier, was once Mother had a roster, the ship would disappear forever.

Everything she knew and loved left behind and that hurt but Aggie didn't want to leave Mother either. Since Mother got inside her head, Aggie didn't know if that desire for space was planted or natural. The idea that somebody got inside her thoughts was a big freak out. What right did Mother have? Aggie's emotions were a mess. Last night in bed with Mel didn't help improve Aggie's mood. Bubbling up through it all was the realization she owed Mother big time. How do you pay back someone that saved your life?

Aggie was in no hurry to start a crew although Sanderson insisted time was short. The ship had to go before the Feds attacked again. Aggie didn't want to leave Earth but if her parents and Grandpa Branford came … but they were impossible to reach. Aggie was seriously leaning toward tapping out and going home for good. She'd have to give up the fleet, then maybe the butthead Feds would leave her alone. *Yeah right.* All this raced around inside while Melisa snored like a pug with a snot-stuffed snout.

She's worse than Dad.

This whole thing wasn't fair. Aggie was the captain but Mother had her own ideas. If Mother didn't need a captain why stay? *Because she needs help. She saved me. I ow her.* Every oligarch in the Military Industrial Complex was going hard after Mother and Mother was stuck here. Aggie wanted to bail, forget the whole thing. Maybe she could hide in Tibet or something. *Just burry myself like a sand flea.*

Aggie slapped her forehead. "I'm responsible. It's on me. Make it right then I'll go home." *Barely eighteen and the weight of the universe is squeezing me like an overripe puss nugget. I'm ready to pop, way over my head.* "One more stressor and I'm toast."

"Mmmm." Mel said, still asleep.

A new thought came on like a storm and Aggie rolled off the bed. Her feet dragged the sheets off the bed. Mel snorted and twisted around. Neither one got much sleep last night. Mel sat up; her oversized black T-shirt, and black hair made Mel's pale face stick out in the dark like a lit channel marker.

Mel put on lamp. Aggie was naked and why not? She was never modest before. She and Mel had many sleep-overs since second grade. Aggie and family were regulars at the nude beach. Hippie dippy Earth Priestess Mom hardly keep her clothes on at home. Funny how Mel covered up.

Last night's attempt at making love didn't go well. Aggie finally decided, after a lot of false starts, that it was time to try friends with benefits. Aggie was clueless but Mel had been with girls before. Aggie looked forward to breaking the ice, release the tension but instead she got upsets and new stress. Mel didn't let Aggie touch her but did all the touching. Mel took charge like a man. Aggie never felt another girl's breasts before. She was nervous about it but still dying to try. Aggie's boobs were tiny. Mel had nice ones. *But no, I didn't even get to see them.*

"Ship, bring up the lights slow." The clock still said 6 a.m. Aggie regretted Mother setting up ship's time to Key West. If it was more like eight, she'd feel better about getting up.

"Dude, you didn't sleep much either?" Mel said. "You got eye bags."

"Sleep's overrated. I was thinking, stuff like … " Aggie trailed off, she wasn't ready to talk about wanting to bail. She thought a lot about how Mother takes liberties with your brain. Aggie woke pissed at Mother. OK, she was pissed at everything. She never asked to be responsible for an alien space fleet. Her dream of going to school got totally trashed.

When I get the crew together, I'll give the ship to Sanderson and Praytis.

"I don't have to leave forever, right? I don't have to be captain: It's not official anyway."

"Dude, you're losing it." Mel put a hand on Aggie's shoulder. "You OK?"

Aggie wrenched her body away. "No, not really."

"I'm not either," Mel said.

"Crew's got to be wired, right." Aggie said. "No way. Mother's not reprograming me."

"It doesn't work like that. All it does is load info; you learn — "

"It's a big world, there must someplace we can hide. We'll all go home, what do you think?" Aggie casually touched one of Mel's breasts and Mel reacted like she was stung by a bee.

"Dude, you're not hearing me!" Mel moved back pushing the blanket off the bed. She sat up straight, took a big breath. "I have to tell something … last night."

"You woke up butch." Aggie said, feeling hurt. Mel wasn't listening. "What's so important?"

"I'm eighteen today. I can do what I want … " Mel sounded grumpy. "Thanks for remembering."

"Sorry I forgot — " Aggie slapped herself on the forehead.

"Dude, that's not it. Something I never told you. Something I've been waiting for, for a long time … I have to tell you. I never told anyone. I'm legal now, my parents can't stop me."

"What from being lesbian, don't you think it's too late? Get real Mel."

"I'm trying. I'm not, yeah I like girls, boys like girls." Mel kicked off the rest of the blanket. Her bare feet slapped the deck hard. "I'm trans Aggie, don't you get it? I'm a dude."

"No way!"

"Way, that's why I had a gym excuse, it's why I always dress to hide my body. It's why I don't want you to touch me. I hate my body. I can't believe you never figure it out."

"That's great, just great. I get my act together and you jump into a black hole. All this time you lied to me. Crap!"

"Keeping quiet isn't a lie. Don't you get it? You wanted me because you sensed it. All you talk about is Jon, Jon, Jon. Maybe you aren't bi Aggie. Ever think of that?"

"Screw you! I know who I am."

Aggie ran to the door, it slid open just in time to prevent her from smashing her face. Her AI probe, Buddy was there waiting like a lonely beach ball. It spun around doing its happy dance.

"At least I can trust you." Buddy was a knee-high metallic ball with the personality of a Labrador, but to Aggie he was simply 'man's best friend'. Right then it felt like Buddy was only one she had. "Come on Buddy. Let's get out of here."

Aggie stomped along the gangway toward the bridge with Buddy rolling after her. Maybe a smashed face would feel real. *How can a robot ball be a dog?* Nothing was real anymore. Grandpa turned out to be an alien reverse engineering defense contractor. Hippie Earth Priestess Mom's a lawyer now. OK Sky Flower graduated law school but she never did legal crap. And Creole fisherman Dad's writing a book. She imagined his book cover. *Po-boy Piper, what kind of name is that for an author?* Everything changed, everything was upside down, everything sucked, no hope of going to college and the one solid, dependable person in her life was all smoke and mirrors. Aggie almost kicked the little gray alien bio-bot as it passed her going the other way. It was then she realized she was going the wrong way and she was naked besides.

The damn ship was two thousand feet long and twelve stories high, there should be arrows, signs, some way to know where you are. *Oh yeah, if you wear a control belt it tells you everything.* Goose bumps sprang up on her bear arms.

"I'm cold. Where the hell's the bridge!" Green arrows lit in the floor. "Great just great."

She stopped at a utility closet because the light over it lit when she said, 'I'm cold.' Aggie took out an ugly green jumpsuit and put it on. The ship read her mind again. She felt cold and the ship provided and it didn't need her brain tuned by ram-ed to get the message. Mother's local AIs didn't need Aggie's control belt or command chair to get the message.

"What about privacy?" Aggie said. Buddy rubbed against her leg and blinked his lights like he was trying to tell her to chill out and accept it. "No way. Not letting alien computers get inside me. I want off, this is too weird. I need a break."

Aggie took a break when she was overwhelmed. Mom taught her meditation and other ways to calm down and it mostly worked. She usually went to the beach or some other nice, quiet place to meditate. Mark had his methods, too. She learned other meditative forms from his karate classes. Hitting Mark's heavy bag would've helped but Mother didn't have one. It was a long walk to the bridge and it gave her time to cool down but she still wasn't thinking straight. The only thing that flew out of her spinning mind was the idea that going back to Earth was stupid. There was nothing there for her, she'd never have a normal life but she wanted to go home anyway. The bridge door slid open and she stopped halfway inside. Overnight Mother had remodeled it … again.

"All I said was I never got to see Hawaii. I didn't tell you to change anything. Crap on a cracker."

Sarah, four or five years old in appearance, said. "Mother wants happy." She was into her coloring book and didn't look up.

The biological robot's pilot station was still a tiny woven reed and grass hut. Aggie had Mother make it because the grays were too creepy and she didn't want to see them. Aggie was used to them now. Why didn't those little creatures chew on their grass hut? Weren't they made out of cow parts? Mel's communications station was the same, just like her desk back home. But Aggie's Captain Kirk chair had been elevated on a platform and it was surrounded by fronds, bamboo and palm trees which didn't reach the high, domed ceiling. On either side of her chair were tiki torches. They lit when she looked at them. Her pet rabbit, Miss Bubbles, was busy chewing up her best pair of straw flip-flops instead of the nice, green grass deck they took pains to install.

"Even my rabbit hates me." Aggie flopped into her chair. "Chair off, you hear me, no getting inside my brain." The chair reads your thoughts if you let it. Aggie sat there stewing over her situation until more trouble showed up.

The entry door slid open and Sanderson hobbled in and went straight for his command chair. He had Mother set it up to vibrate and massage like the ones at the pedicure salon. The chair also provided pain management. Ben was a hard guy and wouldn't let Mother dope him. *He should let Mother do it.* The look on his face spelled pain. Deep wrinkles dug into his regenerated face and made Aggie think of the old Ben Sanderson.

Ben was a hundred years old until regeneration made him physically thirty. He came out of the tank with hair down his back, weird for a guy born in the 1920s. Regenerated because Archer shot him but he wasn't fully healed. Mother didn't have time to finish. *He'll remain in Mother's service until the cost of regen is repaid.* She made Mother save him, he didn't get a choice. *Thanks to me Ben's on the hook, too.*

Ben was caught in a trap but he didn't see it that way, said he felt privileged. *The stupid ship must have put that into his head.* OK maybe it was because he was in the military his whole life so a service hitch wasn't a big deal to him. Ben didn't choose it, she did. His deal wasn't what she wanted for herself. Once wired, Mother owns you. No devices necessary, no chair or belts needed. *Just open up your brain and let the sunshine in, no way.* Aggie was pretty sure the control belt changed your brain, too. *I shouldn't have tried the belt.* Aggie stood up afraid the chair allowed Mother to sneak in. With the fronds no longer blocking her view she couldn't ignore Ben. He was having a very bad time.

"What's with your back, any better? Pot's supposed to help a lot." Aggie hated seeing him hurting.

Sanderson eased himself deeper into his lounger slowly. He pulled a joint out of the top pocket of the cowboy shirt he wore. That shirt was just like the kind Jon wore. A pang of regret fired in her chest as Ben lit up. She should have busted Jon out of jail, but there was no time.

"Got it." He took a few deep pulls. "No better. It's the old alien spine, doesn't want to meld with my new body."

"How'd you get an alien spine, that's messed up?" Aggie could almost feel his hurt. It wasn't the ship making her feel. It was her usual empathy. Buddy nudged her leg; dogs know how people feel.

"Crashed into an alien craft over Japan during the great war. That's WWII. They fixed me up, class-A job too, but it's mechanical, worn out. I have to do something about it, stat."

"Bummer, once we are out of here — "

"It can't wait. I'm going back into regen ASAP. Mother's growing me a spine now. Should take a few days once I'm in the tank. I'll run security from there. You'd know all this if you'd let Mother in. You'll need her help."

"No way, I'm not letting aliens in my brain. What'll you need? Baby-sit while you gestate. Just sit here and vegetate like a lump of poop?"

"That's the idea. You can't go to Earth, too dangerous. We almost got caught last trip. Mother's pulling her hardware. Aggie, you must communicate directly with Mother, that's how she does it. Otherwise she'll guess or misunderstand you … "

Sanderson went on preaching but Aggie tuned him out. He went on and on about the dangers, the world's militaries were after them and they had to know Aggie survived and, Mother had to refit, and on and on. All stuff she knew. But wasn't she captain? *I can go back if I want.* Mother had a big vote but Aggie was in charge, use a control belt and force Mother to take her back. Maybe have Mother dope Sanderson to make him shut up. The only problem was she had to use the belt to make Mother do it. *Not happening.* The idea of forcing another person made her stomach turn. But if she went home who'd see to it that Mother got her crew?

Ben's tough, he's a war vet. Let him solve the crew problem. Delegate, that's what I'll do. Once that's done, I'm out, the further away from Mel the better.

Ben's daughter came up and rolled Buddy out of the way while Aggie built argument steam. Sarah was regenerated and made four years old again, but grew to a five-year-old in just a few weeks. Because she was over eighty and on death's door when they picked her up out of the rest home, a big reset was necessary. She was a cutie pie, too. Why didn't Mother regen Ben better? *Time, they were running out of time. Ben can wait for the repairs. He's the hardass ex-military guy. He knows stuff. That's an idea, get the crew first before his medical.*

"Crew first." Aggie said. Her voice sounded in her ears like she felt, conflicted.

"Yes, get this show on the road, pronto." Ben said. "You'll oversee pickup operations."

"But I need you." She said. "Can't you wait until this crew stuff is set?"

"I'd prefer that if it were possible."

Sarah ran around the bridge in a big loop with Buddy following. She changed course straight for Aggie. The class-A robot assigned to watch Sarah almost fell over Buddy. Sarah crashed into Aggie's legs and looked up with a pleading face. Her cheeks were red. Fresh tears streaked wetness to her chin.

"My daddy's really, really sick. He hurts!" Sarah buried her face into Aggie's legs and wiped her eyes on the jumpsuit. "Daddy needs medicine." The little girl blew her nose on Aggie's loose pantleg.

Sarah was wired into ship systems like Ben so maybe she could actually experience his pain. Aggie didn't know what it was like to have a living spaceship deep inside your mind patching people together and she wasn't willing to find out. She tasted it once when she tried a ship's belt. It scared the crap out of her. Way more invasive than the command chair. What about a normal life? Solve the crew problem first.

Sarah pulled away. "Won't you help Daddy?" She started bawling all over again.

Poor Sarah, she knew her father was hurt bad. Aggie had to do something. She had no idea of what that was. Maybe her overnight self-assessment was right; she wasn't captain material. A captain stuck to her guns. A real captain would keep Mr. Security on deck, and use her men like disposable tools. *That's not me.* Aggie caved in. She hated his suffering.

"Get back to regen right now. You suck this way. The sooner Mother fixes you ... "

"That's how I see it. Mother will add more class-A's to look after Sarah. Praytis will keep tabs as well. You don't have to do nothing. Wait until I'm cooked before you make any moves."

That got under her skin. *I'm eighteen, I decide my moves. Aren't I the big cheese? He's acting like he's all that.*

Sanderson got up with the help of one of the class-A bots. They're bigger, smarter and taller than the other types but still spindly. More aware than pilots. Ben limped over to Mel's station. Sarah and her class-A escort followed. 'You don't have to do anything,' rang Aggie's guilt center's bell. She wasn't good at waiting or doing nothing. OK Earth was off limits for now. But once Sanderson was fixed, she'd go. She didn't need the ship to tell her that once she left it'd be a one-way trip. Aggie wasn't the only one feeling this way. Mel was going back. Everybody knew it.

I need a break. How about Moon City? He didn't say that was off limits. Aggie needed to get away. She was itching to go someplace, anyplace. Anywhere was better than sitting inside a big can orbiting Mars. There had to be people on the moon who wanted to sign onto a starship, right? Praytis said Earth people lived there. That would save a lot of hassles. Besides, the further away from Mel the better.

"Speaking of the devil," Aggie whispered.

Melisa entered the bridge. No greeting, no, 'Oh, hi Aggie' or 'Hey what's up,' or anything from Mel except a dirty look. Mel wore men's tan khaki pants and a man's button-down blue shirt. Mel had always dressed in emo black, but now it's business casual. Her hair was slicked down like Clark Kent.

"Great, just great."

TWO

Archer and the Joint Chiefs of Staff

Archer proceeded deep into the Pentagon's inner ring. He was called by the Joint Chiefs of Staff, the puppet masters' muscle. The people that controlled presidents and bankers alike also owned the Chiefs. Archer had ideas about why he was called. He had reported many times before but not inside the belly of power. Going down to the War Room was calculated. It was a show of force. There was no place on Earth more secure. He guessed the Chiefs thought they were safe from alien observation there. Archer knew better and he'd keep that to himself.

He passed the last checkpoint only to find another at the elevator leading into the bowels of American security. Fitting. One step away from hell. He produced his badge, a Navy Recovery Office badge with Q security clearance. The guard looked it over carefully. He was a private security man. The guard worked for Brinks Security Inc., an insider's boondoggle if ever there was one.

"Navy Recovery Office, hum. It checks out," the guard said. "I was told you were coming."

"Naturally." Archer got inside the elevator and pressed the only button.

Of course, the elevator scanned him every which way on the long ride down. Everything was under surveillance here. But they could not scan his thoughts and if they did, they would be surprised. It surprised him. He discovered it slowly, over recent weeks, that things inside him had changed. Karnack's alien control bracelet employed to control him while a prisoner of the pirate, changed not this mind but how his brain processed and gathered information. The device's purpose was to direct biological robots. It wasn't intended for use on sentient beings. It almost killed him. The bracelet develops brain access on its own and to do that it modifies neuropathways, makes them faster, less jumbled and more direct. The aftermath effects of a control bracelet, a thing never used on a human before, were to let him see himself and everything else more clearly. He used his new found and improved perception judicially.

Never show your cards.

The door opened into a small antechamber. Two marines, top men, searched him, ran scanners over him, checked his ID again.

"Paranoid much are you?" Archer tried his hand at a small grin. He wasn't very good at it. The skin on his face was as tight as a funeral drum. He needed to eat more, force himself.

"Shouldn't I be?" One of the guards said. "We're at war."

"Contrary to the song, paranoia won't destroy ya." Archer said as the other guard handed him back his fedora. They even searched his hat. That exchange reminded him of Aggie Piper and her humor. He was rereading her file. Closed case. She was supposedly dead, but he had this feeling, or was it hope? He brushed off the thought, his bullet had hit home.

The ranking guard pressed his thumb on a wall plate and the inner door slid open. Archer entered and stood on the rim. This big room was ringed with an elevated deck, probably to service the massive computer screens which hung on every wall, each to its own purpose. Archer assumed the Joint Chiefs spent a lot of time with theses tactical displays. The lesser details on the many computer desk screens below the ring eluded them. But Archer learned much at a glance. One screen showed a Navy destroyer in low orbit. Another screen located American MACs. Other screens showed where aircrafts from every nation were. America's hardware was toys next to what Karnack had and that system was now under Aggie Piper's control if she survived. *Adult toys in a child's hand.*

The Joint Chiefs brought him there for a reason. A game, in part, to convince him to play ball. Archer had his own game. In the center of the room was a C shaped table and there sat a handful of the Chiefs. Archer didn't know all their names; he didn't want to know. Does a hunter give game-food names?

"Archer, come down here." It was a Navy admiral.

He took the stairs down and stood before three men at table. The functionaries had backed away. "Yes, sirs." Archer expected no preamble, and got none; these men weren't built that way.

"As promised, you'll take over for Sanderson. General Brinks is running alien relations ... for now."

"You have a uniform? Can't go to the alien's base naked." The Army general said.

"Sir, I've been with Navy Recovery Office for twenty years, my rank is designated as Mr. Black, this black suit is my uniform."

Three top-ranked men conferred in whispers. A normal man would not have heard them, but Archer's hearing was enhanced, his ability to read lips as well. Very little data was required for him to put a picture together with his newly modified mind. They said nothing important. Internal politics prevailed.

"We'll make you an Air Force general, how's that sound?" It wasn't a question. Corps generals don't ask questions.

"Fine sir, whatever you require."

The Navy man leaned forward. Now the real reason they called him was on the table. "See here, Archer, Archer is it? Carry on with the aliens as before, but here's the rub. We need to know you are loyal. Whatever happens, are you with us?"

"Yes, sir. I am with you." *As long as it works for me.*

"Brinks' plot against President Albright was sloppy. The General's a little too cute. Civil war isn't out of the question, thanks to him." The Army man brushed a hand over his jarhead haircut. "If Brinks becomes a problem … " The general made a slashing motion across his neck. "Are we clear?"

Brinks was already a problem. He launched Space Fleet prematurely right after the botched Albright affair. There was a lot of grumbling going on. Technical issues aside, controversy between agencies was settling and they were restacking firewood behind Brinks. Archer didn't know the big plan but war was smoldering. Once the public got wind of aggression against the aliens, sparks will fly and ignite a blaze.

"Do we have an understanding?" The admiral said.

"Just give the word, sir." Archer said.

"I told you he's a good man." The admiral said. "His Navy record's impeccable."

"You'll work with Brinks … for now." The Army man said. "Keep an eye out for us. Do what Brinks says unless you hear otherwise from me." The Army man seemed to be the top dog. They had more up their sleeves for him than that. Little tells everywhere. This was a test.

"I'll wait to hear from you, sir."

The Army general dismissed him with a wave. Archer did an about-face and left. He went to uniform requisition and picked up the basics. He never displayed his medals before and he was handed a blue billboard made for the job. He had an apartment there in D.C., not much inside but dusty furniture and a cot but he also kept his awards there because it was a handy place to store the strongbox inherited from his father. It held his father's Medal of Honor, the only brass ornament he cared about. Before a moon trip, he'd plaster that other garbage on thick, put on a good show, make them think he was with the program. Sanderson always went up to the aliens in full dress regalia.

Archer was still working on his own program and wasn't sure how to go forward. However, his primary interest and endgame desire was just locked in. The question was how to get from A to Z and back again without spilling his motives.

Brinks was a slippery steppingstone, keeping balance won't be easy. Killing Karnack before the GTO withdrew, first order of business. That was impossible without Brinks' indirect help. The tumblers were failing into place one roller at a time, one murder at a time. The first one, Ben Franklyn Sanderson, had already clicked into place. Killing Sanderson was easy, Karnack would be more difficult.

THREE

Aggie and Mel

Mel had taken Sarah and gone to the lunch room. Aggie was hungry too, but she didn't want to deal with Mel so Aggie ordered the ship to bring food to her room. Aggie ate and thought about finding something to do besides hanging around doing nothing. Taking a little trip to the moon didn't seem like a big deal. Maybe it was what she needed right now. Ben was back from a visit to medical and on the bridge when she returned. She sent Buddy to get recharged. The other robots weren't around. Robot free felt good.

The bridge door slid open. Praytis came in with Mel and Sarah. *Great Mel's back.* Did Melisa, or whatever her boy name was, care about what Aggie thought or did? No, she/he went straight to that stupid com station. Mel and Sanderson got right into it and were looking at something and not on a holo screen either so everyone could see. Both faces blocked one of Mel's hard screens. Did they share, no, bunch of buttmunches. Do men ever ask a woman's advice? No. *Great, Mel hasn't even changed into a man yet and I'm thinking of her has a guy.*

"Aaarrgg!"

"What's that?" Sanderson asked over his shoulder.

He didn't bother to turn. He and Mel were face-planted on that stupid computer screen like they had striptease dancers on it or something.

"I said. You don't give a crap what I think. You don't tell me stuff. You never listen."

Ben slowly turned toward her without twisting his back. "Listen huh? You're the one that won't listen, more like you refuse to hear. Put on a goddamn communications belt and you'd know what's happening." Ben went back to the screen grumbling, "I don't have time for this baby-sitting baloney."

It was the same argument they had over the last two weeks, put the belt on, put the belt on, put the belt on. Aggie was about to drop a bombardment of insults but Sarah wheeled around like a drunk and crashed into her legs. The little girl backed up a step, stood on tippy toes and looked up at Aggie. But the child was not there. It was Mother again talking through Sarah. *What a creep out.*

"I understand your frustration, please allow me to enter." Then Mother was gone and Sarah was back. Sarah yelled. "Miss Bubbles!" and ran off after Aggie's black, lop-eared rabbit.

Aggie wanted to tell Mother to go scratch, but it was hard to face a little girl and say nasty things. Maybe Mother had planned it that way. Why can't the stupid ship just talk like a normal person? *Oh yeah, you had to be wired for that.* What that means is Mother wants inside everybody's head. But Mel wasn't processed either so how did she or he, talk to Mother? *Why is everybody working around me, I'm the captain right!?*

Praytis was looking in at the screen as well. His four legs allowed him to stretch his upper body outward in weird ways. His anthropology desk was next to Mel's com station. He tapped Mel's shoulder. Mel spun in the chair to face him. He straightened up.

Praytis asked. "Melisa when and if you undergo regeneration, Mother can convert your body gender rather easily, but of course you'll then be permanent crew afterwards. I'm afraid she can't reprogram your mind, that aspect, one's sense of gender is innate. Mother has confirmed she would indeed accept your application for permanent crew. She would be happy, as would I, to have you join us."

"What're you saying?" Sanderson never took his eyes off the screen. "She's temp. She won't sign on. Damn shame, if you ask me. Why discuss regen?"

"What Praytis is trying to say … " Mel pushed away from the station. Sanderson turned around. "Ben, you don't know. Dude, I'm trans, OK. Praytis is conveying Mother's offer. I'm really a boy inside a girl's body."

Sanderson turned back to the screen. "I know, Mother told me. Ship said it was a security matter. It's not an issue … I waited until you were ready. I concur. We need a good man like you."

"Everybody knows everything except me! This is bull." Aggie said. Mel's morning confession went into ship's records. The stupid ship and crew just do crap without asking. "Why am I the last to know?"

"You aren't permanent." Sanderson said. "Get wired if you want status. Fact is, you keep thinking you're not staying. Why waste my breath on you with ship's business? What'd you expect?"

Of course, Aggie knew that. But she never said she was thinking seriously about going home. OK she told Buddy. How did the ship know? Mother isolates your brainwaves so she can tune in and telepathically speak and share information but without asking? That's rip-off mind reading. Mother did it without an interface device. Mother doesn't need hardware inside your body or an external interface. She just slaps you with some kind of quantum mechanics mumbo jumbo. Spooky communications at a distance. Devices give access to Mother's data but she can just go ahead and get inside you without you knowing? The implication made Aggie feel like tossing her cookies. That control belt Aggie had ripped off Karnack gave Mother the way in. Had to be. It was the conduit that hacked Aggie's mind. And nobody told her. Why is Mel getting information that she isn't?

"What about Mel?" Aggie pointed at Mel. "She gets the scoop but I don't?"

Sanderson stood back from the desk. "He, it's he now, get used to it. Aggie you're pretty damn stupid for a smart girl. Mel's running communications. Mother's on text screen. Get off you duff and call up a screen."

"That won't be necessary, watch." A strong female voice came over the intercom, except there weren't any speakers. It wasn't coming out of Aggie's head either. Around the room and in the ceiling, there were holographic screen projectors situated at intervals a few feet apart. All of the holo system's green indicator lights began blinking wildly. The air between Aggie and Mel's station pixelated and the projection of a goddess-like woman manifested. She was tall, regal, thin, pretty and green skinned but dressed like a bad-girl witch in a studded leather catsuit like something out of a demented Disney movie.

"Woah, is that Angel Eve, dude?" Mel said. "I love old-time movie stars. It fits. Hey, that's the subroutine I've been hanging with, cool."

"Mother! Weeeeeeeeeeeeeee." Sarah took off giggling and windmilling her arms while running around the holograph. Buddy had rolled back onto the bridge unseen and proceeded to follow Sarah.

"Great, just great," Aggie said, "How am I going to compete with that?" Aggie slapped her forehead; that projection wasn't real even if Mother was a real person.

"I've made this image available for interface should you request it." The holo said. "Shall I remain?"

"No, go away, do me a favor if you have to talk, don't do it from Sarah. Just talk." Aggie said.

"As you wish."

The hologram blinked off. The boys went back to work. Aggie had made a demand of Mother up front, which was "stay out of my head." She didn't want an avatar looking over her shoulder either. This was getting like America, surveillance everywhere. But there was supposed to be a big difference. Mother respected your privacy, but did she really? Apparently not. Mother agreed to boundaries and broke them. It wasn't right.

Symbiotic relationships weren't like this. Tick-eating birds don't tell Mr. Water Buffalo where to go or what to do. Bovines don't care where parasite-picking birds' nest. Aggie was nothing but a tick on an elephant's butt. She just had to go somewhere anywhere and get away from Mother. Maybe do something constructive that brought her closer to finishing. Aggie calmed herself down. Negativity wasn't getting her anywhere.

"So, what are you assclowns doing?" Aggie asked of the group around the station. She was trying for her usual smartass casual.

"Working out an open call," Sanderson said. "Mel came up with it. We can't go back. Reports are the Navy has more MAC killing ships in orbit. The militaries have armed with MAC killing projectiles. They're gearing up for something, probably, my guess, they think I'm dead so they figure you, a teen girl, is in charge. I know how they think. You're an easy target. Once they muster, they're coming. They'll take us out, they know we're here. Mel confirmed they heard Branford's call. We're reading command chatter. They know about us although Earth's media hasn't figured it out yet."

"Great just fab, so how are we going to get a crew? Mother won't leave, remember? Can't do a landing party, how's that going to work?"

"Simple," Mel said. "We put out a call on the net, have people file an application. Mother will process and contact the one's she wants. She's wired into every computer on Earth, quantum stuff. We show the people she likes how to find the alien's subterranean shuttle system. Moon City's OK with it … still gotta work out details, but anyway. They come up to the moon and take an interplanetary shuttle from there to us … if we don't get blown up first."

Earth was laced with alien tunnels with trams and space shuttle docks. The Galactic Trade Organization didn't build it, they rented it. Moon City made the tunnels. She used to trade with Earth before it became civilized. She stopped the practice when Karnack caught the sociopath bug. Karnack let religions spring up around trade visitors. Noninterference policy forced the shutdown of trade interactions. The transport system had formally covered the entire planet. But now it was seven thousand years old and in disrepair. Still, there were enough shuttles running to gather up the crew Mother needs. This trade system and more alien things were infused into Aggie's surface memory when she was plugged into Mother using the captain's chair. It's what put Aggie off about interfacing. Too much information all at once. She didn't know she knew that until just then.

"I hate this."

"It's a good plan, safest way." Sanderson said.

"You'd know, you're all about security." Aggie said with a sarcastic tone.

"We'll use the dead man blogs," Sanderson said scratching his beard. "They released. We tracked who watched them and commented positively on social media. We zero in on them first."

"I'll do new blogs, yeah." Mel said. "Trace backwards and narrow it further … "

"No," Sanderson said. "Things are too hot. You must get back before it's impossible. We hardly have time to slip you in. They'll splash incoming craft. Going in is risky. I'll pull off reentry, that is, once I recover. I was an ace flyer in the war, you know. Shuttles leaving Earth for the moon have less risk. Inbound craft is what they're after. Mother has it — "

"Hold on!" Aggie jumped out of her chair and almost took a header off the step. "Mother, Mother, Mother, what about me, my needs, what I want? Ever think of that? I get to pick, too. I'm the captain. I want my parents and — "

"They may not qualify," Praytis said. "Mother will scrutinize interested persons by way of her online applications. She is programmed — "

"That's poop. I have a say. I have authority. OK, I can't go to Earth. Fine. It's still on me to get crew, right. My responsibility. I'll find them myself. What about Moon City? There are Earth people there."

"It's better if you stay and go with the plan … " Sanderson started but Aggie waved him off.

"What if I get them off the moon? Safer right? Everybody's happy. My family can't come, fine, so I'll go home after. I suck at being captain anyway." Aggie crossed her arms over her small chest. She felt like she'd do anything to get off ship. Away from them sounded good to her.

Sanderson was boiling. Aggie had been around him enough to know Ben Sanderson's moods without ram-ed or any other high-tech trick. Being in pain made him even more testy. He was about to launch an argument and took a step toward Aggie but Mel grabbed his arm.

"Dude, let it go."

"I need Aggie here. She needs to filter the applicants. She's got final word. Damn my back. I've had it."

"I'll stay for now." Mel said. "I'll handle social media. You recover, then I'm out."

"That's a team player," Sanderson said.

"What of your body gender reconfiguration?" Praytis said. "Mother's offer."

"I'm doing transition on Earth, the hard way like all the trans men I know. It's my right of passage." Mel spun his computer chair toward Aggie. "Be a childish bitch. We'll do this without you."

"The heck you will. I'm, I'm doing it. I don't need help." Aggie headed for the door and before it closed, she heard Mel say, "She has the watch, we'll be OK, she's traceable."

Ben said, "She isn't going anywhere, it's all bravado."

Oh yeah, screw you guys.

FOUR

Grandfather Branford Flies

He was shaped like a fireplug and just as hard. But Al Branford, the famous grandfather of the famous Aggie Piper, had softened lately, more he woke up to his real situation and what was important. Family was everything. America was temporary, but where will he go when the shit hits the fan? He didn't know how long normal would last but it was on its last legs. Things in America were going bad. He spent more and more time in his intelligence center down in the lower basement of his Washington D.C. home putting the puzzle together, running algorithms and looking for warning signals.

"Son of a bitch."

He made one of his many screens blow up the picture. He was tapped into every camera within a mile of his place. The CIA phone truck that was always in view and there to keep eyes on him had moved out. A gas company truck pulled up in one intersection near his house, two blocks over another gas truck was parked but there was no activity. The antenna on that truck's roof didn't look right. He typed a command. More gas trucks were converging around his home.

He checked the gas companies' work order records. His neck hairs bristled. "Nothing. They're CIA, must be." He leaned back in his chair scratching his chin. *What are they up too? Think it through you lug head.*

"Goddamn, good thing I texted Bryon. She's gonging to be pissed." He gave his daughter no reason. He simply told the driver to turn back "with all speed". His driver knew the drill. Earlier Branford had a hunch and now it was much more.

As a primary UFO technology contractor, he was in a precarious position. With Aggie on the loose, his life wasn't worth a pugged nickel. They'd use him to get to her. That's why he waited so long to try calling in the first place. If his call got picked up that meant the watchers knew Aggie was alive and that made him and his family expendable. Tools of state gone obsolete. He felt the noose tightening around his neck.

Loyalty? He gave the Military Industrial Complex what they wanted, a fly-by-wire system that controlled magnetic aircraft without the need of a robot pilot. That gave him an idea of where to go. With the aliens out in the open, the Complex will take the alien's star drive by force. He wasn't needed anymore. And since he made that call, he found Aggie alive and the Complex knows it too. No way around it. He had to run before they decided to take him down. One jump ahead is how he survived in this game so long and he had long prepared for the day when the wolves turn on him. With his late friend Ben Sanderson out of the picture, his buffer zone was gone. He had to act before they did.

Branford lived in D.C. right where the Complex wanted him. However, he was there for his own reasons. His long association with Mark Levine paid dividends. On one of his security screens he saw his limo outside. The driver, a man he had trained to be leery, was rushing his daughter Sky Flower to the door. Po-boy was already long in this house writing a UFO book no one will ever see. Branford was getting used to calling his son in-law Sonny, Po-boy. That damn Cajun was growing on him. Once Sonny figured out his writing career wasn't going anywhere there'd be hell to pay.

Checking another bank of screens, plainclothes operative types were a block away. A police car was blocking an intersection a block further. Branford pushed the intercom and haled his house man, Jeeves.

"Yes sir," came over the com.

"Jeeves, gather up Sonny and Sky, bring them down to the subbasement, you come too." Branford released the button. Strange how he called his daughter, Sky Flower, her chosen name. His wife had named her Charlette. There was a time he refused to call Charlette her new name or use Sonny's nickname. Times were changing radically and he was changing with them. He clicked the com switch again. "Oh, and grab Po-boy's valise, too. If you don't have a bug out kit handy get one. Text Bryon, tell him to take the car and himself to the airport, double speed." *That'll put him out of harm's way.*

Branford's subbasement computer room was well equipped. For a short, hard man with Popeye forearms and fat, short fingers he was pretty good on the keyboard. He flew over the keys while waiting. Checking, making sure his false leads and other wild gooses were let out. Things were in order and he was ready to run. Once he was done here, and staff was out, this basement will be leveled. The bomb won't go off until the place was empty of recognized bio signatures. He activated it. He designed the "accident" to look like a gas leak. Branford wouldn't give them any evidence to pin the murder of operatives on him.

Sky banged open the steel door. "Dad, what are you doing? I was on my way to meet the service arms committee rep in New York. My first time at the UN Why'd you stop me? I'm not done with Haiti yet, they have to — "

"It's a trap, those bastards work fast. You wouldn't have made it. I've got a man on the men who were following you." He didn't say his man just ran the CIA car off the road. Sky Flower was the CIA's target.

Sonny came in right behind with Jeeves. Sonny's eyes were comically wide. Branford's office just outside the com station was stuffed with alien artifacts. Neither one of them had come down to this level before. They had no idea there was a recon center in his house.

"Ready for an adventure?" Branford said

"Sir, what are you talking about?" Sonny said.

"We have to go, and now."

"What about my book, I got this here contract." Sonny said.

Sky, his lawyer daughter, started firing lawyer jargon missiles but Branford cut her short and simply said. "I spoke with Aggie, she's alive."

Po-boy whooped and hollered and patted Jeeves on the back so hard Branford was sure the thin, quiet houseman would topple. But Jeeves stood like a redwood, the man was as dependable as reinforced cement. Sky cried and screamed and laughed and they all did; even stoic Jeeves wore a toothy smile. But there was little time for celebration. Branford calmed them as fast as he could.

He thought Aggie had survived Haiti but didn't share it. He had to be sure. Two weeks was a long time to mourn the loss of a child that wasn't dead, but Branford had no choice. He didn't want to leave a sliver of light for the spymasters to pry open but now …

Sky caught on. "You knew it all along, but why … never mind I see why. What do we do now?" His bank of screens gave it away. She saw different locations on each monitor and each camera held the same kind of truck.

"We run like hell and keep low."

"What about my book, I got a publishing contract?" Po-boy cried.

Sonny and Sky had stayed closer to him there in D.C. since Aggie had gone MIA and Sonny was writing Aggie's story all over. Maybe to help him deal with the loss. Sonny wasn't getting very far. Branford had a hard time with Sonny's Creole accent but saw Sonny's usual arguments coming. That boy was stuck on it and Branford had had enough of it.

" … dis a lifetime opportunity, I — "

"Stop! There's your damn briefcase, notes, laptop, everything, show him." Branford snapped. Jeeves held it up. "Keep at it but not here, not now, we're going."

"Now, you mean this instant," Sky said startled. "I must pack, what about my files? I have legal actions in process. What will I tell my staff? I … " Her torrent faded away. "We're in trouble, aren't we?"

Branford held up his hand. "None of it matters anymore. I told you they'll go after us to get to Aggie … We can't help her from jail or dead. We run." Branford pointed to the corner where backpacks were piled with his compact survival rifle. Po-boy stood with hands on hips defiant and unconvinced. "Look at my screens, see the gas trucks, the plainclothesmen? They're here to kill us, all of us."

"Da-y beat us like de dogs for a drop o' spit." Po-boy said. His accent got worse when excited. He had been researching and learned how insidious the deep state is. Sonny's face went white as realization struck, "This no lie."

"I can't accept this; you must be joking." Sky said.

"See that?" Branford pointed at a screen. An unmarked SUV pulled into the nearest intersection stopping traffic. "That's a CIA hit team and they're coming here."

"I git it true enough, we best go." Po-boy's voice was dejected.

Branford turned to Jeeves. "David, we both knew this day would come. We'll take the back door south; you follow and go north when you can. If you're willing, stay in the house and run the program for an hour." The program was projectors and speakers to make people outside think people were inside. "That will give us a head start, they won't bust in right away … you know what to do."

"I am willing, sir. Thank you for all you have afforded me and my family. They are safely away."

"What are you saying?" Sky said.

Branford ignored his daughter. "Don't push it, give us an hour then move. I set the charges to blow in two hours. It'll take out all the data banks when she blows. Don't forget to set the door trips."

"I don't understand." Sky slumped her shoulders and fell into an office chair.

"The trip only goes off if someone breaks open this door or my bedroom." Branford waved at the entry of his data room. The only way into the subbasement was by way of the hidden elevator that landed in his alien artifact museum. He had many things down here illegal to own or even know about.

"He means to blow up de house, that no lie." Po-boy said somberly.

"I bought this site because of the tunnels," Branford said. "Like Key West, there are alien tunnels under us. They run all over the world. Most were abandoned eons ago, but the GTO employed the system and kept a good amount of it running. They don't all connect any more. The Complex doesn't know about this one. My guess, that's how President Albright escaped from the murder setup. There's a tunnel under the White House that runs to the Capital building, how she wasn't caught, I don't know. Maybe they have her locked up somewhere. She might be dead. Scuttlebutt says Brinks is behind it."

"I'll be a boiled mud bug." Po-boy said.

Branford wasn't taking any chances. He had Sonny and Charlette change right there. He had clothes for them all in stock there, lightweight shirts, pants and underwear. He wouldn't let them go back upstairs.

"Jeeves run the program from here, infrared projections will fool the detectors. No need to jeopardize yourself."

Branford had and used alien technology that the Complex didn't have or know he had because he wasn't allowed to have it. He had a lot of tricks they didn't know about but that advantage was playing out. No other place stored his alien toys. They got everything that was on his research vessel. *After the bomb, they won't get this material either.*

His research laboratories were watched. MJ-12 only gave him enough information and hardware to work on his security segregated projects. But he had his inroads. The best of the alien tech he had was here and it was better to blow that boon to kingdom come than to let Brinks get hold of it.

Once suited up and ready, one quick look at the perimeter monitors told him the CIA had setup road checks all around his location. They weren't moving in yet, they might not for a few hours. How long before they bashed down his door was anyone's guess. As an afterthought, he armed the upstairs doors. Any forced entry would result in a percussion explosion and smoke bombs. That would slow things down. Jeeves saw it and nodded his agreement. Branford wasn't telling peaceniks Sonny and Charlette that his house was a death trap.

The hidden tunnel's entrance was behind the paneling in his subbasement's lounge. His house was big, but his basement complex was bigger. Should the CIA make it this far, they'd have a hell of a time finding the entry. The three refugees entered the tunnel and there were no lights. Branford provided each with night vision glasses.

The walk was long and slow and despite his good health, the walk wore him down. The backpack had him off balance. The tunnel was muddy and slick and the steel rail that ran down its center was twisted out of its recess here and there making it a trip hazard. Branford hit the deck several times on the way but he didn't curse.

After a three-mile walk, the tunnel dead ended and the sound of muted boat engines penetrated the walls. Branford felt around until he found loosened brick, bricks that were put up by government people a hundred years before. He had had Jeeves weaken them from the inside.

"Take your glasses off," Branford said as he picked up the ten-pound sledgehammer he had placed there years before. He lined up his swing before removing his own glasses. One mighty hit was all it took. Bricks flying out splashed into mud puddle water.

"Where are we?" Sky asked blinking at the sunlight.

"South of Thompson's Marina, on the Potomac. That's where I keep my runabout."

"We taking your boat, that's doggone big." Sonny commented. Branford's little 40-footer must have looked like a yacht to a small boat fisherman like Sonny. The sea was the only real common ground between himself and his son-in-law.

"Of course not, they know every piece of hardware I own. I keep a tricked out flat boat over at Hire's Boat Salvage. Mark set it up for me — "

"Mark, our Mark, you know Mark?" Sky asked.

Branford ignored her and started pulling bricks down. Now wasn't the time to spill that can of beans. The hole wasn't big enough but the old bricks came out easy. Sonny helped. Once opened this bricked in tunnel was hidden by a large bolder blocking the infilled wall. Thick foliage enhanced cover. They had to squeeze and scrape past the boulder's rock face. The bricked section was originally done to plug a crack in exposed bedrock. A low bluestone cliff was above them with a security fence mounted on top. It wasn't an easy climb. On the riverside they'd have to tread water to get around the cyclone fence and into the storage yard beyond. Branford stopped long enough to assemble and load his 22-caliber survival rifle.

"What's that for?" Sky asked wiping her face leaving mud streaks.

"Guard dogs and whoever else might be around. Can't leave a witness." Branford saw Sky's face go white but she didn't say anything more. *She has to know it's us or them.*

They got inside the salvage yard quickly and dashed toward a drydocked boat for cover. Branford scanned everywhere and waited. Not easy for a man of action. They stayed a long time searching but there was no one about. The dog wasn't a problem. Sonny made friends with it on contact. Branford, satisfied, had them move forward to the next drydocked hulk. No one heard the man come up from behind, not a whisper was heard until the man slapped his hand down onto Branford's shoulder. Branford dropped the gun, spun with ready fists but he didn't hit the old man.

"Mark said you'd be along. I'd been waiting two weeks. Come on, boat's this way."

"He saw this coming, that figures." Branford said.

The old man took off at a surprising pace. Branford knew about Mark's network of safe houses, hidden transportation, and off-the-grid associates. He offered to finance Mark's underground railroad and Mark was enthusiastically onboard. He hired Mark to keep an eye on the Pipers and the system grew from there. Sky had no idea that Mark had that inside line. Branford went so far as to fund Mark's activities without him knowing it. Branford never expected one of Mark's contacts to turn up on cue. It seems one watcher was watching out for the other watcher.

The man brought them to a boat tied up in a bulkheaded lagoon. There was a boatlift crane mounted on the dock. The place was used for salvage. The crane hoisted wrecks and not pleasure crafts. Grease, mud and rust decorated everything. The boat below the bulkhead fit right in, it was ass-ugly.

The man handed a slip of paper to Branford. "This here's your next stop. It's Bart's place. Y'all better git there quick afore Bart decides to vacate. This here's Mark's boat, it's got hydrofoil. It's damn fast."

I see now how he spent so much of my money.

The party had to climb down a slick ladder that was bolted to the algae infused wall. The boat was ten feet below. This lift station was designed for big salvage but the boat docked there was a wide, flat aluminum job about 22 feet. It looked the part of a salvage vessel, forward cabin, standup pilot's wheel, small hydronic lift at the stern. Inboard motor box at center. Sonny got into the pilot's seat and started fooling with the controls while Branford was casting off.

"Bodacious, twin jet-drives, hydraulic nozzle controls, and gas-op tolling motor on a prop, she'll run shallow or plain like a race boat, doggone, this here's got Mark all over it." Sonny flipped a switch and the hum of an electric motor was heard. "Yup, hydrofoils." He checked the sonar. "It's too shallow."

Sonny reversed the hydrofoils and fired the engines. He departed on the propeller to not make a big wake. The motors were quiet but the power was evident in the way the deck vibrated as they pulled into the river. Just outside the salvage yard boats were tied to anchored buoys awaiting docking. The menagerie gave cover but not for long.

"Po-boy, handle the boat. Sky and I will stay in the cabin. They have face rec all over here. Put on that big hat … keep your face hid, go slow until we're upriver."

They weren't a few yards upriver when a fast police boat thundered past going south. Branford had told Mark to have the salvage people use this boat daily so it was a fixture on the Potomac. The police wouldn't look too hard, at least not right away. That was his hope. Bart's place was a good sixty miles upriver as the crow flies and he was itching to go fast, but Branford knew better. Even at top speed, sixty miles on a winding river was a long ride. Winding made it double the straight-line distance making for a long day. With "no wake" zones intermittent their average speed can only be a few knots.

They proceeded slowly and progressed upriver until suddenly the boat rocked. An explosion, miles away, but so powerful shock waves struck. Branford opened the cabin door a crack and looked into the sky. Black smoke billowed upward from the direction of his house.

"What is it, Dad?"

"It's off time. It's too big. Something's amiss."

He had a hard time resisting the temptation to have Po-boy gun it when his place blew up. Was it two hours already? No. Po-boy steered into the main channel north. That was one hell of a gas leak. Too much smoke over the city. Alarms went off. Maybe he shouldn't have tapped that gas main. It was overkill on his part. But still, that result was over the top. *Did I calculate wrong?*

He checked his Van Ness watch; the same one he used to call Aggie to warn her off. That explosion wasn't by way of his timer, it went up too soon.

They weren't gone long enough. The CIA must have tripped the fuse. He didn't want to kill them, they brought it onto themselves, and of course, they'd blame him. Stupid bastards. If he wasn't a wanted man before this morning, he surely was now. He backed away from the cabin door on shaky legs.

The Cajun got on the gas as another police boat raced past them going south.

"Slow and steady. You'll give us away." He called up to Po-boy. The motors idled down.

A slow boat going fast was a dead giveaway. Branford wasn't about to give in to fear and race off. His granddaughter was cut from that same cloth. She proved brave many times over. He just hoped that Aggie had the good sense to run when he told her to take off. That watch phone was a sharp gift well given but it will cut the other way. Branford opened a porthole on the thought. He removed the watch, pulled out the battery, and pushed it all out of the porthole donating the entire kit and caboodle to Davy Jones. Out of communication was better than dead. He'd have to find another way to reach her, should he ever get a chance.

FIVE

Aggie Leaving

Aggie ran down the gangway. Yeah, she has Grandpa's watch, a gift for her 18th b-day. Praytis had given it to Grandpa to give to Sanderson to give to her before her world caved in. Aggie wanted to dash it on a bulkhead but she managed her temper and didn't even take it off. It was a phone watch, she always wanted one and it came from Grandpa. Why screw up that gift because of buttheaded dick-brains like Mel and Sanderson and Praytis?

Aggie blew into her room, stripped off the green jumpsuit, and put on her usual non-sundress attire, a bikini, old denim shorts, and a tie-dyed tank top. She dressed for action, like she was really leaving. She preferred the sundress but it didn't feel right for space travel. She put that crappy jumpsuit back on over her outfit. Her ships were too cold for summer dress, the only stuff she ever owned in Key West was all thrift shop or homemade warm weather clothes.

Equipped as much as she wanted to be, she put on a pair of rubber flip-flops and went straight to the nearest launch bay. She didn't bother packing a bag, this won't take any time. *I'll show them.* She wasn't going to be gone long, right, right? Half a day on the moon and she'd be back with a crew. Then she'd quit this crap with a clear head and go back home to live like a normal woman, maybe even go to college like she wanted to in the first place.

Aggie slapped herself in the head. Yeah sure, every spy on Earth wanted her head on a pike. At least she had a low-tech solution to get a crew. She liked things simple and direct and non-tech, but in space nothing was that and the flying saucer she was about to board was the proof. As she entered the small one-robot shuttlecraft, her bio-bot pilot was already at station readying the magnetic drive engines. Mother was one step ahead as usual.

It felt good, she felt like she was doing something, like she was independent. Excitement rose as the bay opened and her craft floated out. Sanderson was always going on about teamwork. No team she was ever on really wanted her. *I don't need help I'll do this myself.* Once parked on the moon, and off this ship, Aggie would be out of reach for real, she thought. *Everybody off my ass.* The idea was both freeing and scary.

Aggie didn't give the order to move out. The small ship held stationed next to Mother. The relative position holo screen came up automatically. Maybe walking out like that wasn't such a good idea, she thought as her phone watch rang. Aggie pressed accept. It was Mel.

"What, I'll be back before you know it." Aggie said.

"Whatever dude. I'm tracking you OK?"

"They'll hear us, the stupid Feds tap in."

"It's cool, countermeasures, I'm ping-ponging the signal. What're you doing, that's the question?"

"I'm getting the crew OK, just leave me alone. I need a break. I'll call if I need you."

"Aggie you just can't — "

Aggie clicked the phone off. Fine, track me, this was worse than homeroom detention. Aggie had every intention of a quick visit to the moon and, OK, maybe this was more about cooling off than anything. Mel coming out like that threw her for a loop. Aggie needed space.

But Sanderson was right, play it safe, stay out of reach. Finding crew people on the moon was safe, right? Earth military can't just land on the moon, right. The stupid Feds wouldn't screw up their chances of making major space bucks and attack the moon, right? *They can't be that dumb.*

"OK Ship, proceed."

A lot of crap went through Aggie's mind as her shuttle pulled away from Mother. She avoided the command chair and sat on the sofa where she could see the pilot's holo screens. The moon Phobos was close, it looked like a big potato. It didn't take long to clear local gravity. She had no idea how fast they could travel but it had to be half of light speed. On one monitor her little ship was accelerating. One holo showed a relative position. All kinds of data streamed on the scroller. The only thing she caught was estimated time of arrival. She was in for a six-hour ride.

"OK genius, how you going to find people once you get there?"

The biological robot turned toward Aggie, it had to be sending a signal, but she wasn't wired and had no idea what it was saying. A holo popped up like it read her mind and Earth words scrolled but Aggie ignored it and instead, she kicked back for a nap.

******

On Earth, an NSA operative who unofficially worked for Brinks picked up the transmission. Hers and many agencies received Piper's signals, they were all hunting for the Piper girl since Branford's call was recorded. Shannon, like everyone else, was fascinated by it all, that aliens were here and, if you could trust the Piper blogs, they were making deals with Earth for trade. A lot of people were up for having trade with spacemen. Shannon didn't agree.

As a longtime NSA operative, she was allowed to work at home. She knew not to trust anything or anyone inside or outside the company. There was so much disinformation out in the world she'd be a fool to trust the blogs or her own agency, and she was no fool.

When agents working for Brinks had visited her, they gave her a device that attached to her home cellphone cradle. She didn't trust it. She tested it. It was a link to Brinks office that was hack proof. It was new technology from Van Ness Industries, she was told. She didn't trust Brinks, but she trusted the money Brinks provided.

Shannon started her countermeasures and picked up the phone. Brinks himself answered. She reported the conversation she had overheard between Piper and that Van Ness kid.

"No idea where it originated?" Brinks asked.

"I don't have access to that equipment, but the ping-pong effect was mentioned. It was a strong transmission, my guess it came from Earth. The girls must be on Earth and have something that bounces transmission from tower to tower. We have that same capability, as you know."

"It's a trick," Brinks said. "Keep me posted."

Brinks hung up. A trick, what kind of trick? Brinks wasn't saying. Shannon had seen Haiti blow like everyone else. It was splashed on all media. The source of that video was unknown. Insiders say it came from Piper's spacecraft, but no one really knew. She had a suspicion that Brinks knew. Could it be that Van Ness girl again? No, Van Ness was under surveillance, they had her transmissions nailed down. No visual on her yet, but the CIA was closing: That's what came down the pipeline.

Shannon didn't know what to think or believe, the only thing real was the money. She switched off her blockers and turned to the computer. A voice came on.

"Where'd you go?"

"I had to pee, I'm allowed to pee, aren't I?"

She went back to work. Her house was wired, someone was watching her work, that guy on the phone. But he wasn't very smart. She had hacked the house system that the NSA installed and put in a loop of her in the bathroom on one view and the empty workstation on the other.

Every time he watched her pee, he saw the same footage and he didn't even notice her clothes were always the same. Maybe she should change the footage, but she wasn't worried, the guy they hired to watch her wasn't watching very well. Shannon put on the loop of her working and reset the catcher program that was tuned to pick up the Piper watch, and resumed her game of solitaire. She didn't know if the Van Ness hardware recorded her exchange with Brinks, only the inventor of it could know that.

SIX

Aggie in Transit

Mel, Praytis and Sanderson were on the bridge when Aggie's shuttle said it was separating and going for the moon. Mel was still pissed but he wasn't going to be stupid about it. He finally let out his biggest secret and the one person he thought would be OK with it, acted like an a-hole. Meanwhile everyone else already knew, thanks to Mother. It didn't seem like a big deal for the rest.

His computer desk was just like the stuff at home, Mother made it that way so he could use it, but this setup was way more advanced. Mel was still learning how it all worked and was glad for the regular monitors because holo screens floating mid-air made him seasick. A message like an IM popped up. Mel called it out from his computer station.

"Looks like Miss Bad Temper took a shuttle. Mother says she's heading for the moon. She's such an a-hole."

Praytis was behind him and said, "I'm sorry Melisa — "

"Just Mel OK? I thought you were OK with it." Praytis always called him Melisa. He immediately felt bad having snapped at Praytis. People always freak when a trans person comes out, it wasn't his fault. "Dude it's cool, it's me, my fault. Aggie worked me up, that's all. Sorry, dude."

"Yes, of course, no need to apologize, Melvin."

"Melvin ... I like it, I'm going with it."

Sanderson was in his back support chair with holo screens all around and a keyboard floating in space. Because of regen Ben interfaced like a lifelong nerd; it was sort of unsettling especially since before regeneration he was a throwback from the 1930s. He still hadn't cut his hair either. Admiral Benjamin Sanderson was bodily thirty, barefoot and wearing vintage jeans, cowboy-style flannel shirt complete with an old rock band T-shirt underneath. He just didn't look right. But it felt right. Maybe those were all the clothes Mother had laying around for him to wear? The dude is 6'4" so how did random clothes even fit?

"I don't get it," Mel said, thinking of Ben's fashion statement.

"I told her to stay put." Sanderson said. "She can't screen crew if she's not here, not with communications blackout in effect. I need her on deck. When I get out of regen … Mother wants me tanked pronto. Sooner is better. This delays me."

"He is correct," Praytis said. "The regen process, that aspect that installs a missing body part, works best in fast succession. I'm afraid Ben wasn't fully … ah baked … when Mother thought it necessary for him to help with our quandary. His new spine won't last long in suspension without a body attached to it."

"We're up shit's creek," Ben said with a groan. "Damn military's getting more MAC hunters airborne every day. They'll reach us here. Mother needs to put down to refit. It's not safe, she'll be exposed. Somebody's got to mind the store. You, Melvin, you got to git before Mother goes into refit. She can't launch shuttles in first stage." Sanderson adjusted his seating position. By his voice, his condition was worsening by the minute. "I'll get back to the tank once we're shipshape."

Mel spun his chair to face Ben straight on. Ben was gritting his teeth. He had to be in more pain than he'd admit. *Wow, Ben's cool with me.* "How long does she need, Mother and you?"

"Says we'll finish refit and me in three or four days, maybe less. Her active mind will be busy. Subroutines will handle mechanicals, life support and the like. Tank medical will wake me intermittently. I'll reach out to the com here and there. Underway, if Aggie doesn't come back, Praytis is first mate. We still have a chain of command."

"It is my pleasure to watch over your daughter, but I'm not good with technology. I am an anthropologist, after all, and very slow responding to technical matters, I'm afraid."

"This is why we need crew and fast." Ben said. "That tears it, I can't leave the bridge."

"You must before it's too late — " Praytis said.

"I'll stay." Mel said. "I'll hang until you and Mother are cool. I already know half the other stuff anyway and I got communications down cold. Subs and me get along."

"I'm not sure Mother agrees," Praytis said. "A temp on com duty is very unusual. Under refit, Mother requires trusted crew as she will be vulnerable. That's when Karnak modified his control belt, the one that robbed her of independence. Mother wasn't watching."

Mel checked his main screen. Mother hears all, but she didn't respond to the open question. Nothing on Mother's text window. Maybe Mother was being a bitch, taking after Aggie or something. Mother was complex. Mel had a hard time accepting that Mother was a living being. Why's she expressing herself by way of computers and machine avatars that only represent little parts of herself? *Does a pancreas tell the brain what to do?*

Mel pieced together a few things. Mother needed people but exactly why wasn't clear. Might be for companionship, or purpose, or she needs mobile living beings that think creatively to maintain physical systems and contribute Life Force to power it all. Whatever the case, Mother had her own ideas, whatever they may be. Was Mother too big of an intellect to narrow her focus enough to talk with crew directly? Mother's full attention was hard to attract. Only subroutines answered inquiries.

An answer to Ben's question came. The door slid open and a robotic wheelchair with two class-A bio-bots entered the bridge and went directly to Sanderson. Sarah ran to her father. Mel called the medical computer and checked. Ben needed help to get out of his chair and medical knew it in advance. His condition was critical. The bots and medical chair stopped before Ben.

"Oh, no you don't. Goddamn it, I'm on duty."

Sarah tugged on Ben's arm and cried, "Daddy, Daddy, don't be sick. Let Mother fix you, please, please, please. come on!"

"Fine, fine. Make it fast. Praytis, Mel keep an eye out for Aggie, whatever she does make sure she doesn't go to Earth, you hear me?"

One bot on either side of Ben's chair took his arms and helped him up very slowly, and, he let them. Ben was having a worse time of it since this morning. Badass-Ben had tears streaking into his beard by the time he was lowered into the medical transport retractable.

"Not to fear, sir," Praytis said. "I will instruct the pilots to not venture earthwards. As first mate, I control the pilot robots." Praytis touched his control belt. He had a new one made to fit his tiny thorax-like waist. It was a thin leather belt. "They shall go no further than the moon."

"Goddamn it." Ben said as the two bots escorted him off the bridge. Sanderson spread his arms at the door and the chair stopped. He yelled over his shoulder in a nasty tone. Mel jumped. "Look you two, don't do anything stupid, all right. Lay low until I'm out of sick bay. Lay low, will ya."

Sarah had run ahead but stopped on the gangway. "Daddy come on!" The grays manually removed Ben's arms and the chair proceeded on. Once the door closed, Mel relaxed.

"Well, I guess I'm hanging out for a while." Mel said.

There wasn't much to do but monitor Earth and take evasive or electronic action if a U.S. MAC showed up. But why not proceed with finding crew? The idea was to locate and screen applicants over the internet then swoop in and grab them. But Mel had a better idea. Why not use Moon City's shuttle system? Better than doing it hit and run.

"Praytis, what if we use Moon City's shuttles to run people over to us here? She's OK with bringing people up to the moon, right. Didn't she rent them to the GTO, you think she'll expand the deal?"

Praytis rubbed his skinny chin. "We did consider it." He was on the moon for an ungodly long time, he knows how it works. Praytis manned his control station next to Mel's as data streamed. It was just a metal desk like Mel's Ikea look-alike but taller. Praytis didn't have the ability to sit.

"It is true Moon said she will not interfere with us … I wonder." The bug-man said.

Holos came up and the four-legged man swiped and gestured in the air. No need to vocalize. It was all done telepathically. Negotiations were going too fast. Mel couldn't follow on his screens. He wished and not for the first time that he could get plugged in and have access to that computer power. The info Moon and Mother passed between them overloaded his signals bounce program.

"Moon City will allow shuttle access. She will help process our call-out. I dare say we should proceed immediately. Moon City is preparing to vacate. I fear there isn't much time."

"All righty, let's get to it. First, I'll set up the search program." Mel started working on his keyboard.

Finding people was easy, getting them to the moon and all the way to Mars was the hard part. It will take time. Mother tapped into the NSA's data servers because those butthead's watch everyone that's got a computer, TV or phone. Just put the application out, run an isolation chooser and see who responds to his video blog. The government can't shut everyone down without killing the whole internet. In recent weeks the Feds tried cutting the web off and Mel overrode the attempt each time. The government shouldn't have trusted Van Ness Industries' programs.

Mel had options. Buddy or any probe in orbit could suck up his internet data and relay it home. Finding people was part A, part B was to get them off planet and that was dangerous. What Ben laid out had holes. With him in regen they can't ask or tell him anything. If there were problems, they'd have to figure it out. Mel had an idea, a preemptive measure.

"Let's rattle Earth's cage, yeah? Use the dead man blogs with added spice, what do you think? Stir the pot. I'll make new ones that'll keep them confused. They know we're alive, well Aggie anyway. It'll distract the crap out of them."

"Earth's population doesn't know we survived. Ben said we must remain incognito. As an anthropologist I predicted the likely response of the public should it be made known that Aggie is alive. I'm afraid the reaction against the government will double. The outrage over blowing up Haiti has quieted, but this may well reignite protests. Riots had shut down Washington for several days, as you will recall."

"Perfect," Mel said. "The more confusion and problems for the Feds the less time and energy they'll have to mess with us."

"I'm not sure that is advisable, perhaps we should check with Ben?"

Mel opened the medical status window. Ben was in the tank and under sedation. Too late. *I should think it over.* He considered pros and cons and came to a flash conclusion. "Ben's knocked out. Let's do it."

"Alerting Earth will cause tremendous and immediate disorder," Praytis said. His voice had a warning edge to it.

"That's what we need. Good idea Praytis, why mess around? What happens when people learn Aggie survived is an open question, so, let's take away the what-if part. Aggie's always for the direct approach. Let's tell the world. Set a fire. You'll help. You know psychology and junk, right?"

"Oh, dear."

Praytis has a tick. When upset, or thinking and unsure, he lifts and sets down his four feet two at a time at opposite corners, like kneading the ground. He was doing it now. He makes this side-to-side front-to-back rocking motion that reminded Mel of the old coin operated rides he loved as a child. The horse ride outside in front of Bixby's Game Room was a favorite. His childhood fantasy was to become a real cowboy but he was a little girl then, one with a cowboy deep inside. His inner cowboy was ready to bust broncos.

"Aggie's not going down, she's safe. We get messages out on the web. Her folks, they'll feel better. We're calling for crew any way, yeah. More people will want in if they know Aggie's OK. Talk about a smokescreen with massive side benefits. What can go wrong? Am I right?"

Praytis stopped his nervous dance and stood tall on his back legs making him more upright.

"Melvin, if I may, I see your point. I do believe … what is the phrase, smoke and mirrors, a mirror screen is in order. But Mother's breadcrumb communication system is being withdrawn. How will we transmit, sending additional messages from here … won't that increase our risk? They will trace more easily, isn't that so?"

"Oh, ye of limited geekery. We'll load up Buddy probe, he's in transit chasing Aggie's shuttle. No problem for tight beam. I'll have him dump our data into the cloud. Setup time releases. OK, it won't be continuous real-time two-way but we can still receive ambient signals here without them tracing us. Buddy will pick up the hot stuff directly and tight beam it back. We'll do crew stuff back and forth that way. Who detects tight beam? We'll see what's happening. OK maybe not instant but we'll get data."

"I was assured Moon City will cooperate as well." Praytis slapped himself on the forehead like Aggie does all the time. "I see why Mother desires Earth human crew members. Earth type humans have interesting problem-solving skills, very creative, indeed."

Mel went to work figuring out more ways to get around the military's trace software. He found the Feds had tech to follow tight beam. That's why Mother pulled her probes in. But Mel discovered he could project a modified beam one way into Buddy and then bounce it directly into the government's com satellites from Buddy. They'd use the government's junk the same way Karnack had done. He'd save that approach for an emergency. It was better to go the roundabout way and use media satellites.

Mel understood the military sat-link software. Van Ness Industries, his dad's company, had made it with Mel in a ringside seat. Sanderson didn't know if the spooks knew that Karnack had tapped into NSA satellites. For now, one-way communication into Buddy was the way in.

Mel checked Aggie's watch phone. It was better not to call, but Mel saw where Aggie was on route. He'd call her once she was closer to the moon. Just in case.

Mel got to work setting up a new bounce-signal program. Calls to Aggie's watch from here will first bounce off Earth's towers. They'd be able to call Aggie before she touched down and it'll look like it came from Earth.

Having set up the bouncer, Mel worked up a little video blog and sat back. This one he'd shoot right into internet servers from there and then shut down the tight beam fast. It was risky. The government had hardware on all the public's internet hubs. It wasn't exactly the safest way but it will get things rolling.

"Praytis, check this out." He came over and stood behind Mel. Mel pressed play and the blog rolled.

Hi, this is Melisa, you all know me. I'm Aggie's planetside communications person. I have heard from Aggie. She is fine, she survived America's attack on Haiti and the Feds are still after her big time. So, Aggie is hiding out in space right now but she wants me to pass this on. Aggie and Starship Mother are taking off and they need a crew. Mother wants 40 volunteers so if you'd like to see the universe just make a video blog, post it on social media and tell us about you and why you want off the planet. Mother will keep an eye out and pick you up before we … they go. I'll post more details later, but for now I'm outta here. I can't let the NSA trace my location. Peace out space nerds!

Mel stopped the recording's playback, "What'd you think?"

Praytis rubbed his chin and rocked for two minutes before saying. "I see no issues; it doesn't give our location away. I like how you made it look like you are planetside in a tropical location. That you continue the gender ruse is clever as well. I like it."

"Dude, I'm the man when it comes to this stuff. Send it, yeah?" Mel wanted to make sure it got out and if anything, just to see how far it went. This first shot was a heads-up for the next one. He had more blogs already in mind. He'd expose government data that Karnack had collected. It made the best whistleblowers' stuff look like high school newspaper reports.

Praytis gave a thumbs up and Mel hit send. Praytis was picking up a lot of Earthling nuances lately. The tight beam shot directly for one of the TV network's satellites which was linked into a huge planetside internet server. Even at the speed of light, from Mars' orbit it took a while to reach. Mel had to keep the channel open until sure the signal arrived. Confirmed, he shut the transmitter off. The though occurred that if the Feds had any spy crap in space between here and Earth's orbit, they could figure out where that tight beam came from. Mel crushed the idea. It went out smooth. He had a perfect shot, everything lined up right. That pathway won't happen again until they completed another orbit. *What could go wrong?* He thought of one thing.

"Oh, balls."

"What is it?"

Looked good on Mother's end. But would things stay good? That beam could only travel one path, if the NSA figured out which satellite received it and when, from what direction … They just gave away a traceable trajectory.

"Nothing, it's nothing." Mel said. "Let's get more stuff ready. We got a lot to do."

A thought came to him as he worked. Rather than use the NSA's junk, why not park Buddy in orbit and go direct? Mel was going to have the probe move around, but they might catch his movements. *Have Buddy latch onto the International Space Station.* They might trace relays to there but they'd never shoot down the ISS … would they? These buttholes blew up the Twin Towers, so they were capable of anything. If they find Buddy there, he's cooked. As far as the Feds knew Aggie and her fleet weren't anywhere near Earth.

"This could backfire."

Mel started preloading instructions to send to Buddy in one data dump. He loaded blogs and programs for local relay and more stuff that taps into Earthside hardware. The little AI could work more independently if it had a plan and more tools. Too many beamed instructions might give away Mother's location. Less direct communication was safer. Mel sent the info package. How Buddy tapped in was up to him now. A lot depended on how smart an AI probe with the personality of a Labrador retriever really was.

SEVEN

Archer's Move

Archer made a detour back to his apartment on his way to report to Brinks. He laid the uniform aside and went to his desk. He had a relative back on the reservation, a distant aunt they didn't know about. He wrote to her once in a while. She knew about him, what he did. Writing was a way to ease his soul. He pulled pen and paper and wrote longhand.

I want to leave truth behind. Chances are good I won't be around to explain and people should know.

They never stop, the deep state. They used me like a tool. That's what I agreed to. I knew what I was getting into. This is what tipped me the other way.

I was called to Washington without R&R after surviving that sea monster's attack and consequent sinking of an armored rocket platform gunboat. After my transport killed Haiti, and I killed a man that didn't deserve it, I needed rest. I didn't get it. It's over two weeks since Haiti as I write, and I'm still very tired. Its small things built up over time pecking at your soul that forces clear sight.

Archer had to tell her something, something she would accept and share. Soon he would go deep. Auntie won't see or hear of him again.

The Life Force explosion created it; Haiti became a life accelerator. The people left behind, that the U.S. government murdered, grew gigantic. Trees were thousands of feet tall and that monster seen on Aggie's Face-Plant feed was born out of a lizard. They all died fast. Even so, that sea monster had time enough to sink the ship I was on. The eggheads in R&D never imagined this result. So goes military research. None of these details will ever appear in the media. The footage Aggie Piper's alien associates splashed all over the internet was real. Please don't accept the whitewashing media's propaganda. The aliens didn't attack Haiti, America attacked the aliens unprovoked.

I never told you how I got involved. My service in the Middle East came to their attention and they called. I didn't ask. I was then a can-do Special Ops man. I thought I was serving my country. I justified it. You know about my role in the Navy Recovery Office. It's no secret that the empire must do certain things illegally. They are downright brutal in fact. Anything to maintain power. We must do this and that for America is how they sold it. I believed. Dad gave his life for America, he was my example, but I took the wrong rail.

Longfoot died protecting women and children in Vietnam. I was only a little kid, as you know. My hero was used like a cleanup rag for the messy truths that were spilling out of the media and I missed it. I thought the military was right. The empire subverted media then as now and I bought in. No more bodies on TV. Lesions learned. I learned too late.

Media never reported Dad's real life, the poverty he suffered, the hardships of oppression. Just the hero story. But I don't understand. Dad came from a place where Uncle Sam crushed him. He came out of a reservation school with white teachers and white perspectives and white propaganda. Dad was programed into gung-ho American. He joined the army; they didn't draft him. There he took abuse and ate bigotry for breakfast and all in support of his oppressors. What is the term for when the abused embraces the abuser? There is a medical term for it. I fell for it too.

Like him, I believed but I also believed in not taking it. I believed in making money. Special Ops offered first class indoctrination, big money, better food. I swallowed it all until Sanderson reminded me Dad died protecting women and children. I said on record I'd never kill a child. This to honor my father's memory. Sanderson quoted me and in anger I shot him dead. That was my breaking point. I shot Sanderson and Aggie Piper too, a child. I dishonored Longfoot. For this I will make amends.

Thirty years-ago in Cryersville I was ordered to shoot an alien who appeared to me as a child. I refused and caught hell for it. Refusing orders was a mistake that almost ended my career. It wasn't a child. It was an alien biological robot. I did not refuse the next or any other order since and I should have many times.

Archer leaned back in his chair. No point in soft words. A hard thing to face required hard words. She was not soft. Little things over time unravel the best hypnotics. Shooting a child was not a small thing. *I must have hit Aggie with a through and through.* Archer's wheels had been spinning since. Sanderson knew his weakness. The Admiral must have read Archer's file. Sanderson pulled Longfoot's sacrifice out of his bag of psychological tricks. Archer wasn't ready to face it and he took it out on Sanderson. Had Sanderson lived, Archer would owe him. Sanderson resurrected what Archer had buried and that from a man who lied for a living.

And post-murder, after two days in the water clinging to a tree, just minutes after being plucked away from death's door, MJ-12 called. They wanted him back in Washington that same day.

The fleet was disabled as seen on satellite observation and the Navy sent help. But due to residual effects, pickup was delayed. I was put on a fast chopper within minutes of rescue, dripping wet, hungry and cold. The Life Force bomb's wake had disabled every ship within 30 miles of Haiti. It was two days before recovery commenced. Two days of hell fighting for my life and that was all the time I was allowed. This is not a little thing. R&R later, they said. Half dead, they shipped me out to report. If I had a last straw, on that day it was broken.

Those operations were top secret, and if the state found out he shared it: They would jail him. More state's secrets came to mind. His life was mixed into the blend. He could not explain himself without tipping Pandora's jar. Archer wrote on.

Karnack the alien pirate had given me a wider perspective. I learned how widespread the empire really is. How they work. How deep is their reach? It's too deep. With Karnack there wasn't any misdirection by compartmentalization. From Karnack I learned how insidious and callus empire is. I didn't mind deep down, not until later. Life Force raiders had harmlessly milked mankind for thousands of years. And we, the NRO, shot them down since WWII. Most successes were only probes, anti-nuke robot probes sent to stop us from killing ourselves by way of nuclear war. The powers weren't having it. They want, no, need, the ability to destroy everything and the aliens prevented it. We should thank them, not shoot them down. That was in my mind when I met with the Joint Chiefs this morning. The Powers have made our alien saviors the enemy. We are already at war with them.

People should know we live under a ruse. Tell it. The game is power. Democracy is a tool, like me, to keep power. They fool the people and are very good at it. So good I forgot who I served. I forgot who I am. Everything I thought, everything I knew as a soldier was a lie. On my way to Washington I became free. The chains of conditioning unlocked.

My question is, what do I do now? I'm in Washington to figure it out. My desire to kill Karnack, a need programed into me, is wrong. He was a tool like me. We tools mustn't be enemies but Karnack deserves death. I won't tell my superiors I've awakened. Let them think me willing.

Archer put the pen down and stuffed the handwritten pages into an envelope. He addressed it to Longfoot, general delivery and put down the reservation's post office address. His aunt would get it, no return address was required. On his way to Brinks, he dropped it into a mailbox. A taxi stand was nearby and he took one.

Archer arrived back at the Pentagon an hour after he had left the grounds. He paid the taxi with a c-note. Money didn't mean anything to him. Operatives got as much as they needed and more. He made it to Brinks' office in the outer ring of the Pentagon ten minutes later. Brinks was busy inside his office; orderlies were running around in a panic, Archer took a chair in the reception area and watched through the soundproof glass French door. He heard what was happing inside without a problem. Sound waves vibrated the glass, it was enough.

"What do you mean dead in the water!" Brinks was waving his hands around. The aide shrank a little.

"Sir, the aliens penetrated our shields, they shut the nav-computer off, life support is intact, but our destroyer is stuck in orbit."

"Moon pussies don't like to kill, interesting." A smile appeared on Brinks, something seldom seen and it usually meant some sort of cruelty was forthcoming. "Can we block their signal?"

"Working on it, sir."

"Get going, keep me informed." Brinks checked his watch and looked through the glass. Archer waved.

The aide left the door open when he exited and Archer didn't wait, he walked straight in. No alarms went off, his plastic gun wasn't detected. He tucked that bit of intel into his internal ready file.

Brinks started the dance. "Archer, the NRO is now under my control. You aren't needed there; I have a new mission for you. As promised, Sanderson's position is yours. You are our contact liaison. We want you to take over as trade representative, deal with the moon aliens, buy me time. Give it a whirl?"

It wasn't really a question. Tool makers don't ask tools questions. "Am I otherwise operating as Mr. Black?"

Brinks laughed. "We don't need men in black anymore. I need you to distract the Galactic Trade Organization."

He was right. The cat was out of the bag. Aliens weren't a secret anymore and the Navy's space fleet was about to be exposed and made public. They didn't know he knew that much and more. Archer never volunteered information. Information is like any weapon; keep it holstered until needed.

"Can you handle it?"

"What do you want me to do?" Archer asked the loaded question.

Brinks, sizing him up, bore holes with dead eyes. It was no secret that Brinks didn't trust the aliens or Sanderson. Brinks previously made it clear he didn't trust anyone on the alien contact team. *I wouldn't trust me if I were him.* There was more to it, there's always more than what is said. Whatever was rolling around inside that bag of tricks wasn't going to leak. Brinks' practice was to only give enough info for an operative to accomplice the mission. Archer would discover the rest on his own.

"I want you on the moon. Press them hard. I'm tired of kid gloves. Tell them we aren't dicking around anymore. Either they trade or they suffer consequences."

"Let me consider it." Archer said. "I need to explore how to go about it, what I'll say."

"Distract them, I need time. You'll have the file. Simple mission. Questions?"

"No sir."

It was better not to ask questions. Archer understood the game. The GTO and America had danced around trade deals in closed-door sessions since WWII. Piper blew those doors off their hinges. Was MJ afraid the UN or somebody else might beat them to the honey hole? Why was America still playing empire as Rome burns? The people were in revolt. The masses backed against a wall. Empire doesn't care. MJ might open trade to ease mass unrest and uncertainty but Brinks wasn't there for trade. If the government didn't give people another bone soon it'd be too late. At its core, empire has no brakes. Why stop with Earth when there's a universe to ravage? *He wants me to jam the gears.* Delay tactics for what? To make ready for war, of course.

An orderly came with papers for Brinks to sign. Archer stood by.

This is opportunity. Archer had his ride to the moon. He'd kill Karnack although he didn't have much heart for it lately. Still, Karnack deserved it. Threatening the aliens into compliance won't work. It wasn't about that anyway. Delaying tactics also gave Archer time and intel. If he pulled it off maybe they'd let him retire.

Archer was a deep insider. Nobody told him coming in there weren't any exits. His source said Branford was to be assassinated. Branford the state's primary reverse engineering contractor was a tool used up. *They'll off me the day I retire.*

Brinks finished with the orderly. "What do you say Archer? You in?"

"I'm not a talker, more an action man. I won't be nice about it."

"That's what I need. Good attitude."

Brinks wasn't satisfied, a flicker of doubt stiffened his appearance. Psychopaths attract each other, use each other. The smartest dominate the dumber. Archer had lived the dumb part. Heartlessness was the job's requirement and a thing he wasn't. He was bone tired of that act. He didn't project the willing fool as well as he should. *Get him back on my rail.* Lies and misdirection came easy to Archer from long practice.

"Shouldn't I remove the GTO honcho? I can't shoot her like I did Sanderson. They won't let weapons in. But I'm good with a knife."

"No nothing like that. Follow protocol." Brinks said handing over the job file. The title said 'Trade Strategies.'

"How do I get there?"

"Sanderson's office, he has, had that is, an elevator down to the alien's tram system, leads to a shuttle bay."

Brinks wasn't happy to let that information out. Archer had chased and wreaked skyborne targets for a living and the idea of underground alien bases on Earth never occurred, nothing like that was ever mentioned. Need to know reigned supreme. That was a thing he needed to know before now. Archer didn't react. Let Brinks assume he already knew.

"I don't have clearance." Archer said.

"You do now," Brinks said. "Pick up a flight line pass at Key West administration. It'll be waiting when you arrive."

And that was that. He was in. In so deep there was only one way out. All he had to do was decide what to do with the time he had. Brinks had ordered Sanderson wasted when plans changed. How long until they did the same to him? He'd take out Karnack first and after that … what did it matter? What was life if it had no purpose? No reason to be?

Archer made his way to the nearest military airfield to requisition a jet. He didn't wait long. Brinks was one step ahead and ordered it before he arrived.

EIGHT
Mel's Call

Mel reentered the bridge with Sarah close behind. The second the door slid open; Sarah bolted for Miss Bubbles. The rabbit wasn't having it and took off. Miss Bubbles had a new litter of bunnies. Somehow that lop-ear managed to make a nest under the robot's station. How those androids didn't step on that rabbit and her offspring was a mystery. Miss Bubbles took cover under the pilot station and Sarah retreated. The robots protected the rabbit. Mel could ask Praytis anything, he kept forgetting that. Mel wasn't permanent crew but the computers and the others didn't mind answering questions. Honesty was an actual survival necessity in space.

Mel took his chair at the communication desk. Praytis was already on the bridge. Sanderson was due to be revived inside the tank and available for a few minutes. He wasn't coming out, but they had a window to speak briefly.

"Hey Praytis, how come the robots don't smash the bunnies, robots aren't very dexterous?"

"They have artificial intelligence, and as such, they aren't capable of doing harm to any living creature. Karnack had overridden their program, which is why they were in poor condition when we inherited them. AI's will do no harm and that is one of the reasons why the Galactic Commonwealth had hoped to hire Earth humans for police work among other things. Earth people have no qualms about killing each other and anything else which may hinder them, as you know."

"Sorry I asked."

"Come here Miss Bubbles, pleassssse!" Sarah said.

"This question of police workers is an issue." Praytis said.

No point in trying to stop him; once Praytis got going, he'd roll on. Mel was all ears.

"One needs police to deal with unruly less evolved sentient beings. We had experimented with genetic modifications to enhance one's ability to be more ... what you may call Earthlike, so to say. That is how Karnack originally went wrong. He absorbed the virus that activates the sociopath gene and inadvertently introduced a new variation on Earth when the sickness adapted. Interesting how the gene-mod spread rapidly and did not hamper the majority of humans. Only one percent of Earthlings are affected negatively. But oh my, how they who are susceptible responded to that stimulus. Most negatively, indeed."

"And there is no cure?" Mel said with half an ear open. He was busy grabbing Earth signals.

"Of course, there is. But it would take a generation or two to take effect and I'm afraid Earth doesn't have that long before civilization collapses, whereby that proclivity may become helpful. Such an event my well cause the species' end. As to how the robots, as you called them ... "

Mel turned in his chair. *Earth doesn't have long?* Boy was that a mouth full. Mel was learning that Praytis, when prodded, was an information dump. He was about to ask Praytis another question when the com chimed.

" ... not to mention," Praytis was saying, "They are made from cows and thus take on the better nature of the bovine species. How and why this works, we don't know. The — "

"Daddy, Daddy, Daddy's coming!" Sarah ran and leaped onto Mel's lap spinning them both around. "Show me."

Mel wasn't very big or tall or heavy as men go and he was still in the form of a girl at 5'2" and a hundred pounds. Sarah crash landed like a ton of bricks. *Maybe if I go in regen Mother can make me taller. What am I thinking! I'm not staying.* With Sarah in his lap, Mel turned to the computer terminal.

Sanderson's voice came over the com. There was no video. Mel envisioned Ben was half apart while the new spine was being installed. Good not to let Sarah see her father that way.

"There's my girl." Ben said. "Are you being good?"

Sarah slipped off Mel's lap and put hands on her hips like a scolding parent. "Of course, I am! Me and Praytis picked strawberries and I got the most. I'm a big helper!"

"That's my girl, that's fine." Ben said. "I'm proud of you. Save some strawberries for me, will you?"

"Strawberries?" Mel said. So weird to hear Ben act this way, soft voiced and kind. When Ben was an admiral, he was a huge buttmunch.

"Yes Daddy."

"Honey, I only have a little time, let the adults talk, OK?"

Sarah put on her fake sad face and climbed back onto Mel's lap, "OK Daddy."

"What's the situation?" Ben asked.

As the head of security Ben was a business first kind of man. Mel reported. "I've set up a satellite relay so we can send and receive without getting traced ...

I hope. Me and Aggie had a fight. She took off to the moon, soon we'll be able to call her without being traced." *At least I hope so.*

"Goddamn it, I told her to stay put. Mother's landing for refit. We need all hands on deck. We'll worry about securing crew after. Refit is priority. What was she thinking? But, good work Mel, we'll need to talk to Moon City. Mother reports Moon is pulling up stakes. Goddamn it, that puts the screws on."

"Shit," Praytis said.

Mel did a doubletake. Praytis began his unhappy dance.

"Daddy, Praytis cursed!"

"I'm sorry Honey, I'll have a word with him later. Look, Mel, ring her up and tell her to get her ass back … no belay that, tell her to stay put until we get Mother fixed up. Aggie is not to move unless security clears it. If confirmed no enemy eyes on her, get Aggie back here pronto. Mother's got an alternative idea about picking up crew. Ship will project it into your station. We'll go with Mother's idea if the timing works out. Seems like you're already on the same wavelength. Continue with it and for God's sake don't let the Navy find us. We're sitting ducks until I build defenses. I've got ideas. Foremost keep your heads down. You copy?"

"OK, Ben, I get it. Tell Aggie to chill until I clear return flight. Me and Praytis got this."

"That's fine. I've got to go. Pain blockers are failing. Whatever happens Aggie stays put until we figure this out. Something big is coming down the pike. Sarah, you be a good girl for the boys, OK Honey?"

"Yes Daddy."

Ben went off line. *Be good for the boys? Ben's cool with me.* Mel didn't get a chance to tell Ben anything about it, to explain himself, before Ben got tanked. *I'm a dumbass.* Ben's wired and the ship knows everything. Mel felt a little jealous. He was, after all, a tech geek beyond this century and Ben was an analogue man from 1923. Ben's an antique with access to the smartest computer in existence. A message came into Mel's text window. Mel scanned the text.

"Dude, cool beans. Mother has the same idea or she ripped us off. The test application is out on the internet and it's getting results. Says here, Mother's already processing applicants and I haven't even released the general call. That first one only hit Aggie's Face-Plant fans. Pick them up off the moon is confirmed. Way cool. I was afraid we'd have to go down to Earth ourselves."

"Going below is ill-advised. Moon agrees to assist. How will people find Moon's shuttles?" Praytis asked. "The system is secured and restricted. Without reservations, one cannot activate it.

"The accepted applicants will get instructions online. We tell them how to access the nearest underground shuttle station. Says here, the GTO's lease on Moon's transport system ran out so we're all clear. We're renting it. I say open it to anyone that finds it. We make sure our people get there first."

"Most unusual that. As ship's anthropologist, I foresee problems. I believe an open call is not a good idea. What if the military moves to block access?"

"Dude, it's cool. I got this. We sew all kinds of confusion, get the Feds chasing false leads. Tie their panties in a knot. Like we'll project fake secret communications that say where tunnels are that aren't there at all, see? We'll mess with them until their heads spin, this'll be great. I'll send nonapplicant people fake directions, send them chasing their tails, have them storm the military bases. Stuff like, 'hey there's alien access at … ' how about White Sands? People will mob the wrong places, how's that for cover?"

"I do not think that is wise, we should consult Ben first. He is, after all, the security chief. Oh, and there is a shuttle below the military's White Sands test facility."

Mel brought up the security AI that heard everything, of course. No flashing red lights. Buddy was almost in place. The Navy wasn't anywhere near. Odd that of the half a million pieces of space junk orbiting Earth, about a third was gone. Maybe Navy MACs were cleaning house? That made sense. They were launching more and bigger MACs and they didn't want their hardware splattered. Nothing to worry about. Mel moved around the security program. No immediate threats near them but the Navy was watching the moon for sure.

"Dude, Ben won't be out of regen for a couple of days, it's up to us. We can't wait to consult him; he'll be out of communication until Mother lets him out. You're first mate. Say yes."

"I don't know … "

"Clock's ticking, tick, tick, tick."

"I suppose if we are careful, oh my."

"Back burner, I'm calling Aggie." Mel punched in Aggie's watch phone. The Feds must be dialed into it, but they can't trace it, not after all that work Mel did. Mel started a blocking program that cuts the signal if a tracer locks on.

"Mel to Aggie, hey butthead what're you doing?"

"Mel, sorry. I should've known. It's just that … I haven't wrapped my head around it. It's not every day your best GF tells you she's — "

"Dude, it's cool. I expected it, typical. But listen, I talked to security. He said don't do Earth, no way. Bad crap's going down really soon. Stay where you are until cleared to return."

"What about crew?"

"Mother's getting them. Not sure how exactly yet but — " There was a chime and the signals were cut.

"Crap, I didn't tell her details. Better not spill it over the air anyway. I'm calling Moon City. She needs to ground Aggie." Mel tried to set up a tight beam but the com would not respond. "Double crap, the Navy is pinging like mad. The communication AI won't let me send. I'll try after breadcrumbs redeploy. This sucks cow poop."

"Cows, I want to see the cows!" Sarah cried.

"Oh yes, I did tell Sarah I would show her the ranch." Praytis said.

"Ranch, we have a ranch?" Mel said.

"Yes, of course, it is necessary to harvest cows for biological robots and food. This ship is more than adequate for the task. We have forests and gardens as well. Everything necessary for interstellar travel is here. Karnack was ready to make his exit when Aggie disrupted his plans." Praytis touched his head. On Mel's monitor Praytis was accessing the ship's storage log. "We have seventy-five head of cattle at present and the holds are full of other necessities. We can leave at any time though I would dare say our new crew will want to stock their personnel materials. Therefore — "

"Dude, how big is this ship?"

"We are currently one Earth mile long and some, how do you say … fourteen stories high and wide and growing."

"That's bigger than I saw, I don't get it?"

"Mother has begun refit, but we will land to complete the process. Actually, she is in the process of docking now."

The relative positioning holo showed the ship approaching a little moon with Mother's ass end facing it. It was Phobos.

Sarah was tugging on Praytis' overcoat. He often wore an overcoat over his jumpsuit. The little girl was ready to go and Mel thought it was time to take the tour, he needed a break. Since coming on board, he never made it past the spaceship docks behind the bridge on the upper levels. He asked about the bays and Praytis said they were for transporting smaller ships. Only mother ships had star drive. Mel figured that was the ship's main business, transport services. But there was much more to Mother than that.

Praytis and Sarah were at the bridge door when Mel asked. "Hey, mind if I tag along?"

"Of course not, and along the way perhaps you would be interested in seeing our gold stores. It appears Karnack had … what is the term … cleaned out, yes that's the expression. Cleaned out Fort Knox some years prior. Quite industrious of him I would say. This is why America went off the gold standard in 1971."

"So, what about the cow mutilations? UFO people say it's alien robbers, yeah, was it?" Mel asked.

Praytis laughed. He didn't do that often. He sounded like three people were inside him when he did. It had something to do with how his lungs worked. "Oh that, that was your government at work. They have quite a large disinformation program in play. It is remarkable how much money is spent to fool the public, fully one-third of America's budget."

"Wow, no shit."

"Yes actually. We may well find copious amounts of it in the pasture. We only have two scooper-bots clearing cows' droppings … Earth humor, no?"

"Close but no cigar."

"I prefer to avoid cigars."

The small group took the lift down two levels and boarded a tram car. Mel had no idea they had a tram system. Was it new, part of the refit? Mel had more questions than answers and he felt that it would take more than one lifetime to explore and understand this ship. Too bad Mel wasn't going to hang around long enough to do that. Once Aggie was back and they had a crew Mel would go home and start transition the old-fashioned way. The hard way. He'd experience becoming a man like all the other trans men before him. He had this in common with Aggie; both of them had to do things their own way. But in this case, he wanted to do it the trans-man way.

NINE

Branford on the River

Al Bradford was uneasy. Another police boat powered downriver toward D.C., the fourth one in only a few hours. Laying up in the cabin while Po-boy piloted the boat north slower than dirt was about all he could stand. He was a man of action stuck in neutral. Despite his stocky frame, he could move like a locomotive given the chance. The steady drone of the docking motor put Sky to sleep. Her head leaned against a greasy bulkhead. *Fine, her crazy haircut might improve.* He almost wished Sky had her dreadlocks back.

The forward cabin was dirty as hell, the galley kitchen was splattered with cooking oil, but at least there was food. The boat played its part too well. He didn't mind the grime, the old seadog he was had birthed on many old tubs. It wasn't his surroundings that bothered him, it was the waiting, waiting to get to Bart's place and Bart wasn't expecting company. They might make it only to get their asses shot off. Branford touched the 22-survival rifle. It was no match for whatever war vet Bart was packing.

When Po-boy steered away to port side he was glad for a break in the mundane. He looked out of a tiny brass framed porthole. Po-boy was making for another police boat that was moving slow along the opposite riverbank.

"Goddamn it. What's he doing?" Branford woke Sky. "Police, keep quiet, head down."

"But Dad — "

Branford stopped her with a look. His daughter slunk deeper into the old bench seat. Branford sat straighter and cocked his ear toward the cabin's door.

"Howdy officer," Po-boy put the boat in neutral. "I'm looking fer a derelict. Y'all seen any upriver? I done covered this here ... she mighta sunk. Owner suspects kids took her out and pulled the plugs."

Branford felt the police boat bump off the gunwales and too hard. His sleeper salvage boat was lined with old tires on both sides, but still, that was bad manners, bad seamanship. *Land lovers.*

"Salvage huh. Look, sucker you don't wave down a police boat." The cop's voice was over-the-top angry. "We have a national emergency. I don't give a damn about stolen boats. Stay clear. You hear me?"

The cop didn't wait for an answer. He gunned his engines, spun out and was off. His wake caused the flat boat to pitch and yawl. Sky Flower got up, probably to give that cop a few rash words, but when they pitched, she fell back into her seat. Branford could almost laugh but that damnable Cajun had called that police boat over.

"Jesus Christ!" Branford clenched his fists.

"What's wrong, Dad?"

"Your goddamn husband is what's wrong. I'm going to chew his head off once we're clear."

Branford slapped a wall hard. Sky shrank back away from him. She hadn't seen him go off like this in years, not since she refused to work for his company. All their years of estrangement was written on Sky's face in that moment. Why she left wasn't just ideology. She was afraid of him and he had to admit it. He tried to pull it back but his temper didn't abate. Branford wanted to punch something, or better yet someone and Sonny was up on deck. Instead of going top side, he balled his fists and chocked it down. He had been behaving well since the Pipers arrived at his home. He wanted things cordial, make up for lost time. But now he was wound up. He checked. The police boat was still in sight. He hated waiting.

When he was up and coming in business, he took too much stress out on his family. There were too many smashed dishes and holes in the wall board. An image of Sky, Charlette then, as a little girl cowering during one of his rants came up and broke his heart.

There she was now, backed up like a beaten dog. Same look as when she was five years old.

That's why she disowned me right out of college. He did too much damage back then and he hated what he had done to his own. Hindsight played over and over in his mind all the years they were estranged. He finally pushed the anger away.

"I'm sorry Honey." Branford put a hand on Sky's shoulder. She wrenched away.

"I thought you changed; thought you were better." Sky turned her face to the wall.

Branford sat forward and put his head down. He covered his head with his hands. He didn't know what to say. Sorry don't cut it. *I'm a monster!* He felt a light touch on his arm and looked up. His hippie daughter took making peace seriously. Another woman would have rightfully told him to drop dead.

"It's OK, we're OK," Sky knelt on the deck before him, reached for him and hugged him like she meant it. "Po-boy was just being himself. He was fishing … fishing for news."

Unable to find softer words he said. "I'm an idiot. That was a good ploy, you don't call the police if you're hiding from them. I should give him more credit."

"You're just being you."

"That's bad. Who am I? Navy spaceships couldn't fly if I didn't back engineer alien flight controls. I redesign it and handed the power of gods over to mortal men. Because of me, government will war on the aliens. I made this mess same like I did at home. I laid foundations of conflict for a filthy buck."

"It doesn't matter now. You did what the universe needed. You did what you were destined for." Sky eased away and patted him on the arm. She took her seat and sat closer to him. "I love you Dad."

"You're a good daughter," he said. He never could say I love you.

Branford just told his daughter top secret info that nobody was allowed to know. His compartmentalized role in this wasn't public information. When the powers catch wind of a leaker — he wasn't supposed to know that — the guilty parties paid with their lives one way or another. He knew much more than he was permitted and sharing it was a crime. *Now I go and blab to family, the ones I'm supposed to protect.*

"Jesus, I made a mess of it." He said thinking of his failures as a family man, memories of failures keep coming. "I wish I was a better … father."

"That's past. Let it go." Sky pulled her bug out bag closer, rummaged around in a side pocket and pulled out a small hardcase full of joints and a lighter. She lit one and took a couple of deep pulls. He had Jeeves stock her up, her habit wasn't his to judge. "Care to join me? It'll help you relax."

"We're out of Washington, it's not legal here."

Sky laughed. "Everything we've done since this morning is illegal. I'll lay money on a bet, and I don't gamble, that most of your government contractor activities until now weren't constitutionally legal, either."

"My daughter the lawyer. I'll take counsel's advice." Branford took the joint.

He never thought of smoking pot before, it was never on his radar. When he was younger, he drank too much and had to stop for business's sake. Everything for business and nothing for anyone else. But he did quit smoking cigarettes when Sky was a baby. The rare cigar he smoked since then was one of his few pleasures. Al Branford took a couple of big hits and didn't hack and cough.

Sonny called down. "I smell somethin's a cooking, coast is clear, pass it up."

Branford took a fresh one out of Sky's case and went up on deck with a lighter. All those years of anger at Sonny for taking his little girl away were wasted. Everything was different now. All the old flotsam was washing out to sea. A little bonding with the son-in-law, a thing he avoided, was in order. If the plan he had cooking in the back of his skull worked out they'd be spending a lot of time together in close quarters.

Branford lit the thing. It was time to bury the hatchet. When Sonny took the joint, he did so like they were old pals. It was like nothing was ever bad between them. Branford knew he was the only one aboard this tub with a hatchet to bury.

"I wonder what the po-lease were fussing about." Po-boy said before tossing the roach over the side. "What's this national emergency, we got one every other day anymore."

"One way to find out." Branford turned on the FM radio. Nothing was on the marine band except a recording telling boats to keep the airwaves clear for the emergency. Branford dialed in a local right wing talk radio show. He couldn't spin the dial without hitting one.

"… that's right Ned, it appears we are under attack."

"It could be a gas leak; the AP reports gas utilities trucks were in the vicinity."

"I'm not buying, it's a whole city block? I bet the aliens have some kind of death ray … "

The war drums were beating as expected. Branford switched to one of the public broadcast stations he regularly used that featured big band and classical music.

"This just in. The center of the explosion appears to have originated at Aloysius Branford's estate. Mr. Braford the industrialist, known for his involvement with military weapons development, was reported to have been at home with his daughter, Sky Flower Piper, when the explosion occurred. We go now to an interview with Tom Riggers, CIA spokesperson … "

"We believe America is under attack. Mr. Branford was a primary contractor relative to the development of our space fleet. We believe the aliens are responsible. Branford's skills are a threat to — "

Branford shut it off. The color ran out of Sonny's face. Sky opened the cabin's door but didn't come up.

"You blew up the whole block! All those people … " Sky's face was stricken with grief.

"Not me, it was the CIA. They took the whole block out just to make sure I'm dead. Jesus H. Christ!"

"But the news — " Po-boy stammered.

"It's bull," Branford snapped. "Don't you see the propaganda here? You saw the gas trucks on my monitors, the police cars. Two birds one stone, take me out and blame the aliens, or blame me, that's the second trick." Branford felt woozy and grabbed a hand hold to steady himself. "They think we're dead … we'll use it."

"No, I can't accept it! They can't be that insidious, that monstrous … I, I … " Tears rolled down Sky's cheeks as she came up out of the cabin. "Tell me they can't … it's an accident it has to be, must be. If it's true, they killed all those people just to … just to — "

Branford held his daughter. That was his answer. Yes; they can, and they do, and they have done much worse. Aggie's blog was correct, every word. He thought about telling her about 9/11 and some of the other nasty things her government had done, but what was the point? Maybe another day. That was enough deep state truth for now. Sonny's interests in conspiracies were righter than he knew. Po-boy stood there at the helm like a knowing stone. Branford reached to him, and pulled him into the family embrace. A man of action, that was an action long overdue.

All Branford had left was them and one missing granddaughter. The young lady who saved the world: The one person the powers-that-be will stop at nothing to destroy. He and the rest of his family had just joined Aggie's club. The day was hot but he shivered in the sun.

Branford and Sky went below. Police boats came and went. He wasn't going to put his two cents in again, two captains running one ship didn't work. Sonny had a handle on it.

Later near sundown things were quiet. No police boats came around after dark. Sonny eagle-eyed his way for a time in the inky night. Still, somehow, that Creole found what he said he was looking for. Sonny pulled off into a little waterway and went upriver a few bends. He found a tree-shaded shoal, beached and tied up. It was a good place to overnight. No lights near. The boy was right, they'd never find the turn off into Bart's lagoon in the dark. The canned food was tasteless and the fold down bunks hard, but the comfort of family softened the situation in Branford's mind. He slept well for the first time in ages.

TEN

Aggie on the Moon

Aggie's shuttle landed. She got the message just prior, "don't go anywhere." She thought it better if she didn't even get out of the ship, just take off and go back. That'd show them she'll do what she wants. But flying six hours back sucked. *I'm here, why not check out Moon City first?* Aggie had the feeling she ought to go back — and now. Her intuition was usually spot on. Besides, Sanderson said he needed her back there. What if they really, really needed her back there? Going now was best. But curiosity won the internal debate.

"Pilot, open the door."

Aggie took the gangplank down into one of Moon's many hangars. It was weird that nobody met her as before. *Duh, I'm not an Earth guest anymore.* She half expected Praytis to come flop footing toward her from a hangar hatch. What was weirder was that the place was half empty. It looked like the same hangar, but that place had ships parked all over it. Big starships and smaller local transports were scattered around like discarded toy bricks. She focused her attention on the giant hangar space. It wasn't the same one as before, there were no student rooms above the main floor and this space was a lot bigger. But otherwise it was pretty much the same. How many hangars did they have anyway?

"Whatever."

Aggie noticed a couple of aliens off in the distance and walked toward them. It was half a mile at least and when she got there, she was sorry she bothered. It was only a couple of tall gray robots, the class-A kind, smarter, but still machines and she didn't have the ability to communicate with them.

"Hey robots, where's the city?"

One of them turned from its task of loading boxes into a ship's ground level hatchway. The ship was big, but not super big, more like a smaller version of Mother. They had Earth boxes, boxes of beans and canned veggies and junk like that. The pallet truck was loaded. In answer, the robot put a three-fingered hand to its ear, paused and went back to loading boxes.

"Bunch of crap, fine, I'll find it myself."

Aggie found the nearest hatchway and exited. The hall outside was the same, dull white metal floors and walls, nice doors on the hangar side and dirty, rusting hatches on the other side. She walked about a mile, testing door after door until she found one that wasn't tacky and the round hatch lock spun freely. She didn't understand the script written on the door, but it looked familiar. She could almost read it. That brush with ram-ed when she was here before had put some of the alien's text inside her head but it didn't last.

"Here goes nothing."

She pulled the door and was affronted by dust, the smell of oil and sounds of machines, regular machines like metal shop in high school. The light was poor. A little robot like a lawn mower zipped by and made her jump.

"Space rats, great."

She went in and waited until her eyes adjusted. This was like backstage for the Wizard of Oz. Gray and rusted metal walls with cables and wires and conduits and junction boxes all over the place, but no sign of moving parts other than little utility robots scurrying around. They reminded her of rats in a ship's bilge. The space, ten yards wide, ran in both directions and curved away. It ran parallel to the spaceport hall. No doors on the inside. It also curved away in the up direction, up and out of sight. She started walking and looking for an inward door. Aggie realized she was in a big dome's outer shell like the hangar's dome. She had a vision in her head of domes inside domes like Russian nesting dolls. Was that her idea or was it planted like the other junk that brush with ram-ed put inside her head? She found a door back to the main hall and backed out, closing the hatch.

Aggie called into the empty spaceport hallway. "Hello, anybody home?" No sound returned to her, not even an echo. She called over and over, louder, more frantic. She pulled open a spaceport hangar door and looked inside that vast room. She didn't see her ship. The nearest shuttle was an old rusted Earth shuttle like the first one she rode in, but nothing else was recognizable. *How far did I walk?*

Aggie looked at her phone watch. Call Mel and get position? How would Mel know? Wow, it was late, too. Her stomach didn't like skipping lunch, much less dinner. Aggie started walking fast, she didn't know if it was the right direction or not. She made it to where her ship should have been, ripped the door open, but it wasn't there. She had gone the wrong way.

Aggie cried out. "Hey buttholes, where's Moon City. I want Moon City!"

The floor opened like on her shuttle but this time she was in the middle. She tried to jump clear, hit her chin on the edge and fell into the void. Dazed, the gravity well tunnel trip was a muddled dream and short. She was dumped onto a padded floor and the jolt made her come back to herself. She had blood all over her, the cut under her chin gushed. She sat on the floor with her legs wide, eyes blinking trying to wrap her head around what just happened when a mechanical robot rushed up on her. It had tentacles and spindly mechanical arms and a spray bottle on a stick all waving around like some crazy art project. Aggie backed away but the thing came in close and fast and shot spray into her face. She fainted.

Aggie didn't know how long she was out, but the robot was gone and she had a bandage on her chin. The blood was mostly gone but what remained was dry.

"You dope, medical emergency robot, duh." Aggie slapped her forehead.

Had she kept her wits; she might have followed it to civilization. Now she took stock. Her landing was high on a dome wall. The landing was like a bus or train station platform. There were stairs leading down into the bowl. Moon City went on for miles and faded out of sight. They must have ripped the city's plan off an old sci-fi movie. Gridded streets, low, flat buildings none higher than six stories, and neon lights everywhere. Signs climbing the dome wall above and aside her. She stepped down one stair tread and saw a creature like a six-foot-tall snail without a shell worming past the stair's exit below her. It had a dozen eye stalks waving in every direction. One eye stalk zeroed in on her and fear seized her legs in place. It moved on but Aggie stayed there petrified.

"OK, OK, you hate bugs, but that's not a bug, it's cool, really, it's OK."

She tried to convince herself to move on but it wasn't working. The longer she waited the more creatures that made Praytis look normal passed by. Finally, what looked like an Earth person appeared a few blocks away. She called, the guy turned and looked, but he kept going.

Aggie rushed down the stairway and straight into a maze of weird beings. She dodged a giant slug, got around a tall gray humanoid that smelled like bread and avoided a number of garbage can shape robots before she got to the spot. At least she thought it was the place. The guy was gone. Aggie spun around. There were smooth rock streets and adobe buildings lit with bright neon but no Earthlings.

None of the signs had words she understood, the letters, if that's what they were, were more like hieroglyphs. Right after that run in with ram-ed, she kind of understood some of it although most of it had since faded. Praytis said the effects of incorrectly tuned ram-ed wouldn't stick and the stuff Mother tried to put inside her was going too. She wished to Goddess that it stuck better. The one sign she recognized said "spaceport," but there were a couple different signs pointing in different directions. She didn't know which spaceport was hers. She didn't even know where the gravity well she came in on was. Aggie realized she was lost.

"Great, just great."

Aggie moved toward what she thought might be the center of the city. This place was on the outskirts, more like a suburb if the suburb was Duval Street. They had to have some kind of public buildings, right? Maybe a town hall or a welcome center, right? Maybe she was in the wrong hood.

The only people she saw weren't humanlike. Didn't Praytis say only human variations were allowed to interact with Earth people? She saw the reason for it. People would freak out if they meet one of these creatures and the robots weren't much better. The slugs ignored her. The birdmen, way more birdlike than Karnack was, ran from her. The giant bi-ped that passed for Bigfoot, looked down at her and growled when she asked it for directions. Everybody else ignored her. The only thing she could do was keep looking for humanoids that spoke Earth or hit herself in the head with a hammer so a medical bot might bring her to a hospital, but she couldn't find a hammer either.

Aggie made it to what she thought might be the center and nothing had changed other than the ceiling was out of sight and some of the buildings had metal parts. The majority of aliens were different and there were more of them, more varieties as well. There were more of the Moby people and the tall gray-skinned beings with big eyes and pointed chins who looked just like her class-A robots. None spoke English when she stopped them.

She came upon a tall, angelic human person who could have been born in Norway and a bit of hope sprung to life.

"Excuse me, sir, I think sir, right? Anyway, any idea where I can find the GTO?"

The person backed up. Its long, slim, fingers shot up in front of his face like Aggie was a monster. It jabbered some kind of high-speed language, turned and took off. Its long legs carried it faster than Aggie could run.

"What, I smell bad?" Aggie called. She lifted each arm and sniffed her pits. Maybe that was it.

There was a long rectangular metal box set along the curb like some kind of utility thing. The streets here were not really streets, more like wide sidewalks between buildings. She checked her watch. "OK, I'm done, I better call Mel." Exhausted, she sat on the box to make the call. The box moved. She jumped off and the thing stood upright. It was a stupid robot.

"Can't a girl get a break! Where do people get rest around here, what about food?"

"Rest," the robot said in a pleasant salesman's voice. "Let me tell you about the finest Earth human watering hole in this sector." Its body lit with an ad on its flat surface. It said "Kowalski's Bar and Grill."

"Yes sir! Kowalski's has the finest human foods fit for refugees. No adaptive digestive procedures required. Genuine Earth food and drink!"

"OK, robot, where's the city offices, town hall, something like that, where's the people in charge. You know, take me to your leader and junk."

"Kowalski's is the leader in authentic Earth food and drink!"

"You aren't an AI, are you?"

"For the best AI services, go to Kowalski's! We serve artificial beings and humans alike!"

"OK, I give up, take me to Kowalski's Bar and Grill."

"Follow me sir, for the best Earth human food and drink in this sector!"

"I'm not a sir, that's Mel's thing." *Should I ask how many sectors? No, forget it.* "OK, take me there."

"Right you are sir, follow me to Kowalski's!"

The box opened and three wheels came out, two in the back and one in front. It looked like a mailman's three-wheeled letter caddy with the letter box in the caddy rather than on a sidewalk. It wheeled on its tripod rolling away in the opposite direction that Aggie had come from. Both sides lit and flashed, "Follow me to Kowalski's Bar and Grill."

Aggie shrugged her shoulders and followed. Maybe this Kowalski spoke Earth. As they progressed inward away from the dome wall, she noticed more Earthlike people but she decided they must be aliens, too. A group of knock-offs were chattering in that weird language. It was a mixed group with several kinds of aliens walking together. The group seemed to notice Aggie and they sounded like they were laughing at her. She wasn't sure. Back in Key West lots of kids in school had laughed at her. She heard it all the time. The jokes stopped when she became master of an alien fleet. So why would these assclowns laugh at her? It wasn't that. It had to be something else. She was glad when they turned off onto a side street.

She had gone a long way. This part of Moon City was pretty shabby like the perimeter. The buildings were unpainted or almost painted and made of moon-brick. Some were adobe with steel parts mixed in. To her eyes the ones with paint were once brilliant but had long ago faded. More slug people were around and it smelled like garbage there.

Aggie was about to turn around and skip out on the escort when she saw a gaudy neon sign at the end of a dark alley that was written in English. There was an airplane propeller attached to the sign under that message and a pair of martini glasses lit by neon in windows on either side of a split swinging door. It was just like the dive bars in Key West. The place had Earth written all over it.

An Earth guy stumbled out of the door drunk. Aggie had seen a million drunks while living in Key West. Drunk was the local pastime back home. She didn't miss that part of living in paradise. Aggie hurried toward the place. The guy said something in that odd tongue as she approached him.

"Sorry, what'd you say?" Aggie asked.

"American, a refugee already. I need to get myself together." He pushed past her, staggered into the street and yelled, "Taxi!" A tube descended from the ceiling, sucked him into it, and retracted.

"I hope the drinking age is eighteen. I think I need one."

The ad-bot sang out, "Right this way sir, Kowalski's features the finest drinks in this sector!"

Aggie put her hand on the door. The ad-bot stopped blabbering, turned smartly, and rolled away. A quote from one of her favorite books came to mind. It was the part where the dragon character named Argolis stood before a magic door, and he had no choice but to enter. Argolis didn't know it was a trap. Argolis said, "There's nothing for it then," and proceeded onward. Aggie was out of options. She pulled the door open and didn't see anything inside that qualified as magic.

ELEVEN

Mel on the Bridge

Mel was still in the body of a girl but he dressed his true gender. It was way past time for him to be himself. Strapping his breasts down hurt. Losing the black stovepipe jeans and a death metal concert T-shirts was a pleasure. He didn't feel a need to express the interior blackness that overshowed his life anymore. Man-tailor shirt and slacks were much better. There was no need to hide his body on starship Mother like back home. He was really tired of ugly, baggy clothing and combat boots.

Mother knew everything about him anyway. Mother had made quarters for him even though he wasn't committed to staying. She gave him a little multi-room apartment duplicating his pool house lab and a sitting room like the one in his parents' house he favored. Mother even produced his old bedroom's interior, right down to his flaming skull boxer shorts. The room on the moon they had made to trick him missed many details. He'd lose the old house's stuff after tran-sition anyway. Coming out to Aggie freed him to become himself. How much Aggie freaked was nothing compared to how people will usually react. He'd deal with all that later, right now survival was the thing.

Mel was checking his communications station on the bridge while scratching a beard he did not yet have when Praytis entered. Funny how that dude didn't even flinch when Mel came out. Praytis just knew stuff. He'd find out what makes the bug-man tick later. Right now, he had more important things to do.

"I am quite impressed with your ability to adapt to our communications systems and utilize them effectively." Praytis said as he situated himself next to Mel. "Moby, Karnack's former first mate, from what I could gather while a pris-oner, handled all the technical aspect of ship systems. Apparently, Karnack, an anthropologist like myself, did not have suitable technical skills. Their ability to elude capture was quite a feat."

"Dude, it's nothing, really," Mel said. "It's all concept, yeah. If you get how it works and what it can do, you decide what to do with it. How to use it is the thing. The rest is just figuring out which button to push. Look at this." Mel had several holographic screens open floating around along with several hard screens. He pointed a finger at a holo and swished it onto a hard screen. "See that, it's the tracker. It's the same kind of junk my dad builds for the military. Same concept, same stuff. I've been playing with such ideas since I was little."

Praytis bent lower to the hard screen. It was a monitor like any planetside one. With four legs he couldn't get that low easily. Praytis splayed his legs outward like a spider carrying a brick to adjust his height.

"This is why Mother greatly desires your service as a crew member."

"I don't know Dude? I got a life back home. 1 want to do this right like the trans men that came before me."

"I'm afraid that won't be possible … Oh is that tracking Aggie's watch?" Praytis pointed with a long finger.

"What do you mean not possible?"

"Mother has the ability to regen your body with modification so you won't need to suffer the process that Earth offers to transsexual persons. Of course, Mother can't change your innate character. If she could, she would not. One's sense of self is one's own. She won't modify one's brain as Aggie assumes but she can — "

"Dude, why not on Earth? Spill it!" Mel cut him off with an aggressive tone. He let the man he'd been hiding for so long out more every hour.

"Oh dear, oh my … I … well … Oh dear … "

Great, now I upset him. "I'm sorry, OK? You want me to sign on. Tell me what's up with Earth. Give me a reason to stay."

"I have studied Earth humans for seven thousand years and … Oh bother, it's hard to say. It makes me quite sad, sad indeed. I've grown quite attached to Earth people. After all we are all related. All humans hail from the same source … the signs are in place. The AIs agree, even Moon City … my data is good, there is no doubt … But Earth humans are resilient … and — "

Mel slammed his hand down on the keyboard. It felt good letting frustration fly. His adopted brother got away with it all the time but he never did as a girl.

"Spit it out, right now — what's happening?"

Praytis drew himself up and backed from the station. "I'm sorry to tell you … Earth is doomed. Your civilization cannot survive and there is little time left. This is why the GTO became aggressive in their attempts to make a trade deal … Oh dear … The GTO has begun withdrawing … that is a bad sign."

"Not good enough, why, how?"

Praytis made himself as erect as was possible for his body form. His way of being formal.

"As you know the pollution and CO_2 levels are beyond repair and accelerating and that is no small thing. Coupled with the mass extinctions of flora and fauna now in progress, soon there will be no food. That the military oligarchy has over-thrown the government of America has and will generate intractable wars. The GTO, as you have seen, has removed its satellite system. Its purpose was to prevent nuclear weapons from operation. A great many thus far have been launched and disabled. The governments know their ICBM missiles cannot work, but once they learn they are free to use them … " Praytis made a big round sign with his arms indicating an explosion.

"There is the ongoing problem of rule by sociopaths. It is a genetic disorder that drives the worse of humankind into positions of power. There is no easy solution for this, any of this, there are no political solutions."

"Hope, what about that? There's no way out?"

"As before on Earth and like dozens of other planets, advanced civilizations fail and in so doing remove survivability. Mass die-offs will occur. Many human worlds have suffered this, and ironically, usually at the very moment of qualification into universal citizenship. In the recent past a meteorite collided with Earth and acted as a reset but no such thing will occur this time. I am afraid, due a combination of a docile, normal population over-lorded by true monsters, and that Earth's resources having been poisoned or used to exhaustion, I'm sorry to report only one outcome is possible."

"I don't buy it, I can't. How do you know this! There's always hope."

"This is how my home planet met its demise." Praytis bowed his head so low his pointed chin rested on his pidgin chest. "I'm afraid this pattern has often been repeated in the universe and the results are always the same."

Praytis went on to describe his ruined planet, which was reduced to a combination of landmass deserts and huge, lifeless oceans. His people had managed the lands for time immortal until the population increased and the capitalist class captured control of the resources upon entering their industrial age; thus, the countdown began. Praytis was one of the few survivors of his dead world. Like him, the ones that could leave did. He hitched a ride with a Life Force raider and signed on as crew for starship Remus. Later, he was hired, rather his contract was bought out by the GTO, and he remained in their employ for seven thousand years. He witnessed the end of his world and many others like it during his years as a starship anthropologist before joining the GTO. *This dude knows his stuff.*

Mel wasn't convinced Praytis' predictions were accurate. What about hope? Isn't Earth unique, Praytis said as much. Mel kind of knew all this horrible crap but could not face adding it up. His hope of a normal life on Earth, if you can call a trans man's life normal, was circling the drain.

Mel was heartsick. And just sitting there doing nothing made him feel worse. What could they do? Mel recorded Praytis' words. He'd send that conversation to Earth in a blog. Maybe people will hear what happened to Praytis and wake up. Mel and Praytis talked long and the whole time Aggie's watch didn't move from Moon City's low-income section.

TWELVE
Aggie Meets Kowalski

The front door looked like every other pub's front door in Key West, dirty brass handle, faded paint and all. Aggie hung near the door getting a better look at Kowalski's Bar and Grill thinking what could they be grilling on the moon. *Oh yeah, cows, they like cows.* She had the feeling that cow wasn't on the menu and she didn't want to know what was. Cows were used for robot parts around here. What would Jon Colbert think of that? Her almost boyfriend came out of cattle ranching. On thinking of him, her heart yearned.

The signs on the walls advertised Barth beer. OK, so they have beer on the moon. That kind of made sense, there were enough Earth people here to want beer, right? It was dark inside and tables around the room were hard to see. The bar was on the back wall with a door behind it going into a kitchen. There weren't any waitresses in skimpy outfits like when she worked at Bixby's. Just a weird looking blue guy hunched over a mug at the window table and an Earth guy behind the bar polishing glasses. Aggie ventured deeper inside.

Pubs opened to the streets on Key West's Duval Street and as a result the streets always smelled like second hand dinner and pee. Aggie edged forward. It didn't smell like puke on the moon but inside this bar … somebody had a bad night. She held her breath and grabbed that nasty door handle to leave.

The guy called out something unintelligible. She turned. He had a poop-eating grin on his three day's growth face.

"Sorry Mr., I don't speak moon … not yet if ever."

"Hey, don't go."

The guy came out from behind the bar by flipping up a section. He was maybe thirty, wore an old blue Navy shirt and regular blue jeans. Normal enough. The crew cut was out of fashion.

"Hey you speak English. Scuttlebutt says a lot of people are coming up." He spoke as he glided across the floor. Gravity was lite in this part of the city. He stuck out his hand. "Kowalski, Chip Kowalski, welcome aboard. Can I get you something?"

"I'm not old enough to drink and I don't have any money."

The guy busted out laughing. Aggie didn't shake his hand. "Money, you don't need it here. Nobody told you? Food, medical and drinks are free, for a donation of LF, that is. No drinking age here. That's fine, fine, how about I give ya something on the house, on the house."

"I am kinda hungry."

"Man, oh man, it's good to see Earth people. Not enough of us here, but that'll change pretty quick. Say, you're a refugee, aren't you?" The guy pulled a hot dog out of the rotating grill on the bar, put it in a bun and handed it to Aggie. "Hot dogs are free, free to enjoy."

Aggie inhaled the hot dog. She never got them at home. It was always fish and veggies or burgers and fries at Mark's Marina if she could justify spending her money. She couldn't tell if it was a good dog or a bad one, or if there was a difference. She didn't know what to make of the food, him or what he said.

"Tell me, what's your name?"

Her internal alarms told her to shut up but she blurted it out anyway. "I'm Aggie Piper, Captain of Mother."

"That's strange. You don't look like the girl on Earth's news." He went to this old fashion looking brass cash register and punched a few keys. A picture of Aggie from last year came up on the TV behind the bar. It was a still shot from a network news show with her previously long hair blocking her face. She was wearing a pretty yellow sundress in the picture. *I miss that dress.*

"I'm Aggie, so I changed. So what?"

"Aggie Piper has very nice long, straight, blond hair. You look like something the cat dragged in." Kowalski pushed a few more keys. "Says here you don't have a credit module on you, no ship belt either. Captains wear control belts and dress well. Never saw a captain in such piss-poor condition."

Aggie checked the ship's coveralls she wore. Yeah, she looked like a janitor. "I'm telling you I'm her. Ask Moon City. She has me on record. I bought ships from her. You don't like my hair? That's bogus. It's the latest thing."

"Really?" The guy laughed hard. "I guess you can afford the good stuff. I'll take silver or gold. What else brings you? How about a highball? I got whiskey and soda. I stocked up when I heard. That guy Sanderson isn't with you, is he? I hear he's trouble. I don't want to tango with that ass-rider. What can I do for you? I'll take Earth cash if that's all you got."

"I'm here about a crew." Aggie snatched another hot dog and talked while she chewed. "I'm looking for starship crew. Mother needs bodies. We're cutting out."

"You and everybody else. Didn't you see the rosters? Every ship in this quad's looking to take on crew. Me, I'm not budging. I'll make bank when the refugees come. I'm stocked. Traders are stupid. Moon City's where the money's at."

"Crap, no one for hire, no Earth people? I know there's some here." Aggie said. Her voice sounded like she felt, dejected. "How do I put the word out? I'm new here."

Kowalski laughed. She smelled alcohol on his breath. "Lady you're barking up the wrong tree. Fine, if the shuttles were running, you'd go on down and ask. Used to be the military won't shoot down GTO ships, but not so lately. You're screwed. Scuttlebutt says the Navy's got open season on Mother's ships. Only way down is with raiders. Shuttles aren't running." Kowalski picked his nails and blew air on them. "I know how you can get below." He said with slyness in his demeanor. "I know this raider, see and — "

"Forget it". Aggie said. She had seen a lot of hustlers in Key West. Everybody was trying to sell you something until you said you weren't a tourist. But Aggie was curious. "If I wanted a ride down, how'd I pay for it? I got credits. I'd transfer, right?"

"Sorry, credit's no good if you don't have a module. I'm not stupid. This isn't spaceport. City's not dialed into outworld economics here. Now if you had something to trade. I know a guy that knows a guy looking for hardware. Got any spare parts? What about that watch?"

Aggie looked at her watch. It was a gift; she'd never trade it away. What was she going to do now? Go back to her freshly repaired ship and yank off parts? No way.

"No thanks. I'll keep my watch. I might have stuff for ya back on my ship." She lied. *I'm not going anywhere.*

"I really like that watch. How about collateral? What if I get you a ride? I'll hold it until you come up with something I need, say, a matter thrower motor. I'd bet Mother could whip one up nothing flat. For asteroid deflection, not a weapon, see?"

Kowalski winked at her like he had a loose eyelash. She wouldn't get close enough to hear him whisper. Moon City didn't listen if you whispered, that was the rule. She smelled the booze on him from where she was and that was the repellent. Moon City AI's recorded everything in the spaceport anyway. She learned that the first time she was on the moon. It only respected privacy if you indicated you wanted it. People could and did mislead the AI. It was the only way to live in a total surveillance environment Praytis said. Kowalski was trying to put something over on Moon City. She didn't know what he was really after but she didn't trust him. And it seemed like he didn't trust her either. Besides all that, Sanderson said, "whatever you do, don't go to Earth."

"I'll think about it." Aggie said. "How do I get to the main spaceport or do I have to bribe you?"

"Ouch, fine you got my number. Can't an old war vet make a decent living? Exit, one block to the right. It's on the corner. That one goes to Main Port. Just say taxi. You refugees really need a module. Local transport info is available on it."

"OK, cool, thanks, by." Aggie had to bite her tongue. Refugee, really? She was at the door when the bartender called.

"Change your mind, come on back. I got a man that'll do it cheap. He'll ride you down no problem."

Aggie pushed the door and was outside. The air was way better. The taxi station wasn't far. It had to be a transport tube like Mother's. Nothing to be afraid of, right? Still she closed her eyes when she said taxi.

When she opened her eyes a few seconds later she was standing inside an alcove situated along a busy hall outside the main hangar. It wasn't the place where she parked but she had been there before. This was near the student quarters she visited on her previous official government moon trip.

The place was crowded. A lot of people carried duffel bags like they were leaving. The word refugee hammered inside her. What did Kowalski mean by that? Refugees coming or going? Next order of business was finding the roster wherever that was. Getting her request listed was a big step toward her goal. Mother was famous and surely somebody here would rather go on Mother than one of those lesser ships?

Aggie activated the phone and called Mel. "Hey, can you look into listing us on the Moon's roster, the one asking for crew?"

"After I'm done. I'm kind of busy right now. Can it wait?" Mel said. "I'm right in the middle of blogging. I'm writing about Paris, cool, yeah. This place is rad."

"Whatever, just let me know, K." Aggie closed the feed.

Paris, really? How's that more important? Oh yeah, a ruse. They didn't want the Navy tracing Mother. How does Mel do it anyway? He has some way to override everybody's software. It's like he invented the junk. Aggie hated all that spy crap. She was always a direct path kid. Just go and do what needs doing. In the hallway her direct path was blocked by a crap load of space people. She remained inside the taxi alcove thinking.

Kowalski's offer came to mind. What better way to get crew than go to Earth? A new idea hit, what if she went to Gitmo and busted Jon out? If she had Jon to back her up, they'd go after Mom and Dad together. Old times. They were unstoppable together. Aggie wondered if she might get a raider to drop her off in Cuba?

Forget it, that's not happening. Stupid idea.

Aggie leaned out into the hall. The place was mobbed, no signs pointing the way. She was out of ideas. Maybe a stupid idea was better than no idea. She rejected that concept. There had to be a way forward.

THIRTEEN

Archer in Ben's Place

Archer had long ago changed his name from Longfoot, his father's name, to David but he never thought of himself in that name. Archer is all anyone called him for all his time in regular service and he had been in the military since he was eighteen. He joined after learning how his father died in Vietnam. He wanted to emulate old Longfoot but he had gone far afield. He started life by seeking a hero's journey and wound up a tool of state serving an empire with no morals. Never ask why just obey. When commissioned to run the NRO's field operations they gave him a new name. Mr. Black. He didn't complain. The powers thought well of Mr. Black. Let them think that. Tool-hood is good cover.

He was thinking more and more of the past as his future unfolded ahead. It was strange pulling up to Sanderson's old office on Key West's Naval Air Station. It wasn't long ago when he and Sanderson locked horns here. The home office of the man he killed became his. *The spoils of war.*

Like Sanderson the building was plain Jane. Just a simple brick building on the end of a seldom used flight line. Normal enough, but it was full of tricks. Sanderson was also stuffed with mysteries and sleights of the hand but Sanderson could not trick the bullets that ripped him apart.

Archer silently moved through the foyer and entered the main reception area. Sanderson's old waiting room was down the hall. Stealth was an old habit he no longer needed. The building felt empty except for the hardass MP sitting behind the front desk. Archer reached the desk before the MP looked up from his novel. Startled, the man launched out of his seat.

The MP went to attention and delivered a sharp salute. "Sir!"

That was strange, so much strangeness. It was a long time since he wore a uniform. He wore the black suit and fedora of the rank called Mr. Black so long he forgot how to return a salute.

"At ease," came slow to his lips. NRO men didn't use formalities. *Never give away your rank.* The marine relaxed but Archer wouldn't call that stance at ease.

"General Archer, may I escort you to your office, sir?" The man was stiff as a board. "I was told you would arrive today, sir."

"That won't be necessary. I know the way." Archer looked at his guard's name tag. "Jones is it, a fine American name."

"Yes, sir!"

Archer resisted the idea of telling Jones to stop with the formalities. He had to keep up the ruse. The guard was faced with the uniform. Archer had to put on a different continent. He wore his ribbons and medals which were light on his chest but heavy in his heart. He didn't like it. After today he'd scrap the uniform. He had forgotten the uniform's hat. Having worn the fedora of power, not wearing a hat felt good. Generals don't have to be in uniform. He caught his image in a hall mirror. His hair was too long. Since his run-in with Karnack's control bracelet his black hair had streaked gray.

Archer walked the short distance alone. Sanderson's office reception area wasn't occupied. That yeomen who was there before, he had no idea she was CIA, was sent by President Albright to spy on Sanderson. *What was her name? Jennifer Nostrum.* That woman went missing. Probably on a deep cover assignment. Everyone spied. MJ was no doubt watching him now. But why is this building open and only one guard? Were they setting him up? Testing his loyalty? It didn't smell right.

He went past the secretary's desk. Sanderson's door was behind it. He opened the door half expecting it to set off a bomb.

Everything was as it was before except that ugly green phone was gone. He took Sanderson's old desk, pulled Sanderson's old laptop case up, and punched in the wall code. Sanderson's bookshelf came forward and spun 180 degrees. A wall of screens and a server with madly blinking lights replaced the antique navel manuals and other old books. Half the eight screens were dead. He'd figure out how to access them later. The other half streamed data too fast, but not for him. Sanderson also had alien enhancements, and perhaps he could read them as well. Archer made the library wall come back. Whatever Sanderson was into, he'd let it alone for now.

He could swear Sanderson's old phone was still there before the man died. Where could it have gone? Did the dead man come back for it? The thought made him shiver. Maybe Aggie Piper beamed down and stole it. He looked further; it was in the trash can. Archer carefully placed it back on the desk.

He pressed the intercom, "Jones I'm good. You can go. Take the day off."

"Sir, I was told — "

"Whoever gave your orders consider his rank is lower than mine. Dismissed. Take the week off."

"The week, sir?"

"You heard me."

Archer didn't bother to check if the man left. Rather he went down the hall to Sanderson's lounge. The door was locked but the file provided the combination. Likewise, the bathroom was locked. Achieving entry, Archer pressed a tile and activated the elevator door behind the shower wall. It was just as the file described. The tile wall slid away and a stainless steel elevator cab was behind the slider as expected. It was dirty inside, rust on the walls, dust and mold.

The ride down took time. He did not know how deep but the cab traveled fast. The alien transport hub had to be deep. The entire ocean crushed down upon the cavern system.

It was as the file told but seeing it was different from reading about it. This cavern was impossible. How did they do it? This deep down it should be over one hundred degrees.

Archer got into a tram car which rolled on many miles and stopped at a terminal. The cavern was huge and obviously not natural. More impossibilities. The car pulled into a station of sorts. Many tunnels radiated out from this space. The car stopped at center. A device rotated his tram like the train museum's steam engine turntable he saw at the B&O Railroad Museum in Baltimore as a kid. That museum was organized and clean but this place was rusty, dirty, uncared for. When the turn was complete the door opened. An alien shuttle was waiting, gangplank down. He didn't see it arrive.

"You people should take better care of your equipment."

Archer boarded. The gray alien biological robot pilot was there and it didn't talk as expected. He had seen plenty of dead bio-bots but this was the first one he met alive enough to be functional. It didn't address him. Instructions came verbally from some other source and most likely a recording. "Please be seated at the center couch and secure your seatbelt."

He didn't bother to strap in. The moon flight took 31 minutes as expected. The file said every flight was the same. The ship parked without a bump and the gangway silently dropped open. What he saw once landed wasn't expected.

The moon hangar was gargantuan to be sure. But it should have been filled with craft of every description. Packed like canned fish. The place previously had two-thirds of its capacity filled. Where did all the ships go? The report didn't have anything on increased alien flight activity. The NRO monitored all alien traffic. Strange, of late, fewer alien crafts were reported than normal. Where had they gone? Archer smelled evacuation. The Defense Department will be pleased to learn there were fewer alien ships. Less counterattack vehicle potential was good news for war hawks. He had read all of Sanderson's reports, none of them described these conditions. Archer wondered what Sanderson would have thought of this.

He stood a long while searching the hangar. Alien people moved here and there at a distance. Some types he knew, others were more alien than the usual but he was too far from the nearest for details. Sanderson's report said their GTO hosts didn't let Sanderson linger in the hangar. Sanderson thought the aliens were limiting observation time to prevent a true assessment of the fleet. Strange, no one came to greet the new Earth representative.

The GTO always sent someone to escort Sanderson. Sanderson was never left alone. Archer took the time to check his plastic gun. This one had nothing metal, not even the bullet tips. It was more than enough to kill Karnack. *Once that was done … retirement.* Ridiculous idea, they never let you retire.

The ceiling of the hangar lit. It must have been a mile up. A section shimmered and a shuttle penetrated the hangar's solid roof. Sanderson was never allowed to see that. The small craft glided down and landed near the furthest perimeter. His craft was parked near the center.

He turned away searching the walls for signs giving direction. An Earth woman with spiked multi-colored hair wearing a jumpsuit came through a hatchway. She looked around and stood there as if she were looking for someone. That door was a hundred yards or more from him. His eyes were good but he couldn't see her face in the shadows.

"Aggie Piper, can it be?" Archer rubbed his eyes. "Aggie Piper!" He called. The girl was too far away. She didn't hear him. She looked toward him but exited via that hatch and was gone.

"Was that her? She's dead." He wasn't sure. If Brinks knew Piper was still alive, he wasn't telling. *But why? I'm Brinks' man and he lies to me? What's his long game?* Archer saw why there were holes in Sanderson's reports. No insider tells all he knows, it's protection, insurance. If that was Aggie Piper, he'd keep it to himself. He was sure he hit her when he shot Sanderson. Piper might have survived but that island blew up. He decided it can't be her. That haircut was popular.

Archer hurried toward the nearest hatchway. He opened the door but didn't see her. There was a wide hallway left and right bending away in both directions, and one hall across from his hatch leading out and away from the hangar. It was full of aliens, all kinds in every direction, many he never heard of. That girl's door was around the bend, if she went the other way, he missed her. His attention shifted.

The aliens were going about their business and ignoring him. Archer straddled the hatch with his mouth and the door hanging open. He was stunned. Sanderson never saw anyone but GTO people. It was as if they cleared the decks whenever an Earthling was in town. An alien tapped his shoulder from behind and spoke in a language Archer never heard before. He looked normal for seven feet tall, his jaw was too big but the giant's one piece jumpsuit could pass for a U.S. Navy flight deck overall.

"I'm sorry, I only speak English." Archer moved out of the exit. The big man squeezed through the hatch; it was like any other ship hatch; solid steel complete with spin lock.

The alien man adjusted a device on his wrist. "I see, Earth person. Moon City said to expect refugees. First thing you should know is keep airtight doors sealed. It is the most basic spacer rule."

"I'll keep that in mind. Could you please direct me to the Galactic Trade Organization offices?"

The big face put on a puzzled look. "I'm not used to this, you aren't wired. City says forty doors down on your right." He pointed down the hall leading away from the spaceport. "She says they have disbanded although former employees remain temporarily."

The big man closed and secured the hatch. Archer moved into the flow of passersby traffic. Nothing was as described. Was Sanderson pulling MJ-12's chain all this time? Every visit to the moon was a fact-finding mission but what was known in the reports didn't add up to what he saw now. Moon City? Refugees? What is all this activity about? Bigger question, how much of this should he report?

"None of it. I'm here for my own purposes."

Thoughts of killing Karnak were once foremost on his mind as he recovered from the bracelet. When he boarded his flight to Key West this morning, killing wasn't on his mind. This profusion of alien life took his mind to another plain. The moon was alive with people, all kinds of people, all working together, all living together. A sick feeling came over him.

Brinks would destroy it all to consolidate his power. What Archer wanted was only one alien and the chances of finding him were slim. The GTO disbanded. What does that mean? Archer wondered in a daze absorbing all he saw. He spent several hours moving from one spaceport to another and back again. Many aliens were leaving with luggage. The largest hangars held mother ships, many more than what was described in the reports.

"What's going on here?"

Archer took another turn into a long hall that was full of people. He went against the tide and without looking for it, found the door with the number forty marked on it. No doubt Sanderson had IDed the correct room. It said GTO under the number. Every sign he noted so far was in alien script. He moved closer and it opened automatically. The room was as described, off white walls, ceiling and floors. The conference table Truman gave to the GTO in the 1940s, and matching chairs, was as reported. But no people. Nothings else, not even a post-it note.

"Gone fishing I suppose."

Archer lay his briefcase down, took out a note pad and wrote a message. *General Archer, Earth's new trade negotiator, was here. Please contact me via my cell phone.* He wrote the burn phone's number. It wasn't traceable to him. He laid the note on the table and left.

The hall wasn't as crowed this far from the spaceport. He went back the way he had come and ducked into the hangar; his transport was still there. Nothing to worry about, he went back into the hallway. At a distance he saw two winged humanoids. He hurried forward. They were moving toward the spaceport at a fast clip. Seven-foot-tall people have a long stride. He hid his face and moved past them, palmed his gun, and followed. Tapping one from behind both creatures turned. Was that Karnack? If so, he had changed. The other he didn't know.

The female started squawking at him with birdlike speech. Once she finished, Archer said, "Sorry I'm from Earth. I don't understand."

"Mr. Black, my how you have recovered and all for the better. And a promotion as well." Karnak said. "I am so glad you survived, quite surprising actually." He extended a hand. "I've not much time to chat. We are flying out soon and we must confirm the condition of our accommodations."

Archer took his hand. W*here the hell are you going*? The alien's grip was weak and it should be. Even at that height there wasn't much to Karnak. He was a flight capable human; light and thin with hollow bones. As Archer gripped Karnack's hand, he fought the urge to draw the alien in for the kill. The timing wasn't right. People were everywhere. Something else stopped him, too.

"How is it you aren't in chains after all the harm you caused?" Archer said as he slipped the little gun back into his jacket pocket. This was personal and not the kind of question he was sent to ask.

Karnack's laughed, his birdlike cackle was raw and grating before. But now it was musical, soothing, friendly … strange.

"My dear fellow, we are not primitives. Medical cured me of the virus which enacted the sociopath gene response. I am now immune. The cure was discovered eons past, but of course, while a criminal I avoided the treatment. I am very sorry that I transferred this malady to Earth. As you know, I was out of my mind and that was the case for seven thousand years prior. No more. We advanced races don't … what is the word … grudge. We don't hold a grudge. Rather, we address the cause of trouble and repair it. We move on. Is that not logical?"

"If I kill you right now for what you did to me, I would be forgiven?" Archer was incredulous. One hand reached into his pocket. He fingered the plastic gun.

"Of course, now that Earth has been adjudicated an advanced race and accepted as a citizen of the universe. You would be taken directly to ram-ed and cured of the desire to do such a tasteless thing. I on the other hand would be revived. On occasion city residents do die and are revived. As you are a guest you will likewise be properly cared for. Corporal punishment is so very archaic, don't you think? It has never worked on Earth. I am correct, of course. Would you agree?"

"I don't know what to think. What about trade deals? I've taken over for Sanderson."

The female sang and squawked incomprehensible words.

"Oh, my sister is quite right. We have an appointment. I'm sorry but the GTO's contract has run out. Anyone on Earth that has the ability to get here is welcome to come and make their own trade arrangements while the opportunity last, that is. Many goods traders have shops here. We of the GTO no longer have exclusive trade rights."

Bird-lady squawked more forcefully. "I'm afraid we must go." Karnack said. "Good day to you Mr. Black and the best of luck."

"It's Archer. Mr. Black is dead." Archer called as Karnak walked away.

"Goodbye Mr. Archer. I really must go." Karnack and his sister blended into the stream of people moving toward the hangar.

Archer pulled out the gun and aimed. A larger, hairy man got between Archer and Karnack. There was no taking the shot. If he hit the Yeti, Archer was sure he'd only piss that giant off. He returned it to his pocket. *What good is a gun here?*

Not all aliens there were getting ready to leave. Many must have gone already. GTO people? Archer leaned against the wall and watched Karnack and the other until they were out of sight. The plastic gun in his pocket felt like a thousand pounds around his neck.

What would happen if I blew my own brains out? They don't have me recorded; I'd die.

The old Mr. Black would never think that. Kill others for country by command and even himself if called to do so, yes. The old Mr. Black had a mission and the mission was everything to that shell of a man. The mission was all he once had. He didn't feel that way now.

"Mr. Black's dead." He whispered as he wandered down a hallway. "Karnack killed him."

It hit him; he didn't have a worthy purpose. Mr. Black was dead, dead like the Galaxy Project. He'd never admit it not if he wanted to stay alive. He won't go out like Sanderson like a used up monkey wrench. For the first time in thirty years, Archer felt human. His old self, the self that honored his father's memory and life was back. A new plan and mission began to jell.

He opened a hatch in the long hall, opposite side of the GTO office. There was a vast city inside. He shut the hatch and moved toward the spaceport. He noticed an alcove. A sign above it said in English, "Bar and grill." He stepped inside the booth and was whooshed away. He landed next to a pub. He went inside and found the place was run by an American expat named Kowalski. He had seen other Earth people around the spaceport but this was the only one that spoke normal.

He never got his R&R so Archer proceeded to get drunk. The barkeep didn't ask for money. Earth money was good here but unnecessary. Guests of Moon City drank free. Archer had his fill of Mr. Black and drank enough to drown out what was left of him.

He pulled the gun out and played around with it. He intended on leaving it on the bar and call it a tip. He milked usable intel out of Kowalski, more than Sanderson ever knew. Some gratuity was in order and the least he could do before staggering back to the spaceport. But Kowalski wanted nothing to do with a gun so Archer laid what cash he had on the bar. Archer didn't need the gun anymore. The bar had a garbage bin. He decided the trashcan was where guns belonged while sipping his last rock and rye. But old habits die hard and he slipped it back into his pocket without thinking before tipping off his barstool.

As he made his way back to his transport Archer realized he had a better use for that specially built plastic gun. It cost a lot to make. *Why waste it?* A tool of state for a tool of state. Fitting. He got back into the shuttle with his head swimming in alcohol and subversive ideas.

FOURTEEN

Back to Kowalski

Aggie wandered around among the people asking questions and getting no answers. She wound up back where she started. The taxi station was near an intersection of the hallway that went around the main spaceport. She was there before on tour with Sanderson but the halls were empty then. All she saw of aliens before were students like Tall Gray and Moby types. They must have let her see them because she was already used to them.

The hall was flooded with people, really interesting people, but she hated crowds. She never went to Sunset Pier or Duval Street if she didn't have to. Some people there were the same kind she saw in Moon City but others were so strange she almost freaked out.

That thing she saw coming her way was ten feet tall, and just like a giant spider crab, but wearing clothes. It wasn't around when the taxi shoot dropped her or she would have crawled back up that tube. Worse, it smelled like crab too. She hated crabs. Aggie almost barfed. She pressed backwards into the taxi alcove and looked up at the low ceiling thinking she should crawl into that hole. But the thing passed quickly and rather than leave, she stepped out into the busy corridor. There was a rush of air behind her. She turned and the alcove's ceiling hole was gone.

"This is crap." Aggie said as she waded into the crowd again.

Most of the moon people were going from the interior toward the spaceport and directly into the hangar. Others split in either direction and went down the perimeter corridor to further hatches. Some marched further on and out of sight around the curve. Aggie hung out at the intersection randomly calling out her questions.

"Hey, where's the spaceport office, where do I post a crew request?"

A big guy all hairy like Bigfoot stopped. The guy was like the one she had seen earlier but had white rather than brown fur. It grunted at her. It was talking but she didn't understand. It understood her. Weird that aliens understood English. It tried to help but all it could do was grunt and point up the hallway — the way everyone was coming from.

"OK, OK, I get it. That's where the office is, right?"

The big alien grunted out something that sounded like it said GTO. Great the GTO isn't what she wanted at all. They were in cahoots with the U.S. Government. Praytis said that the GTO were just contractors and not a big deal on the moon, more like slimy used car salesmen. Thinking back to Kowalski and all the shops and neon signs, Aggie figured the GTO weren't the only cheesy operators in town. The only difference between Moon City and the tourist trap she called home was variety. This whole place felt like a bowl of spaghetti with everything twisted together. No ends anywhere.

"Hey everybody!" She yelled loud as she could. "I need crew, anyone looking for a starship job!"

A lot of them stopped and looked her way but they all kept going. This was getting hopeless fast. She took a few deep breaths too clam down and decided to use her eyes and not her voice, which was getting horse.

Look for Earth people. Maybe they'd talk to me at least. Down the hall, a couple of winged people like Karnack were heading her way. That creeped her out big time. The memory of Karnack and his evil was still fresh. She started moving in the other direction and back to the main hall, when someone in an Earth military uniform came around the corner up by the spaceport.

"Duh, somebody had to replace Sanderson. What will it be, dumbass? Get creamed by alien killers or a government killer?"

No brainer. The government wanted her dead and the aliens didn't give a rat's butt about her. She plunged into the crowd and walked against the tide. She managed to get around the angel people without being seen. Checking back, the military guy stopped to talk to the angels. The lady angel pointed toward her. She ducked into an alcove. There were alcoves up and down the halls but only one had a sign she could read. This one didn't.

"Great, just great." She said and the ceiling opened.

Aggie peeked. The military guy was coming right at her.

"Taxi, Kowalski," she said with no idea if it would bring her back there. Anything was better than running into a government guy. The tube shot down and sucked her up. In a few seconds she was back at the curb within sight of the bar.

"I could get used to this. I wonder how they charge my account?" Aggie said as she reentered the bar.

The blue guy was passed out and sleeping on the table. Kowalski had that big poop-eating grin on his face again. He reminded her of a shark considering an easy meal. She didn't like that slimy guy but at least he was an Earth guy who wasn't out to kill her.

"I knew you'd be back," he said. "I told you there weren't any sailors available. You want crew, Earth is where you'll find them. I heard sluggo's are seeking crew positions." That cheesy smile returned.

"Maybe I'll just go back to Mother … But I do need Earth people. OK, you win. Nobody here is for hire. I'll have Mother send a recruitment party." Aggie didn't sound convincing even to herself. She never was a good liar. She didn't have a party to send. She was it.

"That's not smart," Kowalski said. "Planetside news is General Brinks has America on high alert. Orders are shoot down alien craft. Mother's crafts are the target. But I know how to get past the blockade. I know a guy that has a guy with the very best cloaking gear. It also has camo that makes one ship look like five. They'll send fighters chasing ghosts. I can get you to Earth … but it'll cost ya."

"How do I know you won't keep my watch? OK you want collateral, I get that, but this thing isn't worth much."

"Lady this is Moon City. She sees all, knows all. If we make a deal it'll be recorded. Terms are if you don't come back, I keep the watch. Call it a pawn deal."

"Why, what good is it?" Aggie said perplexed, it was just a phone watch and nothing special except to her. OK Praytis had improved it, but still it wasn't special by alien standards. *He knows it's special to me. He knows my motivation.* "You're reading my mind. That's so disgusting."

"No, on the contrary. It's not like that. Earth tech's collectible especially because she's about to … Moon City isn't pulling out for laughs. Not for nothing, but it's about to hit the fan. It's on the feed. Moon's shuttles are one way only. Up and out is it. There's no more two-way passage. Artifacts are fast becoming scarce. Values are up and climbing. I'm in business to make money and … "

The guy rattled off his justifications so fast Aggie didn't absorber it all. *Yeah, he's a used car salesman with a lot full of lemons.*

One thing seemed true. From what Praytis said, things were about to get really bad back home and really fast. Mel and Sanderson didn't have time to set up the plan. Mr. Security is out of commission. Going down to pick up crew was dangerous, and the longer they waited the more dangerous it was. This was serious. She felt like she had to do something before it was too late. She'd never get there on a Moon City shuttle. That was her backup and it was toast. Her ship refused to go to Earth. Take the offer. What choice did she really have?

Aggie activated her watch. "Hey Ship, this is Aggie. I need to talk with Praytis."

"Hello Captain, I am glad you called. I have much to report. First — "

"Wait, listen. How is our security guy mending? Will he be in medical much longer?"

"I do believe he will be released soon. Late today ship's time is possible but tomorrow is most likely. I must say — "

"OK, I'm going out for a little while. I can't tell you why. The stupid butthole Feds might be listening so I can't say. Don't wait up for me, OK?"

"Captain, I know your mind, after all I am an anthropologist specializing in Earth studies and if what you are thinking is what I suspect you are, I do believe you are making a mistake, such as — "

Aggie clicked off the signal. "Whatever." *They aren't ready. Sanderson can't tell me no.*

"OK, Chip, get your raider." Aggie took off her watch and spun it by the band on her finger. "When we settle, I get my watch back. The price is ten credits. That's all I'm paying. Ten LF credits for a two-way ride there and back again. Take it or leave it."

"I think we can do that."

"I want Cuba, Guantanamo Bay." Aggie said. "In and out with a passenger."

She'd work out some stuff with the raider crew and hire them to help spring Jon without Kowalski involved. Once she was in flight, she'd get them to help her. She had the money. She just couldn't get to it now. Kowalski gave her a big clue. They're capitalists so they'll go for extra cash. They're raiders, right. They're in it for the money. Working together, after getting Jon, she'd get them to help find her folks. She'd get that much crew before Sanderson was even out of the tank. *That'll show Mr. Security I've got it going on.*

"The crew won't go there directly. They have a scheduled LF gathering first. It's a collection operation. Just a small detour. Two-way transport is not a problem but you'll need to wait a little. Jamaica first."

"Close enough. I'll take the ride. Moon City recorded this, right."

Kowalski came out from behind the bar and said. "Moon City, play back the contract, please." What was just said came back. No speakers anywhere, the conversation was everywhere in the air. "Satisfied?"

"OK, cool."

Kowalski walked over to the passed out guy, stuck what looked like a pen into his arm and pushed the cap. The blue guy bolted upright in his seat like getting shocked and started jabbering. She was sure he was cussing up a blue storm.

"Earth English, damn you. Where's Andy? I have a side job for you. Earth customer, she's here."

"Earthman, this better be good. I just spent a tenth credit getting drunk. We aren't supposed to go for another two hours."

"I'll give you a free drunk when it's over. Alert your ship."

The blue guy put a hand to his ear. Weird how Chip told the blue guy what to do. Who worked for who here? Maybe the raider crew wasn't up for a side job? Too late now. Aggie was committed. The blue guy must have been communicating with his crew. Aggie waited. Chip had his hand on his ear too. Everybody was talking moon talk without her. If she had gotten a belt maybe she'd understand or maybe not.

"Ship's on stand down," the blue guy said. "She's in the trader's pod. Operable in thirty minutes." The blue guy got out of his chair slowly, obviously hung over. "Going on raid anyhow."

Aggie sized up the alien. Blue guy pretty much looked like any normal person except for blue skin. The bald head wasn't unusual. He wasn't much taller than

Aggie's 5'10". She'd take him if she had to fight. She took out 7-foot Karnack no problem. Nobody expects a girl to know how to fight. If she hadn't trained with Mark, going with a strange man would be crazy. She wasn't crazy or worried.

"Hey you're that guy in the old Blue People Plyers stage act. I saw videos. They performed in Key West. I wondered what happened to them. They were kind of fun."

The blue man smiled. His teeth were blue. *Oh, that's how they communicate, it's blue tooth.* Aggie stifled a laugh.

"That was a good scam." The blue guy said. "We packed them in and collected a good measure of Life Force. I didn't have to use holo, either. Too bad your government caught on. They forced us to cease operations. The current collection point doesn't pay as well."

"Oh, OK, whatever. Let's go."

The blue man exited the bar with Aggie and they proceed across town on foot. Apparently, there weren't any tubes going to the raider's pod. Blue man complained, saying Moon City didn't accommodate them so well although City AI was happy to accept their money by way of docking fees, rents and the ambient Life Force each crewman emitted. Raiders were outsiders and tolerated but not embraced. Aggie identified with that. She was an outsider all her life and now she was way outside. So far out the Navy would shoot her down on sight if they had the chance. Maybe it was good to leave Grandpa's watch behind. No watch meant one less way the Feds could find her. It didn't occur to her that Mother would have that same problem.

FIFTEEN

Brinks and the Blog

Since Brinks gave the order that blew Haiti away, the Defense Department suffered a public relations nightmare. Americans wanted blood after dead gargantuan men, bizarre beasts and U.S. sailors started washing up on Puerto Rico's shores. A sizable faction of the Department of Defense stood with the public. He was boxed in. It was time to kick down walls.

He couldn't pin Haiti on President Albright. He neutralized her too soon and that was a mistake. It was necessary. She had to be taken down ASAP but his men weren't fully prepared. The operation was cobbled together and poorly executed. Too sloppy. That's how Albright escaped. He needed to get more radical to ensure control. Brinks ran a tight ship and he detested loose ends. Things were out of control and now this. Goddamn if Aggie Piper's dead man switch blogs didn't keep popping up. He called the NSA's head man, Jimmy Door, to his Pentagon office to see about staunching this bleed.

Door was sent right in when he arrived. Brinks pushed a pile of briefs and security reports out of his way to make room for Door's laptop. Door was a short man of Hungarian descent with bushy gray hair pointing in every direction. A disorderly man. Brinks hated him on sight. Door placed his laptop before the general and had a hard time reaching in to manipulate the computer. Door's nasty sideburns brushed against Brinks' cheek as that pissant scrolled with the finger pad. Brinks almost elbowed that dweeb off his feet.

"Take the computer off my desk. Tell me, don't show me."

The NSA man snapped up the laptop, rounded the desk and took a chair. "I've never seen anything like this. We can't locate where the blogs originate. We know Aggie Piper and Melisa Van Ness made them in Key West but where they are stored is at issue. She releases them from different servers each time. We get close to an archive and it jumps away."

"You mean to tell me the NSA with all its equipment — years ahead of China — can't figure this out?"

Door visibly cringed. That was a low blow. China was winning the technology war. It was like China had an inside line to the aliens. Door shrank in his chair. Brinks leaned forward. He took pleasure in his effect on others. His moniker, General Mayhem, was well earned but it also kept others from telling him what he needed to know. The fear he generated had its down side.

"I, I, I was trying to show you … it's complicated. It's a worm. More like a quantum tunnel. Van Ness Industries is stumped. Mr. Van Ness says his main engineer has gone missing. I bet the Chinese kidnapped him."

Who is lying here, Van Ness Industries or Door?

"Put your best men on it. I want that blog stopped yesterday. Do you hear me?"

"We have top men on it. The problem is after we killed the old blogs, they came back. I think we have a new set. They're still making them. That Van Ness girl … " Door dropped his head and started mumbling.

He doesn't want to say it. The problem is how to take out the girl without killing Van Ness Industries' enrollment. The NSA relies on Van Ness hardware. It gives them the ability to manipulate the entire internet. Maybe a big kill is the answer. Employ direct controls and shut off the net permanently. Do what it takes.

" … so … I don't know … I mean … this is a real quandary …

"What quandary, say it."

"We suspect Melisa the daughter participates in Van Ness design engineering. She was placed there, after all, due her genius. A child prodigy and — "

"I'll handle the girl. Not your problem," Brinks said. Door looked relieved; he wasn't a killer. Too many luncheons with the Van Ness clan under his belt. "Where's the girl now, still under house arrest?"

"No, she took off right after restrictions were imposed. We've tracked her. She's in Paris but we can't find her."

"How the hell!" Brinks pounded on his desk.

Door radiated misery. He's a tech man, not a field operative. Unfair question. A different sort of spy did that. Brinks was asking the wrong man. He'd have the CIA in next and relight that fire. Brinks pulled himself together. He was about to chew the man's arm off but intimidating the NSA never worked out. Door wasn't a political appointee. He was a deep state lifetime bureaucrat and Brinks needed him for the final move.

"Next item," Brinks said. "You're ready to pull the big plug."

"Yes sir, we are a go on that."

"Show me the Van Ness girl." Brinks didn't know what she was about. He didn't read her file. He only met her old man once. Small potatoes until now.

Door pressed a laptop button, turned the machine around and placed it before Brinks. Melisa Van Ness appeared. Door explained it didn't look like the previous blogs. The background wasn't Piper's house. In this one Van Ness was filming outside the Eiffel Tower. Brinks wanted to ask how that can be without French security cameras capturing her but he held the question. The NSA hacked every security system in the world. Alien tech was how they did it. *That goddamned Piper girl! Keep cool Brinks.* Aliens also explained how the Van Ness girl escaped out of country. Brinks made a note to add Melisa Van Ness to the kill list. He underlined it three times.

The girl wore a man's dress shirt. Her chest was strapped down flat. The wild hair was cut short. A girl's styling wasn't in evidence. A disguise? Brinks' neck hair hackled. The girl was smart, too smart.

"Hey everybody, guess where I am? Sorry if the sound is funky, it's a little windy here … "

Brinks pressed the space bar and stopped playback. "Find out what day this was. Search the background. Find out when the wind was blowing. I don't see those flags waving."

"We'll get right on it."

Brinks continued the recording.

"Dudes, so, like, I'm doing this walkabout, yeah. But Aggie's been in touch. If you haven't heard, Aggie survived the attack. That's right, America tried to kill Aggie for real. What a bunch of buttmunches. They did a job on that Sanderson dude. They killed their own guy! Shows where they're coming from. You all saw it on the video, yeah. I'm hanging loose, moving around because they'll try and kill me too, even if I'm not that important. I don't know how she does it, but Aggie's spaceship can find me wherever I am. Cool right? Even so … Any-who I have a message or two from Aggie.

Brinks stopped the playback. The girl held up a phone to read from. Good, they'll trace the phone's make. More clues. The little bitch has a tripod and camera. That should have been easy for French security to spot but they were compromised. Brinks made a note for the CIA to tap every local phone they could. No doubt Piper killed the security camera's view. Maybe a private citizen caught it. He hit the space bar.

"First, Mother's computers looked at the murder tape and President Albright didn't do anything. Mother captured the White House's security system before the event. Besides, any nerd with decent software can figure out how they faked it. Hint, hint. But we have records of how they set it up. Look out for those. Aggie will put them out at random. Trust me, Jane Albright isn't a crook, OK."

"Here's the other thing. Starship Mother is leaving soon and she wants a crew of Earth people. I don't know why. People suck. She's like the NSA, she records everything. If Mother thinks you'll make the cut, you'll get an application on your computer. Do your response video and close it. No need to put it on the net. If accepted, you'll get info on how to get to Moon City. Oh, did I mention, there's a big city on the backside of the moon. cool, right?"

"I'm out of time. I got to go before the Feds trace me. Peace out. Oh, the other thing, I'm really a dude, I'm trans. Sorry Mom, I'm done waiting."

The screen blanked out. Brinks pushed back his chair. He had leaned toward the screen for a better look. Jimmy Door shrank deeper into his leather seat no doubt waiting for Brinks to blow his stack. But Brinks wasn't going to do that. Rather, he was calm. Calm in the face of trouble is how he managed to stay alive in war. This was war.

"Door, find out where the Van Ness couple are and pick them up. I want that girl. Pass it onto the CIA. I want it done now, understand? Research the Pipers data again while you're at it. Arrest extended family if they have any. Sonny Piper survived. He wasn't there when Branford's place went up. He's in the wind. All agency APB. Find him."

"What are you going to do? I won't be a party to — "

Brinks raised his hand and pitched his dead-eyed cold stare at Door. Door shriveled up like an anorexic grandma. In a real democracy he would never say what came next. But Brinks, the NSA and all the top men in security and military were all outlaws and all in. They were criminals. They go along to get along, like it or not. Some had more balls than others. Brinks had the biggest balls of them all.

"Whatever it takes to crack the Van Ness girl and take Piper out is authorized. Kill or kidnap the families if that's what it takes. You will do your job. No limits, back to work."

The NSA chief took off fast. Brinks kicked back into his chair. Piper was alive and he knew it. That was top secret information. Now the public knew it as well. Branford wouldn't have made the call if Piper was dead. Everyone knows Piper survived. That played into his hands. The more people agitated and up in arms, the more excuses he had to crush them. It was perfect. When his big event went down, he'd blame it all on aliens and Piper. He made a note to have media ramp up that angle. He wrote, "Make Piper into an alien invader," and underlined it three times.

SIXTEEN

Countermeasures

Mel and Praytis watched the entire thing. The communication's AI alarmed when Mel's mole hit pay dirt. They had a tap into Brinks' office off the NSA guy's computer. From there Mel was able to get into Brinks' local network.

"He wants to kill me. Good luck dickhead." Mel said.

"Very clever Melvin. How did you accomplish it? We did not release this yet. Buddy is in Earth orbit waiting, did the Americans … hack … yes that is it, hack our probe?"

"They wish," Mel said. "Nope, I fed it directly into the NSA's computers via their own satellites. I made it look like it came from outside on the net. If they search online, they won't find it."

"But how did we see them?"

"The same program we'll use to sort out our applicants, yeah." Mel was feeling pretty smug but the feeling didn't last. Reality rang a bell inside his skull. *The NSA will figure it out, they have my software.*

"I'm inside the NSA dude's computer. I'm telling Buddy ready the cast." Mel typed a command. "I also sent a copy of Brinks' meeting to Mr. Branford. They'll take the hint and split before the hammer comes down. But I don't see him anywhere. I can't locate his computer. Mr. Branford's offline. I don't get it?"

Mel typed and clicked. "I sent a warning to my parents; they got the Brinks thing … just received … Dad's watching it now … Branford will get it, too when he goes online. Dad must be freaking out. He thinks his stuff is unhackable. Thinks he's safe, that's a joke. I love tight beam … I should release Brinks' meeting on the net, yeah?"

"I do believe this will cause massive unrest … are you sure this procedure is … I've studied Earth for … oh dear … oh my … "

"Dude, it's cool. Why not?"

"I can think of a number of things." Praytis said. His tone was miserable. "Revolution comes to mind."

"Fine, I'll hold Brinks back for now but not the blog. It's got to go."

"I suppose my noninterference pledge is void … Oh dear. As this is an Earth ship after all … Oh bother." Praytis gave Mel a thumb's up.

Mel wasn't sure the Brinks recording would do that. Taking a cue from the deep state's usual game was their best defense. Use the enemies' crap against them. That's what kept Karnack safe. The state sowed conflict and caused chaos all over the world that way. It was CIA playbook 101. *Confuse and control.* He typed the code, "ET go home," sent it and watched it bounce around the universe for a minute or two before Buddy picked it up and splashed Earth's media satellites. Every time the NSA cleared Aggie's and Mel's blogs Buddy will reinstall them via the government's own system. But now Buddy had a more important job. He'd also track and forward recipients.

A lot of orbital hardware was suddenly powering down. *They must be trying to stop me.* He'd have to look into that. Turning the media satellites back on wasn't a big thing. It was kind of fun. But some were more than idle. They were turned off all together. *Wow.*

"Buttheads are killing their own media satellites, boy that's desperation."

Ben said get a crew. First step was this announcement, done and done. They had better get results fast and decide who's coming before the internet was shut off for real. Mel checked blog progress. The "Aggie is alive" message went out. Hits were piling up like crazy. And right behind it, the call for crew started zeroing in on candidates. Social AI thought it would take a week to ID the right people. Buddy had to receive the applications and send them home. Mel juiced the program. They didn't have a week. They'd be lucky if they had three days. Alarms went off. NSA countermeasures were attacking the new upload.

"Damn, that was fast, we'll see about that." Mel said.

"Oh my."

Mel began a barrage of electronic torpedoes. He had one aimed at the NSA's mainframe in Virginia loaded into the ISS's navigation computers. *They won't shoot their own space station, will they?* Virginia was the source of the counterattacks. Mel's little worm might not wipe the entire NSA thing, but is sure as hell was going to make a mess of their search and destroy software. That gave Mel an idea. He told Buddy to physically attach himself to the International Space Station but do it really carefully. Buddy was just behind it following it in orbit so it was still possible to shoot him down. Given that the ISS was made into a forward observation station, what better place to hide a little probe?

SEVENTEEN

Aggie's Ride Down

Aggie was confident people below would join her as she followed the blue man across Moon City. Moon wanted Earth people too. Why would anyone want to live here when a starship had room? If all of Moon City was like this, it was just one big slum.

The blue guy wasn't very nice. OK he answered questions but he also walked too fast. If Aggie hadn't been in good shape, she would have lost him. Aggie had to trot to keep up. The further they went the dirtier the place was. Metal parts of buildings were rusted. The lights were low. No ad bots anywhere. Hardly any paint on the cement plaster buildings and very few with neon lights. Moon dust was on everything. In comparison the spaceport was as clean as an operating room.

Aggie asked questions along the way but the guy never slowed down until she said, "Hey this whole place is like this? This city's a pile of crap."

The blue guy stopped. "You insult my home. Better than anything on planet, this is. Our pod is not favored. Moon City tolerates but does no more than needs be. This condition is not our fault."

"Sorry I asked."

They reached the trader's spaceport. Like the main one, this hangar was ringed by a corridor. They had doors like submarine watertight hatches same as the others. When he swung a door open, she was blasted with icy cold air. It smelled of garbage. Aggie wore a thin ship's coverall over her regular beach stuff and that outerwear didn't do anything to protect her.

The hangar's inside was smaller. There was only room for one starship and a few dozen shuttles of different kinds. Every ship parked there was butt-ugly. Their hulls were dented and streaked with rust and black scorch marks. It reminded her of the beat-up resistance fighters in the old Star Fighter movies. Ships here were patched up like quilt blankets with different metals that didn't match the hulls.

The trader's ship blue man was heading for was saucer shaped with a top hat on it like every other bad UFO picture Po-boy had shown her. *Old-school crap.* Only Blue's ship had its gangway down.

Blue man ran up the ramp and Aggie followed. Inside was surprisingly clean. The interior was tiny and had just enough room for a three-person-one-robot crew. Ships were self-cleaning, so these raiders weren't necessarily the shipshape kind of guys. Two regular guys, one white the other black, were sitting on the round sofa. They stood as soon as they saw her. The white guy's eyes locked onto Aggie's chest. She was small chested, so why bother gawking? She checked. Her nipples were hard from the cold. *This never happens in Key West.*

"Hey pervert, keep looking, I'll punch your lights out." Aggie moved toward him ready to strike. There wasn't much room but enough for her to clock him.

He was in Bermuda shorts and a faded blue Navy T-shirt, a short and stocky man. *No problem.* She had moves for foes shaped like Grandpa. The black guy had similar shorts but he was taller and thin. His tie-dye tank top was cool. Not a threat.

"We don't see many dames up here. Cut me slack. Back up or I'll back you up."

The black guy fell out laughing and said. "Bill if that's really Piper she'll knock you apart." Then his voice quieted. "Chip's right. She doesn't look right. This bird has a punk haircut."

"I'm not taking any baloney from anyone," Bill said, moving in. He reached out.

Aggie pulled him in, twisted his hand into a thumb lock, got his arm behind him and drove him to the deck cracking his knees before the other two took a breath.

"That's not how you treat a paying passenger," Aggie said putting more pressure on Bill's arm. He squirmed. A tear ran down his cheek. He wasn't big but he was weighty. She used his girth against him. "You buttmunches don't want the work, OK fine. I'll get another ride." She twisted his arm again.

The blue man backed up like he saw a momma bear with cubs. The black guy put his hands up and said. "Look, e's harmless, let go. Yeah, we'll take the job, please refrain." The black guy sounded English. "I'm Andy. Sorry about Bill. You mustn't expect much of 'im. My mate here's not real smart. 'E was picked up with Chip, Chip's tail gunner. 'E's a bull in a china shop, that one."

Aggie eased her grip as curiosity fell in but didn't let go. "What do you mean, what's a tail gunner?"

"World War II, they put the dumb ones in a bomber's tail section. First place shot up, that."

"I swear I won't screw with you no more, let me up!" Bill cried.

Aggie gave Bill's arm one more twist to drive home an impression and let go. "Try anything funny and I'll tear your arm off."

"Do I look like Henny Youngman?" Bill said and backed away as far as the cramp space allowed. He let himself down onto the couch slowly while rubbing his shoulder.

"More like Jack Benny, that bloke is." Andy said.

Aggie wanted to ask more questions like who are Jack Benny and Henny Youngman but she didn't want to look like a novice. Word War II? Sanderson said he got picked up over Japan during a bombing run. An alien ship crashed into his fighter plane. Such accidents must be how Earth people got to the moon. They can't all be by accident. She got the message that there weren't many Earth people in Moon City, especially girls.

The blue guy grew some balls after things settled and took the command chair. A gray bio-bot was already running when Aggie arrived. The others called him Blue, go figure. His real name must be too hard to pronounce in English. Whatever, she didn't plan on hanging around long enough to find out more about them. As soon as they touched down in Cuba, she and Jon were out of there. This crew didn't act much like pirates or Life Force raiders. They seemed harmless enough but she wouldn't let her guard down. Thankfully, the flight was short.

Aggie watched the monitors and saw the damages as they flew over Haiti. That wasn't their destination. Andy had Blue fly over to scoop up LF bomb residue. She and Mel had reviewed the footage of the bomb's aftermath. Trees and people had grown giant instantly. Little animals had morphed into monsters. Lizards became dragons and the birds were dinosaurs. Too bad they didn't last.

What happened to Haiti wasn't on mainstream media. Like how everything died soon after the LF bomb did its thing. The bodies washing up got around the internet and lots of people were questioning the official narrative. Of course, the military blacked out the alternative news feeds. Mel's flooding the internet didn't last but a day. Somehow the Feds figured out a way to shut Mel's internet attack down. She could have done it again on the day, but that would have given away the fact they survived. All they were able to rip was military satellite views and not much of that before the feeds went down. Mel got more info about it from blogs. People had recorded and posted dead sea monsters washing up.

Flying over low and slowly made the damages horribly evident. Everything was piled up, everything dead and rotting. Aggie could almost smell it from inside. Trees thousands of feet tall had laid down, massive amounts of foliage on top and under them. The bones of giant creatures were mixed in like bleached bamboo shoots. *What a morbid salad.* The scene was grim as they circled over the place before proceeding south. It made Aggie's heart hurt. She was glad when he moved on.

"Hey," Aggie said, "aren't we going in the wrong direction? Cuba's north of Haiti."

"Cuba, who said anything about Cuba. We're going to Jamaica." Blue said without taking his eyes off the navigation screen.

"I told Chip I wanted Cuba, what's going on?"

"We will get you there eventually as per our contract. We have other business first." Blue said. "Our window is closing; we must gather while we can."

"Yup, we got us a first-class scam in Jamaica," Bill said, slapping his knee. "Voodoo church, the marks come in, get all high. Oh boy they dance and chant and whatnot and we collect the LF. They don't even know Blue here's alien. They think he's some kinda teacher. What a riot. No abductions, it's legal, right Andy."

Aggie turned toward Andy who had a big grin on his face. He had nice teeth for an English guy. "E's right, the longer they stay the more we collect. Voodoo keeps them going all night long, right-o."

"All night?" Aggie asked.

"Sometimes they go on for days on end, bloody good take that, I'll say."

"We got to get while the gettin's good before Moon City up and leaves." Bill said.

"What are you taking about?" Aggie was exasperated.

"You'll see, missy, you'll scc." Bill said.

The main holo screen showed them descending toward a tropical jungle. She scanned the outlying landscape. It was much like the aria around the observatory in Puerto Rico. Before Aggie could get the next question out the craft was down — touched down in an isolated tropical jungle. From what she could tell on the holo screens, they were miles from any habitat. It made sense. They didn't want to waste power cloaking. She'd have done the same. She caught herself thinking like a spaceship captain and shook off the feeling. It also meant a long hike to wherever this stupid Voodoo gig was. *I can't wait that long.*

Aggie started out playing hooky, but this wasn't a game anymore. Ben will be out of the tank any time if not already and she needed to get Jon and get off the planet and back before Sanderson pitched a fit. But now …

"I'm so boiled. cooked, stick a fork in me."

"It's not bad, what." Andy said. "The temperature's a bit difficult, I must say, but we have air in the church."

"And a LF sucking storage tank," Bill added.

"How long's this going to take?" Aggie said miserable.

Her mom ran something like a Rasta church on the beach. Sometimes Sky Flower would keep them smoking 'sacrifice' half the day, especially in the winter when it wasn't so hot. The homeless didn't mind participating because Mom fed and stoned them. Down here on the Equator it never cools off. It's always hot as hell. No food on the ship but these assclowns have air conditioning in the middle of a jungle? *That's one way to draw a congregation, I guess.*

The spacecraft's door split horizontally and the hull opened up like a gaping clam. The heat of the jungle rushed in. It was pitch black outside. The term dead of night felt right but the noises of the jungle weren't dead. The humidity was so bad the walls took on droplets of water before she could reach the gangway. Aggie slipped out of her ship overalls. She wore denim shorts, a tank and a bikini underneath. The same stuff she always wore when not in a sundress. She tied the overalls around her waist like a belt just in case. Mark always went on about preparing for contingencies and it sunk in.

"Why's it dark?" Aggie slapped her forehead. *Duh.* The fly-over holo adjusted view to normal light. She didn't expect to arrive at night. Then a mosquito bigger than any she ever saw landed on her arm. She killed it and Blue flinched.

"Activate your force skin, the insects here are vexatious," Andy said.

"I don't have one." Aggie slapped another bug.

"She ain't no captain. Chip's full of it. She's got no control belt, no force skin." Bill said. His voice was incredulous. "How we going to get paid?"

"Do not worry," Blue said. "Chip has collateral. If she doesn't pay, we get it from him."

"Here nor there, mate, let's go. It's a bloody long hike and Mass is early morning." Andy pulled up his shirt and touched the thin belt he wore. "Miss Piper, stay between us, we will deflect some of the foliage. Bill, hold the fort."

"What about bugs?"

He didn't answer. The trip downhill was long and difficult. The plants were super thick. If it hadn't been pitched black, she'd have had a better time of it. It took hours that felt like weeks. She was full of scratches and bites. Her shorts were shredding, her tank top was tattered and one of her flip-flops was on its last legs. She cursed herself for not putting that jumpsuit back on when she had the chance. It wasn't any help worn like a belt. This circus wasn't stopping for anything. Blue and Andy were on a mission.

EIGHTEEN

Branford and Bart

They started north early morning and proceeded upriver slowly as they searched for the cutoff. Branford was itching to land, the longer on the water the greater the risk. Branford, his son-in-law and daughter managed to make it to where the instructions indicated the way into Bart's place was without any more police boats stopping them. Police boats had raced past many times along the way and Sonny waved smiling at them each time. No police were on the river yet. Branford had watched Sonny through the cabin door's hazy plexi window. The boy had more on the ball than Branford was willing to admit … before now. The police must have radioed each other about the salvage boat heading north; they surely didn't have time to check every boat on the river. But that was yesterday.

Sonny shut the engines down to idle and they drifted. The river wasn't very wide or deep here.

"Coast is clear, I don't hear no more motors." Sonny called from topside. "Dis got to be de place."

Branford and Sky came out on deck and he snatched the slip of paper out of Sonny's hand. "Let me see that … " Branford skimmed the directions. "How do you know this is the place?"

"I know de river ways!" It was the first time Branford heard the Cajun get pissy. "I been on de rivers my whole life."

"Don't test me, I'm a real seadog you goddamn river rat!"

"Shut up!" Both men turned to Sky Flower. "Dad, you are a fucking idiot sometimes. Put your dick back in your pants and listen to him. Po-boy tell us, where is it."

"That's de creek outlet leading into Bart's place." Po-boy said pointing the way.

The entry was narrow and trees hung very low over it. The banks were high on either side. It looked like a drainage ditch cut. Branford saw nothing but foliage beyond the entrance.

"There's all kind of tributaries running into here, trees overhang all of them. Spillways are every fifty feet for Christ's sake."

"Look at de water, it's deep there. The others have mud shoals, weeds, no eddies flowing around junk in de water. He got to get his boat out, no? He fishes, how he gonna get de boat out?"

"All right you got me, let's go." Branford was steaming, he hated being wrong.

That damn Cajun … he was starting to see what his daughter saw in the man. Sonny had him and Sky go up on the bow, one on either side, to push back the branches as Sonny motored in slowly. They didn't break a single bit of foliage. Branford was skeptical, it was so narrow the boat hardly fit, but once inside about twenty yards the creek opened wider and deeper still. Somebody keeps it dredged and dressed. The hard part would be finding the dock, but Sonny had the right eyes for it and spotted it right away. Bradford looked on and didn't even see it. Po-boy maneuvered the boat 90 degrees to the banks. Branford and Sky poled the boat through thick foliage and into a boat slip that was cut out of the bank. Sonny jumped off and tied up to a tree.

Everyone heard the sound of a rifle bolt and stopped dead. Branford had one foot on land and the other on the boat. The worst place to be in a fight.

"Y'all just untie yourselves and skedaddle, ya hear me?"

Branford looked up. He knew the man. It was one of the men that worked for him as a diver on a treasure ship salvage job. It was a side venture. Mark had sold him on this man before Aggie was born. Bart aged 100 years since he last saw him. He was craggy and bent, his hair was long and gray as was his scruffy beard. But the AK-47 in his hands was shipshape.

"Bart, Mark sent us … we need help."

Bart spit tobacco and got some on the stock of the gun. "Al, that you Al, I never … I should shoot you now. Y'all screwed me outta ma share."

Bart put the gun down lower but didn't click the safety off while Branford gained the ground. The two of them stood toe to toe with Bart fingering his trigger. Nothing but the sound of the wildlife stood between them. Branford thought he could take him, but what about the gun? A smile started to form on the old man's face and Bart slapped his knee.

"He-haw, scares ya, didn't I?" Bart let the gun down, pointing it more to the ground. "Awl, ya don't owes me nothing, Mark says you put up the money. Come on, follow me."

Bart put the safety on and marched up into the woods light and sure as a mountain goat. It was swampy all around but the path was dry. Traveling through the woods Branford noted another boat slip off to one side and Bart's boat was in it. This man had a hell of a hideaway. It was good to know his money was well used. The cabin was on stilts and blended into the landscape like it grew there. The barn further on could make the same claim. Inside was surprisingly well appointed, antique furnishings, stuffed book shelves, wood burning stove, modern and vintage kitchen implements and no TV. The main space and kitchen blended into one big room.

"Coffee, I got me some good beans, none of that supermarket garbage."

Bart didn't wait for an answer and put together a pot. Sky helped him by putting out dishes. Sonny stood by and the two rivermen yapped about fishing and trapes and crawdads while Bart stoked the wood stove. Sonny and Bart hit it off like brothers. Meanwhile Branford sat at the round kitchen table pushing down his go-juice. They didn't have time for this. But from what Branford knew about Bart from before, there was no rushing the man. Still, they were safe for the moment. When Sky put down a plate of cookies and little round cakes, Branford thought, *I'm off my diet now.*

Once all of them were seated, and introductions when around, Bart asked around a mouthful of cake, "So what can I do you out of?"

"We're on the run," Sky said. "They want to capture us, so they can get to Aggie. Can you help?"

"We need the safe house up in Ohio, transportation and directions." Branford said. "I'll pay whatever you want."

"Now that's rich. Money ain't worth nothing no more, see. And I don't need any anyway." Bart fluffed his beard; it was full of crumbs. "You don't ow me nothing. Mark sent ya, that's good enough. I'll pass you folks down the line, but that house taint safe no more."

"Why what's this all about?" Branford was incredulous. He had spent a fortune setting that place up. He went so far as to buy all the property around it, all private land zoned industrial. His industrial renters didn't have any way into the spot. The safe house had swamp all around it.

"I'll show you."

Bart got up and proceeded to the wall that had one door leading into a bedroom and another door into the bathroom. He tapped a spot on the wall and the old rolltop desk retracted its rattans. Several screens and a laptop lay inside the false front. The desk proceeded inward deeper than the wall and the void was stuffed with electronic gear. Bart booted up, clicked around and waved them over after a short time.

"Look here, you see it? That's the house."

Branford leaned in. It was an aerial view and he saw the car. "So what, didn't you just tell us Mark had a police car?"

"That aren't the one he took, see. That-there place been compromised. Maybe they got Mark. Nothing in the blotters yet. They ain't got him. That girl's not in the spook-news either. I told you he was going that way."

"What girl?" Sky asked. "It wasn't Aggie, was it."

"Naw, some pretty lady about forty-five, and next day her little sister came looking and was gone like the wind, too. I didn't get names, see. You don't take their names; you don't look too hard."

"Glory be … Jane Albright … Mark's gone and got the president." Sonny said.

"You didn't hear that from me, I'm never gonna say who." Bart pressed a button and the desk top rolled back into place. "She wasn't no Jane who'd-ya-say, you're mistaken. I'll find a ride for ya, where you go that's on you. Ohio house is closed." He pointed at the desk.

"And if that one is closed so is the next and the next … goddamn it." Branford rubbed his short hair and took a breath. "No matter, we don't have time to jump house to house. We go direct. Bart, I'll take the camper."

"I figured. You didn't see me, ya git me? You were never here."

Bart lead the party up out of the swap into the woods. He had an old pickup truck stashed under brushy trees. Sonny climbed into the truck's bed and the rest of them squeezed into the front seat. Bart pulled out and lugged the truck across a small, muddy field. There were industrial buildings up front in the distance, but the back forty was still farmed. Taking the farm equipment road along the bottom of the felids, Bart got them to a junkyard complex of buildings and yards two miles away. They entered the property through a side gate. Branford thought the buildings were real junk there and worth far less than the car parts they housed.

Bart pulled up to a metal barn, shut the motor off and got out. "Stay here, le' me smooth him over."

A longhaired old man came out of an attached garage wearing a veteran's baseball cap, a sidearm and a scowl on his long face. Bart talked to the owner a long while.

The two of them walked back to the truck. Bradford readied his mind for a fight but it didn't come.

"Mr. Branford, gimmy your hand, I got a lot to thank you for … " He pushed back his cap, it said Vietnam on it. The man reached into the window and took Branford's had with a mechanic's grip. "Don't worry, I never saw ya, let me get the rig out and you and yours best be getting under them trees so none of them flying over sees ya."

Branford, Sky and Sonny beat it over to the edge of a garage where a couple of bushy trees were furnished with a pair of folding chairs. Bart went inside the hangar like structure with the owner via a side door.

"Dad, he's got to thank you? You know this man?" Sky asked.

"No, I don't know him, not really." Branford rubbed his thick hair wondering how he was going to say it. Sky never knew any of this. "I better tell you the whole thing. He's part of the escape network I set up. I did this with Mark … never thought I'd need it."

"Mark our Mark? You're telling me he's deeply involved with you! Damn it, Dad I — "

"Hush Honey, let im talk," Po-boy said. "I had a feel'n about it. How's Mark sell me da boat so cheap, de engines worth more than I ever made in a year? How's we never get evicted? We were squatting illegal, make no mistake."

Branford was thankful Sonny stepped in. Once his daughter got revved up there was no stopping her. Po-boy had a calming effect on her, one more plus from the Cajun.

"You had Mark spy on us!" The look of sudden realization crossed Sky's face and tuned to anger.

"Hush Honey Peach. Let him talk." Sonny took her hand in his. "Use your heart, this isn't just de facts, no."

"I asked Mark, no I paid him, but listen, he didn't take the money, he put it all in an account for Aggie, to send her to university. He never touched the money. I asked him to keep an eye on you. You ran from me but family is family. I didn't turn my back on you."

"But, but what about Mark, he … I don't know what to think. On Daddy why didn't you tell me?" Tears formed and ran down her cheeks, she moved to him and Bradford embraced her. She buried her face in his shirt. "You looked after us … I thought you stopped loving me … I … I." The tears came on.

Branford the man hard as nails, a man that never let go, never lost control stroked her weird hair and patted her back. A tear fought for egress and escaped his own eye. He had not held her like this since the day she had left for collage, after her mother had died.

After a time, he said, "Would you have listened? I'm not the monster you thought I was but I've been one. I set this up because I know real monsters, the people I worked for … I knew this day might come. They're done with me. My life's not worth a plugged nickel."

"You covered us the whole time … but Mark … "

"Mark screwed up, he fell in love with you and Sonny and Aggie. You're the family he never had." Branford said just as Bart entered the shade of the tree. "All bets are off. They'll take Mark out if they find him. I wish I knew where he was."

Bart scuffed his feet in the hardpacked dirt as he stood near. "Seeming as bets are off, I'm going to skedaddle myself. And see'n no more reason to keep my trap clamped. Mark was here two days ago, like I said." He hesitated and rocked back and forth on his feet. It must have been hard for him to spill what he was told to keep secret. "Jane Albright was with Captain Lavine, it was her, the president. That house, that's where they were going but that their car ain't the one, like I said."

"Albright's still alive." Branford said. "That helps us."

The junkyard man pulled an RV out of a tall work bay. It was an older class-A model like a bus. Branford calculated that such a one won't attract attention. If Mark had the work done that Branford wanted, the rig would be full of equipment and a stock of cash. He'd activate the spy gear as they drove, dig in and find out what was happening. The place he had in mind was a long way from here. He had time to work out the lay of the land.

Just before pulling onto the road, Branford had Sonny stop. He looked up through the big front windshield to check for drones but instead what he saw was a pair of America's magnetic aircrafts streaking across the horizon toward Washington: The sun was low but there was no mistaken that they were classic flying saucers. If the Navy pulled out the stops and exposed themselves like that, it could only mean the shit was hitting the fan sooner and with far greater force than he thought possible.

Those stupid bastards must have attacked the moon. He had thought they might in the back of his mind while working on the MAC control project. The Navy asked for and got enough of his hardware to outfit a hundred MACs. It sure as hell wasn't the usual boondoggle government contract. Higher up, he saw larger objects. In the right light one could see the International Space Station if you knew where to look. What he saw now wasn't that. It was a giant space rock in low obit, one hell of a big chunk of moon and it had no place to go but down.

"We better roll."

"Where too," Sonny asked.

"New Mexico, to start with, and step on it. I'm going to the operations room to see about stealth."

Branford walked back to the rear of the bus and it was just like he ordered it. This land yacht was equipped with the kind of gear that the CIA wished they could afford. He hoped it was enough to get them from there to the real Area 51 without getting caught. What to do once they arrived, he wasn't sure. As far as the underworld was concerned, Al Branford was dead, blown up with that city block they leveled just to get him. They think he's gone and he planned to keep it that way.

NINETEEN

Brinks and MJ-12

Brinks entered the Joint Chiefs' regular meeting room on the first floor of the Pentagon's inner ring. Nothing remarkable about the conference table except it often seated top brass.

Archer was on the moon and out of communication and so Brinks had one less person on his daily agenda. He didn't trust Archer. Brinks wasn't sure which way the man's loyalties leaned. What Archer reports will decide loyalties.

The Chiefs were done with Archer for now but Brink's wasn't. He'd use the man for special operations if Archer proved a good enforcer. As to the Chiefs they will go along or suffer reprisals. Brinks was about to show them how terrible crossing him can be. He wasn't using an operative for this. Brinks will do this himself. He felt it time for a show of power and the like had never been seen in Washington before.

None of the military's high-ups normally cooperated with each other. Agreement was always a battle even within each branch. *Too many cooks in the kitchen.* They needed a strongman to lead the way. The Navy proper didn't know what the Navy Recovery Office was up to, but Brinks knew and he knew how to make better use of them. With Archer's help he'd mold the NRO into his own government payroll jack-boots. He'd blend that force into Brinks Security Inc.

"Brinks, you saw Archer." The general read off a memo. "Says here Archer's airborne. Is that right?"

"I sent him to the moon like I proposed. He'll distract them while we muster the fleet. MACS are at full capacity. Colonel Archer is handling the GTO."

"It's general now." The Navy man said with pride.

"Archer will always be Mr. Black to me." Brinks said. "He fits the NRO slot perfectly. I'll keep them together."

The men there, top brass from every branch with their aides, showed signs of disapproval. The NRO no longer had a purpose and it was to be disbanded. That budget money reallocated. Brinks needed those operatives. The Galaxy Project was being defunded as well. *Very soon the budget won't be a consideration.* With Sanderson out of the way and the president handled, it was time to pull his big move.

Brinks was offered a chair at the table but rather he remained standing to address the group. Admiral King was boiling over the Archer remark. King had made it known he wanted the money and he didn't like Brinks or Brinks' methods. King launched a tirade about the money but Brinks didn't listen.

The public fallout over the attack on Piper's spaceship, that Brinks had ordered, put the screws on the Navy and pushed King into a bad position. The official propaganda wasn't taking. Even the mainstream press, 90 percent under state control, could not squash public outrage. The damn blogs, not only Piper's, but every other malcontent's soapbox had the population in a tizzy.

"I'm not done with Haiti, Brinks." King said.

Launching mud pies, are we?

"Sanderson said it can't work and you did it anyway." King spit it out before Brinks could open his mouth. "You pushed for this, this, disaster. You blew it, you don't get first choice. I need those men. Enlistment is down. They're going AWOL in droves, thanks to you. Your bonehead move has us sailing backwards. You owe me the NRO men. I'm short because of you."

That wasn't true in Brinks' calculations. His "bonehead move" got him somewhere. The military's leadership was too soft. Too many years of easy targets with everything under their control. But "from chaos comes order," a new order. Brinks was about to impose his idea of order.

"Get off my ass, Frank it wasn't me." Brinks said. "It's MJ-12 pulling the strings and you know it. I only deliver the messages but it doesn't have to be this way. Before I get into that, be advised, you read it right. I took command of the NRO. They're mine lock, stock and barrel. Your ocean fleet manpower needs won't matter after we take the moon."

The table exploded with arguments. Frank King was promised the NRO men but Brinks just stepped all over him touching off the debate. MJ-12 gave Brinks the weight. King and the rest were pissed about that imbalance of power. As MJ's secretary, Brinks held the only access card. The Chiefs were tired of being controlled by MJ-12 at a distance. More reason to act now.

The Army's secretary raised his voice above the others. "Brinks, you bastard, Frank has dibs. How can you say it doesn't matter? How the hell — "

"Shut up Paul! All of you." Brinks yelled viciously. Tommy Brinks was known for his dead eyes and cold heart, but his big voice is what reinforced it and what stopped men in their tracks. Their arguments were diddly squat.

Brinks stared down every man in the room. One by one they regained their seats, grumbling curses. They all had the same problem. Nobody likes playing

second fiddle. They thought they were in charge. Thought they had real authority. Nobody overrides MJ-12. That's who they fear. Brinks had to stifle a nasty
smile. *Whoever masters MJ, masters all.* The table finally settled.

"That's better. We don't need to play MJ's game. It's time to take over. Let
me ask you this, if MJ was pushed out, will you support me? What if I make that
happen?"

The room erupted with arguments all over again.

Nobody asked that question before. Since World War II, Majestic Twelve
controlled the Joint Chiefs. MJ called the shots and set the policies. None stood
against them. JFK and later Bobby tried and were taken out. From that the
Chiefs understood the futility of resisting MJ's will. The military's round table
didn't pull the John Kennedy or Dr. King trigger. They quickly learned who did.
MJ ran the security state and were capable of anything. Buck them and you're
dead.

The Complex needed war and MJ delivered the gift of 9/11. Acting against
them was inconceivable. Working with them got you where you wanted to go. If
war was what you wanted, MJ provided. The war racket was why each man there
had cash stuffed pockets. Behind it all was MJ's push for a one-world government
with America leading. The Complex liked that aspect. A one-world trade organization is the only way aliens will trade.

None there understood the big picture or that that the GTO's plan had failed.
That game was over. Now it was Brinks' gameboard.

He let them hash it out. Sure, they'd let him do his worst and claim they weren't
involved. They all wanted MJ-12 gone. Some of them hated the oligarchy. But they
knew this democracy was a lie and always has been. MJ holds the international
purse strings. They control the central banks and military manufacture. If MJ
didn't glue them all together the republic would have died long ago. The irony they
didn't see would have made Brinks laugh if he remembered how.

Brinks made his big ask. "I need assurance, if MJ ... let's call it disbands, will
you support me? They're connected to the aliens but that situation has changed."

One by one the table agreed to stick together behind Brinks should MJ vacate
and things fall into place. As the country was in disarray, and the new unelected
president wasn't popular, a military coup was on the table and they knew it.

"What about Piper, what if she shows up?" An aide asked. The conversation
started anew.

Aggie Piper's dead man blog about 9/11 was still making huge waves. As
far as the public knew Piper was dead, killed by government murder. Murder
as usual. The ghost of Piper was busy. Van Ness' claim that Piper yet lives isn't
substantiated but people are buying in. Piper herself hasn't appeared. Brinks was
attacking that problem but it was small potatoes. What he was about to do would
overwhelm public discourse.

"I'm working on Piper. It's not important," Brink said. "What matters is
you're with me. And you who aren't." Brinks made a gun with his finger and fist
and let the hammer fall. "I'm heading out."

Confident that they were handled, Brinks gathered his notes and picked up his briefcase. If things did not go as planned the case would have been left behind. He had a better use for it now. He decided to walk. His car was waiting in Lot C.

Archer was on Brinks' mind as he marched. Archer the lapdog. Service was all that man knew. It was smart making Archer the GTO contact. Archer had seen enough aliens dead and alive. He won't balk. Archer shot Sanderson as ordered. Brinks didn't trust anyone but Archer didn't need to be trusted. The man was programmed to know what is expected. Archer will kill the GTO's leader. Brinks didn't need to give that order. Dogs understand their master. Archer is a ploy to create confusion.

Brinks didn't care about trade. He'll take what he wants. Archer doesn't know the GTO deal was off. Brinks felt the cogs falling in. Nothing was more satisfying than a plan well executed.

Once outside Brinks noted that the sky around Washington was ringed by columns of black smoke. The city's slums were burning. Branford's place burning with it. It reminded him of his time in the Middle East. Brinks inhaled that brown air. It tasted like victory.

Brinks had placed a note in Archer's moon file. It said, "Kill one, anyone, doesn't matter who, before you make demands." Brinks had nothing to worry about but something didn't feel right.

Archer was stronger, straighter and more upright since Brinks first met him. The NRO man had physically recovered from Karnack's controls. But Brinks' source said Archer was mentally damaged and reduced to nothing more than a human machine. Exactly what Brinks needed. The big plus, Archer's NRO men were loyal. Things were falling in. Just one more job and the world was his.

Brinks stopped at the entry to Lot C and checked his briefcase. It was in order. He hated to give up that old leather case. It was a gift from his men when he left Baghdad for Washington. It was given out of appreciation, they appreciated him leaving.

Brinks waved for his car to come up. Everything was set.

He had the driver circle the Pentagon's secure zone. D.C. was under Martial Law but his staff car wasn't restricted. The driver skirted the slums. The riots were over. The rich section of town where Branford died was inaccessible. Brinks pulled his phone and thought better of it. Archer was out of communication range. Good.

"Driver, back to the Pentagon. Officer's mess."

Brinks went inside and took lunch. He didn't hurry. His car was back in its spot waiting when he returned outside. He took the short ride.

Brinks breezed through the security at the Capitol building. He was a regular and wasn't searched. That his security firm manned the gates was a bother. He might be questioned afterward, but who would question him? He made straight for the elevator that went to the subbasement where his security man was pinned. Like always, his man stood waiting as he exited the lift.

"Is everyone here?" Brinks asked the guard.

"Yes sir, room three. Twelve men."

Brinks entered and they were all there in person as he requested. A long table was against the far wall and all the seats faced him at the door. Extraordinary times called for this meeting. The English banker, the Saudi oil tycoon, the Aussie media mogul, the Greek shipping magnate, the Chinese industrialist, and the rest; in a nutshell, the men that controlled the money and thus the world. A quote from Rosschild came to mind, "I care not who governs, he who controls the money controls the nations." It was that simple.

"Stop there, Brinks," the Texas oilman said. They were a careful bunch. Brinks noted the bulletproof glass erected in front of the conference table. It made the men behind the screen blurry, somewhat unrecognizable. They could not hide. He knew who they were.

"You instructed the military. They will stand down and let the GTO depart without harassment?"

Brinks didn't tell the Chiefs what the GTO had in mind, that they were leaving and trade was declared open. Why they decided to vacate, Brinks didn't know. Archer will provided that answer. Life Force raiders were moving. Brinks saw the game. Raiders were keeping his MACs busy. He'd save his best ordinance for Piper's mother ship and not waste it on the exiting GTO.

"They agreed to back off. I'll tell NRO next."

"The GTO's exclusive contract ran out." A fuzzy figure behind glass said. "We want you to make trade partners of the remaining aliens. Moon trade's opened. That gives our competitors economic equality. We can't have it. Beat them to it. Get that contract."

Trade prevents war. Exactly what I don't want. The GTO must smell it coming. That's why they hit the road.

"The Chiefs will do what you tell them." Brinks said and it wasn't a lie. "If Albright shows herself or not our deal is on. Archer is there now. We have our one-world trade corporation set up. The aliens will sign. I'm on top of it."

"What about the GTO's security? No harm should be done. We can't have the NRO shooting."

The question wasn't about their own safety. Why would MJ protect the GTO? Long-term strategy perhaps? *Screw long-term.* Brinks deflected by changing the topic.

"We'll go around the Chiefs and the GTO. Archer's handling the moon as we speak." Brinks sidestepped to the small table and chair they placed for him. He was the newest member and relegated to some separation as was their tradition. Many of these meetings took time. He set his briefcase down and took the seat. Brought up his notebook.

"Aggressively pushing the GTO works against us," The banker said. "Call Archer. Have him offer them a contract. Get them to stay."

"Earth will soon be publicly declared an open trade species." The Greek was saying. "Trade will proceed. The GTO stood in our way but no more. Once they see our intent, they will join with us, no? The market is free to exploit. If we offer our protection, is good, yes?"

Last time they met, Brinks proposed aggressive tactics and the group balked. MJ-12 had gone back and forth on plans to implement a trade deal so much Brinks thought it would never happen. Why trade when you can take? Ironic that Earth finally had a one-world trade cabal that met the alien's requirements and the rule makers leave. The board talked back and forth and Brinks heard it all before, same old bull. If he didn't know any better, he'd say MJ-12 was on the GTO's side.

Brinks started to take notes but he was told to lay down his pen. They didn't have much to say he didn't already know. They called the meeting to decide how to proceed in this new world. It was agreed that despite the threats Brinks has Archer delivering, there will be no attack on the moon. That was MJ's track, not his. Brinks had his own way. He didn't show that hand. When he was dismissed, he left his case behind. Nothing was resolved. Whatever Archer reports would have informed MJ's next move.

Brinks arrived at the elevator and called the guard to him. "Murry, I left my notes, go get them for me."

"Aye, aye sir."

The guard turned away and Brinks got onto the bombproof evaluator. He went up one floor and pressed the remote. The explosion knocked him to the ground. He was surprised. He didn't order one made that powerful or with that fast a trigger. *It's good anyway, I'm alive.* He looked like a victim.

Brinks should have been angry but he wasn't. That glass shield might have saved a few of them. A bigger bomb was in fact better. It took a few hours for the firemen to dig him out, but Brinks had gone through worse and worse was yet to come.

TWENTY

Majestic Twelve

Twelve important men were gathered on Horse Head Island. This private reserve in the Caribbean was actually a fortress. They faced each other as the table was round. But they didn't see one another as their computer screens blocked the view.

"I told you he would try a bloody bomb." The British banker said. "I predicted it."

The banker was good at that sort of thing. Number One did well to assign him that task. Knowing where and when opponents moved and for what purpose wasn't difficult. They had access to the GTO's social psychology AI. Earth's people had their patterns. The banker had studied Brinks. Majestic Twelve followed Brinks' every move. *No, it wasn't unexpected,* Number One thought. *Brinks is a movie you knew the end of.*

When militaries learn the GTO's antimissile system has been withdrawn fireworks will ensue. Brinks would be the first to run a nuclear attack … unless someone killed him. Number One made a note. He and his will be long gone before that happens. Earth's sentient species' self-destruction was assured. Emotions generally superseded reason within this strain. Number One controlled his emotions. Some Earthlings were capable of emotional control and that is why the GTO made those seated their partners.

"It is good he did not detect our holographs. That he thought we would come in person says much about him." The Chinese industrialist spoke in moon standard. It was the one tongue they all shared.

"It is confirmed, Brinks will attack Moon City." Said the banker.

"Should we let him know he failed?" Said the media man.

"And give him reason to act fast, no." Number One said. "Let him think he has won. He feels safe, it opens him to … let us say problems. This gives us more time. Moon City has been in place a long time. She cannot move quickly."

"Let us go. Home office is prepared for evacuation. I rather leave with the first wave." The industrialist said.

"That isn't possible. The GTO anticipated correctly and are shortly boarding to leave. In fact, they have begun. The second starship is ours."

The Galactic Trade Organization usually installed and aided locals in preparation for open trade. Unfortunately, Earth, a newly recognized trading species, was too dangerous. The GTO's planetside local members were free to operate as they saw fit. Moonside did not manage Earthside affairs. The noninterference rule loophole allowed the GTO to partner with local indigenous persons of majestic character.

"Let the Life Force raiders have at it." The media man said. "I've had enough."

The GTO cares for their employees no matter the outcome. GTO's planetside partners were welcome on GTO starcraft the same as any other GTO employee. *Why not leave this profitless proposition?*

"No point staying." The shipping magnet said.

"I could not agree more, old boy." The banker said.

It was decided. There was only one possible outcome. The end could well happen sooner rather than later without the GTO controlling economics and war preventatives. *Even without total war Earth must fail and soon. It is inevitable.* No amount of money was protection enough for what was to come.

"It is fortunate our families are already in Moon City." Number One said in agreement. He alerted Moon City with the click of his mouse. It was the word she waited for. Moon's evacuation from local space was thereby confirmed. Her recent preparations were not in vain.

MJ-12's own evacuation commenced immediately. Each in turn took the elevator three thousand feet below the ocean. Each took a different tram to a different country where they would each finish putting affairs in order.

Many more UFOs will be spotted around the world this night, Number One thought. A dozen UFOs leaving may be marked but many more will be ascending and descending giving MJ's craft cover. Raiders were already on the move gathering their last bit of LF. Moon City's forthcoming call for refugees will add to the confusion. MJ-12's sophisticated spacecrafts will slip out within this traffic. The Navy had not yet launched its full space fleet but will soon. The window was slim but wide enough. It was time for the company's planetside counterparts to accept retirement.

Number One felt relieved and sad as he took the lift down. *I will miss Earth.* However, new possibilities will surely fill that hollow place where his affection for Earth now lives. Keeping this suicidal planet in his heart so long was challenging. That struggle was officially over.

TWENTY-ONE

Aggie's Voodoo Morning

They arrived at a clearing near a little river at daybreak. Blue called it Toms River. There were a bunch of outdoor benches made out of logs and crap. The little shack there was made from plywood and shipping pallets and painted wild yellow with blue and orange trim. Above the door was a sign that said, "All Are Welcome."

"Where'd you guys get paint? Let me guess, colorblind paint salesman, right?"

Nobody laughed. They went about their business. Aggie pitched in. She had nothing better to do. Blue started a generator. They uncovered an outdoor podium that was under a worn green tarp. Andy lit tiki torches while Blue unlocked the hut. Aggie sat to let the bug land that was attacking her. She killed it with a quick slap leaving green goop on her leg. Thank Goddess the insect army faded with the sun. Aggie was fading too for lack of sleep and food.

The hum of the air unit drew Aggie into the makeshift building. Candles everywhere and more of those crude bench seats. The roof was thatched and it had to leak air. The old window unit pumped cold air, and the hut leaked it like water through a spaghetti colander, but it felt good anyway. Only two windows; the one without the air unit was made from a sheet of hazy plastic. In the back was a big chair like a throne. Aggie sat there and nodded but she didn't get to sleep long. Blue shook her a few minutes after closing eyes.

"Crap, what's going on?"

Blue explained. "The people are due. They come by raft upriver. We start outside and invite them in. Once we get a good number inside, we start the LF generator. After the spliff goes around," Blue held up a bag of weed, "I'll invite them in. I play the part of the Blue Bud Man."

"How long's this going to take?"

"That will depend on how many come." Blue said. "Only a few, we will end it. Staying won't be productive. Bill's collecting jungle's ambient LF even now. But it takes too long, it's not worth the risk. We need concentrations. If we have good attendance, we'll continue all day and into the night. The goal is to acquire as much LF as possible. After which time we will see you to your destination."

"Crap on a cracker. I forgot. I wanted to work out hiring you guys for another gig."

"We will confer after we are done here." Blue stood taller and his head tilted. "They are near. Make ready."

How does he know? Duh, Bill's up there running sensors. People started coming and they didn't stop coming. The outside got to be standing room only before 10 a.m. The people were locals, no tourists at all, and most of them didn't look happy. The only ones having fun were the expat surf bums.

She stood out but not too bad. She was Key West tanned and so fit in with the few white locals that showed up. The people didn't notice her much. She wasn't recognized. Just another American beach bum. She received sidelong glances when she refused the pot going around. Pot was illegal in this province.

"Why so many today?" She asked a random guy.

"De world has trouble," He said. He showed her his I-know phone "Mon what you live in de jungle? Now, now American be fallin', we need prayer."

"Ah but theses here, me no trust. Some — " A woman started.

"Hush woman, no say." The man had a grim look about him. Aggie got the feeling something else besides church was going down.

The Blue Bud Man was supposed to start pontificating at noon, but the surrounding clearing was too small to hold them all if they kept coming. The pot ran out fast and Andy had to send somebody downriver to get more smokables. The crowd there was getting unruly, people were shouting. Everyone was trying to push closer to Blue. He stated his preaching ahead of time. Non-worshipers were yelling insults. The believers were yelling back. Things were getting ugly.

With so many people around Aggie was forced to back up to the river. Crowds made her tense and the undertone of this one pumped anxiety. There were a ton of rafts tied off up and down the waterway. Aggie could have walked to the other side. Rafts were made from logs and rope. A couple of long skinny boats were there too but nothing was seaworthy.

"Miss, come, come, sit with One Love." A guy on a raft called her over. His raft was pretty far from the hut and on the edge of the flotilla.

Aggie really needed some out-of-the-way quiet. One Love seemed like a decent guy. He was tall and thin so Aggie's thoughts automatically went straight to her tall-guy defense style. His big smile and cool dreadlocks ejected her ideas about fighting. Karnack made her knuckles itch but this guy was a hug-fest. *One Love's the right name.* His vibe was Aggie's kind of people.

Aggie still wasn't sure if she should trust the guy. As evident by her current location, she wasn't making a lot of good choices lately. "Hey One Love, you aren't a pirate, are you?"

"Me!" He laughed deeply. "No mon, me lost me cannon."

She laughed and jumped onto his raft. Standing on One Love's a rickety float was better than wading up to her ankles in jungle-rot mud. The church was on higher land and it was swampy everywhere else. Besides, the crowd started pushing and shoving.

"Many people, me no like."

She wasn't the only one that didn't like crowds. One Love stayed on his raft for that same reason. He and she were on the same wavelength. She relaxed. Things were going OK for Andy and Blue, sort of. Lots of people there meant these raider clowns would get their LF and get out sooner. But that changed.

Aggie and One Love were chit-chatting when the crowd roared. Andy was out front waving his hands and yelling for people to move back. The locals were yelling insults and waving sticks and guns around. Blue was preaching at the door but Aggie couldn't hear what he was saying.

"Arguing over getting inside?"

"Bad mojo." One Love hopped off the raft and untied one of the two anchoring ropes.

It was the act as described. He'd invite people inside any time now. That was the plan but it wasn't going to happen. Wind came ripping in overhead. Trees swayed and bent but it wasn't wind. The trader's spaceship popped out of holo crushing down treetops. The center hatch swirled opened and Bill's reddened face thrust out from the hole's edge. The people backed up and a few fell. Many started wailing.

"Emergency! We gotta go!" Bill's voice boomed via projection.

"Crazy bastard," Andy yelled. "What are you doing?" The ship picked up Andy's voice and projected it.

"Incoming! Moon's leaving!"

"Of course," Andy said, "We have time."

"Mayday. Mayday. Incoming!"

"Bloody hell! Blue, EVAC, EVAC!"

"Crap," Aggie stepped off the raft. "The moon can't leave."

The crowd was surprised but the people's shock didn't last but a hot second. People started flinging fruit and whatever their offerings were at Andy and Blue. Andy touched his belt and pushed through to get at Blue. Andy embraced Blue in a bear hug. Someone fired a shot at the ship. Aggie didn't know if they both had force skins on or not but Blue acted like he didn't. A tractor beam grabbed Blue and Andy and pulled them up into the bottom hatch. As the ship slowly rose the people went nuts, shouting, throwing sticks, more gunfire. The ship took off, leaving Aggie standing in the mud.

"Hey! That's my ride!" *They want blood, how long before I'm spotted.* "I'm so screwed."

"Space girl, come." One Love reached a big hand out. She took it. "Mon da hate space peoples."

One Love was holding his raft in place with one leg on land and the other on deck. The raft's bow had spun facing downstream. He had already cast off the other line. The river was strong and the raft wanted out. *Space girl, he knows who I am.*

"Come, come. We go!" He pulled her hand.

Aggie's foot made a sucking sound as she was pulled out of the mucky bank. She boarded. Muddy feet were better than getting ground into the mud. "Thanks man." Her flip-flops weren't yellow anymore.

One Love let go, took his pole and pushed downstream hard. Nobody paid attention. They were busy shooting at the sky and tearing down the church.

When the raft Andy had sent down stream departed earlier, Aggie wished she was on it. The raiders weren't supposed to leave anytime soon. She thought she'd do a little sightseeing to kill the time and escape that nasty pot smell. But she got distracted and missed that boat. She had to wait it out stuck there. She was stuck before, but now she was really stuck.

One Love poled like his dreads were on fire. They were well downstream before he slowed. Not wanting to rock the boat, and to keep her head down, Aggie took the only chair. It was rickety, made of bamboo and fronds, and not easy on her bony rear end but it got her out of his way.

"Why'd you bail me out?" She asked when he finally relaxed.

"Me know." The man bent low to her and whispered. "You Aggie Piper."

"Crap, don't tell anyone, OK." If the people that came to church knew it was her, they'd think Blue's people were her people. They had to see the fakery. They'd blame her for it. Worse, America had a price on her head. These people were poor. "I'm in big trouble."

"One Love no tell … Take me with you, bargain?"

"You mean space; you want on my crew?"

"That yes, make deal?"

"You got it. Except, I have a little problem. That was my ride, not my guys. I lost my guys. I'm MIA and stuck here. Help me get back and you can come with me."

"I will."

Getting a crew was easy, just ask. Mel and Sanderson had it all wrong. They thought it would take a week. She didn't have to worry about One Love. Nobody could hear them with all the yelling going on upriver. She was about to ask him a question but the sky back there suddenly lit.

Was it the spaceship she came in? It rushed in and hovered over the compound, a big, shiny disk. She wasn't sure if it was her ride. Gun shots cracked and echoed. Voices rose to a riot pitch. Cool, Andy came back for her. He'd pick up her bio-scan. Squeezing One Love into that tiny ship was a problem. They'd have to adjust for it.

She stood on the raft's bamboo chair. Making room for One Love wasn't a big deal but she discovered what was. That MAC wasn't Andy's ship. That ship had writing on it and it said U.S. Navy. They were after Andy and Andy was gone like a wayward wind. The Navy ship rotated and shot off. Aggie thought maybe Andy would pick her up downstream. They had a contract but rescue wasn't happening. Andy's not going to hang out and get his tail shot off.

"They bailed. My ride's totally gone. I'm a dope. I should have listened to Sanderson. I'm a big fat butthead."

Upstream the sound of splashing. People were getting back on their rafts. The river bent and twisted back on itself so directly across the jungle was the church. They were only fifty feet away from a lot of pissed off people.

One Love pushed the raft downriver with big, long pole strokes. "Me go hard. Da want no spacemen. Cutis say he kill de space ones."

"I can't trust anyone. I thought those guys were cool. I can't believe they left me."

"Dis me know. People say Blue Man was false. I say alien. Dis me know. De people angry."

"I'm way, way more stuck. What am I going to do?"

A biting fly landed on her shoulder and dug in. She slapped at it and missed. That was the last straw. Aggie started bawling.

"Now, now miss, no cry. One Love be here."

"You don't understand," Aggie said sobbing. "I screwed up. This is all on me. I never listen. Why can't I act right and cooperate?" Aggie cried some more. "You don't understand."

"Me understand. Miss Aggie Piper. You make me spaceman. Dis planet be failing now."

"How did you know? I can't even fake anyone out."

One Love pulled an I-know phone out of his cargo shorts' pocket. "Dis."

"Blue's not coming back! I've got to get to a shuttle." Aggie fell into the bamboo seat with her mind spinning negatives. "The shuttles are in Puerto Rico and Key West. I give up. I'll turn myself in. Go to your government. Mel will find me. But what if … if it gets out? The Feds will get me. What am I saying? I'm so stupid. If I can't get to PR, I'm toast. I'm toast anyway."

Aggie's mind was racing trying to put something together. She thought if she could get into the media her ship would find her, but so would the CIA. But the media was locked down. She stopped the merry-go-round inside her head and cried some more.

"No cry woman. Be happy. One Love has a way."

"What was I saying! That's not going to work. I'll never get to Puerto Rico. I'm so screwed. I got to get to Guantanamo and bust out Jon, Jon … Jon knows how to fly airplanes."

"Me have fishing boat. Dis time tomorrow we in Cuba. Me space team mon."

That stopped her mind spinning on the word "team". *I'm the worst team player ever.* Aggie snapped upright. The bamboo chair fell over. "I need a team. Get me to Jon. Drop me off at Gitmo. I'll send a shuttle for you. Trace your phone. This can work. You sure you want on a starship?"

"Why you thin me visit false church alien? Me try stowaway but … " One Love held his long arms out wide and shrugged his shoulders.

Aggie and One Love had a deal and he meant to keep his part but could she keep her part as well? Mother had her own ideas about crew. Aggie was still the captain, right? One step at a time she told herself. Cuba wasn't that far from Jamaica, right. He has a boat, right.

Once she got crew settled in and was sure Mother was set, she'd have to resign. She failed. She had to admit she wasn't captain material. One thing at a time. Snag Jon, get to PR, find One Love and get off this rock. Then she'd get serious. She hated to admit high-technology was the answer. She had to admit a lot of mistakes.

Her imagination ran wild. She'd grab a ship and find her parents. She'd scoop up Mark. She'd make the butthead government act human. She'd fix Earth and make everything all right. *Yeah right.* Unrealistic ideas swam in her head as the raft floated toward the coast. Her dreams weren't possible but that never stopped her from pushing ahead before. She had one thin hope as logic bubbled up. It might work if she could get out of her own way. That's what she told herself, but she didn't really believe in luck or hope or her ability to resolve this alone. *I need help. But I made the mess. It's mine to fix.*

Aggie's trajectory was usually based on facts. Cuba wasn't that far and she had sailed much farther before. She became calm and more thoughtful on the long ride down Toms River. She decided plan B would work. But once she arrived at One Love's fishing boat, and saw the condition it was in, her old facts were drowned by a new set of facts. First, One Love's boat was a piece of crap. Second, it was really late and Cuba was really, really far away. A leaky wooden boat was just the thing for sinking her hope.

TWENTY-TWO

President Albright

President Jane Albright tried to keep track of where they were from inside the back of a decommissioned police vehicle. Her jail was the K-9 unit's rear dog compartment of the SUV Mark had stolen. Such accommodations smelled of dust-laden fur, dog food and dog waste. She didn't have anything to do but think and watch while her captor drove aimlessly. She felt like they were going in circles before, but now she confirmed it. The windows were blacked out, no one could see in but it was made so dogs could see out. Her captor just drove past that same Thompson's Hardware store for the third time in as many hours.

One-way glass was for the dogs' benefit. People passing won't be drawn to the animals and bother them. Albright saw the wisdom in that. Less interaction between police dogs and citizens who might influence the dog's behavior positively. That was better for the police. Not so good for the dogs. If her jailer would only pull into a parking lot, she'd bark and howl, outperforming this transport's previous inhabitants.

"I must have lost my mind. I'm the president and all I can think about are police dogs?" Albright pounded on the plexi between her and her captor. "Hey I need a bathroom!"

"Shut up! Just shut up back there."

By her reckoning they were still in Ohio and heading west again. He mentioned a relative of his. She still didn't know the security man's name. He said something about Aunt Ro's place. The young man was no doubt still suffering from his head injury. Mark had knocked him silly. They should have left this man-boy behind. *Why did I make Mark save him?* But was he saved? His actions were confused and unsure. His driving went from erratic to slow and back again several times. Was he lost? Brain bleeding?

Many hours passed since leaving Mark unconscious and bloody on a safe house floor. She didn't know if Mark's injury was fatal. Mark needed medical attention and there wasn't a way to provide it.

Mark was her only hope, but another hope crossed her mind. Her jailer still hadn't called the security company he worked for. Did that knock on the head cause forgetfulness or was this tour the indecisiveness of youth? She hoped he was mulling over his country's situation. As it stood, he was a traitor to the Constitution.

"What ever happened to the rule of law?" She yelled on impulse.

He should know better. His job was guarding the White House from a boat on the Potomac. "Perimeter guard," Mark called him. It wasn't the kind of site location one used a talented security man for. Mark was probably right. The boy had washed out of the military. To have incapacitated Mark, a retired Seal, this boy did something a true Special Ops man could not accomplish without tribulation. In this case it was dumb luck. This boy and his jarhead haircut, well muscled body and otherwise hardass appearance, was put to work out of harm's way. Why. He had to be connected to someone important. It was the only set of facts that added up.

"You're a failure," She yelled. "You didn't cut it so they gave you a plum job."

"Hey shut up back there, you hear me, I told you no talking!" He stepped on the gas.

"Do what's right and honor your oath to the Constitution, you, you putz!"

Poor thing, I made him angry. Despite the plexi wall between them he heard her via the air holes. Albright applied her stock in trade. If a politician didn't know how to sway people they didn't last. On the ride she worked on him all day. She tried talking sense into him, sew doubts, plead for mercy, appeal to logic and nothing worked. She was tired of playing nice. The last few miles, as her bladder expanded, she had to push harder.

"Hey, don't be a maroon." She pounded on the plexi open handed. "Think what you're doing, don't be an idiot!"

He slowed down. He wasn't sure what to do. *Good, he's off balance.*

"You're breaking the law. You, sir, are a kidnapper! It's illegal to — "

"Will you please knock it off!"

"I'm in the back of a truck. I'll talk all I want." Her tone was harsh. "What're you going to do? Rough me up like a Mafia bully? Is this how you treat your president? Didn't you swear an oath to my office? If you're going to kill me do it already. Save the traitor military some effort."

"Just stop it. Just let me think!" The boy rubbed one temple with his free hand.

"Pull over. I need the restroom!" Jane was serious this time. She had filled the last soda bottle with urine hours ago. Peeing into a bottle was a skill she never wanted to learn.

"We're almost there."

"Fine, I'll piss right here. You won't mind the smell!" She saw his face go sour in the rearview mirror. He didn't like that idea. *Maybe I should dump a bottle?*

"Almost there!" He yelled like he was the one that had to go.

As he turned his head at a stop sign his tension was evident. His jaw muscles were pulsing as if he were grinding his teeth. That boy was boiling inside. The question was what will happen when he erupts.

"We're here."

Where is here? The SUV entered a highway on-ramp. They were in the middle of nowhere, just farms and fields. The ride north and west was all back roads up until they entered the interstate. But that ride didn't last. Two exits and he was off the highway again. No good. She didn't see any location markers. Miles passed, then a dirt road. The SUV stopped at a gate in front of a little saltbox house. He got out and opened the gate. The sign at the gate said, "Brinks Gunsmithing". And in small letters below that it said, "Buck and Ro."

"Brinks, you're not related to Tommy Brinks, General Tommy Brinks?!"

He didn't answer. He got in the car, drove inside the gate, and parked near the front door. He slammed the car's door and marched up to the stoop. He pressed a doorbell and knocked on the house's front window, but no one answered. There weren't any cars in the driveway. The boy helped himself to a key under the mat.

"Hey come on I got to go, let me out of here!" She was faking before but that wasn't the case any longer.

He turned, hearing her plea but rather than respond, he opened the door and disappeared inside. Albright redoubled her effort to hold it. She wasn't going to let someone find her body smelling like piss. That was no way for the first woman president of the United States to die; soaked in ammonia. She was convinced he planned to kill her by the way he acted. He drove to build courage.

Maybe he was a killer and screwed up overseas and that's why they put him on ice. Security was the ideal job for psychopaths. They're allowed opportunity to kill and satisfy the state's needs while avoiding arrest. Insidious how the State Department operates and only recently did she learn how far they will go. Maybe he's gone too far. Wild thoughts ran her mind since this morning. *Why didn't he report in? He's a sadist and I'm a plaything. He needs a place to do it.*

She, Mark and this boy were three days missing. He spent much of it unconscious in the back of this SUV while she and Mark made good their escape. Then the tables turned. Now he's driving around in big circles, for what? To decide where and when to murder her? Farm country was a good place for that, her body would never be found. But if he works for that psychopath Brinks? Albright shuddered despite how hot it was in there.

It seemed like a year but he came back outside in two minutes. He opened the back hatch of the car holding an AK-47. He had a semiautomatic pistol tucked in his belt. Mark's high-tech plastic gun wasn't evident.

"Get out."

Albright slowly emerged. Her legs were weak. She hadn't eaten much in the last few days. Unable to move around in the dog compartment had made her sore and stiff. She thought about trying to take him before, but now she could hardly stand. He had improved physically. He helped her out of the truck and was unexpectedly gentle about it. Ted Bundy was also a polite murderer.

"On the news they confirmed it. She never turns the TV off. Wolf News says shoot you on sight."

"I'm entitled to a fair trial — "

"Radio, Ma'am, it's on the radio, too. My uncle says never trust media; I don't know what to think."

"Uncle Buck?"

"That one too."

He guided her into the house passed the living room. He had jimmied a gun cabinet's door and left it wide open. Badges and trophies were inside with more guns. Police memorabilia on the walls. Maybe he came here to ask Uncle Buck's advice, or share reward money, or get a shovel to bury her body. This was her best opportunity to engage him. She forced fear down.

"Uncle Buck's a retired cop, is that so?" She wanted to push the rule of law idea on him, cop relatives were a good in, but nature made her rush on.

"You're sharp Ma'am, this way."

He led her to the bathroom. He had gone in before now and removed anything she might use as a weapon. The boy wasn't dumb in that regard. She looked for a weapon anyway. The man of the house was a gun nut, he might have a piece in the loo. Who else would have a gun cabinet in the middle of their living room? Retired cop, gunsmithing was likely a hobby business.

Albright checked the mirror. She was an unrivaled mess. Her short business-cut hair was a rat's nest and dirt somehow got smeared all over her face. Her cheeks were hollow and eyes bloodshot. She smelled of wet dog. No one would think she's Jane Albright, president made criminal. That gave her one small comfort. She didn't look anything like the person to be shot on sight.

Once finished in the restroom, he marched her into the kitchen. He had her open the refrigerator but it was almost empty, nothing but condiments. He had to be as hungry as she was.

"They went to the lake house," the boy said.

"Look at me Brinks, nobody will recognize me. Let's get food, that diner you passed. I'm famished."

"How the hell I'm gonna do that?" The boy looked hard at her. "You got my name, how'd you guess?"

"I put two and two together. That's your picture on the mantel, Kyle, right? Is Tommy Brinks your father? You look like him." She said.

"No, my uncle, not my favorite. What's it to you?"

"He set me up for a murder I didn't commit. Like I been trying to tell you — "

"That's crazy, he, he … he's not that bad … Just a badass. Not a murderer … I think."

"If that's what you think."

Kyle Brinks didn't look like he was convinced. They were family but one with a black-hearted monster in the mix. General Brinks was someone anybody that had contact with him was afraid of. Kyle being in the same family could not escape the General's brutality. The young man must have suffered much for it. Tommy Brinks wasn't called General Mayhem for nothing. She shivered to think what it was like growing up around that monster. This boy didn't like the General, it was written all over him. But, commonly, minions hate their masters and follow anyway.

"Who ordered I be shot on sight?" Albright said quietly trying to make him think about it and not emotionalize. "It was General Brinks, wasn't it?" Kyle gritted his teeth. She hit a soft spot. "Shoot me before the truth comes out, fine. Can't I, at least, have a last meal? You aren't like him. For the love of God and all that is good, let me eat before you kill me."

"I'm nothing like him! Sit, sit right there."

"A little food for God's sake." Albright said lowing herself into a kitchen chair. "You'll collect the bonus money if I'm fed or not. Then you can deliver my head on a platter. Uncle Mayhem would like that."

"Up yours, all right. Just sit quiet. Let me think." Kyle jabbed the AK toward her butt first as if he wanted to club her, but the rifle's stock didn't connect. Maybe this boy wasn't a killer.

"Don't want blood on Buck and Ro's floors?" She said. He moved in front of her.

The boy's face was red. One hand went up to the fresh stitches Bart had put in his head. Did he remember Bart opening up his skull to get the brain's swelling fluid out? Or was he angry or embarrassed? His face contorted. A battle was going on inside him.

He loosened grip on the rifle. The handgun was tucked into his belt rather tightly and out of reach. Albright watched the long gun sway looking for a chance to grab it. She was well practiced with handguns, that fact may well have gotten her elected, but she had never shot an AK-47. She wasn't sure she'd find the safety fast enough. She wasn't the type to shoot a man, but things change.

The boy backed closer to the wall, never taking his eyes away. He picked up the wall phone. It was a regular old-fashioned dial phone. It may have been bright yellow at one time but now it was dull tan. He dialed a number that he must have memorized. Maybe that's why he wasted the day driving; trying to remember, trying to get his brain working again after that concussion.

"Uncle Tommy, it's me Kyle."

Albright heard the General's voice blow like a sudden gale.

"Kyle, where the hell are you! You're AWOL, ungrateful idiot. I had to pull strings to get you that job. Explain yourself."

"I have her, Jane Albright. I captured her."

"What! Where are you. You're sure?"

"I'm at Aunt Ro's house. I have Albright tied up."

"Don't move. I'm sending my crew. Don't do a damn thing until they get there, understand?"

"Yes sir, whatever you need." Kyle said. He cowered at the General's barking voice and held the phone away. He seemed to shrink by half as the General ranted. He gripped the phone like handling a deadly a snake. "I'm hungry, we need food. The Minnie Mart's — "

"Damnit Kyle, stay there! Don't move. Don't let her see the TV. No media. Don't be stupid you moron!"

Kyle flinched at the word "moron". So that's how it is. He's been a target of emotional abuse.

"But Uncle — He hung up, he always does that, never listens." Kyle put the phone back onto its receiver. "I'm not stupid, he always says I'm stupid. Get up, come on. I'll show him."

"Where we going?" Albright asked.

"Food, he always treats me like I can't handle it. I'm in charge of this, this … situation. Prisoners get to eat, don't they? I'll show him … I'm not stupid."

He pointed the way with his long gun into the living room and onto the front door. She had one hand on the knob when he said, "Stop there, hands on your head, face me, back against the door."

Brinks the younger backed up and took a police badge off the trophy shelf and a pair of handcuffs. He pinned the badge onto his shirt with one hand. He checked his gun's action and waved the rifle toward her at the door. Albright went outside first and headed straight for the passenger door. He made her stop while he put the long gun in the back. Brinks didn't try to detour her, rather he opened the front passenger door for her and told her to buckle up. *Buckle up, now he cares about my safety?* Albright didn't argue. She felt the winds changing and it wasn't time to counter the blow.

Kyle with keys in hand had drawn a pistol even before he set down the rifle. He got in and kept the handgun in his lap facing her. If she tried anything, he had an easy shot. He proved dexterous and started the SUV and put it in gear without wavering using his left hand. Kyle drove about ten miles with one hand on the gun before pulling into a diner's parking lot. They had passed this place before.

"You wanted a last meal, here it is. Don't try anything. I'll shoot. Put the handcuffs on."

He handed them over and she put them on loose so she could slip out. He helped her out of the car and pointed her toward the eatery. He stopped and made her tighten the cuffs. Albright entered first with the cuffs on hands forward. There was a small foyer with a reception and cash register desk just inside. The hostess, a middle-aged woman, stopped Jane at the inner door.

"No way Miss. You're filthy, we don't let homeless in here. Go around back. I'll have Cookie get you something."

Brinks pushed her through the door and pointed at his borrowed badge. "Officer Brinks, she's with me."

"You related to Buck?"

"Never mind, give us a table on a wall, I want my back to the wall."

The hostess led the way, grumbling, "That's Kyle, he must be."

This diner wasn't only the classical long, skinny building with a counter and stools. It had that setup but wider and there was a square room on one end. The addition held a dozen tables. Brinks had Albright sit facing the window.

He handed her the keys and let her take one cuff off to eat. *He's getting smarter, more careful.* Brinks sat back with the handgun pointing her way. His eyes darting around.

"I'm gonna eat like it's Thanksgiving." He said.

The head must be much better. He hardly ate anything the last few days. He was too sick.

Brinks appeared alert and focused. Hunger did that to a person. Up until this morning he was out of it. He was over the brain swelling. If she had an opportunity to strike him, she'd go for the head. Mark's friend did a remarkable job with that impromptu operation. The stitches in the boy's head were well done with no redness around the sutures. A solid blow will surely undo Bart's efforts.

Good going Albright, you insisted Mark save his life and now you want to kill him.

They ordered food and Albright ate her eggs and hash browns like a trucker behind schedule while Brinks killed two oversized hamburgers. Other people in the room noticed them as she stuffed her cheeks. She watched the room in the window's reflection. There were a lot of people in for lunch. She also heard people murmuring. "Is that Albright, looks like her, what happened to her, nothing in the news."

Brinks heard them talking as well. He stood up. She turned to face the room.

"Look, this here's a fugitive, you all never mind. Go about your business."

Albright went back to her plate but saw in the window that the room was even more restless. People were shuffling and whispering and pointing at their table.

Someone called, "Officer, if that's the president, you best be letting her go."

Another voice said, "Yeah, we need her. They did her wrong. Didn't you hear?" People got out of their seats and were moving toward them. "What's the matter with you, Kyle? Ain't you got no sense?"

Brinks stood up, a hand firmly on the sidearm. "You all just back up. What in the hell's wrong with you people?"

"You didn't see it, did you? Benny, put the news on." The hostess said. An old man at the counter picked up a TV remote control.

"Daggone thing," Benny said as he worked the remote.

Others in the room started raising their voices with pro-Albright slogans until they were drowned out by the sound of police cars racing by, heading toward the Brinks' farm. A big military truck full of troops also rumbled by the big plate glass window. She didn't know if they were heading for the farm to kill her, or save her but it didn't take long to know the answer.

"I got the recorder thing going." The old man in coveralls said as he clicked around. "Gosh darn thing, here it is."

General Brinks was on the screen, a rerun of him giving a speech. He announced the coup, said the president was public enemy number one. He wanted Albright's head. He said flat out she killed the VP. He said the law didn't matter. No trial. He was in charge. His last words before the short announcement was over was, "Albright is a dead woman. A million dollars, tax free, for her head."

"What, when?" Jane cried.

"Yesterday," someone said.

No one in the room supported the coup. Rather the people there became more agitated upon hearing General Brinks again. This was an open-carry state and several people were packing iron. Nobody pulled a gun yet but she could almost feel their itchy trigger fingers. Many hands hovered over holsters. If Kyle wasn't a local boy, they'd shoot him.

Brinks the younger bolted away from the table like a sudden jolt of high-voltage ejected him. His chair fell. He pressed his back to the plate glass, fingering his gun eyeing the room. Albright herself felt the shock. A coup. Washington was finally and utterly broken. The rule of law was no more. Anything goes.

"God save us." She pushed her chair away and faced the people.

"This is a coup, he's … Brinks is a dictator." A drop of sweat ran down her dirty cheek. She kicked over a chair. "This will not stand! He can't do this, this is America!" Her voice was vicious — hate, shock, anger exploded out with her words.

"Damn right!" the room erupted in curses and insults directed toward General Brinks. Albright wondered if Kyle would try to shoot his way out. He was out gunned. *I'm in the target zone.*

A siren sounded. This time coming from the farm toward them … and it was getting closer.

"We must, must … Revolution," Albright called. "Who is with me?"

"I'm down," Kyle said. "Screw Uncle Tommy, right up his ass!"

Kyle brought out the key, laid the handgun aside and unlocked the other handcuff. He tossed the cuffs away and laid another gun on the table. A detective's special she didn't know he had on him.

"You know how to use it, take it. We gotta get outta here." Brinks the younger faced the room. "What's the best back way? Got to ditch that K-9 unit." He ripped the badge off his shirt and flung it away. Another cop car screamed past the diner. "You all going to help or what?"

It took only a minute, but someone grabbed Kyle's keys and pulled the police car around back. A man tossed his pickup truck keys to Kyle and said, "All you folks, get your cars, block the road. Make Road 420 into a parking lot. What do you say?"

An old-timer with long hair, a peace sign headband and Grateful Dead T-shirt faced up to Kyle. The old hippie said, "You do your daddy proud, son." He turned, put his fist in the air and yelled. "Down with Tommy Brinks! Screw the coup!"

That was a rallying cry. Conservative, liberal, it didn't matter, the people there were of the same mind. Phones came out, calls were made, people got their cars moved into the road. Before Jane Albright knew it, she and Kyle Brinks were driving fast down a narrow farm road in an old pickup truck. When she looked back down the lane a John Deere harvester was pulling onto the road behind them.

TWENTY-THREE

On the Hunt

Mark Levine lay on the floor of the safe house fighting his way back to consciousness and losing the battle. When he first came up onto one elbow, the blood oozing from his head was wet, hot and sticky. He observed what he wiped off his face. It was movie blood, someone else's reality. He thought of a stuck pig. His stomach turned sick. Images of dead men, men he had killed, flashed before his eyes and he passed out. Next time he woke the blood was crusted brown.

"Get going, Levine. She needs you."

He pushed himself upright, but the rush caused him to blackout. At one point he opened his eyes and it was still morning until he blinked. Next, he knew the sun was lower. It was late, too late. There was nothing he could do. His training told him to sleep, to mend. An operative was no good dead. Mark laid his head down once more without hope of picking up a fresh trail.

He felt light footfalls on the floor and opened his eyes; was that President Jane Albright? She's a toothpick like her sister Jen. Ten years apart and they looked so much alike. Thin and pretty, nice hair, eyes that danced like twinkling stars. He let his eyelids fall.

"Mark, Mark, you home in there?"

Someone touched his cheek. It was a nice dream. He felt wetness. "I'm bleeding." He startled and tried to get up.

"No, it's water. Easy Mark, it's Jen, do you know where you are?" She patted his forehead with a wet rag. "Answer me, where are you?"

"I'm in failure land," he said, slowly rising to a sitting position. Sunlight low in the window filtered into the room making the dusty air twinkle. He wasn't out as long this time. Maybe an hour had passed. "Jane's gone. He took her."

"Shit, shit, shit, Mark how'd this happen?" Jennifer said.

She came like she said she would. He had told her about his safe house system. "We had a prisoner; Jane wouldn't leave him to die … "

"I know, Bart told me. Come on, let's get you cleaned up." Jen said.

Jen helped him up onto the bed. She got fresh water and a medical kit, finished cleaning him, dressed his wound. The cut wasn't bad, the knot on his head was worse. He drank and felt better with water in him and a pill for pain. No sign of concussion. She gave him a power bar and put on coffee. His head hurt but Mark felt like he was ready. He had been through worse. But where to, what's next?

"This kid, you stole the boat from, know anything about him, his capabilities?" Jen said from the stove. Always a pro, digging for information.

"I make him a loser. He had Marine Corps tattoos and was pumped up, a body builder. I make him a wanna be. Either no balls for regular service or he washed out and can't let go. I figure that's why he was stuck on perimeter duty. Surprised me.

"No shit Shirley, you look surprised. That was slick of you. Taking a security boat, but you should have drowned that rat." She said. Jen set aside the med-kit and reached for the coffee she brought in and lowered herself onto the bed next to him. She handed him that cup of Joe.

"I'm retired." He drank a sip. "I don't kill for convenience anymore. He's just a dumb kid."

"You're right. But he's not that dumb, he took you out."

"That was my fault! Ouch." Mark touched the bandage on his scalp. That big knot throbbed.

"Dumbass. Relax, let's think this out." Jen said. "There's an all points bulletin out, some GI-looking dude knocked over a gunsmith's house. He took three guns, an AK-47 and two handguns. The APB is a shoot to kill order, kill all parties. Must be your guy."

"Sounds like him. I'd bet Jane's still with him. Nothing in the news? If he reported, it'd be all over the media. The president's capture … wait, how're you getting this. You didn't call in, did you? Your CIA credentials … it's too dangerous. I hope you didn't — "

Jen burst out laughing. Despite the situation, Mark was glad to hear good humor. A little relief was what he needed. It was funny testing her. She was still in the game and in top form. Mark didn't need to school her. More and more as he aged, he knew he was slipping behind the curve. He was fifty-two and she thirty-something and in her prime. When he was active, he would have killed that kid without a second thought.

"OK you got me," Mark said with a crooked smile. He ambled out into the front room. "You have an I-know phone, but you won't use it, too easy to trace. If you searched the junkyard you would have found the car we took and traced it here, but you didn't use Sky-net, you'd know they'd trace your trace. Bart told you where we were. So, if not the I-know phone, how'd you know what the cops are up to without tipping them off? What've you got?"

"I got this idea from you a long time ago." Jen said. She walked over to the shotgun shack's front door and opened it wide. A police car sat there. Heat was still coming off the engine. "The best way to know what the cops are doing is cop equipment, right? You told me that in Spain, remember?"

Now it was Mark's turn to laugh. Back in Spain she played him, but good. He had no idea she was a double agent then. She got more than her mission's objectives. Natural talent gets you far in Special Operations. And to think he almost blew her cover.

"You've got balls, steal a police car. How … never mind, don't answer. It's risky, but let's go."

Mark checked the trunk and found a few useful items. He put the police hat on which covered the head bandage. No sooner did Mark get into the driver's seat an all points came over the radio. The car that was associated with the robbery, a retired K-9 unit, was seen less than ten miles from the crime. The kid was still around. Coordinates came into the patrol car's computer and Jen switched on the GPS. The report said Sky-net didn't see the car. It must be parked inside somewhere out of Sky-net's view. They'd keep an eye out for a garage. Dispatch said the perp might be on foot. It was only ten miles away. Mark put on the lights and they zoomed away.

What bothered Mark was how and why the kid knew to rob a gun dealer's house? Just dumb luck or did the kid know his way around there? The gun dealer's name was Brinks. Was there a connection?

The kid had better than half a day to make tracks and he should be miles from there, but he hung around? Why? Mark doubted the robbery was done by his man but it was a place to start. They'd visit the victim and see if it panned out, but first recon. Go see why all cars were called and heading to a man-on-the-loose call. He thought about using the I-know phone. Accessing real-time satellite data would help but that would also show his hand. Dispatch said shoot to kill. Why, to kill Jane Albright and any witness with her. She didn't look much like a president right now. Maybe she'd get lucky and miss a bullet.

Jen quickly explained General Brinks pulled off a coup yesterday. Brinks said on TV that he wanted Jane's head. If that all points call was about Jane and his man, that shoot to kill dispatch had a solid reason. Mark stepped on the gas.

In no time they came upon an intersection. A parade of patrols cars moving fast with lights on zipped past the side street where Mark stopped. They waited there, not wanting to follow too close. A personnel carrier full of uniformed reserves rolled by. Mark pulled out behind it but hung back. Jen's stolen car was from another department, had DEA numbers. Mark counted off about two minutes and engaged lights and siren.

Once they got near the location, Mark pulled off onto a farm road and parked well off that dirt track. They proceeded on foot along a creek boarding a farm field. Coming to a thicket near the house where the police cars were, they stopped to observe. Cops everywhere. An old lady was waving her hands mad as hell. The old man off to the side was yelling at her to shut up. Mark and Jen had to stay put, no talking to the couple now, too many cops.

Jen whispered. "How did you make it this far? Every cop in the world's looking for Jane. Roadblocks everywhere. I didn't think you'd make it to the safe house; Bart had doubts as well."

"That was easy," Mark said. His move was clever. "Can't go wrong with a police K-9 cruiser. Decommissioned. Nobody looks for a car that isn't missing. Perfect cover."

"White SUV, big black and red letters on the sides?"

"Yeah, how'd you know?"

"I just saw one parked under the trees next to a diner."

"Balls!"

Mark and Jen backed out of the brush, skipped the creek's cover and ran across the farm field. They got back in the car. Mark pulled onto the dirt track ready to fly but he had to wait. A SWAT truck following a K-9 unit blasted past their position forward on the main road. *They're setting up a manhunt.* Mark wanted to slap himself in the head the way Aggie always does, but his headache was improving and he had enough setbacks. More headaches were sure to come without his help.

Mark and Jen made it to the diner having wasted several minutes. The SUV was gone and no sooner had they pulled in; people rushed outside. Why were they parking in the street? As he got out of the car a pickup truck pulled in behind, blocking his cruiser.

"What the hell are you doing!" Mark yelled, going for his authoritarian voice.

An old man got out, white beard and coveralls. Keys danged from his fingers. "Fuck the pole-ece."

"We aren't police, dumbass!" Jen screamed. "We look like police?"

Mark tossed the cop hat back inside the car's open door. The bandage on his head was revealed. He still had blood on his shirt and head.

"Say you didn't steal that car, did ya?" The old man looked at them cross-eyed.

Mark had a gun. Jennifer's piece was hidden as well. Several armed people came up behind the old man. Jen had given him a 38, it was tucked into his belt behind him at the small of his back. Jen was packing too but Mark didn't know where or how; the locals didn't stand a chance. But he needed intel. Talk first, shoot later.

"What ya got here, Benny?" Someone said with a Glock in hand.

Three more civilians nearby closed in, drawing handguns. Mark wasn't ready for a bloodbath. He didn't want to kill innocent people. Bad crossfire situation. More people were coming outside from the diner as a few more cars pulled in. He didn't have time for this. Jen put a hand behind her back. Mark chose his first targets.

"Be damned if I know, they don't look like no cops."

"We aren't cops!" Jen screamed. "I'm Jennifer Albright. I'm looking for my sister."

Mark expected shots fired and not a blast from Jen's mouth.

"I'll be damned. She does look like the president."

What a surprise. Mark was sure Jen would start shooting. But all they had were five-shot vintage police revolvers. The civilians had more firepower. One of them was holding a 13-shot auto. Mark raised his hands and nodded at Jen to do the same. But she pulled her gun instead.

"Look assholes. I know Jane was here. I'm trying to help her, so either you people help me help the president like patriots or get the hell out of my way. Fucking traitors!"

"I'm not no damn traitor!" The bearded man screamed back.

"Nobody here's a traitor." The man with the auto said, but he didn't lower the gun. His voice was even, experienced, maybe retired military First target, Mark thought.

Jen dropped the gun to her waist. "If that's the case, will you please help us?"

"Don't know about you folks, but I'd bet hard money she's with us." The bearded man said. He rounded the truck and put his hand out. "Benny Taylor, won't you'll come inside a spell, we'll get you sorted out."

More people had come over from the street and parking. Another pair of regular cars pulled in. Benny went inside and Mark followed. It didn't take long to sort it out. Jane had just been there. Benny made some calls and had a good idea of which way they had gone and said so. Half the county was blocking roads and got word to let Mark pass. Mark and Jen weren't there ten minutes before they took off and with luck they'd catch up. They were just two steps behind Jane, but only one step ahead of the police. It won't take long for the police to figure out the manhunt around Brinks' Gunsmith was a dead end. The dragnet was about to widen, of that Mark was sure.

TWENTY-FOUR

Mel and Praytis Walk

Aggie had split and gone to Moon City, and Ben wasn't due out of the regeneration tank until tomorrow. Mother was pushing regen so Ben won't be revived again until done. No more advice coming.

Aggie wasn't answering her wrist phone. Mel spent his time learning the ship systems and weirdly a lot of it made sense. He figured out why Mother has subroutine AIs running every aspect of the ship's material functions. Her mind was so expansive and old that she couldn't focus all of her attention on any one thing. Most of her focus was on getting ready to leave. There was much more to Mother than that. He didn't accept it at first but since changed his mind. Mother is an actual living being. *This ship's nothing but the clothes she wears so people can live with her and accept her. He had done that himself.*

Why'd Mother even want people? Praytis said it was a symbiotic thing. Yeah, she needs Life Force and people to operate the machinery, but she doesn't need machinery to live. Mother is millions of years old. But why she identifies with humans nobody knows. He learned humans were everywhere in the universe. Mel thought it was just because Mother likes the company. Life would be boring otherwise. Maybe it was like a reality TV show for Mother, put a bunch of a-holes together and see what happens.

One thing Mother needed, like everybody living needs, was direction and purpose. Too bad that dick Karnack had forced Mother to do what she didn't want to do. No wonder Mother was hot to get out of here.

Mel still had a lot of questions. But he was tired of reading the manuals, if you could call them that, and he drifted into info rabbit holes a lot. Currently he was on the bridge looking at the surface of Mars when Sarah and Praytis came in with a class-A robot. Sarah carried a small rabbit cage and proceeded to cage Miss Bubbles and her baby bunnies.

"Dude, what's going on?" Mel asked.

"As it happens," Praytis said, "Miss Bubbles' offspring, children I should say, are having issues. The litter suffers a lack of water and variety of feed. Sarah and I are bringing them to the wildlife reserve."

"Her babies need ... We have a reserve? I didn't see that on the ship map."

"Storage pods aren't part of the ship proper; Mother adds them to the ship's core as needs arise, just as Moon City does. At the moment she is making ready for star travel, adding quarters and releasing her pods. Karnack had been preparing to leave for a century. Thus, Mother has quite a menagerie. In fact, we are rather well stocked. Sarah and I are going down, care to join us?"

"Do humans live in a gravity well?"

Praytis did a double take. That was the first joke he ever recited. Mel and he had worked it out what felt like years ago. It was only a few months. Praytis' lips parted showing his Chiclet teeth. His version of a smile. He said quoting Aggie. "Hey, that is my line!"

Praytis, Mel and Sarah laughed. Sarah grabbed Mel's hand and pulled him to get out of the chair.

"Come on! Miss Bubbles is gonna feed her babies nice grass!" Sarah said, picking up the cage. Sarah almost fell over as the cage was too big for her. Mel grabbed it.

Mel, Praytis and Sarah took the lift down six levels to one of the halls that went straight aft for a mile. The gangway here was dirt and grass. Old cow pies and other signs of animals were evident as they went and it smelled the part besides. The air wasn't musty as he'd expect on a spaceship but rather the air on this level was farm fresh, that is, fresh fertilizer mixed with hay and grass. They passed environment pods on each side. The doors were clear so he saw a jungle here, a desert there, and other environments along the way. It was a regular Noah's ark except for the cow pasture, which was very deep and stretched half a mile front to back.

"Dude, how, I don't get it. This ship isn't this big, how is it pods are so deep. It's weird."

"Simple really, it's dimensional shifting. I would liken it to the British TV show called Dr. Why. Yes, that is a good comparative. Small on the outside but larger on the inside." Praytis didn't slow as if he was speaking of the weather. This blew Mel's mind.

"But how is it possible?"

"No one knows."

Mel stopped in the middle of the path, put the cage down and grabbed Praytis' arm. He saw a lot of weird stuff in the last year. More since he boarded Mother. He thought he had figured stuff out but that was a curveball.

"Wait, what. What does that mean?"

Sarah ran ahead and yelled. "I found it, it's the bunny field." She ran back, took the cage, and walked through the force door like a ghost penetrating a wall.

"Where's Doggy Doo when you need him," Mel said thinking of the old cartoon ghost hunter.

Praytis did his version of a chuckle. It sounded normal but in stereo. "I suppose it's all right to tell you. The GTO had strict rules against informing Earthlings and as I no longer work for them ... still it is odd to speak openly ... of course, you are not permanent crew ... but Mother hasn't leveled such a prohibition and being as Aggie isn't here ... still Ben might not like it ... but still ... Should Earth ever learn of this ... but as the GTO is obligated to leave ... Oh dear."

"Come on spit it out, if you want me to sign on. Mother wants me for crew, yeah, so convince me. What are you hiding?"

"Very well. Earth wasn't supposed to know, but we of Spiral Arm Six, that is this region of the Milky Way and all the other civilized races hereabout have no idea how mother ships bend dimensions. We don't know how star drive works either. Ironic no? It is what America's elite most desire. We are barely able to harvest and store Life Force, a commodity of exchange mother ships require to function mechanically."

"What about our shuttles, don't they work the same way? You all came here from lightyears away, how's that happening?"

"Of course, we have mastered gravity control. MAC crafts operate by way of a combination of a self-generated gravity pocket that isolates the craft from local gravity and the use of magnetic reflection to give propulsion and direction. They sail on magnetic winds, if you will. However, no MAC can travel between stars. There isn't enough gravity and there is a lack of strong magnetism to utilize. MACs can only work in local space where planetary bodies reside. Earth will soon master MAC crafts. The magnetic aspects are understood and as Element 115 was discovered, it is only a matter of time before they understand how to make gravity pockets."

"But, dude, how did you get here?"

"Mother ships. Mother ships transport advanced civilizations. Moon City and her like are also living entities with the same needs. You did notice while visiting how many large ships were in hangar seventeen, no?"

"Hangar seventeen? That many?"

"Moon is a small city, only twenty-four hangars all together. The city that once fed on Mars' biomass, before Mars was destroyed, of course, was much larger. Phobos was where that forgone city lived."

"Dude, so we are like fleas on a dog. Not cool."

They had continued walking toward the environment pod where Sarah had gone. Mel felt dejected until he saw Sarah inside running over green fields covered in wildflowers. What a great place for rabbits. It lightened his heart. But the idea of becoming permanent crew soured in his mind. This place was fantastic, but it wasn't home.

"I feel like a leech. Next to Mother, we are. I kinda get where Aggie is coming from."

"Oh no, it is not like that at all." Praytis said. "Fleas aren't invited. They are parasites, we are not that. We are more beloved pets, and in some small way, actual partners. AIs are benevolent. Benevolence is a state of balance no human species has ever achieved without the guidance of an AI."

"You mean controlled, like training a dog. Where's the freedom?"

Praytis laughed loudly. His voice echoed down the corridor.

"Melvin you should know, there is no such thing as free will. We, all human types, suffer the same maladies. We are programed by our lives and cultures and the innate workings of imperfect minds, and we act accordingly. AIs make civilized living possible otherwise, like Mars below, like most human varieties, we spaceborne will have blown ourselves up before maturity evolved. Just as Earth would have had not the GTO's program of subverting nuclear weapons had not been approved by Galactic Central."

Mel felt shocked. He could not grasp the implications. Mars killed itself and Earth would have done the same? He grabbed one of the million ideas doing battle inside his head and blurted it out.

"But why, how … " Mel dropped down onto the grass pathway and sat cross-legged. The weight of it all pressed him to ground. "How can this be?"

"Earth's biomass, of course," Praytis said. "Cities harvest ambient Life Force. She, Moon City came here before the dinosaurs. It is a shame such a nice planet is failing. The GTO, for the sake of the LF market, endeavored to delay Earth's progress and keep the ambient LF market open."

"But now aliens are exposed." Mel said miserably. "Let me guess, Earth is on its own, no more help, weapons free to fly and we're too stupid to keep a lid on our monkey-brained impulses, yeah?"

"I am afraid that is correct."

"So, what now? What can we do?" The question was asked seeking solutions to save Earth.

Praytis was kneading the ground with his four feet. He tended to do that when worried or upset.

"We are leaving," Praytis said, "leaving before, as Aggie might say, 'the poop hits the fan.'"

"Is there any hope for Earth?"

Praytis rocked back and forth on his four feet and didn't answer.

Mel asked but he knew the answer. He spent enough time studying to identify patterns. He knew history and it was the same as it ever was only now Earth had the ability to wreak the whole thing and no one could or would stop it. The worst of the worsts were always tops. In the news, as always, everyone was itching for war. The media was bent on bashing Aggie and aliens. Media beat war drums for a living. And it made sense since the U.S. bombed Haiti. The government needed a newer, bigger war to cover their asses and distract the public. Add to that the mass extinction in progress and pollution, over population and natural human insanity, and the numbers looked bad, really, really bad.

Mel asked quietly, "Have any others like us survived?

"Many unlike you, yes. A few of your like kind only because natural disasters set them backward, such as the meteorite Earth suffered 13,000 years ago which drove civilization back to a stone age … very interesting … Oh dear. But, of course, there are those who accepted AI control and so flourish.”

“I see. That’ll never happen here.”

Mel moved into the environment pod. He watched Sarah pick flowers and chase rabbits for a while. He hardly noticed the mechanical robots tending the environment. Biological bots were reserved for more complicated stuff. Praytis went to one of the bots that was offline to check it. Maybe going back for gender transition wasn’t such a good idea. It was nice here. The outside was inside. He hated the real outside.

Mel didn’t ask how long Earth had left before it went completely off the rails. Praytis studied it for thousands of years; he’d know the timing. Mel didn’t want to know.

He wanted to do his big change his way, the hard way, the way trans men respected. Did he have a choice? There is no free will. He had to do it the way he must even if going back might be a death sentence. *A man has got to live with himself.*

Ben’s daughter had her fill of chasing rabbits. Praytis asked if she’d like to go and see the cows again. That explained the fresh milk served with breakfast. It was decided. The party headed back the way they had come but Mel had no more questions. He walked in silence reeling within and failing to ignore the doubts and questions that hammered his logic into new shapes.

TWENTY-FIVE

Jane and Mark

Mark left the parking lot without lights or sirens. Benny passed info up line by phone, ironically, by landlines. All the old farmers thereabout were still using house phones, even Buck Brinks. Mark had learned a trick from Sanderson years ago. The NSA doesn't monitor hardwired phones. It wasn't in the budget. Everything was predicated on high-tech money, that's what made the national budget more expensive. It's what feeds the Complex's lust for cash. Mark was more an analogue man himself and for once it paid off. Like Aggie, he appreciated low-tech solutions to complex problems.

Mark rolled up to a harvester that was stuck in the middle of a country road, got out of the car and confronted the operator. The man said he broke down. Mark wasn't buying it.

"Better check with your wife," Mark said. "She got a call, about us. Go and see."

"No sir I'm not going nowhere. People steal your batteries; you know how much they cost? I'm not leaving this here machine till the repairman comes."

In the distance sirens were going off. Mark didn't know the roads thereabouts, but it sounded like a car was heading toward them. He was about ready to jump up there and drag the man off. He had no time to fool around. Jen got out of the car. Knowing her, she'd knock that farmer for a loop. But he heard a motor in the distance and signaled Jen to hold. The man didn't hear it, he was standing too close to the harvester. Mark was back far enough where he could see the field.

An old woman on a 4x4 ATV wearing a housedress was flying across a muddy field. A hair roller flew off her head and into the sky. He watched the thing fly and saw that the moon was lit up and big chunks were missing. She entered the road a little behind where Mark had parked. She gunned it and fishtailed. The clock in his awareness ticked. Benny didn't relay a destination. Jane wasn't aiming for anyplace in particular. The farmer didn't know to let his car pass.

When the lady skidded to a halt, she stood on the pegs and yelled at her husband. "Harvey, these folks are with us. Let them pass right quick. Sheriff's coming this way."

The farmer grumbled but he got up in the machine's cab, fired it up, and pulled up enough for Mark to squeeze past. He backed it up again. Last Mark saw of them they were riding double on that 4x4 and running across the field at top speed.

A half dozen miles down the road Jen grabbed Mark's arm. "Stop, back up, back up." Mark hit the brakes hard and backed up. "There, look," she said.

Fresh tire tracks went off into the woods. The driver must have tried a tight turn onto the path between fields going too fast. The back of a truck was just barely discernible in the thicket. Jen held the road and Mark charged into the woods; the airbags had gone off. Too dense to make out any prints. They couldn't have gone far, but where, what direction?

A gun barrel pressed against Mark's neck. "I'd shoot you for what you did to me, but she needs you."

The gun was withdrawn. Mark turned. The kid beat him twice. Brinks stood there smiling like a cat that got the mouse. *I'm too old for this.* Mark was about to disarm him but Jane stepped in.

"Mark! You're OK, how'd you get here?" She said stumbling out of a briar patch. She hugged him and he returned the same.

"Ask her," Mark said separating from the embrace.

Jane turned. The kid had his hands up and the smile was gone. Jen had a gun against the kid's head.

"Jennifer! My God, I don't believe it. He's with me."

"So, they said at the diner." Jen didn't release her grip on the gun.

Jen patted Brinks down from behind with one hand. She stepped away and lowered the gun to her waist but still had a bead on him. She held there until Mark raised his 38 to cover Brinks.

Smart, she won't break procedure.

Jen rushed forward. Jane and her sister had a quick hug. The two exchanged information so fast that if Mark didn't already have a headache, this would start one. The happy reunion didn't last long. They had to make tracks and fast. That cop was back by the farmer's equipment, cursing up a storm as he reported over the car's police band radio.

"I sure hope Harvey took the tractor's keys," Jen said.

As if on cue in a low-budget movie, the sound of the John Deere's big diesel starting up echoed over the fields. How many cops can run a harvester? *Farm country, maybe all of them.* Mark didn't wait to find out. He had everyone pile into Jen's police car. Jane's ride was out of sight, but he had another police car problem. The one they were in was stolen and soon to be, if not already, a neon beacon. A military helicopter was not far off, flying low and it appeared to be setting up a landing at the diner. *Special Ops?* Jen's car, like all police cars, had a roof number.

TWENTY-SIX
Aggie at Gitmo

Aggie sat up on the prow of One Love's fishing boat, tired and dejected. She and the boat had that in common. She was a mess. Her shorts and T-shirt were ripped, one flip-flop had broken and her hair was matted flat with crusted salt. The only thing she wore that wasn't turned into crap was Mother's coverall tied around her waist and her covered up bikini. Her appearance matched the good ship *Lazy Days*. Lazy was once painted bright blue but had faded into gray. It brought memories of her old Vespa scooter back in Key West. Homesickness smacked her. Like her Vespa, Lazy Days looked bad but ran well. Lazy didn't even leak … much.

The overnight crossing between Jamaica and Cuba was hard. The seas were rough and Lazy plowed constantly, splashing water over the bow. It wasn't capable of anything else. Lazy didn't have the speed or power to plane. And the seas were weird, the wind blew one way while waves came from the wrong direction. A break in the clouds showed the moon falling apart but Aggie didn't have time to sky watch. She spent the night bailing in between naps and running the helm.

This boat's way slow. She didn't think they'd make it in a week much less overnight. Finally, at daybreak the seas were calmer. Land was on the horizon, the high ground anyway. The haze didn't yield the shoreline, only what was seen above a low fog. And it was quiet, weird after a night of contrary winds, whitecaps and bizarre wave action. One Love steered for land but it was still a long way. Another hour of slowly chugging along finally brought them into shallow waters as the fog began to lift.

"Hey Cap, why'd you shut off the engine?" Aggie called toward the stern. She didn't need to yell. "That's Cuba, right?"

One Love came forward and handed Aggie a bottle of water. "Me go no closer."

"What? Told you I'd make you crew if you got me there, you got to land."

"No, mon. Me in Cuba's three-mile limit. Cuba waters. Me go no closer, dey shoot." One Love's eternal smile was gone. His easy personality had jumped ship. He spread his hands. "Dis Cuba, shoot now ask tomorrow."

"Crap! What am I going to do, swim?" Aggie sank down to the bench seat. She was exhausted, she hardly slept at all last night.

"Ya mon, you say you good swimmer, no?" But then One Love laughed. "No worries, last mile's shallow. You walk."

One Love lifted the door off the live-well and pulled out a faded lifejacket, it didn't look like it could float. He handed it over. It only had one strap and it was kid sized. It was the only lifejacket she had seen on the boat. They didn't even have floatie seat cushions. *This'll never fly with Mark. His boats were safety first.*

Aggie held it up. "Lucky we didn't sink."

"You lucky one. Wind blows for you." One Love looked all around shading his eyes "Patrol boat. You go. Me draw dem away. Follow de wind. Me go quick now."

Aggie had half a mind to turn around and go back and find another way. But she wouldn't chance One Love getting caught with her. Last she heard; her head was wanted on a platter. She saw Brinks on One Love's phone last night. Brinks wants her and anyone with her dead. She was lucky One Love didn't clock her for the money. The motors of the PT boat started revving. Must have spotted them. She checked One's Love's phone's GPS. The Cuban's boat and they were outside the three-mile limit but the military was heading toward them anyway. It wasn't fair.

"One Love, look, after I get Jon I'm going to PR, there's a cave below the south east face of the international radio telescope, it's below the rim. It's hard to find, there is an elevator takes you down to a tram and the tram takes you to one of the alien's shuttle stations. If I don't make it … anyway that's how you get off the planet, OK."

"I know de place mon, me see you there."

Aggie took the life preserver, slipped the one good strap over her shoulder and rolled over the side facing shore. The moment she was clear, One Love fired the motor and started chugging back the way they had come, only more east toward PR. Aggie started treading water northeast with the wind and hopefully toward the beach. She couldn't see the shoreline from water level.

The sea wasn't wild like last night but it did roll in big swells. Once or twice when she was on top of a swell, she saw the PT boat tied up to One Love's rickety craft. She heard the PT's engines idling. *They must be searching Lazy.* He was a long way from home. Aggie stroked away toward shore, methodically as to not wear herself out or splash and become more visible. She pushed until the motor sound faded.

It was a long slog and just when she had enough, energy fading faster, her foot touched something solid and cut her. Her flip-flops were left on the boat. "Great, I'm bleeding, what's next, I get shark attacked or what?"

She wasn't going to hang around and find out. She doubled her effort and that wasn't much because she was exhausted. When she got to waist-deep water she didn't even bother scaring off the blacktip sharks that tracked her blood. She focused on the jungle ahead and ignored the insects that beat the sharks to a free meal. The last hundred yards were muddy and that gave relief to her cut feet. But there were rays and crabs everywhere. That old stingray injury on her foot started throbbing as she marched on.

"I hate stingrays! OK, universe go and mess me over!"

Somehow, she avoided stepping on anything harmful and managed to make it onto the beach. The sand was already hot and it was only an hour or two after sunrise. The wind had blown the fog out and revealed a jungle, the jungle she had to go through to get anywhere. Gitmo was still miles away, but where? The base had the entire bay and the bay was huge. Jon's jail might be all the way inland or on the tip of the bay, she didn't know. She pulled the little toy compass One Love gave her out of her shorts pocket. It still worked.

She wasn't sure how far east or west or north or south she was in relationship to Gitmo and she didn't have time to think about it. That PT boat was moving inshore. OK maybe One Love didn't have anything they wanted. Did he rat on her? She left her flip-flops behind; they might think he had a passenger. She wasn't going to wait and see. Aggie plunged into the jungle and stopped only when she figured she wasn't visible from the water.

"Think Aggie think." She sat on a vine-covered log to rest.

Santiago was west of Guantanamo Bay. There were two natural jungle preserves on the south side of Cuba facing Jamaica, one on either side of Santiago. One preserve boarded Gitmo Bay. If she started west and hit Santiago, she walked in the wrong direction. Straight north across the jungle, miles and miles, there was a road that went east and west. If she made it to the road the going would be easier … if she had shoes.

"Yeah right, hitchhike on the highway, good idea." Aggie slapped her forehead. "Excuse me Mr. Trucker that doesn't speak English, how do I get to the American jail complex?"

The PT boat's engines revved and way too close. Aggie flopped down on the ground for cover. Why did she leave her stupid phone watch behind? *Oh yeah, that's right, bribe a pirate.* She wanted to cry and might have if that would solve anything. She slapped a bug instead. She forgot to check the GPS for location. *At least you know where the three-mile limit is.*

"Great, just great."

One Love was pretty sure they'd wind up west of Guantanamo. All she had to do was walk along the shore east. East was right of her when she faced inland which was north. Maybe it was a mile, maybe it was twenty miles and then she'd have to get around the bay. It felt impossible. A character from one of her favorite novels popped into her head. It was Argolis, a haphazard dragon, not real smart, who had to do all kinds of hard stuff. What did Argolis say when he had to face piles of crap? "There's nothing for it then, let's go." That stupid dragon would just pick himself up and move ahead no matter what.

"OK universe, If I ever have a kid, I'm naming it Argolis."

As the PT's motors faded in the distance, Aggie got up and started east along the jungle's tree line within sight of shore. She was hungry, tired and smelled like a locker room. Her hair felt like a hat made of salt straw. But there was nothing for it, she had to keep moving.

A few hours passed and she was getting somewhere. Signs in English, no tres- passing signs appeared. She became more careful, moved slowly, had her eyes out. When she got to the first fence it had been swallowed by the foliage. Yet along that plant-engulfed wall there was a footpath. *Somebody walks around here.* She followed it down to the water's edge and got around the fence. Pressing on, the next fence was higher and in better shape. Through the chain links there shimmered a bay. The bay was bigger than she thought and so was the base. It was a little city. This wasn't the out-of-the-way jail enclave she imagined; this was a full-on Navy base. A big aircraft carrier was parked on the far side of the bay, there were docks and buildings and an airfield's control tower beyond the docks.

Something about that ship bothered her. She looked carefully. It wasn't in the water; it was parked over it. It was a freaking spaceship with MACs chained down to the deck like Grandpa's ship. That thing had guns sticking out every- where like porcupine quills. Men were all over it working frantically.

Pain stabbed her heart. The idea of Mother dealing with that monster made her knees weak. She stood there reciting a mantra. She had no time for medita- tion. Reciting helped shake off fear. She couldn't let herself fall apart. She had to figure out how to get around the fence and the next one. *Swim in form the ocean?* Cut feet and scratched skin in shark-infested water is a bad combination.

"How am I going to get to the jail?" Aggie was too tired to smack her fore- head. "Aggie, you're an idiot."

"I'll solve that problem for you."

Aggie turned slowly, yup a Navy security guy. "Oh, hey, hi, I'm kind of lost, can you help me. I was camping and — "

"I'm sorry Miss Piper, that's not going to work."

"Crap, I got to stop talking to myself."

"It wouldn't have mattered; your face is everywhere. I should run you into Central." The guy pushed his helmet back a little like the sheriff of Tombstone sizing up the Clanton brothers. But his face sported half a crooked grin. "I have a better idea. This way." He pointed down a trail with his big ugly rifle. The path went along the fence toward the interior. "You walk ahead of me. I know about your fighting skills, heard all about it, stay well ahead and behave so I don't have to shoot you, copy that?"

"What, shoot a national treasure?"

"If you like, now move."

Aggie went along as told. Before long, more fences appeared behind that long one. Many layers of fences with barbed wire and electrical lines on top. Signs in several languages warned about the danger of electrocution and getting shot. But inside the compound there didn't seem to be anyone home. The prisoners from the war were gone, they had been sent to a super max or let go when Jane Albright took office. The guard towers were empty. Low flat buildings inside were empty, no lights, and the inner gates were open. A few MP type guys milled around the main gate smoking cigarettes and not acting very military. One of them was drinking a can of beer.

"Hey, what's going on? You guys Boy Scouts or something?" Aggie said as they arrived at a gate. "Isn't Jon locked up here?"

"It's decommissioned," her escort said. "We can't finalize shutdown until this one prisoner is relocated, or charged, or released. He's in limbo. Problem is, the admiral who dropped him off is dead. I'm guessing you know that."

"I don't know what you're talking — about."

Jon Colbert strode toward the gate on his long legs. He wasn't in uniform. He wore a new black cowboy hat, a Navy T-shirt, cut-off blue jean shorts and cowboy boots. He was well tanned. Her heart skipped. Last she saw him; he was as white as a ghost except where sunburned. Above his sleeves used to be a no-sun zone. He looked darn good. The guards didn't react to the loose prisoner.

"Colbert, look who I found." The escort guard said. The other two behind her weren't paying attention to her other than to whistle and cat call as she was marched past them and taken inside by her captor.

"Colbert's gone and done it again." One of the gate guys said from behind.

Jon came up fast and stood toe to toe with Aggie. "I'd knock her teeth outta her mouth if'n she wasn't a girl. I'm not so sure about that neither."

"Jon, Jon, I'm — "

"Shut up. I got a bone to pick with you." Jon pushed his hat back. "Bring her to the mess. I got me a plate plumb full of ass chewing fer her."

Jon Colbert turned and left, walking fast. What was he so pissed about? The MP waved his gun barrel in the direction Jon went and Aggie took the hint. The escort called to the two at the gate. "One of Jon's girls. Domestic problem."

The beer drinking guy of the gate slapped his knee. "She missed her period or what?"

She was hungry. One Love didn't have much food on Lazy Days. She'd get a meal ... maybe. Jon Colbert wasn't going to be dessert. Deeper inside the compound she hesitated. She was barefoot and the hardpack ground hurt but she decided the pain was worth it. She looked back thinking to run.

The other two MPs had closed the gate.

"Crap on a cracker."

TWENTY-SEVEN

Archer and Brinks

Archer made it back from the moon in one piece, drunk, but in one piece. Rather than call in, he passed out on Sanderson's couch. He woke in the deep of night and stumbled out of his make do bunk and straight to the flight controller's office. He requisitioned an unscheduled red-eye back to the Capital. They knew he was on it, no need to report. Shuteye was priority. He needed to be alert. He rested until the steward woke him for landing.

Instead of calling in, he went to his apartment and peeled off that beer-stained, moon-dusty uniform. He collapsed into an overstuffed chair and remained until a knock on his apartment's door stirred him. Checking the wall clock, he hadn't been in town an hour.

"No rest for the weary."

In flight, the message received and ignored said to report ASAP. Brinks or the War Room? Archer would report on his own schedule. *Position has its privileges.* He opened the door. An orderly was there. The same man he saw in the War Room hovering around the Chief's table. A trusted functionary. The man might be a fake. An operative in disguise, but he wasn't that. Alien enhanced, nothing got by him anymore even with a hangover. It was indeed the same man.

"Sir, General Smith says to report, in person, directly after your mission. I have his message." The man handed over a note, written on plain lined paper. He saluted and left.

Archer stood at the door in his underwear, fingering the paper. They sent a messenger, nothing conspicuous like sending a car or an MP. Delivery on the sly. He'd follow procedure and burn the paper after reading. An old habit. Archer unfolded it. Same handwriting that was in the Sanderson file. It said, "Brinks is a liability."

"No shit." He crumpled the paper and tossed it aside.

On the flight he heard enough. Somebody blew a hole in the Capitol building and he didn't need to guess who was behind it. Brinks went from being rescued out of an elevator directly to Congress. They had evacuated legislators and gathered them in a secret location for safety. Brinks delivered his coup there. Still covered in dirt, he mounted the government's TV stage and announced the coup publicly. Said he was in charge. This all went down during Archer's moon flight while out of communication. Brinks made further announcements but Archer had seen enough.

"He's in charge huh, we'll see about that."

Archer had laid his uniform flat on the bed in case he needed it again, as if that would help it recover from last night. He didn't want it wrinkled worse than it was. He was like that. He paid attention to details and considered contingencies as one of his habits. He didn't plan on using the uniform long enough for it to require cleaning. Things change. He had bought just one. One was enough.

He pulled the plastic gun out of the jacket's inner breast pocket and laid it on the bed. Showered and dressed in his old uniform. The black suit was better. Dirty work required the right uniform. The Chiefs will trust him after this.

Archer arrived at Brinks' place in the Pentagon within the hour. Brinks' office was whirling with activities. People rushing in and out. Archer took a seat out of view of the French doors and watched the security guards sizing them up. He didn't report to the secretary at the reception desk yet. He observed instead.

Apparently, the Chiefs weren't concerned with his moon trip. Brinks didn't call for a report either. Either Brinks sent him to put him out of the way or was too otherwise occupied to deal with moon relations. It was the former. Archer can use the latter. Busy people are distracted, less keen. Brinks will call him in.

Archer, informed of the layout, got up, told the receptionist he didn't have a scheduled meeting, took a seat, and waited.

The phone rang, his official cell phone, it was Brinks himself. "Archer get over here, we have a problem." The general hung up.

"I'd say you do, and you are not alone."

Archer fixed his tie, leveled his hat, checked the plastic gun in his side pocket, and proceeded to the reception desk. She buzzed Brinks. Archer tipped his hat at the security man standing next to the French door. The man wore a Brinks Security uniform. He won't be a problem. The secretary, a pretty little woman, spoke to Brinks in the inner office by phone. She gave the nod and the guard opened the door. Six people were in the room, one was a tactical officer from the Navy that he recognized from his days chasing UFOs.

"Damn that was fast." Brinks said.

"I anticipated your call, sir." Brinks didn't comment about Archer being out of uniform.

The men in the room were stressed. No doubt the war wasn't going well. Was that space destroyer parked in Guantanamo Bay still inoperable? Funny, no one on the moon was overly concerned about a coming war. He didn't hear anyone mention it at the bar. Kowalski said Moon City was leaving. It's hard to kill a thing that isn't there. That did explain why so many moon people were taking passage on starships. Maybe Moon City didn't fly as fast. Archer wasn't about to tell Brinks that.

"Archer, what have you got for me, make it fast. I'm up to my eyeballs."

"Sir, this is for your ears only." Archer nodded at the tactical officer. The man had a grim face, he wasn't on board with Brinks. How many people there were?

"Fine, everybody out, take a break." Brinks said, he ushered them out himself. Brinks was known as a hands-on man that took pleasure in micromanagement. "Take ten, don't go far." Brinks called as the last man exited.

Brinks shut the door. "Aliens are everywhere. Life Force raiders I make it. Too many to shoot down. At this rate the moon people will slip away before I knife them. Our MAC fighters are engaged here. How do I mount an attack? That damn Piper girl is on the loose again. She's helping them, I'd bet my last dollar on it. What'd you get out of the GTO?"

Aggie's alive, or is it misdirection? His lips can't be that loose — Sloppy bastard.

"I'm afraid I didn't get much." Archer said closing the curtains at the French door. "The GTO office is closed. I spent hours trying to hunt down anyone that would tell me anything. They left, they are gone."

"Gone, Christ almighty. Learn anything about the moon we can use?"

"They're leaving, the entire city is a spaceship. All of them are going soon. It's confirmed."

Archer read the look on the General's face. Disappointment was just under the man's lust for war. Brinks wanted a fight and was afraid he'd miss out. Brinks would love to know that nukes were back on the table. Archer wasn't about to tell him that. The Chiefs had this office bugged. Brinks was watched and recorded by others. Brinks wasn't trusted.

"Sanderson would have gotten more, you killed him too soon, Archer." Brinks said. He was building a head of steam.

That's rich a tool maker blaming his tool.

"I did exactly what I was told to do if Sanderson turned tail. You said to take him out if that happens. It happened." Archer was careful to keep his voice even, unemotional. Business like. Brinks preferred reserved discipline. Just the facts. *We're just a pair of psychos talking shop.*

"Did you get anything at all?" His tone switched to that of a desperate man.

"Just this, an artifact. It might help, it's technology." Archer put a hand into his jacket pocket.

Brinks stepped closer, held out his hand. "Show me."

Archer pulled the gun up that was hidden in his palm. He grabbed Brinks' arm with the other hand and pulled while rushing the gun forward like a striking snake. As Archer thrust, Brinks' eyes went wide. Buried in Brinks' gut Archer squeezed. The sound was muffled. Archer had pointed up toward the heart from gut level. Brinks collapsed in Archer's arms. Dead. Before blood could pour out,

Archer dragged the body to the side and out of sight of the door. All in one fluid motion like a robotic machine.

There was a wall mirror above the ruin of Brinks. Archer fixed his tie and checked himself for blood. There wasn't any on him. He chambered another round just in case and pocketed the little gun. It was a clever thing, that gun. Modeled after 19th century palm pistols, it worked well. The special plastic it was made from was a gift from the aliens and a show of good faith. It was a new super-hard nonmetallic product. A product that wasn't known to the public. Just another drop of state secrets in a sea of state lies.

Archer cracked open Brinks' door and called to the receptionist. "He said give him ten minutes."

Archer stepped into the outer office and shut Brinks' door. A Brinks Security man opened the outer door for him. Ten was enough time to get to the War Room. He was sure the Chiefs' saw it on camera and just as sure nothing would come of it, not against him. He walked at ease on his way to the inner ring. He didn't kill Karnack; Karnak wasn't a monster anymore. All the monsters were here and he was invited into their deepest lair. The worst of their lot was just decommissioned. Brinks was a good start.

TWENTY-EIGHT
Jon and Aggie

Aggie was led deep inside the jail complex's fences. *Ugly buildings.* The architecture was gray cement and flat roofs. Moon City's faded paint was more appealing. The sign over one door said administration. Everything was the same Navy gray, even the galvanized fences and cement. And fences were everywhere. It must have taken an army to man all the inner gates. But only three uniformed MPs were there — and Jon. Nothing but monochrome except for the white coral gravel sprinkled with pink and blue particles. OK, one of the guards had green teeth, but that didn't count.

Jon walked well ahead like he owned the place. The guy that found her outside walked with her, but he wasn't on guard. His gun barrel faced the dirt. Why was easy. Only one way out and two guys behind a shut gate were there. Aggie's curiosity kicked in.

"Hey what's happened here? I thought you MP guys were hardcases, nobody cares?"

"Why should we? We haven't been paid. No pay orders coming down since Albright disappeared. With Brinks running the government why would anyone give a shit?"

"Who's Brinks? The new president? What about the old one, what happened to Jane Albright?"

"Brinks is an Army general. He ran the coup, I think, nobody knows who's really in charge. People said screw it and took off AWOL."

Aggie stopped in her tracks. "Albright, she's still missing, right? I bet they killed her. If she turns up dead … I don't want to think about it. People are going to freak big time."

"They already have." The guard said with a strained voice.

"Is the whole world going crazy?" Aggie could hardly catch her breath and it wasn't the 100 degree temperature compressing her chest. *Holy cow, a coup, really?* "America's gone mad."

"You ought to know, you started this corkscrew."

"I saved the planet!"

"That's not what's on TV. Forget it. Can't trust TV. You aren't the problem."

Aggie and her escort rolled up to a building that had windows that weren't barred. The plaque said Officers Quarters. Just inside was a dayroom. There was a hallway on the far end leading to apartments, she guessed. Jon was pacing back and forth in front of the pool table sucking down a beer he must have just opened. He stopped, crushed the can, took two beers out of a mini refrigerator and tossed one to Aggie's guard. Aggie thought she could take the guy if Jon would cooperate. Easy, she told herself. Don't blow it.

"I got it padre, I'm good." Jon said but the guard didn't leave. He sat at a computer desk. The PC was already running.

"Why'd you go and do me like that?" Jon took a big swig of beer. "Y'all was supposed to watch my back. I been here a dog's age. I'd shoot Sanderson down myself if'n he wasn't dead already."

"How do you know he's dead?" Aggie wanted to say more but she bit her lip. Let them think he's gone. That cat stays in the bag. "OK, I'm sorry he didn't get you out of here. But that's not my fault."

The guard interjected saying, "Sanderson was killed. Everyone saw it. A man in a black suit shot him. Your alien buddies splashed it all over the internets."

"Here nor there, "Jon blurted out, "Y'all have all that tech. Y'all should have busted me out."

"Why didn't you just leave!" Aggie was hot. "They aren't watching very hard."

"Just go and fart around enemy territory like Custer having a picnic in Indian lands." Jon pushed his hat back and finished half his beer in one big gulp. "I knew you wasn't killed. Took too long Aggie, I'da gone if'n you wuz quick about it, too late. I ain't leaving."

"What! Are you crazy? I went through hell to get here. You got to be kidding."

"Do I look like I'm funning you?" Jon had another pull on his beer. "Look here. Things are bad. America's got real trouble. I can't up'n leave now, not with the coup and all. Somebody got to do something about it. I ain't gonna cut and run when Merica needs me."

"I don't get you. What's going on is … it's over Jon. America will never be what it was. It's all falling apart. The economy, the ecosystem, it's all dying. The whole world. Don't you get it. America's toast."

"Cut and run if'n you like. I'm staying." Jon turned away on unsteady legs and walked away into the single officer's quarters singing God Bless America.

"What's he doing? This is a chance for a better life. It's survival. How'd this junk get inside his head?"

"I'll tell you how," The guard said. "My computer's here. Your callout for ship's crew. I did the application. It's an AI thing, according to what Mel said, the program goes after the ones it likes. I got the second invitation; I'm asked to join Mother. Jon wasn't. Besides, he's a white gung-ho Texan. My name is Sanchez. I got no horse in this stake."

He brought up a screen and said. "Ben and Jerry on the gate, they don't know about Mother. They're with Colbert. They'll join the revolution if and when it goes down. Nobody knows what we're about." Sanchez clicked.

"Hey, that's Mel."

Aggie was taken aback, Mel's really taking this trans thing seriously. He cut the hair off like a military do and wore a man's dress shirt like the one Mel got off Ernie a million years ago in Puerto Rico. Aggie watched as the message played.

"This is the third message I got."

Hey everybody. By now it's out, that Aggie and Mother survived the attack. Opportunity is closing. Like we said, we'll show you how to get into space. If you were chosen you got this message … well here's the dope. There's an alien shuttle system here on Earth, I mentioned it before, yeah. Underground spaceports with shuttles that go to the moon. But here's the problem. Moon City is taking refugees so if you want on Mother, you got to get to the moon fast. The link below shows you where the nearest shuttle is and how to access it.

Not all of you will make it. Mother wants about forty people but she might take more so don't freak out if you make it to the moon and see a bunch of people, OK. So, click the link below and remember the location because that link will evaporate after you see it. Have a pen ready. That's it. You won't find me on ship. I'm staying. Good luck space cadets.

"I clicked the link," the guard said, "But I don't remember the details, it's in Puerto Rico, that's the nearest one." He stood up and checked out the window. Aggie did too. Jon wasn't around and the two at the gate weren't on alert. The guards were away from the gate and under a shade tree.

"Miss Piper, I'll help you out of here but only because I'm leaving anyway. We do it my way."

"I have a spaceship waiting in Jamaica." Aggie said absentmindedly. PR was a bitch, that jungle hike was terrible. But then again, Ernie and his dad were there. Maybe they'd join. After all, she came to get crew members. Why not Ernie and his dad?

"OK, first thing, what's your name." His name tag said Sanchez.

"Tony, Tony Sanchez."

"OK, Tony how do we get to PR?"

"I have a boat on the other side of the island. We'll go overland avoiding the police. It won't be easy. Jamaica might be better. My boat is sailing today with or without me. What about Jamaica?"

"Screw those assclowns. I hitched a ride with some aliens, not my guys and they split on me."

"We better go. Ben and Jerry think you're Colbert's base employee girlfriend. He gets time off. He's been all over the base but not off it. He wasn't arrested officially. There's a big reward out for you, you know. Those guys are broke." He thrust a thumb over his shoulder pointed at the window. "They'd cash you out. Stupid, money isn't worth boo. Economy's in the tank."

"What if Jon changes his mind?" *Maybe if I hang around a while, he'll improve his attitude.*

"That's the problem. He might be calling security right now. Go now while we can."

"Poop."

Tony brought her to the back of a nearby building. Aggie stopped cold when she saw it. Some kind of old car was there. It had a chalky white and rust primer body with a faded blue roof. The car was huge. The front grill had big metal teeth like a giant robot with dental problems. If the chrome wasn't peeling, it'd look pretty cool. Aggie put a hand on the hot fender and yanked it away. Coral dust coated her burnt hand.

"What's this a tank or a car? Where's the cannon? I'd ride shotgun but I hate guns."

"Funny, I heard you were funny. It's a 1950 Buick. I fixed it up right here behind the guards' quarters. Nobody comes back here. It's our ride out."

"You got to be kidding, in that?"

Aggie felt like things were going from bad to worse. She didn't really know this guy, maybe he was full of crap. But he did fix this old junk car. That was something. Maybe Mother will put him on maintenance. But then again … Aggie gritted her teeth.

"You're unconvinced. She'll get us there," Tony said.

"Drive all the way to the other coast? They'll spot us a mile away."

"All the locals drive them, that's all they have." Tony said as he handed Aggie his gun. "Here, hold this."

She held the gun away like it was a snake and dropped it in the dirt. Tony started stripping out of his uniform. Aggie thought maybe she should pick up the gun. Why's he undressing? That back seat was big enough for an orgy and she wasn't interested in testing the idea. She readied her mind to strike him. Shooting him with his own gun wasn't an option. She suddenly caught on.

"Is this what they mean by sex traffic?" She joked. This is Cuba and Tony wasn't going to drive anywhere off base in a U.S. Marine uniform. "Flying saucer boxers? That won't get us far."

"Do me a favor." He said, hopping on one foot tangled in his pants. "There's clothes in the trunk get a shirt and shorts for me. The suitcase not the duffel. There's some stuff you can wear. You look like a homeless crackhead."

"Thanks for noticing, you look nice too. But I was going for the meth addict look." She pulled out a loose Hawaii shirt and slipped in on over her ragged out top.

How and where he got that car, she didn't ask. Driving past Ben and Jerry wasn't going to be easy. He told her to duck low and stay down under all the garbage and blankets in the back seat until he gave the word. Tony rolled the car up to the two at the gate. Aggie heard the gravel crunching under the tires. She expected the motor to be loud and obnoxious, but it was smooth and quiet.

"Hey Sanchez, where's the chick? Who is she anyway?"

"Some base girl. Colbert had her out camping and left her out in the woods."

"Where she now? Civilians can't be running around in there."

"Makeup sex," Tony said. "I'm going for cigars. I'll bring you some."

"Sanchez, you got balls," the other guard said. Aggie couldn't see which was which. "Driving into enemy territory. Christ, if they find you, you're done."

Tony said something in Spanish and drove out. They sailed out of the base's main gate. MPs must know all the other MPs she guessed. He slowed and they waived him on because he didn't stop. Tony talked while he drove and said he had been planning his escape since the attack on Mother. He spoke in a low voice. Aggie liked how Tony had made plans. Maybe he would make a good crew guy. He's like a Boy Scout getting prepared and junk like that. She thought he was OK. He showed guts and ingenuity. Too bad she wasn't going to hang around to find out how he works out. Once Mother was stocked her promise was finished. She had it in her head to come back, find Jon and make amends later. She owed it to him to patch things up. She was the one that got him into this pile of crap and it was hers to make it right.

The car pulled over some miles away. Tony said to come up front. Aggie tossed off the blanket she was under. There was plenty of room on the back seat floor even with all the beer cans and fast food trash but it was hot as hell and it smelled like French fries. She sweat through the borrowed shirt and discarded it, too.

"Junk food much?" Aggie said as she closed the front door.

"The instillation has everything, more fast food than local stuff. I got nothing else to spend my pay on other than what I give my aunt. That's where the boat's at."

"Wow, it's big in here. Love all that chrome on the dash. Turn the air on. I'm toasted."

For the first time since they met Tony wasn't a straight hardass. He laughed like hell.

"Aggie, they didn't have air in 1950. Get used to it, it's a long ride."

"I'm so screwed. We'll never pull this off."

"Look, I pass for local." Tony's voice went serious. "My parents immigrated from here. I got relatives in Cuba. People that'll help. If the police stop us, don't talk. I'll tell them you're my deaf and dumb sister."

"Great, I'll shut up. You know I'm not good at shutting up, right?"

"It's never too late to learn."

It turned out Aggie didn't have much to say. She had too many things on her mind. The question of staying with Mother or not nagged at her. Mother had taken root. And if half of what the anthropology AI says was true, there wasn't one good reason to stay on Earth. There soon won't be enough Earth left worth staying for. If Mother can collect more like Tony Sanchez, she didn't need Jon Colbert. His rejection stung. Jon might not even be a good crew guy. She had to face it, she wanted him more for herself than anything else. It was stupid to put herself before the ship. The dumbest thing was risking her life and Mother for a man she doesn't even know. The side he just showed wasn't the same guy as before and not the guy she really wanted.

OK you convinced yourself Jon sucks, but it still hurts.

What about her parents? Grandpa said they had to hide. She'd never find them. More and more realities were smacking her in the face and Jon Colbert was just one blow. The one and only person left that she felt like she could depend on wasn't ever a person. Her probe Buddy was just like a loyal Labrador but he wasn't there. He was in orbit relaying the crew search message.

I messed up; I should have listened to Sanderson.

Aggie sank low into the big oversize seat and watched the scenery pass by. She soaked it all in. This might be the last time she saw a tropical place like this. Space, jail or dead were her options. The island made her miss Key West. This place was much like the Florida Keys and she knew deep down she could never go back there. She was going to miss a lot out in deep space.

"This is hard, really hard," she said.

"I know, the shocks have had it. I'll slow down." Sanchez said.

Slow down, there was no time to slow down. Too slow and she would miss her ride off this planet and that thought rang a bell. The pit of her stomach felt the impact but she wasn't ready to listen to her guts. Even so, she willed the car to go faster.

TWENTY-NINE

Mel Gets a Belt

Mel manned his communications station that he had designed himself. But still, he could not keep up. It was primitive by Mother's standards but Mother needed someone on com and he was the guy. It was handy that he invented the stuff his dad's company sold to the National Security Agency. Nobody inside the Complex had figured it out … yet. Mother with all her tech must know how it all works. Or maybe not. Mother's stuff was way past Melvin's capabilities but he was learning fast.

Praytis monitored his systems and took care of Sarah as well. Praytis was good with the little one. Why not, he was a human psychology and social science geek. Who better to help a 90-year-old lady trapped inside a child's body? Mel could relate to Sarah's wrong body plight.

"You are exhausted," Praytis said. "You have been on station too long. It is not healthy for your mind or your eyes. You did not sleep but a little last night and here you are back on station so soon."

"But we're touching down. Mother needs help. And I keep getting something like a distress signal down on Phobos. You said nobody lives there." Mel adjusted a screen. "I don't get it, what if it's military? You know, sneak attack."

Praytis put a hand to his ear like and old-fashioned radio operator. "Mother doesn't seem to have an issue with the sender. In fact, she is requesting that you go and retrieve it."

"Me? It, it's an it?" Mel liked scary alien fiction, but this alien wasn't fiction. It, whatever it was, was real.

"It's an encapsulated being. A baby of Mother's kind, a living entity inside a machine. It was left behind when the city that once inhabited this moon withdrew, much like Moon City is doing now. When Mars lost its atmosphere, Phobos City relocated."

"But that was millions of years ago."

"More than a mere many million, certainly. We have a record — "

"Hold on Skippy, how can a living intelligence last like that?"

"On hope, but … Mother reports she won't last another ten thousand years. Mother intends a rescue. It is the least she can do in exchanges for the raw materials we are harvesting even now. The encapsulated one won't live long enough to incorporate into a living society. She has no partner and so is without a maker of hard materials for her. Earth should have advanced more quickly after its last reset." Praytis spread his hands. "Not all who are born live on. Not even immortals."

"Dude you're blowing my mind. So, I have to go outside, yeah? Like moon walk. Like spacesuit and all that crap? I got to think about it. Maybe once we land … I don't know. Dude, that's nuts."

"We landed. Six standard Earth hours have elapsed. Mother is proceeding with material harvesting."

"How am I going to run com? Somebody has got to stay, yeah? Sanderson needs relay to the tank. I'm watching Earth military. Buddy's out there alone and somebody's got to watch him. And, I've got this blog see, and … crap. I don't know how I'm going to do it all. I can't leave the com."

"I do believe I have a solution. This is not ideal but this will help considerably. Of course, you must rest your body but this will relieve mental fatigue." Praytis pulled a thin belt out of his station's only desk drawl. It was a brown leather belt with a flat gold buckle. Mel wrapped it around himself. It'd fit the slacks he wore.

"OK, what's this?"

"It is a communications control belt. You may operate the com with it from where ever you are. Mother is allowing access. Highly unusual for a temporary crewman, I must say."

"I don't know dude." Mel handed it back. "Aggie thinks it's poison."

Mel was fascinated with alien tech. Most of it wasn't understood by current end users but he was dying to learn it. Mother was far older than any of the aliens in local space and they didn't have a handle on it. The belt was key to deeper understanding. As a tech geek, that device dangling from Praytis' slim fingers was like a bottle of 100-year-old whiskey to a Tennessee alcoholic. He didn't resist the temptation long. Mel took it back and gingerly threaded it through his empty belt loops.

Mel fastened the clasp and his mind lit up. "Holy balls, dude!"

A world full of icons, formulas and text sprang into Mel's inner sight. Reams of information scrolled thought his awareness. It felt like falling off a cliff but he wasn't afraid. He began to grapple items as they flew near. He was used to screens so inside his mind the items he reached for became screens before his closed eyes. A million-bit chunk passed by like flotsam on a wild river and he knew; he knew he wanted to dive into that river and be carried away. It was a nerd's wet dream, all that information, all that power.

"How do I use this?"

"It will take a few seconds for the belt to acclimate and provide an acceptable interface."

New reams of text flashed passed his mind's eye, it was an overview of capabilities. Somehow, inside him, he knew he could call up what he wanted. It was his com station plus a thousand and a lot of other stuff as well. How to access it? Inside his brain, subtle changes were taking place. The belt was tuning his brain to use it. It addressed every thought. He had the ability to stop it or idle it. All at once he had a grip on it. This was just a rudimentary device; a real control belt would make this one look like a toy. No wonder Aggie was afraid of the ship's command belt. It overwhelmed analogue Aggie.

"Dude, I like it. this is mad cool. No, I love this, love, love, love it." Mel stopped it on a thought and he was back in local reality.

"Quantum computing would be addictive except that Mother will not allow it." Praytis' voice was reassuring. "Most unusual, a typical Earthling would go mad before he was able to embrace it. This is why ram-ed is normally required first in order to adjust one's … perceptions."

"Maybe that brush with it on the moon opened me up."

Praytis shifted his feet and pulled on his chin. Previously on the moon the bug-man was forced to help the government put Aggie and Mel into a ram-ed chamber without their permission or awareness. That trick backfired, thanks to Mel. *Thank you very much.* By Praytis' demeanor he was still feeling guilty about it. *Spilt milk.*

"A man could get used to this." Mel said. "I'm setting up a personnel sensor array to monitor my soundings, alarm systems, capture search results on the fly. Dude, this rocks."

"Indeed, and this basic model also has a force skin. Any energy that contacts your force shield is either reflected or absorbed as its power needs require. You will be safe from radiation on Phobos."

"So, I just walk — "

Mel had a question but it was answered before he finished asking. The force suit aspect was not an environmental suit although it would power one indefinitely. He needed a spacesuit. He dialed back the belt so it wouldn't answer questions unless asked for. The belt responded affirmative. It was still learning.

"Oh, so Mother is standing on end along the obelisk, yeah. Good, cover that. I take the tram down, sideways from the moon's perspective, to the fantail's airlock and I'll find a spacesuit there. Mad cool, I see the whole thing."

"The airlock will rotate and project to the surface so you are in the correct position for the planetoid's gravity. Gravity is very light; you must be careful. Avoid Mother's harvesting robots as they are not smart and may well run you over."

"Dude, this is badass!" Mel said, thinking of the ship's computers and its power. He was not really thinking about going outside, or the idea of actually leaving the ship. That part hadn't sunk in yet.

"Your ass seems to be fine, medical doesn't report any change." Praytis said, and laughed in his odd way.

Mel deadpanned a quote that Praytis had said many times since they first met. "Oh, I see, Earth humor, very good."

Praytis did his rendition of a double take. And they both laughed. Sarah, who was taking a nap on the bridge atop a pile of blankets that had been laid out for a picnic breakfast, didn't stir. Mel tiptoed off the bridge as to not wake her. Sarah was always afraid of missing out and would follow like a puppy. That's what they needed, a couple of dogs. Mel missed Skipper, his neighbor's dog on Key West. With the belt on Mel had no problem finding his way to the airlock and he didn't find it weird at all. *What's Aggie's problem, that bitch needs to grow up and take the belt. She's not a good team player.*

When the airlock opened Mel almost lost control of his bladder. Everyone has fears. Maybe he shouldn't be so hard on Aggie's fear of technology. She was the outdoors type and he wasn't. The moonscape was weirdly dark beyond his wildest imagination. No air, nothing alive, hardly any light and the stars were incredible but no help for local light. He tried the night vision and hated it; everything was green. He lit his shoulder lamps and ordered the robots to use lights against Sanderson's orders. The place lit up. There was junk all over. Sharp metals that can rip a spacesuit were sticking up everywhere. Crazy shadows like monsters on Halloween night lurked. Robots dashed around like their circuits were on fire. Silent chaos.

"Dude."

Finding that black box wasn't going to be easy. He didn't have an accurate fix on location. Sensor said covering materials were bouncing transmission. That first step out of the airlock was the hardest first step he ever took. He was an in-the-house kind of dude. He never went outside unless he had to. In Key West it was an easy thing to pull off, the sun was crazy strong. Nobody questioned the wisdom of staying indoors. He never had to tell anyone about his fear of outside. He stood there shaking in his boots a long time before proceeding.

"Man up, you got to do this." He started walking toward the ruins on a pirate's gangplank. But with the gravity so low even tiny steps propelled him further forward than intended. He was afraid he'd launch himself into space if he jumped along like that guy in that vintage moon landing footage did.

Once well outside, Mel was totally creeped out. The vastness of space weighed on him like a millstone pressing down a convicted warlock. He couldn't stop looking up as he walked. Thus, he stumbled several times. Each fault made the fear of sharp objects stab his heart. Avoiding the construction robots was enough of a chore and stumbling around like a drunken sailor only made searching harder. Forcing greater awareness, he still tripped and almost landed on a scrap metal pike that was protruding from a block of concrete. *Focus, you idiot.*

"Dude, pay attention!"

"What is that? Do you need assistance?" Praytis' voice came from inside his head. The belt, of course.

"No, I'm OK."

He was glad to reach the only visible ruins that had an actual structure. It was once a building. Its lower part was made of cement and rocks. Great curved steel ribs were sticking out everywhere and disappeared into the blackness above. Using his suit scanner, he saw ruins like this all around. *It's a whale's graveyard.* Entering the biggest ribcage structure was like getting swallowed by a dead leviathan. But even so, it was good to be inside.

He forgot about running the com altogether. Ship's AI identified this space as the city's control center. It was pitch black and dead inside. His suit lights were not enough. The darkness seemed to eat light. He powered down the lights and watched a while. In that vast room there was a little red dot in the distance, like the eye of a demon winking at him.

His nerves told him to run, fear of the unknown begged him to flee and he almost ran but instead he asked a question as he restarted night vision.

"Praytis, you see what my suit cam sees, yeah, what's that, a light?"

"I do believe you have found our passenger. She will be housed in a small emergency containment vessel, that light is her local distress beacon."

Mel started across the vast space picking his way around and over rubble. He reached the black box. It was the size and shape of a lunchbox and it even had a handle. Mel dug it out of the thick dust and its light turned green. He tucked it under an arm and made fast tracks back to the airlock. This time he didn't look up. The bots running around gave him wide berth. *One less thing to worry about.* But still, he had had enough of the great outdoors.

THIRTY

Parting Ways

Mark was in command but he didn't push them far yesterday. Soon after reuniting, Mark, Jen, Kyle Brinks and President Jane were on the move. Police cars, on the radio and by distant sirens, were busy in every direction. This limited where they could go. The whole county was alive with security forces. Kyle knew a place where an old covered bridge was on a dead end track. The only signs of activity there were old buckboard wagon ruts in the dirt. They spent the night under the cover of that dilapidated bridge's roof. Kyle said local police avoided the Mennonites' private roads. Mark had to trust him and it proved good.

The next day was a waiting game. They made do. The creek water was clean, and the blackberries good, but most of the day they stayed under cover and couldn't forage for a decent meal. The plan was hide under the authority's noses until the dragnet spread wide leaving gaps. Mark's empty belly screamed, everyone was irritable, still he waited until radio traffic died and sirens were few.

"It's time we move out," Mark announced late in the afternoon. Nobody complained about leaving. They didn't like where Mark decided they'd go.

It was counterintuitive. Mark intended to go back the way they had come. His passengers disagreed. He had them get in the back. Trapped, they can't stop him. Any passerby will assume rear seat passengers of this police cruiser had been arrested. Thin cover was better than no cover.

Mark wore the policemen's cap to enhance the ruse. Things were quiet but still hot. Police cars raced everywhere without sirens. The radio was his best friend. The men running satellites surely were on to Jen's trick by now. The oldest trick in the manual was to know what the police were doing use police gear. Better yet, use a police car or utility vehicle. Either way the NSA had technology that would find them. Mark shut the radio off as soon as they were in between hot spots but they were still vulnerable. *Thanks Sky-net.*

"I hate flying blind." Mark cursed under his breath.

Mark whipped the stolen cruiser into a hardware store parking lot, drove around back and pulled into a loading dock slot. The overhang cast a shadow on the car. *It will have to do.*

Jane banged on the window. "Mark, what are you doing?" Sound was muffled. Mark flipped a switch unlocking the back doors and shut off the motor. "I've seen this place before. We're going in circles!"

Jen got out first and helped her sister. "He's getting us cover. Cool it Jane, we know what we're doing."

"But shouldn't we get outta here?" Kyle asked.

"That's what they'll expect," Jen said. "We can't look like runners."

"I hear sirens." Kyle said. "I hate this store. I grew up here. Old man Thompson's a real hardcore redneck. He'll call the cops for sure."

"We'll be long gone before then. I need a few things. Heads down." Mark went inside through the back door on the loading dock. The old-timer there startled, but Mark flashed him a badge. An officer had donated it to Jen unawares.

"Hello Mr. Thompson — "

"Say, whatcha mean coming in ma backdoor? Don't a man have his rights?"

Not anymore, the way Brinks set things up. "Mr. Thompson, everyone around here knows you're a patriot. I'm undercover, on a job. I need a few things. Will you help me?"

"Y'all know I support the police, what'll ya have?" Thompson's tone was grumpy. The old man's face revealed doubts.

Mark laid a fifty-dollar bill on the counter. "I'll help myself, keep the change. I'm in a hurry. Where's the spray paint?"

Thompson pointed the way with his chin. Mark didn't waste time. He grabbed a couple of cans of black and a few other colors, scissors, rags, some stencils, put it all inside a cardboard box and was at the back door in no time.

He showed Thompson what he had and said. "Sir, do me a favor, don't tell anyone I was here. I'm undercover and ... " Mark noted the anchor tattoo on Thompson's forearm. Ex-Navy. "You know this is true, 'loose lips sink ships.'"

"Aye, aye. Got your back, officer." Thompson didn't look convinced.

Looking past the old man out into the front parking lot, a police car pulled into the handicapped space. Mark bolted for the back door. He wasted no time activating his team.

Mark sprayed white paint over the big black numbers on the roof. He had Kyle do the same on the doors. Mark got them in and explained the situation. "Later we'll do new numbers. Right now, we run. Missing roof numbers might confuse the satellite observers' algorithms but not for long." Mark put the car in drive. "By now they must know someone stole this DEA car. Paint's not dry but it won't take long." It was hot for late September.

The passengers lay down in the back and he drove around the building slow. No need to set off any alarms. It looked like a decommissioned car. He stopped at the side of the building. The police were still there, but nobody in the car. Both men had gone inside. Too hot to wait outside. Global warming had done him a favor. Mark pulled out onto the road like an old lady and drove that way for some miles, just in case.

"Kyle, any place near we can finish the paint?" Mark raised his voice due to the plexi. The damn sliding window to the rear was keyed and he didn't have it.

"Yeah about three miles make a right, old dirt road got a barn down a-ways."

This kid was proving handy but Mark still didn't trust him. He was related to Tommy Brinks, the front man for the coup. General Mayhem didn't know it but he was a dead man. It's how the Powers think. The General was a hot potato. His ego too big.

The men behind the curtain were using Brinks and Brinks had a habit of going too far too often and too fast. These hidden men of power won't tolerate Tommy Brinks long. Mark wondered how much the General had twisted Kyle's mind? Scum slimed everyone, even family. *Brinks' mistake is thinking he's in control.* Same mistake President Jane made. Jane should have heeded Jen's advice and gone slower. Instead the president opened the door for a coup d'état and Brinks was ready to jam open that passageway.

Mark found the spot and pulled just inside the barn's open door. It was more like falling off the hinges than open. *How appropriate.*

"We're out of the sun." Jen said. "Freaking hot. Unlock the doors, Mark."

Everyone got to work. He and Kyle made numbers for the doors and trunk with the stencils while Jen handmade bigger stencils out of cardboard for the roof. The roof was key. The last thing Mark did was use a felt marker to change the license plate's numbers. A three became eight and four became nine. It wasn't convincing but it would pass at speed. Kyle took initiative and found an old screwdriver and busted the lock off the driver's side of the sliding rear window.

He looked over everything but had a problem with what Jen did to the roof. "Are you kidding?"

"What, someone has that number?" Jen said.

"What's the problem?" Jane asked as she slid into the car.

"Your sister has a sense of humor," Mark said. "Aggie rubbed off on her. She painted F-U NSA on the roof."

"Make the F into a B and the S into an eight," Jane suggested. "Hurry, I'm cooking. Get the air going."

Knowing Jen, she must have had a reason. Of all the CIA and other operatives Mark ran with, Jen had the deepest connections. Only Sanderson ran deeper. Jen knew people in the NSA, helpful insiders. Always a jump ahead. Mark didn't have time to ask how. Jen won't spill it anyway, deniability is king.

His internal clock was screaming. "That's it. We're moving."

The paint wasn't dry. Mark got in the driver's seat and hammered it anyway. He took police car liberties and beat it back to the industrial park at high speed. He didn't slow until nearing the location. They weren't far from the hole-up. Entering the industrial park, he tossed the hat away and felt where Kyle had clobbered him. The swelling was gone. He tore the bandage off as he drove for the park's back end.

The access road had tire tracks that showed coming and going. He overran those tracks to confuse the story. His mind was still on high alert. It was mania. When he was on, he was fully on. He had switched off last time he was at this safe house and that's when and why Kyle Brinks attacked. Mark would not make that mistake again. He had Jen backing him up this time. If Kyle has any smarts, he won't try anything fishy. Maybe he does have a working brain and had washed out of the Marines for thinking. They don't like thinkers. The kid had a lot to prove either way and that's a dangerous and unpredictable state of mind.

Mark pulled up close to the door and had everyone rush in and out of satellite view. Jen had the good sense to disconnect the car's GPS when they hid before. Mark wasn't taking any chances. He went back outside and pulled the battery cables off.

Inside he realized hunger. It was the first normal human impulse he felt in days. It had been one hell of ride. He checked the cupboard. Canned food in plenty. He opened a can of fatty, preserved meat and started scoffing it down with a dirty spoon.

"Jesus Mark, relax. I'll make us something edible." Jane said. "There's a decent variety here. I'll figure something out." Jane began rummaging through the pantry cabinet.

Jane went to work in the kitchenette while Kyle played with the multiband radio. It was a hand crank job and the kid figured it out all on his own. Jen went over the house checking for bugs and other devices. When Jen went outside to survey the grounds, Mark took a kitchen chair and placed it with his back to the wall where he could watch. It was a shotgun ranch, the kitchen and living space was one room, the other room to the rear behind a single door was a bedroom and bathroom combo. Only one door in. From his position Mark had eyes on everything. He was still revved.

Jane used a couple of cans of stew but added more vegetables and spices. It smelled good. Kyle worked the kitchen's hand pump and made coffee; said he never used an old fashion percolator before. The stuff wasn't bad. The kid had more figure-shit-out skills than Mark thought. Jane was setting the table when Jen came back inside.

"That's it," Jen said. "I did a perimeter sweep; no signs. We're in the middle of a swamp that's in the middle of an industrial park."

"You got it right," Mark said. "Me and Branford set this up. He owns all this land. Rents the industrial buildings to defense subcontractors. His name isn't on the leases. Holding companies handle it."

"Smart," Jen said. "You got Branford's involvement past me. If you hadn't told me this house was here, I'd never have found it."

"Hold on," Jane said. "Aggie Piper's Grandfather Branford, that defense contractor?"

"That's right." Mark said around a mouth full of strew. "His industrial rentals over there are wired. He sees what goes on inside. Another layer of safety."

"I know a bit about the spy world. Jennifer told me," Jane said. "But Jesus, does everybody spy on everybody else? This is ridicules. No wonder nothing gets done and the budget's unaccountable."

"The problem is, things that should not be done, get done." Kyle said. "Just ask Uncle Asshole."

Mark saw the kid with new eyes. He was all right after all. "What'll you do now, Jane?"

"Do I have a choice? She said. "Puppet masters stop at nothing. They'll kill me. The people at the diner are with me. I think most people are. Plain folks see this situation simply. They see America's ending due to the military/banker complex. They understand that is why their lives are degenerating. I must unseat the oligarchs."

"How?" Mark said.

"It's a complicated problem with a simple answer." Jane said. "There is but one way to undo this knot and that is to set it alight. We burn this cancer out. The psychopath class must go. Only a revolution will do. It's the only way."

Mark knew she was right. It had all gone too far. The people have no say whatsoever, it's all contrived, all controlled and people had enough. The only mystery in Mark's mind was why it took so long to get to this point. *Aggie lit the fuse. She saved and doomed us at the same time.* The aliens' gate opened just a crack and America's sewer rat government backwashed in like a hundred-year flood.

"They hurt us too long," Kyle said with a sober voice. "Lied about everything, lied about the aliens. People feel beaten, like dogs. We still have teeth, don't we?"

"He's right." Jen said. "It's time we bite back."

Jane was just the person to rally the bite. But Mark had his fill of it. He was in the game far too long and he'd never break free of it on Earth. Fighting on will be the death of him. He had had enough. He finally made the turn.

"Revolution," Kyle said. "That'll fix them."

"You're right. It's the only way." Mark took a deep breath. "But not for me. I'm out of it."

"What, what are you saying!" Jen said.

"I signed on to protect my family, that's the Pipers. I did my part and now … " Mark splayed his hands. "Jane and I had a deal. I delivered. I'm leaving."

"Family? They're dead already," Jane said. Her voice was bitter.

Jennifer grabbed Mark's arm and not lightly. "A word with you in private." Jen marched them both into the bedroom but left the door open. No doubt to keep one eye on Kyle.

"You're going, that's bullshit Mark." He took her arm and walked her further into the bedroom and out of earshot of the others. "If Jane wants a revolution; I'm giving it to her." Jen said in harsh whispers.

"You don't get it, it's lost, it's all lost." Mark kept his voice down. "Win or lose, America's over. Revolution is pointless. Every time it's the same. It changes everything but always reverts to the way it was. It's the same as it ever was and it will always be."

"That's not the point Mark, Jane's different. She'll fix this, control the oligarchs, the military, the bankers."

"Absolute power corrupts absolutely. She'll win, but she'll be compelled to keep power or someone less … pure, less benevolent will wiggle in and take over like they always do. They never stop. You know that. MJ-12 has its tentacles everywhere."

Jennifer was hot, her face red even in this low light. Mark thought she'd pop a gasket. In all the time they had together, he never saw the real inside of Jennifer Nostrum. Not even as his recent lover. The part no one sees came up front and center. Family's protective loyalty. He had to turn down her heat. He took her hands.

"I'm sorry Jen. Maybe it'll be different this time. I have my own family to look after — "

"I thought we could be a family." Jen squeezed his hands. Her eyes were wet. Mark waited for a tear to fall but she wiped it away, pulled her hands back. "Jane's my family. I can't stop her. I must help her. Come with us."

"Family is all that matters anymore. In that, I'm with you."

"So, what's the problem?"

"I'm twenty years your senior. I was in the Navy from age 18 to 48; I can't do this anymore, Jen. I make mistakes. See?" He touched the stitches in his head to remind her of his failure. "I don't want to spend the rest of my life sleeping with one eye open. If I must it will be for family and not a dead ideal called America."

Mark turned toward the door and took a step.

"Hey where you going?" Jen grabbed his shoulder. He turned back.

"The moon, that's where my family is. They're either there or on the way. Aggie's somewhere and they'll know. If Bart's right, Branford, Sky, Po-boy … Aggie will pull all stops to EVAC them."

"You fool, how are you going to get there?" She pointed at the sky.

"I know a way. You do too. I'll get there."

Mark walked across the living space and into the kitchen area. Jane was handing Kyle dirty dishes. He had one hand in the dishwater. Good place to stash a waterproof handgun. The kid was making himself useful. No dirty dishes left behind for the next time. A shortwave radio channel played. The windowsill's radio had multiband. Talking heads on shortwave were espousing revolution.

"What have you decided?" Jane asked, wiping her hands with a towel.

"Aggie's safe. Branford and the rest have either gone up or will. Aggie's the magnet. The rest will seek her … if they survive … Rendezvous is the moon."

Before he killed the car's radio earlier, an announcement came over the airwaves. Moon City was taking refugees. The tunnel system's existence was exposed. He'd slip into the most guarded access and escape within the confusion. He wasn't going to spell out details or how he'd do it. Plausible deniability. Jen and the rest don't need to know. He'd make Key West in time come hell or high water.

"He's leaving us, he must." Jen said, facing her sister. "Don't get upset. It'll be fine."

"How, why!" Jane said, alarmed. But her face changed with sudden recognition. "I remember what you said Mark, the deal we made when we first spoke. You helped me for the Pipers' sake. It's gone off that rail, hasn't it? For what you've done, you'll always have my gratitude. How are we getting out of this place?"

Skip the guilt. Jane's in good hands. Jen's a top agent. Intuition says Kyle's fine. Mark's part was done but he almost changed his mind.

"What're we to do?" Jane said, her voice sad.

"Easy," Mark said. "In the park there's a garage. In it are a handful of fast cars." Mark pointed in what direction the garage lay. "I'm taking one and you should as well. Take the blacked-out SUV. It has government plates and counter-measures. Use Jen's network of safe houses. I'm going to the moon."

"You didn't say why, why Mark?" Jane asked. Jen stood aside with scorn on her face.

"Family, they're in space. Jane, you understand, don't you?"

"I thought we could be family," Jane said miserably.

Jen's eyes went wide. Jen understood the bounds tied between people in combat together. She had to know romantic feelings might develop. Another reason to leave. Caught between two lovers, sisters at that, was a bad place to be.

"If you're going," Kyle said, "You had better. News is bad. Shortwave radio says the Navy's going to … to attack the moon. So stupid! The aliens cut in again, just now. Aliens, they're leaving for real. I can't believe it. Aliens are here and we chase them away. Stupid, stupid, stupid."

This was news. Mark was too busy running to gathering much intel. He'd get the full story on the road. His bug-out car was stocked. The kid wasn't lying. He saw no tells. Mark had a feeling that the kid's footlocker was full of sci-fi novels. Mark checked the police 38 Jen had provided. He never did ask where she got the car and guns.

"That's it, I'm going now."

Mark said his goodbyes and took off for the garage. It was just like he last saw it. The man Branford hired to keep them running, one of Mark's retired vet buddies, did a fine job. The car would get him to Key West. The question was, would he arrive in time? On impulse before pulling out, he checked the sky. The moon was going to pieces and he could not help but think Earth was as well. He revved the Lambo's powerful engine and prayed the police policy of hands-off rich people was still in effect.

THIRTY-ONE
Missing Aggie

Mel was on the bridge messing with the camera view of Phobos. They were fixed in orbit, riding that moon around Mars. Escape launch windows came and went but it wasn't time yet. The more he looked at the scene below, the weirder it was. What exactly is that tower they're tethered to? It was like the monolith from that old science fiction movie. What was fascinating were the ruins of a city. *Definitely not ours.* He brought up a scale and estimated the size of the black rectangular tower. It stood two-and-a-half miles above the surface. A hard idea to swallow hit home, all that wrecked landscape below the tower was basement space; foundations like below any city. Whatever used to be here was totally ripped away. What would do that? He didn't believe it, but there it was.

"Praytis, that tower, was it an elevator shaft?"

"Yes indeed, very astute of you. How did you know?" Praytis said, not looking up from his computer station.

Praytis' desk was beside Mel's but higher so he couldn't see what the alien was working on. Praytis stood above seat height on his four legs. *He'll never get chair ass.*

"It looks like an elevator, that's how. I saw the Mars Obiter pictures, what geek wouldn't? But I never saw anything like this on NASA's website. That tinfoil hat stuff Po-boy was into never seemed true. He showed us on Aggie's computer what he called the 'Tower of Phobos,' but I checked. It was debunked, yeah?"

"Of course, media has long been captured and usurped by the military. The rulers would not have the public know of such things." Praytis said. "One or two actual pictures slipped past the gatekeepers. Mr. Piper must have acquired a true photo from the internet. I dare say the Complex did such a fine job of propaganda even the scientists that received the original transmission did not believe what they themselves recorded."

"Tell me about it. Government lies even if truth is better for them. But what's all that junk. What was there? I figured it was a spaceport, yeah?"

"It is the remains of a city like on your moon but larger. She departed leaving the husk of a forgotten civilization. It is not known when exactly, but it was here at a time when Mars was inhabited. What disaster drove it out, none can say. This took place ten million years prior."

"You're shitting me. Ten million?"

"No that is not so, I remain sanitary. Would I excrete my favorite turd?"

Mel had to look, yeah, he was joking. Praytis had that tight smile plastered over his even teeth. Mel laughed and so did Praytis. Mel was used to the sound of his mirth. Praytis laughed like a chorus laughing with him. Mel had been teaching the alien man Earth humor right along and it was sticking. Praytis had deadpan down to a science.

"Dude, good one."

"Be that as it may," Praytis said. "Mother had us land as there are raw materials available for fit out. Probes had confirmed as much, and of course, there was the orphan in need."

Mel checked the sky map. Phobos was about to be in telescope alignment for viewing home. "We're sitting ducks," Mel said. "We're exposed, we better leave. Mother's about done."

"As soon as Ben comes out of regeneration." Praytis checked a holo. "I see that he is waking. Sarah is there now. Ben should be along shortly."

"Dude, I didn't think landing was a good idea. We got lucky. Navy MACs are heading this way."

"Might we confuse any search for us?" Praytis offered. "Metallic objects abound here and we can appear as yet another. May we project a false signal?" Praytis' attention was on his desk. He adjusted a control. "Ben will arrive momentarily."

The bridge door slid open and Sarah rushed in. "Daddy's here, yeah Daddy!"

Ben Sanderson, taller and leaner than before strode in. His hair and beard were longer. No sign of pain on his face. He wasted no time.

"Where the hell's Aggie?"

"Still on the moon … maybe. You told me to tell her to stay there, remember?" Mel said. "But Moon City reports she isn't there."

"Goddamn it!" Ben roared. "Mel, I told you to keep an eye on her. I told her to stay here! Christ I was confused in the tank. I thought she took a joyride and came back."

"Daddy don't curse!" Sarah buried her face into Praytis' loose overcoat.

"You are right Honey, I'm sorry. Let me restate that. Mel why didn't you stop her? Didn't I tell you to have her turn around?"

Ben had never said that. Mel was pissed. He stood away from his desk with balled fists wishing he had taken karate like Aggie. He wanted to punch Ben in the face. Mel's newly infused hormones were taking effect. He felt more aggressive than ever but still managed to put aside that flash of anger.

"Have you ever tried to stop Aggie from doing what she wanted to do?" Mel said, with steel in his voice.

"Point taken, goddamn it." Ben took the chair he used before but now the lights were off, no need for it to control his pain. "You're quiet right, my apologies. Double damn, I feel good."

Of that Mel was glad. Ben had softened as quick as he blew up. Mel's anger kicked down another notch.

"Mel, can you raise her on radio?" Ben slapped his knee. "Radio, that's a hoot. I mean tight beam. Is she available?"

"She had her watch but it hasn't moved." He said, retaking his chair. "I don't get it. Moon City should be able to locate her. Praytis says there's private zones there … but still. Weird."

"There was no harm in her going, Ben." Praytis said. "Mother won't allow her ships to go to Earth and Moon City is in the process of withdrawing her shuttles along with our crew members. Aggie simply can't go planetside. With Moon's disengagement in process her sensors might be occupied. Perhaps we should try calling?"

Mel wasn't sure about that. They were leaving so maybe calling's cool. But the Navy was balls out trying to locate them and a big ship was moving toward Mars. He could not have tried the phone sooner. He had been busy on countermeasures and everything else related.

"Want me to try it? Mel said.

"That's fine. Hail her please and give me the com." Ben said, drumming his fingers on the chair's armrest.

"Earth to Aggie, come in Aggie." Mel said, maintaining the ruse.

An incoming reply in text was on everyone's screen before the vocal signal reached location. Mel's electronic runaround was still in force. A man's voice came over the com.

"Aggie? I guess this really is her watch. Blow me down. Who's this?"

"Security, who are you?" Sanderson said in a stern voice. "What're you doing with Aggie's watch?"

"They're pinging us," Mel warned. "It's Navy."

"I'm holding it for her, who wants to know?"

Ben made a slashing motion with his hand and Mel cut the feed. "Goddamn that's a familiar voice. Where's it coming from moon or Earth?"

"The watch is on the moon," Praytis said. "It is good you limited communication. We are being monitored."

"He's right," Mel said. "Navy MACs are triangulating. We can't risk another call until I find another way to bounce our signals."

"Goddamn it, fine, fine." Sanderson drummed his fingers on the armrest. "I'll have to have a little talk with her. Mel, how'd the blog go, any takers?"

"Good response. We don't have a problem filling up crew slots. We might have too many. Lots of shuttles made it out and there's more coming. But how we going to get them from the moon to here without getting caught?"

"I prepared a contingency plan." Ben said. He checked a holo. "When she's ready, move Mother in closer. You men will launch while I'm gone, don't wait. When Mother goes green, skedaddle. I'm going after Aggie, taking our fastest corvette. I'll bring her in. Let's see if the Navy catches on. Call it a dry run. Mother will finish refit in transit if it gets too hot here. Full countermeasures. Batten hatches. Make ready to blow out of here fast."

Mel and Praytis went over their stations while Ben conversed with the ship. Mel got busy trying to disrupt the Navy spaceship's pings. He couldn't understand how they got past his countermeasures. Somebody below must have cracked his surface code. The only one that could do that was Dad. He had a clue how it worked, he had to understand it in order to sell it to the military, but Mel was always a jump ahead and didn't tell Dad everything. He never gave all the details like the software's hidden levels that operated autonomously. Mel had made his backdoor code function like turned-off DNA: It looked dead and unused but it wasn't. A change in environment activated it. He got the idea from biology class. But Dad was no dummy. He'd figure it out soon if not already.

It struck Mel that his own father must be helping them. When Mel released his trace software, he didn't tell the manual writer about backdoors. Dad found one? Dad took the credit for this stuff, but it was Mel's stuff. *I designed it.* His adoptive parents were supposed to put distance between Mel and the state's end users. That was the deal, kept them separated. Mel wanted a normal life without the NSA sucking up every idea he ever had. Dad was supposed to protect him but now he wasn't.

"So bogus, dude." Mel checked his inputs. The CIA had men closing in on the fake location he setup to make them think he was in Europe. "Good luck finding me, Skippy." *Dad had to tell them how to beat my runaround program. Dad sold out. It's the only way.*

"And I want to go back there for gender transition?" Mel thought *delete* and his belt wiped out that false electronic trail. "Whatever those clowns had is gone. Wish I could see those agents' faces. They'd be like, 'Hey where'd my data go?'"

"What did you say Melvin?" Praytis asked.

"Never mind, just thinking out loud." Mel started writing new code in his mind. He had a few ideas cooking. *Maybe I'll malware worm them guys.*

"I'm ready to go." Sanderson said, "Sarah, you be a good girl for the boys. Daddy's taking a little trip, see."

"Bring me a present?"

"I'll see what I can do. Will you be OK?"

"Oh Daddy." Sarah rolled her eyes. Ben walked briskly off the bridge.

Sarah's fine. A good little girl even if she was really ninety-something years old. Sarah's old mind wasn't allowed into active memory. She wasn't ready for adult reinstall. Mother watched over Sarah better than any mother hen.

If Mel was really a girl, he'd be a bad girl. The testosterone was taking effect and he felt usefulness in his growing aggression. He'd find new ways to screw up Navy MACs. *They fly by computers, don't they?* He got into exploring that idea. He'd have a new worm done before going back. All this killer tech at his fingertips made leaving Mother less appealing by the minute.

A warning lit. Ben's ship had undocked. Mother signaled she was ready to detach once Ben's shuttle was clear. A few minutes later Mother let go of Phobos. As Mother pushed away on chemical reaction thrusters, Mel wondered where a ship her size could possibly go and remain unseen.

THIRTY-TWO

Archer for the Gate

Archer did what he was directed to do and the Chiefs will never know why. Brinks had thought Archer was with him and in support of the coup. *He should not have thought so well of me.* Brinks had to know the Chiefs wanted him dead and Brinks took every precaution. Brinks never suspected he, Archer, the man who killed Sanderson in cold blood for the good and glory of military empire, would be the triggerman. It was too easy.

The security around the Pentagon was unprecedented. It wasn't just the riots, the Chiefs had to stave off a revolution. Still, every checkpoint let Archer pass. Archer's eye print had changed and the system adapted. His eye signature was unlike any other since the control bracelet nearly destroyed his mind. And because of that, his mind was better, smarter, more perceptive. He played Brinks and he will play the others just as effortlessly.

They must have seen the hit on camera, Brinks' death in real time. That's why they called him to report so fast. He was on his way when the cell phone rang. The news wasn't out yet, and it might never be, but the big men got it. They sent him. They wouldn't miss that show. *They had to be sure of me.*

He relocated the plastic pistol into a sleeve holster. None of the checkpoints caught it. A shifty-eyed agent caught him on his way and led him into the deepest regions of the Pentagon's ring untested. *They want to see if I'll try anything.* Archer wasn't going to step in that snare so easily. Holding back makes his next move count for more. At the last checkpoint he pulled the plastic gun and left it with the guards at the elevator. It had five shots in it. Archer was good. He'd easily make five kills before they got him. Now wasn't the time. He had a better way. A longer way was jelling in his mind. He wasn't in a hurry.

He entered the War Room far below the main building. The Chiefs were all there with their support men. Twenty big, important military men in the room and a dozen operators. He was surprised that so many were in on the coup. *Psychopaths keep minions, don't they?* If he had wired himself into a ribbon bomb, he could have taken them all out and been done with it. But no, now was not the time. *No suffering in sudden death.*

He stood waiting. They were in an argument. Not everyone knew a handful of top dogs had called for Brinks' demise. All around the room computer screens were lit. MAC movements, aerials of the riots, ship movements. A Cuban PT boat chasing a Coast Guard fast-boat. Troop movements to the problem locations. He memorized every screen taking mental screen shots. The control bracelet gifted him and improved memory with accurate recall. The Chiefs had their hands full. Good. One screen played the murder of Brinks. Archer noted his hair was thinner on top. He didn't remember taking off his hat.

"Archer, good you're here. Good work with Brinks." It was the Marine general; his family was into international banking. Had to be one of the top men. Archer took note. "We'll have more for you to do soon. But for now, we need to get the situation under control." He waved at the screens. "We know Albright is alive. She is your next target."

"I understand."

"Moon opened their spaceport network … Not sure how we handle it."

"You want me to go back up and get them to stop?"

"No, they won't accept any more negotiators. We received word they won't allow our reps access. What do you suggest? You're the alien expert."

Archer put on a show. He scratched his chin and pushed his fedora back. He already knew what he wanted and these traitors opened the door. This wasn't a trap; he passed the test by killing Brinks. *My move.*

"I have an idea, several." Archer said. "Sanderson's office has access to the alien tunnel system. No doubt refugees will try to access it. I would bet if Piper is on Earth, as we suspect, that's her ticket off planet. I'll go there and set a trap. Have base security let refugees in. I'll take hostages if needs be. I might hitch a ride to the moon with one. Give the word. It's our best bet to get Piper. With her in hand, we control her fleet. We'll have leverage to force the aliens into terms."

Archer had read security reports on his red-eye flight. Piper was suspected alive. With Brinks' slip-up he was sure of it. "Her people will show." Archer said.

"What if they don't?"

"I took a gun to the moon. They didn't detect it. I'll get creative. It's good I ditched the uniform."

"I like the way you think. Take off. We'll call when we find Albright. Put your NRO men on Albright as well."

Archer turned and left. He had a fast car stashed. He'd drive nonstop and arrive in under sixteen hours. He wasn't worried about sleep. He didn't need much anymore since the aliens woke his mind to a higher level. With him at Sanderson's gate he could ensure some of Piper's people escape. He may use them to his advantage in other ways. *Who knows, Aggie may well appear.* He owed her his life and he'd return the favor. The Joint Chiefs of Staff he owed nothing but revenge. He'd make better use of Sanderson's equipment. The man had an inside line like no other.

Archer left the Pentagon with the feeling that his dead father would approve. It was good to feel that again after so many years of emptiness.

THIRTY-THREE
Aggie Leaves Cuba

The ride to Tony's relatives wasn't bad except for the heat. *Key West is hot but this is over the top.* All the negative stuff the media says about Cuba made Aggie think the place was a dump. Of course, the media was full of propaganda and most of it was built around slices of truths, or lies by omission, but what they said about Cuba was off-the-charts crap. The roads were smooth and the people along the way seemed content. The fifty-mile drive was slow with lots of delays because of livestock in the road, slower traffic and mule carts. When they stopped at a roadside food stand everyone was nice. That deep-fried bread pocket full of goat meat Tony had wasn't a lot of food but it was better than starving. Tony paid in American dollars and nobody batted an eye. Aggie's flying fish sandwich in a pocket was better than any American fast food fish sandwich she ever had. She wished there was more of it.

After two hours on the road, Tony pulled off the narrow two-lane road and onto a small gravel pad. He turned off the engine. One side of the road was dense forest and the other side was a thick mangrove swamp.

"We're here, put the shoes on. Back seat. We're walking."

"Here, where's here? I didn't see any shoes. Something did smell like cheese-feet when I was back there."

"Funny." Tony reached over the seat, rooted around in the pile of mixed trash and came up with a pair of old sneakers. "Here, put these on," he said, just as a grumpy looking bandit guy busted out of the woods. "Aggie, stay here." Tony got out of the car and stuck his head back inside the car's window. "Zip your lips."

Tony and the woods guy had an animated conversation which took a long while. They didn't even slow down jabbering when a military Jeep full of guys with guns drove by. Aggie wished she had taken Spanish in high school.

Tony and the guy shook hands and hugged; Tony handed him the keys. Tony signaled and Aggie got out. The woods guy got in and drove off. When he shifted, the car's gears ground and Tony gritted his teeth.

"What was that about?" Aggie asked.

"Hate to give up my car. I worked on it two years but Juan isn't going. He'll make use of it. Everyone else is going."

"Going, who's going where? How many?"

"Not your concern."

He's right. Old lessons Mark taught poured in. Mark was a good martial arts teacher and family friend but he was more than that. He was a real philosopher warrior. Without her registering it then, he had taught her stealth and avoiding fights. He imparted strategies that applied to everything in life. A lot of it was about getting around trouble. What stuck out was the idea that the more people you drag along, the easier it is to get caught. She was in survival mode. Streamlining, "cutting out the fat," was how to move fast and sure. Mom would never do that, what Aggie thought, leave people behind. Mom would make sure everyone was safe.

Aggie stood by, caught between Mom's way and Mark's way, while Tony surveyed the swamp. "I hope you know what you're doing." She said. Then in a whisper. "I sure don't."

"Come on," Tony said and pushed on down the road, looking for something.

Did she have a choice? Aggie followed, thinking she was totally at Tony's mercy, and his priorities weren't hers.

They walked further east along the road. When Tony heard a car, they ducked into the brush. Aggie laid in muck. It was that Jeep full of military guys. She held her breath until they passed. The second that Jeep was around the bend, Tony grabbed Aggie's hand and yanked her up. They beat it down the road faster. He broke into a jog and that sucked. Humidity was 100 percent and her sneakers didn't fit. A few hundred yards forward, he stopped.

It was a way into the mangroves but without solid footing. It was as bad as that mess Aggie had to crawl through near Key West. She had clawed her way through a muddy canal and into scratchy bushes to sneak into Mark's place. It sucked. She used to like mangrove swamps but not after that.

"That was close," Tony said, a little breathless. They were moving fast despite the overgrowth. "The police know something's up. Somebody's got loose lips. Jealous I bet. I bet it's Juan. He got paid, what's his problem?"

"Not a team player?" Aggie said from behind.

"You should know." Tony said.

"What's that supposed to mean?" Her heart sank. She knew what he meant only he didn't know how bad she sucked at team play. *Ben's right. I need to grow up.*

The sound of a car came again. They both froze. Was that Tony's old car or the police Jeep again? She didn't know. Once clear Tony proceeded.

"I shouldn't have called ahead. Phones are tapped. I hope they're all here."

"What are you talking about? All, how many is that?"

Tony was well ahead but stopped at the trailhead, if you could call it a trail. Aggie caught up. There was a hidden lagoon. The blue-green sea was just beyond. Overhanging plants almost touched the water and hid the lagoon's exit. The jungle around that narrow waterway had been cut back. A crude dock made of logs was there. In the lagoon sat a powerboat, a big beautiful fast-boat same as the Coast Guard used around the Keys. The only problem was the twenty people around it. Old people and kids, some were on the dock, others in the boat.

Aggie faced Tony. "You must be crazy; we'll never get away."

"It washed up after a storm. Yes, it's damaged, but I've been working on it. She'll run. We got enough gas to make the Turks and Caicos Islands."

"With all these people!? Where the hell's that!"

"Relatives, they're coming. Don't like it, stay." Tony's calm voice snapped into pissy gear. "I set this up for them. You're the liability. I told you family's first. If we make it across then we'll see about Puerto Rico. I don't give a rat's ass about your plans. I should have left you with Colbert."

Aggie opened her mouth to argue, but Tony turned away.

In hushed tones, Tony gave instructions. Everyone got on, took up handmade paddles and they pushed off. There was a narrow channel just outside the lagoon but the boat scraped bottom. The younger men got out and pushed. There were piles of coral on either side of the boat. They must have dug the channel by hand in secret. Aggie imagined them digging at night with shanks around and she felt a shiver race down her spine. The water was shallow in every direction. Deep blue water was a mile in the distance outbound. It sank in, what a desperate plan Sanchez and his family made and she wasn't any help at all. Daylight wasn't a good time to try it.

"This is jet-drive, fire it up." Aggie told him, moving forward. "No problem in shallow water, it's made for it."

"Sure, I'll broadcast our whereabouts to the Shore Patrol, good idea. You aren't as smart as people say you are." Tony handed Aggie a paddle. "Do me a favor and shut up." He didn't say it like he was mad. "If I'm caught, Cuba hangs me. Navy finds me, they'll hang me twice. I'm AWOL and collaborating with the enemy."

How can family be enemy?

Aggie choked down her useless opinions and put her back into paddling. It didn't help that the wind was blowing the wrong way. Progress was slow but at least they cleared the hang-ups halfway out. She watched the water as she stroked and saw a series of splashes. Right after thunder sounded coming from shore. She put two and two together.

"They're shooting at us!" She yelled toward the helm.

He turned. She did too. Flashes from shore. He called frantic orders in Spanish. The last man in the water got back on board. The sound of a powerboat rumbled in the distance. Tony fired the jet-drives. Aggie squinted, it was a PT boat like the one that stopped One Love, and it was coming on fast from the west and aiming to cut off their escape.

Aggie yelled, "Gun it, turn out!"

"We stay in the channel or run aground!"

The PT had a mounted gun, she saw it flash and bullets hit the water behind them. The sound of bullets cutting air whizzed past Aggie's ear. Aggie and the rest ducked below the gunwales as the portside windscreen exploded into shards. The older people clutched rosary beads and prayed.

Tony turned out fast and hard the moment they cleared the shallows hammering the throttles while exiting the channel. People fell all over the deck. One engine screamed while the other popped and sputtered before catching up. It felt like forever before the PT boat lost ground. The Coast Guard boat was supposed to be way faster. It was made to run down drug smugglers inshore. But this one was a wreck. It's hard to believe it even ran or floated. One motor kept stalling and restarting.

As Tony's salvaged boat ripped across the sea with rounds splashing all around, Aggie nearly pooped herself. She was never as scared as this in all her life. While in danger before, she was active, that's why she wasn't terrified. Too busy surviving to freak out. This was intolerable. The boat gave no cover, no place was safe, nothing to do but hang on while Sanchez ran straight with bullets flying.

Tony ducked below the helm diving blind — also unnerving. He should have been zig-zagging but with the motors roaring and passengers yelling in Spanish, Aggie didn't call the warning. She was too scared to do anything. After fifteen minutes of terror, finally, it was over.

The boat slowed. She felt warm and wet running down her leg. *Yeah, I wet myself.* And she wasn't the only one. The teen girl next to her and the boy across also had that problem. The old ladies seemed OK, reserved even. They must have been through worse. One toothless old woman toward the stern gummy-smiled and waved the victory sign. This boat wasn't made for twenty people, the little cuddy cabin below the pilot wheel only had room for three and now it held six just to make enough room on deck. The rest of them were crowded topside. Better on deck, if she sank, they'd get off before it went down.

Aggie wished to the Earth Goddess the boat would move faster. Being over-loaded wasn't good, the craft sat low in the water, too low. Aggie felt low, too.

"I hate this. I'm helpless."

Aggie kept looking back at the Cuban PT boat. It was getting smaller and smaller until it finally turned away. The shells or whatever it was shooting were falling short. As soon as the chase boat stopped chasing, Sanchez backed off the gas and things got quiet but Aggie was still pumped with fear.

"Sanchez, what are you doing! For Goddess sake, go!" Aggie popped up and stumbled forward over people's legs and luggage.

He was in the pilot's elevated seat. "They'll go no further, we're safe. They won't go outside Cuban waters. We're out of range." He backed off on the throttle a little more to prove the point.

Aggie didn't feel safe. "You gotta keep going, what if they break the rules!" Aggie was screaming.

"Cut it out! You're upsetting them." Sanchez addressed the group in Spanish. The panic subsided. Aggie stood there making fists and shaking.

"Back up, I know what I'm doing." Tony said. "I'm not on your team yet. You're on mine. I planned this."

"But, but, but … "

"This boat capsized when you blew up Haiti. OK you pitched in. Thanks for the boat, but that doesn't mean you're in command."

"But what if they come after — Hey that wasn't my fault!"

"The news says it was." Sanchez slipped off the pilot's seat. "Gas is short. We run hard; we won't make port. Back down, I've got to concentrate." He faced the back and said something in Spanish. A young man handed Aggie a bottom-cut plastic two-gallon bleach bottle. "Aggie, you go first. Start bailing, she leaks. We take turns. Got to keep her floating a hundred miles."

Only a hundred miles, that's a relief. Then again, a hundred miles going 5 knots is a long, long day ... and then some.

He turned back to the helm. Aggie stood there like a lump of poop with the bailer in hand. There was a GPS on the dashboard but he made no move to start it. No wonder, wires were hanging all over the place. But that wasn't it, GPS is too dangerous. Aggie didn't have to tell this guy anything. Not only did she feel helpless, she felt useless as well.

Aggie gripped the homemade bailer tight. Bailing was something constructive to do. Just the thing to keep her mind off sinking and the moon falling apart. No wonder the tide was weird. They were lower in the water than before. This sucker was leaking and no pumps were running.

"I better get busy."

Aggie removed the coveralls that were still wrapped around her waist and set them aside. Even wet, her makeshift belt was light, she forgot she had it on. The material was alien, of course, and super strong but light.

The engines were below deck at the stern and the bilge traps were below the motor mounts and service walk. *Typical set up, like Daddy's Uniflight.* She struggled to lift the deck hatch and two people immediately grabbed the handles with her and together they lifted. The hatch had hydraulic rams but they didn't work except to pull it down. Aggie tied off the hatch with her overalls before going in. Two young men helped her down. The hold's wiring was tangled like spaghetti. Everything below was messed up. No wonder the electric pumps weren't working. It was amazing that anything worked on this tub at all. The walk planks around the motors were the only thing inside the engine compartment that didn't look like a bomb hit it.

Given the way Sanchez got that old car running, he was handy with mechanical stuff and enough so to get this crippled boat going. He'd be good on the starship ... If she ever got back there. Right now, it didn't seem possible.

Aggie got off the decking and right into that nasty bilge trough in the bottom of the hull. The water was eight inches deep. Not good. Oily water sloshed around her ankles and smelled like a combination of gas, seaweed and fish puke. The dumpsters at Mark's Mariana, a thousand years ago and a million miles away, smelled better. The pee on her shorts was quickly washed away in skuzzy water.

Aggie bailed, handing buckets up to waiting hands. The young people formed a bucket brigade and Aggie put her back into it. Lifting the buckets up over her head was hard. Nobody complained, or argued and she wouldn't either. Everybody worked hard. They were happy doing this crappy job chatting away happily as they labored.

She imagined them planning a new life as they talked. Hope was in the air. Voices of the grandmas and grandpas on deck sang and laughed. She liked these people. And to think an hour ago she would have left them behind to save her own stupid skin. This family was tight. She felt like an ass.

Sanchez had it right, she was a big, fat assmunch. Her concern was to get away and leave these people behind if that was what it took. *That's really, really crappy.* She was the only one not invited. Aggie spent a long shift bailing, and thinking about what a dick she had been and not only to Tony but to Mel and Ben as well. *Talk about being your own worst enemy. I'm never going to get home without help.* She scooped buckets and hosted them up until her arms felt like they'd fall off.

When she finally came up to rest, she was greeted with food and water and enough love to turn the devil. *Mother will take a few more people.* This bunch wasn't slated for space. Mel's software only identified Sanchez, but she'd ask them to join anyway whether Mother liked it or not.

They were many hours out and still running steady when Aggie pulled the little compass out of her pocket after eating. The heading was northeast, Puerto Rico was south, southeast. They were going in the wrong direction. *I knew that.* Aggie felt like she was doing that a lot lately, moving in the wrong direction. But this time she wasn't going to complain, she was alive. Maybe that's how it was supposed to be. Maybe the universe wanted her left behind when Mother took off. That idea made her sad and she didn't know why. Everyone on the boat was happy and laughing and crying tears of joy and she wanted to cry, too, but not happy tears.

"How long's this going to take?" Aggie called.

She didn't get an answer. She knew her geography pretty well, she could see a sea chart inside her head and it looked more like 500 miles to where Sanchez was heading. Another all day and all night boat ride. OK, maybe it would only take half as many hours, if Sanchez pushed it. Not happening.

"Great, just great." Aggie crossed her arms over her chest and dug into her store of ideas.

Maybe she and Jon could patch things up. Maybe she'd get back home and grab a shuttle and go get him, maybe he'll change his mind, maybe, maybe, maybe. Maybe she'd stop acting like a butthole. Maybe pigs can fly. There were a lot of maybes in her life since this all started and she couldn't do anything about them alone. Maybe when she got to PR, if at all, she'd do the right thing for a change, whatever that was. Aggie felt sick and it had nothing to do with choppy seas. *It's time to get out of my own way.*

THIRTY-FOUR

Sanderson on the Moon

Ben Sanderson had made a cut across is his throat and Mel killed the feed. He eased back into his security station's chair to think. He was sure of it, that man on the other end of Aggie's phone was Kowalski. But how? Kowalski was also on that bombing run back in World War II, that's how. Twelve B-17s launched a nuclear attack on Japan but only two bombers went there and came back again. Kowalski was an opportunist back then and leopards don't change their spots.

"That tears it, I'm going to the moon." He said as he left the bridge.

Fresh out of regen and he needed the beard and long hair shaved off, but he thought better of it. His beard was hermit long and the hair reached his gig-line. He was unrecognizable and that was something he could use. *Let them think I'm dead.* Ben had hurried to the sport model MAC, got inside and was away in no time.

He called the bridge while underway. Mother had cast off. "I'm getting to the bottom of this by hook or crook. Give me what you got before silent running."

"I do not believe this trip is advisable, Ben." Praytis said over the com. "Earth just launched two Space Fleet destroyers. Mother received a message from Moon City just now. Moon says an attack on her, according to analyses, is imminent."

"Dude, Praytis is right, it's hitting the fan." Mel was on Ben's communication holo checking feeds. "Maybe for us too, your call wasn't channeled through my com net. Space Fleet has a lock on us. I'd like to go home in one piece."

"Goddamn it, I'll get you home. I was inside the security state a hundred years, trust me, I know my way around them. Hang with us a while longer, can you do that Mel? I'll have Aggie back before Moon pulls up stakes."

"Daddy, make Aggie come home. I got nobody to play with!"

Ben had six holo screens going and saw the entire bridge. Sarah was chasing chickens around. How'd chickens get on the bridge? He wasn't going to ask. *Goddamn civilians.* He had just gotten used to the damn rabbits.

"I'll do that Honey. Mel, any other sign of Aggie?"

"If she's on the moon, she's lost. I'd bet she's still in Moon City, the bad section."

"Upload the last known watch location and a city map into my control belt. Shuttle's firing for best speed."

Ben had to get this show on the road. He forgot to eat. He patted his formerly large gut and wondered where that hundred-pound spare tire had gone. The food processor ejected a bagel.

"What do you make of it, Praytis? Moon City's up and leaving? What're the odds?"

"I should think there is no question about it." Praytis said over the com. "Earth has launched hostilities; she will certainly go. Given that the recent coup was successful and other negative social factors are escalating, an attack is surely imminent. That is, once planetside social reactions are contained. Massive riots have begun, as I predicted. Even so, the Navy has hunters reserved for us."

"Straight answer, what's the number?" Ben said to cut off Praytis. The four-legged man would talk forever if you let him.

"Oh dear … a hundred percent probability. Moon City is on the cusp as we speak. She is free of her moorings."

"And leave all that LF behind?"

"Life on Earth may well discontinue. As she exits, the moon breaks apart. Much of that debris already rains down on Earth. Her thrusters will make it worse. But that's not all — "

"I figured she'll skedaddle. Look, here's a backup. This is what you do. I laid out a projectile cannon system, big compressed gas guns. It's for deflecting space junk. Make Mother finish them fast and use it if you must. Keep your heads low until I get back, savvy?"

"Sir, my head doesn't go low, my physical configuration doesn't allow it."

Ben laughed at the image of Praytis on the holo. His skinny face scrunched up like a prune. "That's not what I mean. Stay hidden as best you can. Have Mother cloak before you shoot." Cloaking a ship that big cost a king's treasure in LF, but they had to spend it. "Ready our shuttles. We'll pick up our recruits. Moon won't send her ships while dodging combatants."

"Once Moon City launches herself, surely she will not allow shuttles outgoing. It is too dangerous, as you say. She has yet to withdraw all planetside shuttles, which I find curious, however, still, we must hurry. I fear we do not have enough time."

"I wonder what Moon's got up her sleeve? Be that as it may, silent running. Security out." Ben eased back for the ride. As the position of each planetary body constantly changes, Ben launched closer to the moon than Aggie's departure but it was still a long flight.

Mother's intelligence was segmented into many parts each with its own job and priorities. But the underlying motivation was self-preservation and that meant securing the crew she depended on for LF facility management. People were helpful fleas driving a big, happy dog. Ben's job was to keep Mother's fleas alive to defend the ship. Mother missed the details. The flight path holo indicated a flight plan that the navigation AI had loaded. Flight path was too direct, too easy for the enemy to find. Mother 's subroutines didn't think like a scared rabbit, as they should, more like an indestructible whale.

Ben accessed the pilots. He told them what he wanted, an evasive route, and sat back to wait. There was nothing more he could do on his way. Even at the speed this craft achieved, it would take the better part of a day to reach the moon.

Aggie's fear of control belts was due to her misunderstanding of what it is — it's technology that must be used. Ben felt certain that was her problem. Having seen how Karnack abused the privilege soured Aggie. Mother needed direction, a way to focus and sort her intelligence, and yes, love, too. The belts steer Mother; they didn't control her. Mother depended on suggestions and directed ideas for efficiency. Belts were only conduits in this symbiotic relationship. Aggie simply refused that responsibility. *Why isn't she thinking clearly? The emotional interference of youth.*

"Ram-ed would strengthen her out."

Ben made an internal note to himself to make Aggie hear what she didn't want to hear. Karnack subverted the control belt. He found a way to squeeze Mother and used it. This and many other things were learned in regeneration. He would be damn sure to lay it out for her plain and simple. Set her straight. *Maybe the kid just doesn't want to grow up?* Like it or not, Aggie's captain, so he'd have to bend her into better shape if she didn't desert first. He didn't believe she would.

Ben landed in the trader's spaceport. The onboard AI fed him all the information he needed regarding where he was. Moon was the size of New York City including the five boroughs. As he proceeded, he brought up the city map within his mind's eye, and made for the last transmission Aggie's watch broadcasted. He stood there on the curb across from Kowalski's Bar and Grill scratching his beard. It was just like any old, cheap neighborhood gin-joint on Earth. He didn't want to believe it, but by the look of this establishment, it suited the owner.

"Can't be. Can't be *that* Kowalski."

Ben pushed through the double doors. Each one slammed a wall. There was an Earthman at the bar. He saw the man's face in the mirror. It was him.

"Kowalski, you bastard!"

The guy behind the bar spun around with a glass in one hand and a rag in the other. Kowalski wore an apron, and an old Navy utility uniform shirt. A bald, blue human-looking character at the window table looked up from his drink.

"Who wants to know? Hey you … do I know you?" The barkeep said.

Ben strode forward and grabbed the man's lapels over the bar. "How'd you get Aggie's watch?"

"None of your business, it's collateral. What's it to you?!"

Ben let go and backed up. His 6-foot-five intimidation wasn't going to work. Regen made punching someone's lights out moot.

"Head of security, Starship Mother. That watch's ship's property."

The blue man checked a device on his wrist. Ben saw it in the corner of his eye.

"He checks out," the blue man said, "Wow, he's loaded. He's holding a thousand LF credits."

"No problem, you can have it back, just pay the tab." Kowalski said more relaxed. This wasn't Earth, Moon City didn't permit murder. "It will only cost you ten … er … eighteen credits, that's a good price, seeing as the lady didn't reclaim it. I got to make a little on it."

Ben stood by a moment allowing his internal communicator's search. "Bullshit. Tab is ten credits. You want me to report you? That's not why I'm here, I'll give you the goddamn money, but first you tell me where the lady is. Keep the damn thing for all I care, I want Aggie."

"She is in Jamaica, we had to leave fast. We were attacked." The blue man said.

"Damn it Blue, don't give away the game. Haven't I taught you anything?" A dejected face appeared on Kowalski.

Sanderson hopped over the bar and put Kowalski up against the wall. Sanderson's big hands were wrapped around the man's neck. Sure, medical can fix the damage, but meantime it'd hurt like hell.

"This is how it's going to be." Sanderson pressed harder. "You will tell me the truth and for every lie I hear, I squeeze a little tighter. Spill it. Moon City's security bots aren't as fast as I am. They won't hurry for Life Force raider crooks like you."

"Fine, fine, I'll talk."

Ben got the story. Aggie went planetside and was stranded. Kowalski's fake church operation was over for good. That crew wasn't going back there for no amount of money. They couldn't if they wanted to. Moon City restricted spaceport activity to one-way traffic from Earth. Did that apply to free traders? Forget sending these idiots down. Moon recalled her vessels while Ben was in transit. The only way locals flew out was by special permit as he did, or to satisfy contract obligations. Moon was big on contract enforcement and not so big on the needs of raider leeches. *These people aren't going anywhere.*

Ben took the watch off Kowalski and paid the tab with a big tip. Medical was free, even for the LF raiders. The bartender's neck was bruised badly. Ben figured the information was worth a few extra space bucks and he transferred additional credits into Kowalski's account.

Ben put on the watch to call Mother. The signal would also bounce to Earth. Maybe Branford was dialed in as well and copied. Mel was ricocheting their signals all over God's creation. *Good man.*

Ben activated Aggie's watch. "It's Security. I have Aggie's com device. She's MIA. Get Buddy on it, copy." He was careful not to say too much, too many ears pointed his way.

"I need the next message out first. Moon City's confirmed departure. We're screwed. Out of time." Mel had his voice disguised to sound more male. *Smart, confuse the listeners.*

"Do it, then have Buddy track her down. I'm sending a coded message to you. Her last whereabouts. Get the AIs on it, find her. I'll talk sense into Moon City. Security out."

"I know you. You're that admiral the GTO was pulling wool over, aren't you?"

"Wrong man. Do I look military to you? Never met any GTO people." Ben didn't lie. His new self wasn't his old self. That man died when Archer shot him.

Ben left and checked his map outside the bar. The GTO wasn't there anymore. Records show they boarded a starship. It didn't matter. They were about as useful as tits on a beer hat. He located City Administration and started out. He won't move them much but he'd get the real deal. He felt the clock ticking and he didn't trust feelings before. Post-regen he paid attention. Still, he needed facts. He didn't like feeling his way through danger. Old habits die hard. His time as a military politician was over and if intel was right, America's time was about up as well.

THIRTY-FIVE

Aggie in Turks and Caicos Islands

It took forever, half of yesterday blended into the first half of today. She was up most the night taking turns bailing with the others. After that long, slow truck, the former Coast Guard boat was within sight of British island territory. This island group was called the Turks and Caicos Islands. It was way out in the Atlantic and really far away from Puerto Rico. Aggie had no idea how she was going to get to PR. Her plan was to get Jon and get an airplane. *He knows how to fly.* She didn't have much hope of finding an airplane here, and who would fly it? This island chain had been hammered with hurricanes for years, the tourist trade had dried up and the main airport was closed. What she really needed was an airplane.

Grand Turks was the largest tourist trap of them and her best bet. Having done her share of the bailing, Sanchez waved Aggie to come forward.

"Here ya go. Use my phone. Navigate for me." Tony said. She got the message. The other passengers didn't know how to use a complex phone.

"You know," Aggie said, "The Feds have crap that can track any phone and locate it. If this is your phone, they'll know you're gone and where."

"They don't know I've gone. I'm off duty until tomorrow … oh it is tomorrow. Shit. This isn't my phone." Tony said. He was trying to keep the boat pointed right so they wouldn't swamp. "It belonged to my commander, he's on vacation. I cracked his password. Changed the settings. Voice activated, get us a fix."

"That's a bad idea, "Aggie said. "They have my voice print; algorithms will pick me up."

"It doesn't matter, if we aren't long gone when they figure it out … " Sanchez spread his hands. "We're cooked. I need a fix. I have charts but I need bearing. Do it."

"It's your funeral." Aggie started up the phone and the GPS. She used the function that gave relative position. "We're three miles out of Smugglers Bay, due dead east." The phone blinked as she spoke. The damn thing must have captured her voice. "We're off the biggest northern island." She said, closing the phone.

"I need south Caicos, there's Cubans there, the British … they won't take refugees. I'm … I don't know. I have contacts there."

For the first time since they left Gitmo, Tony lost confidence. He stopped in sight of an island and took the boat out of gear. He got a Coast Guard hat from the cabin earlier. He kept pushing the hat back and wiping his face with a dirty rag. He checked the gas gauge over and over. The needle was touching the red empty line. He tapped it with a finger and wiped his face again.

"If I had the gas, I'd turn south." Tony said.

That was their original heading but they wound up way north. Aggie thought they'd be lucky to make shore, any shore. Visibility was good. That speck in the distance was three miles on. Too far to row against prevailing winds with crappy handmade paddles. Too choppy to swim it.

"How we going to do this?" He said. "If we approach Grand Turks, sea cops will nail us."

"No problem," Aggie said, trying to convey confidence she didn't have. "Land nearest place, real sneaky, and steal … borrow a boat, or get gas, whatever, we need to go south, right." *And closer to PR. But then what? The airport is on the farthest north island.*

Tony sprung upright in the pilot's seat. "I should have thought of that." He took the phone off Aggie, tossed it over the side and put the boat back into gear.

Tony guided the boat in toward a cupped bay. There were hotels stacked along the beach with a lot of boats tied up on anchor floats inside the cove. Half the hotels were damaged and empty. At this distance they might have looked like any other boat except for the crowded deck.

Aggie motioned for the people to lay low. She spotted a small yacht and had Sanchez motor up to it. The thirty-foot cabin cruiser was unoccupied. Its storm shutters were down. Thank Goddess it wasn't manned. Tony was down to one motor and that one was sputtering.

Aggie tied up to Stoned Cold's broadside facing the Gulf and hopefully out of sight. She and Sanchez boarded with gas cans and a siphon hose. From shore they'd looked like harbor cops, theirs was the right kind of boat for that. It didn't take long to find fuel. The yacht had an outboard kicker motor for docking with its own detachable fuel tanks. They took the fuel cells and were set to go in minutes.

She felt like a crook and worse when Tony came up from below decks with a case of beer under each arm. She passed the stolen goods down to their launch feeling like a pirate looting Port Royal. She got back on but no Tony? He went back below. *What gives?* Seconds ticked away. Stealing wasn't easy and it was even harder with her heart pounding. Tony returned. Her grip was slick with palm sweat. She nearly lost the bottle of rum he handed down before boarding.

They motored south close to shore still not certain if they had enough gas.

After an hour of slow going, Sanchez found the beach he was looking for. He said it was in the bad section of the island, a shantytown where local poor lived. It's where brown and black low-wage hotel workers hid from the tourists' view. The trade was long gone and these people were left to rot.

Those shacks were way better than what she saw in Jamaica, but not as good as the old bait shop she had lived in on Geiger Avenue. Accommodations were shabby and Aggie felt right at home. Sanchez tied off on a buoy and stood tall on the foredeck waving a white T-shirt.

Rowboats came out and everyone off loaded a few at a time. Aggie and Sanchez were the last to leave. But before disembarking into a brightly painted rowboat, Sanchez went down into the cuddy cabin and came out with a duffel bag. He passed it to Aggie.

"Wow, weights a ton, what's in it, gold bars?"

"No, something we'll need. Guns and ammo. A couple of M-16s and some handguns."

Aggie almost dropped the duffel over the side but she resisted the temptation. As much as she hated guns, Tony Sanchez was right: The whole world wanted her dead and maybe they needed guns. She wasn't ready to meet the Goddess.

The wind blew west so when they cast off that beat up Coast Guard boat, she drifted away toward the Gulf fast. *With no one bailing she'll swamp.* It can't sink due to the hull's foam filling. But still Aggie hated to cut it lose like garbage. It should have been reused, not wasted. Aggie hated a lot of things she was forced to do lately. She had recycling in her DNA and trashing the craft that kept her alive was sour medicine. That boat didn't belong here and it'd be spotted sooner or later. It had to go.

Aggie checked the boat over one more time to make sure they left nothing behind that might identify them. "Great, now I'm thinking like Sanderson." She didn't find anything except her alien coveralls. *That's a big giveaway.* She untied them from the rear hatch and wrapped them around her waist before jumping down into a rowboat.

Two men rowed her and Tony inshore fast. Once landed, happy reunions blew up like a sudden parade. Most of them were relatives, she was told. The Sanchez family was spread far and wide. It made Aggie feel homesick for her own. She didn't have much of one, just her folks, Grandpa and her adopted extensions, Mark, Mel, Jimmy, and lately, Jennifer, and Jane Albright, the missing president. But most of all she missed Mel. She knew where Mel was but the rest of them were in the wind. She felt like an assmunch thinking about how she treated Mel.

Aggie didn't dwell long on her mistakes as there was a party going on. She was soon pulled away from herself. Food came out. Music and dancing broke out. Tony wasn't about to do anything about PR any time soon. After stuffing her face with seafood and plantains Aggie tracked Tony down and asked about an airplane. The music was loud and Aggie had to shout. Tony was dancing and pointed at an old guy drinking beer before he was swept up and carried away by a group of dancing friends. Tony was the star and it wasn't just the rum and beer he confiscated that made him the center of attention. They didn't seem to mind that the moon was falling to pieces. Aggie, frustrated, walked away to chill her jets.

The beach was nice. From shore she watched that disenfranchised boat drift into the sunset feeling like that boat, alone and sinking. PR was a long way from there. It wasn't a few hours away on a fast boat. The trip would take at least a day and more like two days by water and that trip would be sidelong against prevailing winds.

"Crap, what am I going to do now?"

Tony came up and handed her a beer. She took it and drank a big gulp even though she never liked beer. But right then, it tasted good. The first one wasn't great but the next was way better.

Tony wandered off back to the party and left Aggie on the beach. She forgot to ask where the bathroom was. Now she knew why Key West always smelled of pee, beer makes your bladder go nuts. She headed down the beach toward some huts and once there she found them locked. There was a bay going inland but no bathroom in sight. She walked inland along the bay's shore looking and not finding facilities. Finally, she was forced to duck into the bushes. Coming out she noticed a distant gleam.

"No way." She ran forward a few yards. "It's an airplane, holy crap." She ran another fifty yards.

Parked off the bay in a little lagoon slip sat an old seaplane. Its paint was gone. The red shine of sunset reflected off its aluminum skin. Aggie tossed the beer and ran all the way back to the party. Finding Tony, she pulled him aside and told him what she found.

"Forget it," Tony said. "That thing barely flies and besides Uncle Pedro won't do it. He's a prick about it, won't take it up unless you pay through the nose. Accept it Aggie, we aren't going to make it."

"That's poop. Talk to him, I'll talk to him. I'll give anything whatever he wants. Tony do this for me. Ask him."

"No can do, I don't want my head bit off. He's got attitude. My mom's cousin, his sister, won't even talk to him."

"Fine I'll talk to him, you interpret."

"That plane isn't safe; I'm not getting on that thing."

"So, stay here. I'm going if he'll fly. Talk to him."

"Let me think about it." Tony walked away grumbling, and she lost sight of him.

The party was just off the beach but Aggie wasn't in the mood to be sociable and she didn't know Spanish, so she went back to the water's edge. Not long after, Tony returned.

"Think we should get going ... get over to PR?" He asked.

"I thought you were staying, family and all that's here." Aggie said. "You said it's too late anyway."

"I deserted, Aggie. I got no place to go on Earth but the gallows."

"I know the feeling. How about stealing an airplane off Grand Turks? Must be one there. How's that for a crappy solution? The airport's that way, right." Aggie pointed north. "Hello fire, this is the frying pan, the fire isn't hot enough."

"Said I wanted in and I wasn't fooling." Tony took a long pull from his beer and tossed the can. "That seaplane's not in good shape but … " He wiped the beer off his face. "It'll get us there."

"No way, really? You'll ask him?"

"I hate asking. He won't like it. Maybe the beer loosened him up. It's your idea." Tony tossed the Coast Guard hat into the sea. "Convincing him won't be easy. He'll want favors, something. He's a cheapo."

"I'll do him if I have to." Aggie said. "You know, sex … I don't know how but if that's what it takes. Tell him I'm a virgin, it's true."

"Really, no?" Tony whistled. "That might be the only way." Tony said it with a little smile.

Aggie hoped he was kidding. She never did it with a man before and this wasn't the time to learn. If sexing a fossil got them to PR, she'd do it. Whatever it took. Time was short.

Moon City was taking off for sure. Why else would the moon break up? She'd be stuck here forever if they didn't try. The thought made her woozy. What she wanted originally was to take a little space ride and come back later when things cooled down. Staying on Earth for real was a very bad idea. She'd have to hide forever.

Tony's duffel held more than guns. Before he and Aggie took off for the little lagoon where the plane was parked, Tony passed out American candy and cigarettes. He had a big package of Cuban cigars that were carefully wrapped in plastic, too. The cigars weren't meant for Great Uncle Pedro the pilot alone. Tony planned to share them all around. That was his big gift.

Aggie and Tony arrived at the airplane's berth with bribery in mind. Pedro was there going over the plane. Tony gave the pilot all the money he had to cover gas. No profit there for Pedro.

Tony pulled out the last pint of rum. Still no good. He produced a small package of cigars and handed them over. The old man indicated no. Tony took the smokes back and put them inside the duffel. After ten minutes of back and forth. Tony reached into his magic green bag and pulled out a motherlode package of Cuba's finest hand-rolled cancer logs. The deal was made. The old-timer's face lit with joy on receiving them.

"So, I'll have to do him, right?" Aggie asked. "Right here on the dock or where?"

Pedro indicated he didn't understand. Tony interpreted. Pedro laughed like hell.

"Says he's a virgin too, never did girls before, men only." Tony relayed. "He rather not."

The sun was only gone a half hour when they got inside the plane in dimming light. The old guy barely got it into the air. Pedro proceeded to fly low to the water. Tony said it was to avoid radar. Aggie figured it was more because the plane barely flew. Seaplanes, apparently, don't glide well when the motors go poop. Because of the floats, seaplanes drop fast. The pilot smoked cigars the whole 400 miles. She almost wished she gave him her virginity instead. Aggie bit her lip and sucked it up. When the lights of PR were close Aggie felt safer and asked Tony the question that was swirling around inside her.

"So, why are you doing this? I understand about family but what about America, aren't you a military guy, you know patriotic and junk?" Aggie had to shout over the droning motor. "What about revolting like Jon? Save America."

Tony laughed and moved closer to her ear. "You're kidding. I saw your blogs and the others you suggested. Saw it before shut down. Chris Camp, Lee Wolf, Richard Hedges, truth tellers all say it. America's over. Earth too. Getting out while I can. I had one foot out the door but the other was stuck in doubt. You unstuck me when you showed up."

"Oh, sorry about that."

"You did me a favor."

The plane gained altitude and circled, going over the big island so Pedro could scope out a good spot. He was aiming for a lake or river landing. Even thought it was dark and the middle of the night Aggie caught a glimpse of the telescope site in the distance below. Not hard to find, it was on top of the tallest mountain in that jungle and it was lit up. The entire jungle was dark all around for miles. Why not use lots of lights? It tracked radio waves and didn't take pictures, right? But still it felt wrong. The place was kept really dark before.

Spotlights were pouring light downhill. Maybe Buddy was buzzing the place? There were flashes, too. The skies were clear, but why would there be lightning there? *Hello, it's the top of a mountain.* Pedro started his descent. Aggie left her reservations in the clouds. She didn't know why the observatory was lit like a roman candle and didn't care. She wasn't going there anyway; the tunnel, her destination, was below the rim.

THIRTY-SIX

Sanderson and Moon Security

Sanderson knew where he was going. He didn't need Kowalski. The man was holding something back, Sanderson knew it in his bones. 100 years inside the deep state didn't make him cynical, it made him observant. *Screw that guy, he never was worth a damn.*

"No more dithering around."

Sanderson made his way to Center City and hardly bothered to look at the sights. He had seen it all inside the tank while his new spine grew. A smart soldier did that, observed his surrounding and anticipated, thinking ahead, planning contingencies. Mark Levine was famous for it, that guy was always a step ahead and Sanderson wasn't above taking a lesson. He hoped in the back of his mind that Levine might find his way off the Earth. He could use a guy like that and he'd take him as crew if Moon City didn't beat him to it.

There wasn't any point in going after the GTO, they had no power here and they were leaving anyway. That little fact, that the GTO wasn't the big cheese here, was something he never knew as Earth's trade negotiator. The GTO pulled his chain so long Sanderson felt like a sash weight.

The thought struck him funny and he stopped to laugh at himself. "You old fool, they stopped using window weights in the 60s."

Back to business. Sanderson proceeded while searching the local database. All this GTO info was in Moon City's public data stream. He needed more. Sanderson found the City Controller's office and walked right in. The door was open, that was policy. The Controllers didn't run Moon City, Moon had her own ideas. These beings were there for detailed security and facilities management.

Just employees doing what Moon wanted. City living had too many restrictions for his blood.

He found what was expected. Two sluggos working a wall full of dials, holo screens and switches. Sluggos didn't sit, no need for a desk or paper. *Where would a 400-pound slug put his ass if he had one?*

One of the Sluggos projected communication telepathically saying, "Mr. Sanderson, we were expecting you."

Sanderson flinched. He wasn't used to being called mister; admiral was his handle for more years than he cared to count. Sanderson didn't have telepathic capacity but outside words inside his head from another mind didn't jerk his chain. That form of communication was standard aboard Mother. His control belt took care of cross-species communications. He didn't need to speak but he did anyway.

"Of course, you were expecting me, any idea why I came?"

"Sir, we respect privacy. We may only record what is exchanged in public spaces. But to hazard a guess, based on your recent conversations, you are concerned with your captain's whereabouts. Am I correct?"

"That you are. You monitored Aggie's conversations with Kowalski, play it back for me. I need to know where she went, what her plan was."

The sluggo extended one of its tentacles with a slurping sound; it had many more but they were normally kept unseen inside the body blob. It manipulated a dial that was made for handless operators. On a holo the conversations Aggie had at the bar and with Blue repeated. What was said on the trader ship wasn't recorded although her conversations on the way to Traders' Port were. It took a while to hear it all.

"She mentioned a place called Guantanamo Bay." A sluggo pointed out. "She seeks a person known as Jon Colbert. Her emotional state was high. Psychology AI reports a romantic interest."

"I saw it. I should have known." Sanderson scratched his beard. "Goddamn it. I forgot about Colbert. I never did release him." Sanderson engaged his control belt. He wore it to hold up his pants like any other belt. "Ship, make ready. We're going to Earth. Goddamn Colbert."

"Sir, I would not advise it." Sluggo said. "Moon City released her moorings. She is in the process of lifting off this planetoid even now. We do not have a countdown, but she will vacate this sector with all speed."

Moon restricted its local crafts, Sanderson learned, but his wasn't that. No city controls a mother ship's crew. If Moon had it her way, she'd stop all Earthbound traffic.

"Why's that my problem?"

"Massive amounts of projectile debris are released. Such fly in all directions. Local space navigation is unsafe. Known orbital obstructions have become unpredictable. Once she exits her cradle fully, orbital objects will greatly compromise flight. Even now debris fields form in Earth's stratosphere."

"Thanks for the warning."

Sanderson exited. He wasn't far from the hangar where he had parked. It was just a couple of miles. No need to take a tube. The walk wasn't faster but it was useful giving him time to work strategies. As he went, he called home. He had prearranged a protocol with Mel. All Mother's voice communicates were scrambled. But most important, no names were to be mentioned. *Mel better not screw this up.* Sanderson wished that guy was better with the com so they didn't need this rigmarole. Mel was crew already but he didn't know it yet. *He'll accept officially when the smoke clears.*

"Communications, this is Security. Secure protocol. Elvis has left the building. I'm going after rendition, copy that?" Sanderson let go his belt.

"I copy, what about our probe?"

Sanderson was startled this time. Mother made Mel's voice sound exactly like it will once Mel switched body gender. The man could have been a voice-over artist.

"I'll have Moon City transmit our target's latest bio-form reading. Have the probe upload it. Put it on hard search."

"What about the messages? Next one isn't scheduled yet."

Of course, Mel was referring to the crew call. The first two were out and anthropology AI has the applications. The next blog is the final. Navy will block escapees. Risk was mounting. Be that as it may, the AI should have IDed the best before now. They should be on the move. Sanderson wished there was time to review the applications. Too many good ones to narrow it down this quick. He'd need a week. They had a day at best.

"Get last call out now. We're out of time. Moon's taking refugees. Shuttles will get mobbed. Get our people airborne pronto."

Sanderson cut the signal. The Navy might trace it, might not, he wasn't taking chances. Latest report said the Navy launched a squadron of small fighter MACs. More big destroyers went online while he was in flight. Another destroyer was in orbit. It's a race between Moon City's departure and the Navy's attack. Inside his mind he scanned the reports and stopped in the middle of the hall.

"Navy's patrolling right where I need to go. Goddamn raiders alerted them."

A tall Nordic human also stopped, looked him up and down and then proceeded on her way. She was pretty for a seven-footer. He wondered if they were sexually compatible. She was only a little taller than himself. He shook it off. No time for that. He hadn't felt horny since his 75th birthday and that was a long, long time ago. Goddamn if regen didn't have its pros.

Once onboard his shuttle, he wasted no time launching. He pulled the best class-A bio-bot they had and he needed a smart one for this. Navy MACs were in high Earth orbit as well as around Cuba. The damn robot wanted to reverse engines and go home, that was smart. Sanderson had a few not so smart ideas cooking and the guts to execute them. Robots weren't wired to take risks.

"Deploy joystick." He said and one came up out of the deck. It was the same as the P-38 he flew in the big war. "Give me tactical holos." And they materialized instantly.

Sanderson played chess inside his head and decided on an approach. He moved toward Earth. Navy MACs spotted him and formed an intercept configuration. While in the tank, he directed Mother to install tactical capabilities in all craft. She didn't understand the concept, but he was insistent and she did what he had asked.

"Look at that, we'll hitch a ride behind that inbound asteroid. That one. Moon ejected it just for me," He laughed. "Boy she's a screamer. Give me full manual."

The class-A turned from its forward station and blinked. Its thin-skinned eyelids dropped over its big, black eyes slowly. Sanderson laughed like hell as he pushed the stick and proceeded directly into the path of a massive inbound moon rock. It was twice the size of school bus. Two Earth MACs came on hard from below but sensors indicated they lost him in the blinding light and heat as that space rock ignited and out gassed. His screens said it would impact in the south Atlantic Ocean. He didn't need to tractor its course away from populations. Sanderson aimed head on and pulled the stick just before impact. He flipped his ship up and over the projectile, pulling a looping 360. He situated the craft inside its debris stream. Shields were up but his craft rattled like marbles in a tin can.

"Hot damn, like old times!" He yelled as his craft was pelted with ice, tear-offs, and superheated gases. "Gotta love them force shields."

He rode that wild rock all the way down with the navigation AI screaming bloody hell. He didn't know if the Navy tracked him. Sensors didn't work from inside a comet's tail.

Cloaking was designed for oxygen atmospheres. He had to employ cover in space. It was the only option although the ship didn't like it. Despite shields the ship strained to maintain course. Sanderson held on until that rock was on the edge of blowing up. He turned out just in time. They slipped past the blockade with a dirty, scorched hull but otherwise unscathed. If his class-A had the ability to shoot stink eyes, Sanderson would look like a landfill to it.

"This is why Mother needs Earth people, by damn." The computer wasn't happy. "No imagination. OK Scooter, take over, best course."

This ride was nothing like the flights he had taken on the aliens' shuttles for America. For one, he had full control. It took about thirty minutes to reach Cuba, no point in going to Jamaica. Aggie wasn't the kind to sit still.

Arriving, he held up hovering over a mountaintop to scrutinize the situation. He needed recon before dropping in on Colbert. He sent mini-probes to map and note locations and assess the enemy's capabilities. He was shocked to find the jail complex in shambles. He thought it was a trap, did a little research and found it wasn't, just the usual government waste program. Never shut down any facility that drew budget money. The place wasn't used anymore but the public didn't know it. Colbert was still there.

Bio-scan said, beside Colbert, there were two others on location but no Aggie. Trace of Aggie was evident, that could mean anything. He had to question Colbert. No other way. He went deeper into the bio-scans. The entire base was half deserted. "What gives?" He checked the anthropology feed. Mass riots everywhere, internal CIA reports said soldiers were deserting left and right.

"Open door, let's go."

The door wasn't as open as he'd like. He lifted off and that set off alarms below. In a matter of seconds two Navy MACs beelined toward him.

"Weapons!"

Mother's fleet had none. "Evasive action, goddamn it, cat and mouse that's all I need."

Sanderson's ship shot straight up and did a hard turn. It was a pre-programed move that robot pilots used. The Navy ships can't do that. They don't have antigravity, but they were onto the robot's move. They sure as hell figured out a way to track him. Sanderson had no choice but to beat it out of there flank speed and try again later. As they cleared the Navy's sensor range, he took note of the holo that pointed at the moon. The moon was breaking up in a big way.

"Take us down to sea level, under radar. Let me think." He made a looping motion with his finger.

He went over the ship's data recordings while the robot made a thousand-mile loop. He took a good look at that destroyer class spaceship docked at Gitmo. It had fighters, dozens, parked on deck. Moon's sudden haste made sense. Moon City had good cause to pull stakes and leave Earth's supply of LF behind.

The goddamn government would rather blow up the aliens than trade with them. The Complex moved faster than anticipated. Space Fleet was ready and that's not what his secret admiralty reports had said.

"Christ they even fight when peace is crucial for survival." *Going after the aliens is the biggest military blunder in history.*

Every problem's a nail and hammers are the cure. Standing military philosophy was his keyhole. Once that destroyer launched all the local MAC fighters would follow. The military was a bunch of 5-year-olds playing soccer, kick the ball and all the players chase it, even the goalie … or at least that was his hope. For now, he was relegated to sitting under cloak until the smoke cleared.

Sanderson had his probes watching. *Sure as hell, it's going down like I figured.* The big ship lifted off and left. The sky cleared of MACs.

Sanderson raced in at sea level from the west. He gained altitude and flew just above the trees following the island's contour. He found a local road leading to the jail gates. He slowed to car speed and ran along the road a few feet off the pavement in holo. He'd look like Cuban military from above. He had miles to go. It was the dead slow approach, but it was better than dead. A pair of F-16s hunted above. Cuba wouldn't like its airspace compromised, it was against standing agreements to be sure, but with the American coup all bets were off. Cuba wasn't about to dance with that maniac Brinks.

The holo made his ship into an armored personnel carrier. It came right out of his imagination. WWII vintage was good for travel. To the locals and the Americans at the gate, old hardware was Cuban. Cuba didn't have anything modern. Once he got closer to the security compound's gate, he switched the holo into a U.S. armored personnel carrier. Two bends in the road later he sighted the entry.

Sanderson parked twenty-five feet from the gate as one of the MPs brought a rocket launcher to bear. He didn't think his little ship could take the pounding; its force skin wasn't top shelf. Fine against heated gases but a thermite-laced contact explosion was another matter. On screen that rocket packing MP tightened his finger on the release bar.

"Balls! Decloak, open the hatch." Sanderson didn't bother with the only gun Mother had in stock. It was an old WWII 45. He'd use his mouth for this.

He came down the plank yelling, "Stand down, stand down! CIA, back off!"

The two MPs looked confused; they must have seen a lot of strange lately. They lowered their weapons as Sanderson marched right up to them with his hair flying behind him.

"Halt, who goes there!"

"CIA, where's Colbert, Jon Colbert, I need a word with him. National security, you're still Americans, aren't you?" They were or they would have gone AWOL.

"In the Officers' Club." One of the MPs pointed the way with his gun.

Sanderson touched his belt and told the ship, "Resume truck holo." The MPs almost dropped their guns when it instantly changed. "See that boys, that's American ingenuity for ya ... You didn't see that, understand?"

"Yes, sir."

Sanderson pushed his hair over his shoulders and marched straight to the building. He had been there before. Sanderson found Colbert leaning his ass on a pool table facing away. The boy was drinking from a bottle of gin. Colbert was in Bermuda shorts and a Navy T-shirt.

"You're out of uniform!"

Colbert dropped the bottle and spun around, "Sanderson, you sound like Sanderson!"

"CIA, I'm — "

"I saw him die. TV, everybody saw ... holy cow pie." Colbert grabbed the pool table to keep from falling. "Dang ... that's really you."

No point dancing with him, no time for it.

"You saw wrong, you got me. Yes, it's me. I'm with Aggie now. I'm crew. She's the captain. Where'd she go? Why didn't you go with her?"

"How, why I, I ... "

"It's called regeneration. If you had joined, you'd get it too when needed. She was here. You didn't go, you bailed on her?" Sanderson had a hard time keeping the anger out of his voice. He needed information and scarring the bejesus out of Colbert like old times won't get it done. Sanderson switched to soft mode.

"Look son, I'm sorry you didn't sign on. I need to find her. Will you help me?"

"Help you, you left me here to rot! I ain't going nowhere 'til I have orders. I'm stuck. If'n I go I'm AWOL as all hell."

Sanderson had never seen the cowboy blow up like that. He stated pacing back and forth and cussing up a storm. Sanderson was glad that boy didn't have a gun. Colbert was confused and not from his drunk. That seaman didn't know the difference between patriotism and reality. Sanderson didn't have time to explain it. The way the moon was falling apart he'd be lucky to make it off the planet. American hardware in space didn't help the situation.

"Look, Colbert how about I get you released? You want orders so I'll get them for you. Then you can go and fight, whatever you want. How's that? Deal?"

"You'd do that how?"

"You got a CO's office here." Sanderson said scratching his beard. "I'll sign the release form, we backdate it. Say it got lost when the CO moved on. Maybe he never saw it, get me, lost in the mail. My signature's on file. It hasn't changed. I'll have my ship put the order into the Navy's record system. It'll be verified if anyone checks."

"You'd do that for me?"

"Sure, but you'll tell me about Aggie first, whatever you know, deal?"

Colbert picked up the black cowboy hat that was on the table, put it on and said, "Let's go."

None of the inner gates were locked and why should they be, nobody was home, not even the prison's commander. O'Connell was on vacation. Colbert said the place was otherwise abandoned except for him and the guys at the gate, one of whom recently vacated for parts unknown.

Admiral Sanderson had issued standing orders to keep Colbert there without charges. The boy was in limbo. Sanderson would be pissed off too had it happened to him. The CO's office was neat as a pin regulation. Sanderson had known the man but not well. It didn't take long to find form1730, same one used in every Navy brig. Sanderson filled it out and backdated it. He took a piece of notebook paper to write a personnel note. After addressing and dating it, he wrote.

> Bill,
> Thanks for holding this man for me. To be frank, I sent him down to you for intel. I wanted to see what you were up to. You have a stellar reputation and I wanted to confirm it. I can use a man like you on my team, but I wanted to be sure. Please release Colbert and send him back to me in Key West.
> Yours truly.

"That'll do it. I appealed to his ego. If it gets back to him, he'll say he never saw it." Sanderson stuffed the order and the letter into an oversized envelope, sealed it and backdated it.

"How ya figure that'll pass? There ain't no stamp on it. How's they gonna know it ain't cow dung?"

Sanderson held up the envelope. "It's a messenger's parcel; it doesn't go in the mail. Hand delivery only. O'Connell could have missed it. He might have seen it and got distracted and ignored it."

"Glory be."

"You go down to out-processing, tell them you found it while cleaning. The reference caption has your name on it, see? You had an excuse to open it."

"Daggone, I don't know how to thank you."

"Tell me what you know, where's Aggie?"

"I ain't see her since yesterday. Come to think of it, ain't seen Sanchez either. Can't figure where she'd gone off to. Said she wanted the alien's shuttles. Said she was going home."

"I see, walk with me, show me out."

Sanderson tried to talk the boy into coming along but Colbert had his heart set on fighting for America. He had a bevy of convoluted ideas as to who was what and why. Sanderson couldn't convince him. Everything Seaman Colbert believed was bull.

"You can lead a mind to knowledge but you can't make it think." Sanderson said under his breath as they neared the ship.

"What's that?" Colbert asked.

"Nothing, if you change your mind … send up a flair." The ship decloaked and Colbert damn near fell on his ass. The boy didn't like the look of it.

Sanderson boarded alone and ordered the AI to scan all local computers and get the drift on the men there. It searched Sanchez's official record. Sanchez had special gate access in and out. He had family on the island. Handlers thought they'd get local info out of him but they never got anything useful. The ship accessed Sanchez's personnel computer. It was what Sanderson thought. Sanchez got Mel's message and he was directed to Puerto Rico where the nearest shuttle access was located. He must have gone with Aggie.

Good, now I have two search window inputs.

Sanderson had the ship make a Humvee holo and told the robot to drive away slowly. He'd go airborne once the F-16s being tracked were out of range. He called the probes to do a wide search and check boat traffic, aircraft, scan for anything that smelled like Aggie. If he got lucky, they might pick her up in transit. Too bad she had a day's head start and it was a big ocean.

He knew where she was heading but not how she'd get there or even if she'd make it. Her whereabouts and status were in question. What if Sanchez used her? There was that price on Aggie. The Cubans would love to have her as a prisoner. She could be dead or in jail. Anything could happen. He wasn't going anywhere until he knew one way or the other. Mother wasn't ready to fly, but would she wait? *Never leave one of your own behind* scrolled across his mind's eye. Sanderson was determined to find her, dead or alive.

"Pilot, silent running. Take us out to sea. Holo us up a beat-to-hell fishing boat." He kicked back into his chair. "That's an idea. Ship, raid Sky-net. Give me a map of every boat sailing hereabouts in the last 24 hours."

"Working," the ship said inside his mind.

Sanderson decided he'd trace her most likely path and put the AI on mapping probabilities. He might find traces. More and more moon chunks were flying. His tactical display showed American MACs shooting them down. Still, many fiery rocks were getting in. A big one just hit near Iceland. If he was a praying man, he'd pray for one to hit wherever Brinks was. No telling which hole that snake slithered into.

THIRTY-SEVEN

Po-boy's Lie

Sky Flower sat next to Po-boy in the cab of the RV as he drove on just north of Roswell, New Mexico. Yesterday was all Interstate 40. He didn't even know what road they were on now. If she wasn't there supporting him, his guts mighta twisted into a knot sooner. They had stayed in another roadside campground last night along old Route 66, in Tucumcari. Sky wanted to go to the dinosaur museum on the college campus, but old man Branford wouldn't allow it. She and Branford had to keep their heads down. Po-boy did the talking and paid the camp host. It made sense to have him as frontman. He wasn't well known. She was in the news all the time representing Haiti's proposed spaceport, which was Aggie's idea. Of course, the authorities had other plans.

As Po-boy drove closer to the intersection his stomach began pitching fits. Nothing much made him sick, working around dead fish and mud-rot, the innards of caught sharks and even alligator shit never turned him sour. But now his insides were a jumble. A peaceable man, driving into trouble was not his way. *I never done nothing like this before.* Playing cat and mouse with security boats across the mudflats wasn't dangerous. Going to protests against the empire wouldn't get you killed. By the look of them, these empire men were fixing to shoot dissenters.

He felt a hand on his shoulder from behind, a strong solid hand. Branford never showed him any encouragement or affection before. Desperate times had desperate people school together.

"Sonny listen, Sky and I are going back to the closet," that's what the old man called his spy center, "It's up to you," Bradford said. "Show them the fake badge."

"What if they go an' question me?"

"Make something up," Branford turned for the back of the bus with Sky close behind.

Po-boy whispered, "Never been good at fibbin'."

On the road ahead there had to be a thousand cars and RVs lined along the shoulder. Getting in and out of Roswell was hard enough, too many people, but out here in the desert way past town this many cars just wasn't natural. He saw the intersection half a mile ahead. Two roads out of the five-way intersection went right for the military. It was the one straight up and past the military's cut-off Mr. Branford wanted. *Dead nuts north.* The old man still didn't say where they were going. "Plausible deniability," he said, that wasn't helping Po-boy no how.

What was he going to say at the roadblock? *No sir, I got no contraband. Me sir? I'm just an old UFO researcher is all.* Sonny Po-boy Piper was a bad liar if'n he was anything. Just wasn't in the family genes. His tongue already hurt from biting it.

Police usually had control of the roads but there was military ahead too. They were making folks k-turn around. Most wasn't going back no how. Instead folks were diving off into the desert making a hell of a dust-up. That officer just ahead didn't like it none either by the scowl on his face. Even a desert hound respects his grounds and folks was tearing it apart.

A protest was brewing. He had seen such many times before.

When he got up to the spot, a local policeman came to the window. A high-faluting military officer wearing mirror aviator's shades came along. Po-boy's reflection looked back at him. He saw himself looking as guilty as all git out. He swallowed the bile in the back of his mouth.

Po-boy slid the window sideways. The cop's head reached the window bottom. Act natural Po-boy said to himself.

"Turn this piece of shit around." The policeman said.

"This no doggone junk, this here's in good mechanical shape, no lie." Po-boy said. He wasn't lying, that made it easier. "I'm not going up there," he pointed at the roads into the base, "I'm going up yonder. I was camping. I'm … was on vacation. Work called. Said drop everything come quick."

"I don't give a shit — "

"What's going on here?" The military man said.

Sonny held up the badge. "Going up north way. I'm called off vacation. Gotta go that a way, make no mistake." Sweat poured down Po-boy's face and it wasn't that hot.

The military man had a clipboard with many sheets of paper on it. "He might be OK. Let me check the list. What's the name?"

Po-boy forgot what name was on the badge. He had to look but couldn't. Instead he pulled a Mr. Branford move. That is, put it on the other. He leaned outside still holding out the badge and said "What y'all can't read?"

"You don't have to be a dick, hold on." The military man took it from Po-boy and started leafing around his papers.

Po-boy flinched. Nobody ever called him a dick. People say he was nice as sweet tea. Po-boy was fixing to file a complaint but a shot was fired. It was a flair. RVs and cars started racing across the desert like a demolition derby at the county fair.

"Jesus Christ," the policeman said. "Your people better not shoot civilians. There'll be hell to pay."

The military man shoved the fake ID back at Po-boy. "Don't move. I'm not done with you." He pulled up a walkie-talkie. "Bravo Report."

"Permission to engage." The radio said.

"I'm telling you," The policeman said, "I know these people. You start shooting they'll shoot back."

Report of military fire came loud and clear. The military shooters didn't wait for an answer. To Po-boy's ears both sides opened up.

"We have orders. Wait here." And the military man ran off toward the breakout.

Po-boy craned his neck to see behind better. There was too much dust in the air. He didn't see squat but flashing gun fire and tail lights. Protesters were for sure shooting. It was like black powder at the O.K. Corral; nobody could see nothing. The cop stood by with his mouth open.

"That's what you'll git with gun culture, no lie." Po-boy said.

"Madness, this is madness," the officer said, shutting his mouth and pulling his sidearm. "Wait here." He took off running toward the action.

Po-boy sat there gripping the wheel, trying to figure what to do. A bullet hit the police car parked on the roadside and busted out a window and he didn't move. Civil disobedience was one thing but this wasn't that, they'd shoot him if he moved for sure. Po-boy never felt fear like this in all his life, not even when that bull shark damn near ate Aggie when she was a little girl. A bullet hit the edge of the RV's side-view mirror and ricocheted away.

Branford roared as he came forward, "What are you doing, hit it!"

Po-boy snapped out of it and punched the gas. The camper was surprisingly fast. Branford said it was made to look like a pig in a poke but it was setup to fly and he wasn't fooling. Before Po-boy realized it, he was going ninety and he wasn't but a half mile down the road. On reflex he let off the gas and the bus lurched.

"No, keep going," Branford cried. "Go Po-boy, go!"

Po-boy hammered the throttle again but held speed at eighty. No point in getting killed in a wreck. The damn thing handled like what it was, a bus. Once down the road a piece, Bradford, laptop in hand, took the passenger seat. Sky Flower came up out of hiding. The old man checked his spy gear in the back with the laptop.

"Goddamn this is nuts." Mr. Branford said. "The world's gone stark raving mad."

"What is it Dad, what's happening?" Sky asked.

Branford put the computer up on the big wide dashboard. There was room enough up there for a sleeping dog. The thing showed an aerial scene. The old man had gone into satellites. On screen there were men like pixel dots and cars like little bugs all going this way and that. Po-boy didn't have the wherewithal to make sense of it while keeping his eyes on the road.

Branford pointed. "This is us, we're clear. The choppers are busy. Slow it down." Po-boy let off the gas. "I was monitoring. Protesters arranged a run at the base. It's a reaction. Internet, that Van Ness girl's blog, has it that alien moon shuttles are there."

"I'd take that cotton-pickin' ride." Po-boy said. "In a heartbeat."

"Marines started shooting soon as they started. That's not the crazy part." Branford said.

"That's awful," Sky said.

"Their backup, local Reserves I'd say by the radio chatter. They came from behind and started shooting at the regulars. It's ... the cops are joining the protesters." Branford adjusted the view. "Jesus Christ the revolution's on!"

"I doubt Jesus had anything to do with this." Sky said.

They all knew what he meant. Jane Albright had gone on radio and the internet this morning, calling for a revolution. Just after her plea the dang internet went down again.

"If this don't beat the dog's mule." Po-boy said, as the implications sank deeper.

"You did well Po-boy, good job." The old man put a hand on his shoulder nice and friendly like. "Son, we're on our way."

"But what way is the country going?" Po-boy asked. "This'll be the end of it."

"Not our problem." Branford said. "Not anymore, if this works out."

"The people have had enough." Sky said. Her lawyer voice set aside. "All the wars nobody wanted, the way they crushed people until the middleclass was toast. The abuses, the hardships, the lies, people are sick of it, sick of dying for rich men's war. Sick of going homeless or bankrupted because of medical costs."

Mr. Branford hung his head.

Po-boy expected a revolution would come but he never thought he'd see it in his life, and all of a sudden, too. Hell, he never thought he'd learn the facts about aliens true enough. But there it was. Revolution was a shock. The old man showing him respect surely was that too. Two in one day. He never expected Sky's old man to call him son. Changing times change everything and everybody, even Sky's old man.

"Glory be," Po-boy said, thinking will wonders ever stop?

Two flying saucers escorted by two F-16s flew right down the road single file just over their heads going toward the fight. *Answers my question.* Jet thrusters rocked the bus and kicked up a torrent of dirt as they went over. Po-boy managed to stay on blacktop. The saucers didn't leave a trace. He slowed down on impulse. Wonders weren't fixing to stop any time soon. He mashed back down on the gas.

"Steady as she goes, son." Mr. Branford said. "We have quite a distance yet to go."

Sky's old man wasn't saying where the hideout was. Said it was to protect them. They were so far into the outer reaches he couldn't figure where they were going. Canada maybe. The badlands all around were more like the moon than

God's good earth. That old Jackie Gleason TV show came to mind. "To the moon, Alice, to the moon," Ralph would say. If that's what the old man had in mind, they were going in the wrong direction.

THIRTY-EIGHT

Archer at the Gate

Archer arrived at the Key West Naval Air Station early morning. Armed men were stationed along the inside fence every fifty yards. The men at the gate waved him in with only a glance at his ID. But he had questions and stopped. He wasn't in uniform nor would he wear one again if what he planned succeeded. His stock in the deep state was paying dividends.

"I've been on the road all night. What's happening? Why extra security?"

The guard stiffened. "Sir, it's the revolt. Command thinks there might be a riot, an attack on the base. Jane Albright was on radio again last night."

"Nonsense," Archer said. "This is Key West, rich people and servants who drink too much. Do you really think that will happen here? These people storming the gates?"

"No sir, it's not likely."

"If anyone comes to the gate, anyone at all, who asks for Sanderson's office, let them in."

"But, sir, I have orders."

"I'll talk to command; they should already know this. Word hasn't come down yet. I'll go now."

Archer drove off leaving the sentry scratching his head. No wonder he looked confused; anyone would be off balance tracking the news. Too much propaganda. Nobody was buying it. Reality and the news didn't match. The internet got shut down and put back up a dozen times in recent days. TV was hit and miss and controlled. Radio was easy to use. No way to stop radio wave reception without killing every station. Albright was smart. She had someone with skills behind her, perhaps Mark.

All kinds of voices the state can't control were flapping gums and now Albright herself was in the mix. This was getting interesting.

Overnight as he drove an all points came over his car's standard radio. It wasn't an official announcement. Albright herself talked revolution. How she got on-air was a mystery. Break into a radio station? Alien tech? She had to have insider help to pull it off.

Archer heard about coworkers deserting in favor of her. Had to be that. She didn't know it, and never would, but he was with her as well. When he heard the first announcement yesterday his heart sang and he thought it had lost its voice.

The NSA doesn't have the power they think they do. Archer was damn sure it was Piper's alien tech that kept tricking the system into rebooting the internet. From what he saw as Karnack's prisoner, the aliens are a million years ahead in technology. Piper inherited the lot when she took over Karnack's fleet. The president confirmed it when she repeated Piper's message. Piper's alive and seeking crew people.

If Piper wasn't just a kid the Navy wouldn't stand a chance against Mother's technology. Nobody was safe from the alien's tech, not even the NSA. The alien's advantages were driving the Chiefs to distraction. *I will use that.*

Archer arrived at Base Command and an orderly was waiting. The gate must have called. Brass made him into a big shot over night. Fine, use it. When he was there two days prior, nobody took notice.

"General Archer," the orderly said after a sharp salute. "Right this way, Admiral Clinton is waiting."

Archer followed him inside thinking, *general, now I'm a general. If they think rank entices me to play their game, they don't know me very well.* He stifled the chuckle forming in his throat.

Archer reached the base commander's open door and the bloated man standing inside didn't waste time. He came at Archer jabbing a finger. Archer was glad Clinton didn't extend his hand far enough. His impulse was to break that moron's pointer finger clean off. That moment's pleasure wasn't worth blowing his cover.

"What's this, you telling my men to ignore my orders. Air Force doesn't tell Navy what to do, got it!"

Archer pushed back his sunglasses. He retained that dead look in his eyes after his time on the alien control bracelet. His stare scared people. The commander took half a step back.

"The Joint Chiefs ordered you to give me what I need. I'm not telling you to throw open the gates. I'm after the ones Spaceship Mother called. Anyone of them near will come. Let them in and we might catch the big target. Aggie Piper won't come in if the others don't get through. Understand?"

"What if they get away?"

"So what? Consider them wasted bait."

The big man had to huff and puff to show his dominance. He was lucky Archer didn't just shoot the pig. But in the end, the Navy man agreed. Commander

Clinton sent new orders to the gates. Satisfied, Archer made his way to Sanderson's building out on an auxiliary flight line.

No one was in the front reception room. Everything was how he left it but he heard voices. Archer traveled the short hall to Sanderson's reception room with his ears wide. There wasn't any threat in those sound waves. Sanderson's old waiting area held five people milling around. Four civilian types who likely worked on base and one seaman out of uniform. They all looked disheveled like they had slept there. Judging by the body odor, they had.

Archer left his dark glasses on. "You people are here for Mother. I'll help. I know about the elevator; I saw it." That was true. "What did Mother say, where is it?" He said, to test if they were called or tagalongs.

"We aren't sure we ought to — "

"Don't, don't tell him anything, that's Mr. Black!" The Navy kid said.

The five looked at each other and a small argument started. Archer followed their conversations. They had been there all night, had gotten on base before lockdown. They recognized him and argued about that too, good guy or bad guy?

Archer didn't need to explain himself; the whole world saw him near death on the deck of the Contention when Aggie took Karnak. Maybe the Van Ness girl's blogs made them leery. He was a contradiction. People saw him shoot Sanderson with Aggie in the kill zone thanks to Van Ness. Truth got out before the NSA could pull that footage and start counternarratives. Melisa Van Ness made him famous, more so infamous. Her media bypasses tore this all open. Alien tech, or did the Van Ness girl use her old man's security software? It didn't matter. The message got out.

The Navy man spoke up. "Gang, gang," he said, "If Mr. Black wanted us dead, we'd be dead already."

"Smart boy," Archer said. "Best we get you on your way."

The Navy man didn't know which room was what. All they knew was Sanderson's bathroom. Nothing was marked. Archer brought the small group into Sanderson's unmarked inner reception office. Archer unlocked it and entered first. He had been there before and knew how to access the inner sanctum.

He opened a closet door. The uniforms inside smelled like Sanderson. Pushing aside the contents he found the entry. It led into a smaller lounge with a well-stocked bar and an oversize bathroom. If these people had instructions, they'd know what to do. Archer stood by. A pretty girl about twenty-years-old pressed a shower tile and the back wall slid sideways. That's it. They weren't spies.

The five got inside with fear and apprehension on each one's face.

"Good luck," Archer said. "When you see Aggie, tell … tell her … never mind."

The Navy man pressed a button and the door slid shut without a sound.

Archer went to Sanderson's office and dug into the dead man's effects. That antique military phone he pulled out of wastebasket had collected a bit of dust. He wiped it off. Did the man know his time was up when he threw it away? Archer had removed that discarded relic from the trash to honor the man by placing it back on the desk as a testimonial monument. That's where it was when he last saw Sanderson alive.

Archer opened Sanderson's hidden computer center. The password was his daughter's name. Archer had Karnack to thank for better perceptions. Cracking the password was nothing. Having suffered the control bracelet's brain rewiring, he was a better agent. What previously distracted focus were no longer in play; the control bracelet changed him for good and ill. His body suffered permanent damage but improved thought speed and capacity made up for it.

Hours passed and dozens of people came and left by way of the tunnel system. There came a change in that. The first were called by Mother, the rest were invited by Moon City. The more of them that got out the better. A planet with American hegemony making its endgame dash wasn't worth living on. He envied the escapees. He couldn't go. He had work to do.

Late afternoon things slowed down and still no Aggie Piper. Watching Sanderson's security screens, he thought he knew why. There was a mob at the gate. But that wasn't it. Like Mother's call, Moon City had limited time.

All of his screens lit at once. The regular phone rang. His cell phone barked. It was Moon City's last all points bulletin.

"Attention Earth. This is last call for refugees. I am hereby recalling the last of my shuttles. Have a nice day, and thanks for all the fish."

"Aliens like fish, didn't see that coming."

She closed the door. Archer went outside to check the sky. There was a huge, bright object, so bright he couldn't make out its shape. The moon was visible, too, as the sun was low. The object and the moon were dancing. Someone had bit a third of the moon off. Meteorites streaked the sky like chem trails gone mad. Flying in that was ill-advised. Good, that should ground air traffic and screw the military's ambitions. He went back inside.

Sanderson's system had dialed into many telescopes. Archer had his face in the laptop watching Moon City separate. He saw it better now. A cyclical object moved in toward the free-floating City. *A starship?* Sanderson's door burst open. Archer left his gun in the open and out of reach for this occasion. If he shot, he'd kill an unarmed man in cold blood.

"Mark Levine, no need for that. I'm unarmed." Archer pointed at the gun that pointed at him. It was a policemen's 38 special. Levine was dripping wet. He must have swum the mudflats to get inside.

"Archer you snake, I ought to shoot you, stand up, show your hands."

Do wet police guns fire? Archer obeyed. "Look, there isn't time. Moon City just announced it's shutting the door. No time, you want off or not?"

"I know, what about it?"

"Come on, I'll show you the elevator."

Archer didn't expect it, he expected a bullet in his face, but that was the old Mr. Black making a habitual judgment call. In a flash Archer's mind reassessed the situation. Mark didn't know exactly where to go. He was forced to trust the untrustworthy. It was instinct. Mark Levine lived this long for good reason.

Archer believed Levine wouldn't shoot as he leaned into the shower and pressed the tile. He backed away with his hands up. Mark got into the elevator. Levine never took the gun off him. The man had good instincts and acute caution was hardwired.

"I don't understand," Mark said. "Why?" One finger was on the button, the other on the trigger and the second Levine let go, the door closes and that bullet will fly … if the answer is wrong.

He had to say something Levine could believe. He didn't have time to explain why he'd wipe out the Joint Chiefs and make each of them suffer for all they had done. What was done to his father. Mark understood revenge, payback, an eye for an eye but also a gift returned. There was no time to justify the murders he planned. Brinks was just one head of a hydra. Only an insider can tear enough layers down to reach the heart.

"Aggie Piper saved my life. This is payback." *Truth serves better than a lie.*

Levine lowered the gun, released the elevator button and was gone.

Archer went back to the computer wall and watched as a number of alien shuttles left Earth's atmosphere. The military had a new handle on unblocking the alien's signal interface. He also tracked the Navy's insufficient spacecraft dodging space rocks. The alien grays were much better at dodgeball. Smart move on Moon City's part. *Get while the getting's good.* The sun was nearly down and he felt it. Mark Levine was on one of those alien ships or he'd have come back. Archer didn't regret going himself. *I'll do what good I can.*

He continued exploring Sanderson's former intel system. Previously he didn't dig in deeply. Many more pieces of the moon were raining down on screen. *Predictable.* Secured messages said communications were cleared of alien interference. Moon City was free. The destroyers in orbit regained power. Others were on the move. The attack began. But the target began moving and shortly it would be gone. *What's the point?* One of Earth's big ships was hit by debris and destroyed while Archer watched in real time.

"'What if there was a war and nobody came?'" *I'll soon find out.*

THIRTY-NINE

Aggie at the Observatory

Pedro intended to set the seaplane down just under the International Observatory on the Arecibo River, the observatory's namesake. He told Tony a recent dam project made that part of the river wider and deeper. It was hours past nightfall and starlight lit the waters below but not enough to land by. Pedro started his third lap.

It should have been a full moon, but someone had bitten a big chunk out of it. It wasn't supposed to be a crescent. That chunk was Moon City and she wouldn't hang around long. Aggie witnessed more than a weird moon. From above as the plane circled, there were flashes around the observatory. The sky was clear and lighting shouldn't act that way. *Weird local weather?* In Key West it often rained on one side of a street but not the other.

She didn't have time to think more on it. Pedro found what he was looking for and banked hard and into a steep decline. The aircraft squeaked and growled in protest. Outside the window, the wings flexed so much Aggie feared one would fall off. The craft bounced and rattled on landing and it finally stopped shaking. She would have jumped out and kissed the ground had they landed on dry land.

The old man laughed and jabbered after he cut the engines down to idle. He searched the surroundings and aimed for the shore, revving the motor. He laughed while taxiing and took a big swallow off the rum bottle.

"What's he so happy about?" Aggie asked. "He's drunk?"

"He never landed on a small river before. Never between mountains. You'd drink too."

"I get that."

Closer to shore, motors idled lower while Aggie and Tony got out of the passenger compartment and onto the pontoons. Sanchez's duffel full of guns was still heavy but less bulky having unloaded the goodies before they took off. The airplane nosed up and turned sidelong to a clear spot. They stepped off onto muddy but solid ground. It was the outlet of a mountain stream's bank. Aggie was sure it was that same creek she and Mel were on before.

Inland the gorge was dark with mountains on either side that made it hard to see far. The observatory's location was evident. The horizon up over the mountain was lit like a city. No town was anywhere near them.

"How the hell we going to get up there?" Tony said pointing up at a shear climb.

"Easy, we walk the creek between hills. I was here once. We go inland then up."

Their destination wasn't hard to find with the mountain's lights. Aggie thought her luck was turning. The pilot's engines increased idle. She and Tony pushed the plane off. Pedro maneuvered to setup his take off while making a lot of attention-getting noise. Aggie was relieved when that little plane raced upstream and took off.

"We better go." Just as Aggie steeped into the stream's rocky bed, a loud bang echoed through the valley. It came from upstream. Tony jumped.

"Crap, a storm. Just what I need, a wet climb. Waterlogged sucks for that."

"That's gunfire. You said checkpoint's down the road. It came from above."

"No way, scientists up there and junk, they didn't even have security."

More gunfire cracked, this time many shots in succession. "Somebody up there's shooting, damn it, Aggie." Another big boom. "That one's down here, shooters all around."

"No problem. We sneak upstream find the path and just slip under. The tram tunnel entrance is under the lip on the far side of the compound, this side and half way up. It's way below the ring. You'll see. We'll be OK." Aggie said it but she didn't believe it.

Sanchez opened his bag as the seaplane's motors faded. He got an M-16 and put it together in the dark. They didn't have a flashlight. Sanchez didn't need one. Aggie heard more than she saw as he geared up. She caught starlight glinting off the handguns resting on each hip as he slung a canvas ammo belt over a shoulder.

"Take the duffel, I'm loaded down." Tony said. "Not going anywhere without it."

"I hate guns." Aggie started walking but he didn't. Sanchez didn't move. She reversed back and took up the duffel. "Whatever. Let's go." They were upstream a hundred yards when shooting started again. "Crap, I hope they aren't shooting at Pedro." Aggie said.

"They can't. Quiet or they'll be on us next. Don't be stupid, aren't any skyward spotlights."

Aggie took the hint and shut up. She didn't even fire the insult that came up on autoload. They moved upstream slow and easy. The water was cold but the humidity was intense. The stream was between tall hills and she was sure it was the same creek she had traveled before. Go too far and they'd reach the observatory's entry road. Maybe the military guys were shooting. There might be civilians storming the telescope. Everything was crazy, no telling what was going on. They turned a bend and lights from above lit the gorge casting weird shadows.

It was where she and Mel had come down from the alien's shuttle exit. A big skull shaped rock was the landmark and dead ahead. It was a hard, uphill climb from there. They needed to get past Skull Rock to reach Ernie's path and the easier way up. That one zig-zagged around and was way less difficult a climb. Aggie itched thinking of when she and Mel had to practically crawl down that thick, jungle slope. They'd use Ernie's path and drop down from above to get the cave.

The moment Aggie walked into the light; bits of a tree exploded above her. She heard the shots after the fact — *bullets are faster than the speed of sound* — scrolled across her mind. She stood there a long moment thinking until Tony pulled her backward into the shadows.

"Doesn't make sense, scientists don't have guns." Aggie said.

"They do now and they aren't the only ones."

Sanchez brought his rifle to bear and Aggie followed where he pointed it. There were people upstream hiding behind trees and rocks. They had guns but were pinned down. She thought she knew one. Dreadlocks and a rainbow Rasta hat poked out of the brush inside a sliver of light.

"One Love, that you?" She called.

"Ya mon, Aggie Piper?"

A barrage of bullets answered One Love's question. Sanchez pressed himself flat against a tree but Aggie stood there until a bullet zipped just above her head like a wasp on rocket juice. She crumpled down.

Tony hissed, "Aggie get back, over here." She crawled backwards. "You know him?"

"Yupper."

"Good, more fire power. Can he shoot?"

"A shot of rum, but that's about it. He likes pot better. I don't know the others."

Aggie knew enough about One Love after their time together to understand he was a nonviolent peacenik just like her hippie parents. One Love was on his way to where Aggie told him to go. But where did the others come from? It had to be Mel.

Mel was supposed to broadcast the escape tunnel locations to the crew people Mother filtered out. But there were at least ten people there. Crew were supposed to come from all around the world. Something wasn't right here.

"This is poop."

Aggie took off running toward One Love. A few shots rained down but not many. Aggie was a fast sprinter and it wasn't far, she practically knocked One Love over. She gripped that tall skinny man in a bear hug and said, "I'm way, way glad to see you! These guys with you?"

One Love explained. "Dez people not for me crew. Moon make invitations. De whole world mon. She tells every phone. She says where transports be. First come first. Limited time. She says time's up last hour." One Love held up his I-know phone.

"So, the buttmunch military's up there?" Aggie pointed.

"Everywhere no here. Military not on de road. Police join us. Dis where de get da guns. Up der be science men shooting."

Aggie checked out the people. Yeah locals from what she saw in bad light. The two cops were old men and half out of uniform.

The paved roadway up to the observatory was a long, twisted drive and last time she was there, only two MPs were at the checkpoint far below. The military guys had apparently bailed. The cops were locals. She heard enough from One Love to trust the others there.

Aggie's eyes were drawn upward seeking who was up there. The moon was in sight cresting the hill and brighter than before, like it was on fire. It wasn't right, it wasn't the moon, it was something else. Things in the sky were worse than ten minutes ago.

"The moon's come apart! We got to get out of here." Aggie said.

"No move from here."

"I'm sick of this crap. Anyone got a pair of size ten sneakers?" One guy translated on the other side of a clearing where people huddled together. The shoes she got from Tony were way too big. A pair of sneakers came flying over. Aggie put them on. "I'm going up. I'll make them stop. You guys follow when I give the OK. If Moon City won't take you, I'll take all of you … Oh and don't shoot, OK."

Word was passed around. Someone shouted it to Tony in Spanish. Sanchez got the message to cover. Aggie exercised a lot before aliens and got back into it while on Mother. Mostly because waiting around was boring. No time for the zig-zagged path. She jumped over the stream and ran straight up grabbing plants and whatever handholds she found. It was a long, sweaty climb and she drove hard. Out of steam near the top she hunkered down under cover to catch her breath.

"Who's there? Don't make me shoot. Back up, get going." A deep voice mixed with squeaks called.

"Aggie Piper, that's who. You back up butthole or I'll bust your face."

"Aggie! Aggie, boy am I glad you're here!

"You know me?"

"It's Ernie!"

"No way!" Aggie burst out of the shrubbery and shot up the last thirty feet. Yeah it was Ernie and he was bigger, taller. His voice had changed. He laid the rifle down and Aggie hugged the crap out of him.

"I didn't shoot at anybody." Ernie cried. "I wasn't trying to hurt them, just scare them."

"What are you guys doing! These people need help." The look on his face … he was scared and confused. He wasn't a killer, not even close. "OK, you didn't hurt them, what's going on?"

"It's Dad, he thinks we'll be overrun by vandals or something. Once the announcement was made … there's riots everywhere and with Brinks dead, and the alien war, and nobody's got control, it's all falling apart."

Ernie kicked at the gun but didn't hit it. It wasn't military, it looked old. "Crap, this is crap, take me to your leader, but first turn off that spotlight."

Ernie complied and took Aggie to his dad. Frank was his name. He was about fifty yards down the rim's path, holding an old revolver that looked like something out of an old cowboy movie. After a fast greeting. She had to ask.

"Where'd you get that?"

"It's Mitchel's, he's our IT man. Mitch collects vintage firearms … who knew so many were here on the island."

The way Frank handled it Aggie was pretty sure he didn't know much about guns. Like his son, Frank was an unlikely warrior. *I can relate.* He held it by the trigger guard with two fingers like it was a smelly, dead fish. No doubt Frank and the other geeks there weren't into shooting folks. People do weird stuff when faced with weirder stuff. Aggie explained what was going on downhill.

"It's a bunch of local people. They aren't here to mess over you. They want off Earth. Some of them were invited by me, but you know the rest. Moon City's taking volunteers." Aggie pointed downhill. Frank's science people were moving toward them. "I'll take them, too, if Moon City won't." She pointed at the group of observatory people. "Come on, help me. We have to go before military shows up for real."

Frank brushed his hair back with one hand. *He's hedging.* Frank was overdue for a haircut and shave. His clothes were dirty. She'd bet he hasn't sleep in two days. He didn't know what he was doing, just reacting and not thinking. It was time somebody gave directions.

"Are you with me?" Aggie said.

"I don't know … The army called, told us to defend … " He spread his hands out. "As the head of the team, it's my responsibility. We, I must protect this place." Frank said. "I have a dozen scientists here. What about the hardware?"

"Reality check." Aggie said. A couple more people had joined the group. More were heading toward them. *That's no way to defend the high ground. Everyone's in one place.*

"This equipment's crap compared to alien stuff. Your people: Army doesn't care. If they knew I was here they'd drop bombs on you just to get me." Aggie took a breath. It was hot as hell but she needed to chill out. "We have to leave, OK. All of us. If you don't want out, fine. Don't stop us. Stay here. We're going. I'm out of time." She pointed at the moon. Moon City wasn't attached at all. "Let my people go, Frank. The military … they're traitors; totally bogus."

"I concede your point. Let me talk with the others." Frank said.

He didn't have to gather them. The rest were already on the walkway. The lights along the path were dim but she saw enough. Aggie didn't wait for Frank's answer.

"Ernie, turn off all the lights, even the walk lights. Keep the decks on." She said. "Tell everyone to come here."

Ernie looked toward his dad. Frank nodded and the boy took off toward the complex. He shut the spots off as he went. With the lights off the message was sent below. Back where she came up, she yelled downhill telling them to come. Tony crested the top first, armed to the teeth. He must have been on his way up. She wasn't about to fight him over the guns weighing him down.

"Tony, you're in charge of transportation, OK. 'The mission, should you decided to take it,' is help them up to the cave." Aggie said. "I'll organize the science people. They'll help you with the older folks. Hurry, OK."

"Are you sure," he said half out of breath. "You aren't shitting me? It's over?"

"I'd never shit my favorite turd."

Tony dropped his ammunitions belt and the long gun, gave her a thumbs up, and started down.

From the telescope's grounds the tram system was fifty yards downhill. Aggie had the science guys set ropes to make it easier going down. She sent a science guy down with a message. He'd help Tony. The cave was a hundred yards from the bottom. It's faster for the older ones to take the zig-zag path. Getting every-one up was a slow process. It took a while. She had Sanchez take a few down to the tram at a time. He reported the first tram car was loaded and away half an hour after the effort started. Aggie had told them what to expect before leaving.

Ernie came running. "Aggie, Aggie, I was in the radio room. Moon City's leaving! Less than an hour."

"We need more than an hour, crap on a cracker." It was taking too long. People were hauling luggage and junk. Too slow. There were twenty more peo-ple. "How we gonna do this?"

"Tram holds six." Tony said. "We could squeeze more in. I only fit four. Too much luggage. There are two bays. One leaves another comes in. Only one runs at a time."

Aggie remembered that from before. "Going back and forth for sure." Aggie said and turned to the group. "Hey forget your junk, leave the luggage! That is, if you want outta here!"

"I'm not leaving this," A science guy said, he had a big suitcase. "Took years to accumulate — "

"Fine stay here," Aggie said. "No luggage! You aren't going. OK so hold back anyone that comes up the road. No shooting! Bullshit them. Whatever, give us time."

These scientists weren't used to dire straits or direct, fast actions but Aggie put fire under them. She had Tony lead them down. One Love stayed at the tram and loaded. The science people that were going helped the older locals.

Before long, a downhill trail was beaten into the mountainside and the last few had a clearer path. Aggie, Frank and Ernie were the last on the hill. All had decided to go in the end but Aggie still hedged. She knew with Moon City leaving, that was the end of this shuttle system forever. Her escape window was very small.

Sanchez crested the lip for the last time covered in sweat and dirt. He ignored the grime. She thought he'd make a good crew member, tough and focused as he was. Her gift to Mother. The guns he had on his waist were gone. That nasty rifle was still laying in the weeds. His duffel bag full of war stuff was downhill. Aggie felt a tinge of relief.

"Aggie," Tony said. "Time for one more and it's nearly packed." He looked up at the moon. It was misshapen like a giant mouse-chewed cheese gone to pieces. "Let's go," he checked his watch. "We're late, that last car out … it didn't come back like before. Only room for three."

A lot of people were going and small trams came and went a bunch of times, but now they were down to one and Aggie knew it was the last. She didn't need a control belt to know that but she touched the overalls tied around her waist as if it had an answer.

"Going home, Aggie?" Ernie asked.

Too many people for the last car. "You guys get going." Aggie said still struggling within about leaving. "You too Sanchez, they need you."

The word home triggered her emotions and she felt tears forming. She wanted her home in Key West back more than anything in the world, but that wasn't possible. She did what she set out to do, get a crew for Mother. OK, maybe not choice, but they were all good people. Not military buttholes types, OK, maybe Sanchez but Mother needed security, right.

"Aren't you going home?" Ernie asked.

The question ripped her guts open. Home was all she wanted. But Earth wasn't home anymore. Ernie knew where her home was and she didn't. *How weird is that?*

"I got something to do first. The radio room is still on, right? I need to make a call, tell my family goodbye and stuff. Buddy's around. He'll link me to Mother. I'm good, I got a ride." Aggie lied. She didn't know if Buddy could find her and what if he did? She can't go anywhere with him. Mother was a million miles away.

"Know how to operate it?" Frank said.

Aggie shook her head no. She saw that room once before, but only at a glance.

"Not hard." Frank said "Main power's on. The CB, shortwave, all bands work the same. Press the power button and squeeze the microphone switch. Talk and you're broadcasting over the big dish. It reaches everywhere. We were trying to contact the aliens and it didn't work."

A jet raced overhead and low just above their heads. Aggie was glad she had the lights off. The jet kicked in afterburners like it was chasing the wind.

"When you guys get there, tell them to send a taxi, OK." She doubted that could happen. Moon City won't wait and Mother wouldn't either. She felt it in her bones. Another jet screamed past but higher this time.

"Go, I'll be right behind you. When you board, the little gray guys are pilots, just robots. You might feel sick, it's pheromones. You'll get used to it. Don't freak, they're harmless." She repeated that message for the last time.

Frank handed her one of the flashlights and they started downhill. The tunnel was rough cut but it wasn't deep into the mountain. The elevator was only fifty feet from the opening and it went straight down to the tram station. They'd make it.

Weird that there were two trams docked. Last time she was there the two bays had only one car. The one she came in on and it took off as soon as they got out of it. Like somebody was behind it. Two cars were waiting this time. Moon City wasn't messing around getting people off Earth.

"They'll be OK." She said as Tony disappeared out of view.

She didn't need to hold anyone's hand. Aggie took the path around the telescope to the residence building. She wondered how long it would be before people stormed the place or one of these jets dropped a bomb. They'd be way too late in either case. She found the communications room pretty fast. It was five minutes until Moon City said it was taking off. Aggie clicked on the radios and pressed both microphones, one in each hand.

"Aggie Piper here. Mel if you hear this, I'm at Ernie's place. You know where Praytis picked us up. Pull Buddy back home ... home. Don't let Mother leave him behind." Outside the window a car's headlights was winding up the twisted access road far below. She glanced at the clock and pressed the microphone. "I just missed my ride." She let go of the microphone. More lights were farther away in the distance. Cop car strobe lights and others.

"The Man or someone worse."

She went out onto the deck of the residence that overlooked the radio telescope dish and some of the access road. Normally the rim's spotlights were aimed at the telescope but now the dish was blacked out. It was a nice night except for the moon falling apart and the humidity. The insects were weirdly quiet. Everything was dark with the lights out. It was peaceful. The meteorites above were intensely pretty.

"Calm before a storm, right."

Looking down the mountain, she could not judge where the road was except for that car's lights. Well one light anyway, the others were farther away and disappeared around the mountain as she watched. That first car had to be a local who missed the party. It only had one headlight. The law didn't care about broken headlights here. Sanchez's old car didn't even have any. It was really hard for him to give up that car.

A moment later there was no light at all. Just a hum in the air and it didn't sound like an insect. The space in front of her above the dish got suddenly darker. No stars were visible and then all was light. She shielded her eyes. A space shuttle door had opened. The gangway came out but she couldn't see. She felt it touch down on the observation deck just beyond where she was.

"You going to stand there all night?" Sanderson said. "It's time we got home."

"You're goddamn right!" Aggie said.

"Took the worlds right out of my mouth." Sanderson said.

Aggie laughed out loud. It wasn't all that funny but she let her steam whistle blow. He helped her over the rail and onto the retractable gangway. She flopped down into her Captain Kirk chair still trying to adjust her eyes. Something bumped her leg and she reached down; it was her little probe.

"Buddy! You made it. I was so worried about you."

"We don't leave our own behind, dead or alive. Get used to it." Sanderson said. "Permission to get the hell out of here before that MAC killer equipped F-16 I've been dodging draws a bead."

"We can't go home yet. I just sent like forty people to the moon. Told you I'd find a crew, right."

"That you did, Captain." Sanderson had a big fat smile on his face. She never seen him do that before. "Ship, you heard her. Best evasive action to the moon. Then we go home."

Aggie heard him think it. She was able to do that only while in the chair. This time she didn't tell the chair to shut off.

"Yeah, let's go home."

Aggie voiced it, and the word "home" sounded good and right in her ears.

FORTY

Last Man Out

The sun was long down. Archer moved into the common space of Sanderson's little brick building. He had Sanderson's laptop open on the main reception desk. He had tracked alien shuttles leaving all day. Not much surprised Archer but the hundreds of alien shuttles hidden on Earth were beyond his imaginings. Sanderson had first-rate tracking satellite access that identified and counted each one. The Joint Chiefs had no idea how deep Sanderson had dug in. This system's capability was a gift from the dead that he will never reveal.

American MACs had chased a handful of alien shuttles but only splashed a few among the hundreds. The TV was on showing electronic snow. It had gone on by itself. Moon City took over the airwaves for the last time thirty minutes ago. Soon she would be gone. TV had nothing more. Nothing about Moon City closing up shop, no network news, no state reaction.

The last alien message was clear. Only Moon's ships in transit will be received. With pieces of the moon flying inbound, he wouldn't take odds on Earth satellites' survival. Maybe Moon City wiped them out. Who knows if she had that intent? Fewer eyes in the sky was a solid defensive action.

A tiny black man burst through the door. Amazing how well he moved wearing that massive backpack. It was Jimmy Brown, a friend of Aggie. He had studied Brown's file due his association with Piper. Brown was smart, only sixteen, emancipated. He graduated from high school with high honors. Archer noted the CIA didn't have a man on him. Why was evident. The agencies were falling apart. Such was typical disorganization after a coup. *Special Ops 101.* America's operatives were experts at disrupting other countries. They didn't take their own medicine very well.

Brown stopped cold when Archer looked up from the desk. "You, you're that Mr. Black! What're you going to do!?"

"Show you the door, what else. I don't kill children. Monsters only." The kid turned for the exit door. "Not that door, the one for a shuttle. Not much time." Archer grabbed the olive drab antique phone and got up. He forgot he brought it out. Brown curled his upper lip at the old phone like it was a snake. "I'm here to help."

"What, you'll help me? After what Mel said about you on the internet?"

Archer shrugged. "This way kid, one thing, tell Aggie you saw me, tell her … here take this." Archer handed Brown the old phone as they walked. "It was Sanderson's. It was important to him … give it to Aggie, a keepsake. You're very late."

"Why I gotta be so damn late all the time?"

"Don't worry kid, you'll make it."

Archer brought Jimmy Brown to the elevator and pressed the tile switch. With Brown away, he waited in the reception room in case the kid didn't make it. He continued to watch the evacuation on Sanderson's laptop. Fewer shuttles were launching worldwide. The last of them flew even as the alien base pulled away from the moon's carcass. Sanderson's link-ups to telescopes were failing as satellites went off line, but signals also came in on hardwire. Sanderson didn't leave any tool unused. The TV still snowed. Of course, nothing was on network TV. Transmissions use satellites.

"Communications blackout. I should have seen that coming."

An hour passed before Archer lost interest in the computer. Moon City, as a parting gift, uploaded Sky-net software into every computer on Earth. Washington killed what was left of Sky-net soon after. Archer didn't need it. Sanderson's wire feeds still worked. Moon City was still visible and was accelerating. A giant starship had first taken flight. There was nothing left to see. Brown wasn't coming back.

"The Navy won't catch them." Archer closed the laptop's lid.

He secured his new office and put away Sanderson's former laptop. Sanderson left quite a set of useful gifts. The man was always stepping ahead. That's how Sanderson got his ninety-year-old daughter out of Bethesda under everyone's noses. *Maybe he's still alive.* Archer put that vain hope away.

He'd honor Sanderson alongside with his father's memory. The best way to do that was to destroy the men who caused America's downfall. They who kill for power and impose false honor deserve dishonorable treatment. On his way to the exit, Longfoot stopped and removed his fedora. He placed it on the reception desk and left.

FORTY-ONE

Aggie Above

Aggie was pretty wiped out before but now with stress draining and taking her adrenaline with it, she felt practically unconscious. *How much sleep did I have the last three days?* A few hours at best. The lull didn't last. No time for a catnap. Alarms went off. Her shuttle began dodging American MACs. Getting to the moon was a bitch.

They weren't out of danger. Aggie rose from her command chair intending to oversee Sanderson. Her body was on its last reserves but her brain wasn't ready to give in.

Sanderson was forward standing behind the bio-bot and directing the ship's movements. The holo screens above were lit, one was setup like a 3-D chess game. Sanderson was mumbling and cursing and waving his hands around like King Kong swatting biplanes. She had never seen him so flustered. Aggie lost balance as their craft shifted hard and she fell back into the command chair. Sanderson turned around.

"Thought you were down for the ten count." The ship lurched again but Sanderson didn't falter.

Antigravity had its limits with humans on board. In the chair, Aggie saw that those enemy pilots were good. They must have trained for crazy maneuvers. Sanderson was a flying ace in WWII, but this wasn't like that. The chair let her feel his doubts.

The ship rocked sideways. "Damnit. Three on us!" Sanderson cried.

MAC killer rocket launched from quad two. The ship AI said inside Aggie's head. Sanderson was really upset now. Aggie forced herself into calm and tried to think it out as her shuttle dove at an island mountaintop. Sanderson was thinking to run between peaks. Two were on their tail, but the one above had a clear shot. Aggie overrode Sanderson's direction.

"Full stop, 100 percent!" Aggie cried.

Her ship stopped and the antigravity didn't catch up, she flew out of her chair but got up quick.

"What are you doing!" Sanderson yelled.

"Thinking like Mr. Spock."

"Goddamn it, Aggie, another incoming."

Yup two rockets were on them. The rockets maneuvered better than the men in the MACs, they didn't have to deal with inertia. The Navy didn't have antigravity but they had three dogs after one.

Aggie took over the pilots. She had them fly right at the nearest Navy MAC. In a flash they were directly in front of it pacing nose to nose going 1500 miles an hour at forty feet distance. The front screen showed the Navy pilot freaking out. His heart rate, sweat glands pumping, everything was in overdrive. They were flying head to head but Aggie's ship was going backwards.

Aggie checked. Both MAC killer missiles were converging. If they hit, they'd kill their own guy. Aggie hedged.

"Stick with it!" Sanderson yelled.

Sanderson caught on and stopped the pilots' reaction. The grays wanted to evade as programed for self-preservation. Aggie felt Sanderson in her head, overriding them. In the back of her mind, in another dimension of the chessboard, she heard the Navy pilot yelling, "abort, abort!" Another Navy man was yelling. "Too late!"

Sanderson's big voice cut through it all. "Down, down, down!"

Aggie felt the surge of gravity and then she was weightless. Her MAC dropped straight down at three times the speed of sound. In her mind she saw the Navy MAC blow up, the second MAC killer was too close, it was caught in the explosion and got toasted. One of the Navy MACs was diving. She had their craft shoot up again. They nearly hit the diving Navy guy as they ascended like a fired bullet.

"What now?"

"Do it again!" This time Aggie had the pilots drop in on top of the Navy guy. They flew directly over him with only a few feet in between. If the Navy guy twitched, they'd wreck. An idea came to her and Sanderson picked it up.

"It'll work, use the tractor, force him into the ground."

But that was too easy. Her AI read the Navy pilot's movements as he made them and was able to keep the shadow going. Aggie debated with herself while the stalemate raced on climbing to fifty thousand feet. Height won't stop the tractor effect. She knew she could take him out, but the peacenik side of her hammered in her heart.

She didn't mind killing the guy that tried to kill her but this wasn't self-defense. That Navy guy flying under her was a wolf caught in a bear trap. He didn't stand a chance. The other MAC followed missiles ready but if he fired, he'd kill his own guy … again.

"Come on Aggie, take him out, goddamn it."

"No," Aggie said. "Give me a channel into his radio."

The AI signaled it was transmitting. "Hey butthead, look here. We're done playing. OK it was fun for a while but here's the thing. If you disarm, I'll let you live, got it?"

"Who's this!"

"Aggie Piper. Look this isn't rocket surgery. If you don't want to die, disarm. Better yet drop your … what's it called?" Sanderson sent the answer. "Ordinance, get rid of them."

Sanderson was working on something with the AI, she felt it in the background. She needed to stall.

"I can't, it's not set up like that. They load and unload manually."

On the screens she saw how scared he was. This guy was about to die. Aggie felt afraid for him. But she also heard in her mind he was lying. The short-range scanners showed it but Sanderson also thought, "bullshit." Aggie wished the long-range scanner were as good; she'd have to work on that later.

"OK, I'm sorry to hear that." Aggie said. "Do you have a family? Is there somewhere we can send flowers? I'm sure your funeral will be nice."

"What the hell! Mayday, mayday, I've lost control."

Sanderson came over the com. "Attention MAC pilots. I've armed your rockets and destroyed your launch command. You have five minutes to land or eject and get the hell out of here before your ship blows. I am now returning your ship's flight controls back over to you. Have a nice day and enjoy the rest of your flight."

The other MAC guy was on radio. "He's right, we're locked out, I'm going down."

They were too high to eject. The Navy MAC tailing turned out and headed down at a steep angle toward the nearest landmass. The MAC below them did the same. Both on course to land in or eject over South America. Aggie felt Sanderson transmit the new disarming info to Moon City. She got that new defense inroad for free.

"Oh wow, you sounded like that old TV show guy, what was it, Twilight Zone, right. I didn't know you had a sense of humor." No doubt about it, Aggie thought. Old Ben Sanderson wasn't who he used to be. She felt different as well.

"I didn't know you were a warrior. I should have known; you nearly jammed a pike into me once. Where'd you get that move? I never would have thought of it. Anyway, well done, good team effort."

Aggie balked at the word "warrior". But she had to face facts. Her life added up to that and more. She was trained by Mark, a real warrior. She didn't feel bad about wrecking that Navy MAC, either. Mom would have lost her mind over it. Mom and Dad came through too, no point killing if you don't have to, right. Dad killed fish because they had to eat but they never took more than what was necessary. Dad never killed a fish just because and she won't either. OK, that rooster that used to wake her up too early deserved it but she never actually hurt it.

"No doubt you have war chops, where'd you get it, video games?" Sanderson never took his attention off the tactical holo.

"Books and movies, you know science fiction and junk like that."

"I'll have to take up the practice. Let's move while we can."

"'Make it so Number One. Sulu take the com.'"

Aggie got up. Sanderson didn't get the Star Trek references but he took her command chair. She was really, really washed out now, all that excitement was enough for a lifetime. Aggie curled up on the sofa and tried to rest but her brain wouldn't shut off. *Good team effort, he said.* The idea of team stuck in her mind. She wasn't good at team work. All the teams she was on, like the swim team, hated her. They should have, she acted like a big buttmunch. *Playing nice with others is the better way.* She closed her eyes.

When they arrived, Sanderson woke her. "I didn't really fall asleep, did I?"

Aggie rolled off the center couch. The hatch was open and the first thing she saw was Praytis outside in a hangar. It wasn't Mother's landing bay; it was the moon. Aggie, dragging ass, exited the shuttle. The spaceport was empty of ships but loaded with people, Earth people.

"Captain, it is good to see you. Are you injured; your appearance is quite disconcerting, I must say?"

"You look nice too, new jumpsuit?" Aggie was still in rags; her shorts were toast. The T-top she wore was more like a small "t". The ship's overalls she had tied around her waist was still in one piece but not much else.

Praytis held up a finger. "Oh, I see, Earth sarcasm, very good." He kneaded his feet like a kid that had to pee. The plastic-steel deck allowed his feet to make that suction sound but she was used to it. Something was eating him.

"OK, what's up?"

"Moon City has requested we accept some of her refugees. She was too efficient about inviting Earth humans. Far more shuttles were operative than anyone knew. She did not think so many would come."

"OK so we got our forty, right. How many extra are we talking about?"

"I overestimated how many crewmembers might arrive here and adding Moon's ... oh dear."

Praytis turned and swept his hand at the crowd milling around. It was more than her shuttle could hold by a long shot. More than all of her shuttles could hold together.

"At last count three hundred, but more shuttles are on the way. Ben shared his idea with Moon City, that of making weapons reprogrammed to malfunction in flight. She has piggyback probes disarming Earth fighters, very clever I must say. With your permission, we should begin loading. Reports say, however, the Americans are having success overcoming Moon's probes. Defense AIs agree, Earth will soon launch an attack that we may not survive."

"More is OK as long as we got room. But we'll never get them over to Mars."

"That's not necessary," Sanderson said. "Mother's docked here. That's our loading tube."

Aggie slapped herself in the head. Had she checked while in the chair she would have known that.

"There is another problem, Captain. Many here simply won't cooperate. I don't understand it. Should we stay much longer, all will be lost. I tried to convey this but they won't hear me. Rather I seem to … what is the phrase … freak them out."

He's the anthropologist and he doesn't get it? These people are in shock and conversing with an alien with four legs isn't helping.

"It's cool. I'll talk to them, lead on."

Praytis turned and flop-footed toward the gathering. Even from a distance people reacted, some backed up others were sick. Maybe new arrivals were still woozy from the robot's pheromones. She didn't know what was what. Aggie walked beside Praytis to show them he's OK.

Shouts and cries of recognition echoed in the chamber as Aggie approached. "It's Aggie Piper!"

"Hang back," she whispered to Praytis. "I'll get them to chill."

Aggie moved in among the people. People shouted questions all at once, many others expressed congratulations while others called out their fears. What a mishmash. Aggie was happy to see Sanchez and One Love in the mix. One Love was tall and his dreadlocks made him bigger so Aggie zeroed in on him. His hair reminded her of Mom but there wasn't time to pine for Sky Flower.

"Hey people!" Aggie yelled. "Everybody quiet, OK." To her surprise they quickly lowered their volume. That never happens. "OK first, crew people, picked by Mother or me, come forward, I need your help." The people re-shuffled their order. Her crew gathered around her. Way more than forty.

"OK, here's the thing. We gotta leave and fast. America's about to drop bombs. No, you can't go back. There are no shuttles going down. This is it." She waited for the murmur to subside. "Moon City doesn't have room for everyone for real. Moon City's leaving soon as we undock. The only options you've got is get on Mother or stay here. Mother's leaving first, that's safer. Tony, tell them in Spanish."

Sanchez relayed the message. One of the older ladies that came up to the observatory crossed herself three times. She reminded Aggie of that grandmother lady on Tony's escape boat.

"We go before we're toast. Tony, One Love, help Praytis. Praytis is in charge. He won't hurt you people, he's vegetarian. He looks weird but he's cool." That was a lie, Praytis likes meat. She never heard of anyone that was afraid of vegetarians.

"You folks that were selected pitch in. This is serious. We really, really have to go. I'm loading my shuttle." She pointed over her shoulder with a thumb. "I'll see you all on the ship. Hurry."

Aggie moved over to Praytis who was waiting outside the group. "It's on you, get them on fast."

"I will do my best."

Praytis with One Love and Tony began moving them toward a loading tube that had descended from above. Mother was tethered to this pod and loomed large through the clear force-ceiling. Aggie also saw the image of Mother docked in her head but didn't recall when it was put there. She got it from the chair, of course, she just wasn't aware of it at the time.

Sanderson called from the gangway. "Let's go. Back inside pronto."

Yeah, the shuttle wasn't going to fit into a loading tube. Her shuttle had to exit the pod to enter Mother. She got in and gave Sanderson command, he took off without hesitation. Aggie watched as Sanderson handled the craft manually. *Where'd that joystick come from?* Slow maneuvers weren't the gray bio-bots best thing. On screen, Mother had grown and was twice the size she was before.

Aggie was glad to be home but she wouldn't feel right until she apologized to Mel. She wasn't sure what she'd say, but she had to say something before Mel took off.

Mel intended to leave and that was just minutes away. He had to go before they left. Aggie didn't want to part on bad terms. She didn't tell the people there was still a way open to go back. Mel wanted out and Aggie was willing to sacrifice one shuttle. She would give Mel that one-way trip.

When Sanderson docked into Mother's cradle with a bump, Aggie's heart skipped a beat.

FORTY-TWO

Leaving S-4

They had pulled over late last night and slept only a few hours before continuing. Sky Flower was wide awake despite inadequate rest. That run in with the police near Roswell had her strung tight. Since then they drove on and on and were miles from nowhere by twilight's call.

When they arrived at the intersection leading into an unnamed airbase yesterday, she and Dad hid and watched the gathering via satellites. Things soon got worse after their exit. A quarter of a million people flooded the desert juxtaposing nothingness. Roads into the military bases were jammed. RVs and cars parked every which way on the highways for miles around. Many vehicles were still crossing the desert on last inspection. Others remained where they were destroyed or broke down.

So small a number of military people couldn't stop the mob although they tried. Bodies lay about the plains like scattered matchsticks. Before the satellites died, the military base was overrun. All this destruction for a rumor.

"Isn't there an alien shuttle terminal in Roswell, is there?" Sky asked her father.

"No. Nearest one's at White Sands. They're barking up the wrong tree. That was good cover for us."

"All that violence for nothing?" Sky was flabbergasted.

"It's not for nothing, it's helping us." Dad said. "I'd like to shake hands with whoever seeded that misinformation. Aliens, my guess."

"It's the dang Boston Tea Party on dry sand." Po-boy said. "It's not for nothing, make no mistake."

Po-boy was right. They just witnessed history and to think she and her family were tied up into it. Yes, history does repeat, it never fails in that and people never see it coming. No one could predict the new American revolution.

Sky and Po-boy had felt the winds of change but she never thought it would happen like this. Through those breezes came a hurricane and Sky's own daughter brought the storm's catalyst. *The government was wise to keep aliens secret.*

Two hundred and sixty miles on and the day had worn away when Dad had Po-boy turn onto an unmarked dirt road at sundown. The only road signs near all said the same thing, "Government property, trespassers will be shot."

Po-boy stopped the bus. Dad insisted he continue and on they drove. They drove past several unmanned checkpoints. Po-boy ran down each gate. Dad's electronic equipment opened holes in the government's surveillance gear. In her lawyer's mind federal infractions mounted. She counted the jail time by the years they deserved upon her interior's abacus. Legal defense strategies came to mind.

After many more slow miles Po-boy rolled up to a sizable gate of the military complex proper. A tall barbed wire topped fence stretched in two directions and out of sight. The mesas in the distance looked near, but were not. She had been fooled before now and had learned that in the desert, distances were deceiving.

Po-boy pulled up to the gate and shut the motor off. "What you thinking Honey Peach?"

"Looks deserted. It doesn't feel right. Maybe we should go back." Sky said. Her interior sense of danger nagged and she gripped the passenger seat armrests harder. Unease was written on Po-boy's face.

"Nobody home," Dad said. "They're dealing with the riots. Further up the line it's guarded, it has to be."

Sky looked down the military road before her and it seemed to go on forever. It wasn't the same as the washboard road that took them this far. Beyond the gate it was paved. The blacktop went on so far it was reduced by distance into a thin ribbon. The sun was well down but the sky was lit by a rising moon.

"Hiding out on an abandoned military outpost, which isn't abandoned, isn't ideal." Sky said.

"We aren't staying," Dad said.

Upon reentering civilization, if what lay ahead could be called civilized, she expected resistance. Aggie preferred facing problems headlong but Sky was of the mind to avoid confrontations. They were trespassers on this lonely, open road.

Dad had played back a message just before arriving. Secure radio reported reinforcing troops shot dead at the main entry into Area 51. That was three hundred miles away, but Dad said this place was part of that same installation. Civilians were still shooting. The base was being overrun. Dad received confirmations. The dead and wounded were more military than civilians. Bad for civilians but the number of military casualties was greater. They were far from the conflict but it wasn't safe here either.

"There's nothing, nothing here." Sky said. "It's too open, we should leave. What about cover?"

"Sittin' ducks, no lie." Po-boy said in agreement.

"There," Dad said. He pointed. Heat waves distorted the view but miles ahead a standalone mesa and mountains beyond wavered on hot, sunset-red air. It could have been a hundred miles or three. "That's the place."

Po-boy got out and went to the gate waving his badge at a camera but the gate didn't open. Dad followed and put his face to the camera. There was no one inside the booth on the other side of the fence. The power lines were intact, the place was operational. The hum of an air conditioning unit came from the guardhouse. The Jeep parked inside the gate wasn't covered in dust. People were recently there and may return. Despite the heat Sky shivered.

Sky slid over and called from the driver's side window. "There's no way in without creating havoc. We better go back."

"No." Dad got back into the RV via the driver's door. He stuck his head out the window and yelled. "Sonny, stand clear. I'm ramming it."

Sky got out and joined Po-boy. Dad backed up. He didn't need much speed. The bus had plenty of mass. The gates fell like ice-pop sticks. He pulled in and parked next to the Jeep. The three went into the guard's shack. Thank Goddess the air worked. The radio was on. It was one of the many that Dad had tapped with his surveillance equipment. The sign on the shed said it was gate fourteen. Nobody on the radio was calling gate fourteen but there was constant radio chatter. Fighters talking to each other frantically. One voice came over clear.

"I don't care. I'm not shooting Americans."

"Get your squad forward traitor!"

"Says you, I'm out, I resign. I didn't sign up for this!"

"Seven come in, come in. He walked!"

Po-boy turned it off. "Seems folks what swore on the Constitution weren't fooling."

Dad raked fingers through his thick hair. He was thinking. An alarm went off but it wasn't the military, it was Moon City. Same attention sound used before. It was broadcast over the military radio and it also came on the camper's AM/FM. As before, the message entered every device.

Attention Earth, Moon City here again. I'm not taking any more shuttles. The next out is the last. I shut down the tram system. Sorry about that. You people really need to learn how not to kill each other. We are departing shortly. And by the way, thanks for all the fish.

Po-boy fell out laughing and slapping his leg. Dad punched the radio cutting a knuckle.

"What's so damn funny?" Dad demanded with a bleeding finger joint in his mouth.

"'Thanks for all the fish', haw, haw, haw. That's Douglass Adams. Doggone aliens got a sense of humor. It's from *Hitchhiker's Guild to the Galaxy*. If that don't beat all."

"Hitchhikers, you guessed it." Dad said sucking his fist. "Her shuttles are off. She'll refuse Earth's ships. Not a problem." Dad winked at her like when she was a child.

"What are you doing? I thought we were going into hiding? You have a place." Sky said. "Oh no, you can't be serious."

"It's a student model that … er … went missing, so to speak. She'll let it in. We aren't finished yet. Get in the Jeep, let's go. Balls out."

They exited the guardhouse in a rush. Sky Flower checked the moon. It was low in the sky. The red of sunset colored it's bottom. It should be full, but it was more like a crescent bowl. A third of it floated free like a sister moon. She nearly fainted at the sight.

"The moon's broken!" She held onto the side of the Jeep to keep balance. "What will happen?" She cried thinking of the harm a degenerated moon will cause Earth.

"What's happening is we steal a stolen spaceship. I have access. There's a dozen parked there." Bradford pointed to the distant cliffs. "Sonny, get her in, buckle up, it's balls to the wall time."

Dad got behind the wheel and they were off like a shot. He explained as he drove, he had been there many times before, he knew the security men there and they knew him. He was the man that had reversed engineered the alien's navigation and control systems for the U.S. Government. As he approached the second gate, ten miles on, they saw this one was guarded. Dad picked up the Jeep's radio microphone.

"Gate four, this is Branford. I got an emergency. I'm coming on, don't shoot!"

Bradford jammed the breaks and slid sideways to a stop before the last gate. Sky expected to see a dozen men with guns but there were only two. One of them, a big uniformed man, came to the Jeep with his hand extended.

"Al, never expected to see you again. I thought they killed you."

"They aren't that lucky, Tom. Anyone around?"

"Just me and O'Conner. They pulled everyone up front, it's a freaking blood bath."

"I saw it." Branford looked up. So did Sky Flower and Po-boy. Moon ejecta were lighting the upper atmosphere. Fire rained down in two different directions. "I'm taking the student model, you guys in?"

"Do aliens shit on the moon?" Tom spoke into his walkie-talkie "O'Conner, get over here."

The other man exited the guard booth, dropped his water bottle in the sand, and the two of them climbed into the Jeep. Sky smelled the fear on them as Bradford raced toward the cliffs. She heard the expression but always thought it was just a saying. Yet, it was real; fear has an odor. Just as real was the fact that the sky was falling. *Chicken Little is vindicated.*

Something big and on fire screamed overhead and crashed in the near distance. The ground shook. Sky focused on her Kegel muscles to avoid wetting herself.

One of the military men pointed a remote at the cliff face as the Jeep skidded to a stop and the mountain opened like a giant garage door. She ran inside with the rest. There was a row of alien crafts parked there. Dad didn't hesitate. He ran straight for the smallest one and stopped at the ramp.

"You people coming or not?"

"Dad, you know how to drive it?"

"I designed it didn't I … Goddamn it. I … I don't know. It's better than dying. I'd bet Moon's aiming rocks at S-4. Thank God her aim's off."

"I got to pee," Po-boy said.

As if in answer another impact shook the mountain. Dirt and rocks fell from the ceiling and bounced off that shiny, little spacecraft. Sky found her feet and ran toward it.

"Goddamn it, Po-boy, just piss over there." Dad pointed to a piece of equipment and went inside.

Her husband went behind that equipment to do his business. O'Conner followed Po-boy. The other military man was right behind her and shed his armor and other gear before entering. It was tight inside. Dad sat at the controls and maneuvered a joystick that was wired into the dashboard with fiberoptic cables. The stick wasn't alien, it came from a computer game.

"Damn it, forgot how to start it." Dad said as another impact shook the ground. "That's it." She felt the craft vibrate. "Where the hell's Po-boy?"

"Where the hell's O'Connor?" Tom said.

"I'm here," O'Connor said from the door with a handgun drawn and a shovel in the other hand. There was blood on the spade. "You aren't going anyplace, hands up!"

"Where's Po-boy!?" Sky cried.

"Knocked out, hands up."

A huge clang rang out. The MP's helmet flew. O'Connor fell face forward hitting the back of Dad's chair hard and face-on. Po-boy stood in the doorway with a crowbar in hand. Sky felt proud and horrified at the same time.

"Nobody keeps me from family, no lie." Po-boy said. Breathing hard he threw the bar down. It crashed on the gangway behind him and bounced away. Blood poured from his head but Po-boy remained steady as a rock. "Help me get this piece'o whale poop off our ride."

Po-boy took one leg, Tom the other and they dragged O'Connor backwards and off the ship. They rolled him off the side of the gangplank like a sack of beans and quickly got back inside. Dad pressed a control and the door shut. The biggest shock Sky suffered yet was her husband's violent action and lack of remorse. *Dad's right, it's us or them.* Sky felt her nonviolence standards melt into cold reality as the ship lifted off.

"Now we're cooking," Dad said. "Here we go, hold on."

Screens lit and appeared in thin air like a sci-fi movie trick. Dad got it to hover on station. One air-screen showed the ship floating but wobbling badly. He had a hard time finessing the controls. *Didn't the military shoot this one down, does he even know if it can make it? Will it hold air? Are Earth fighters near?* It took some doing but he managed to get it outside the hangar without damage.

Dad pushed the joystick and the ship accelerated into the clouds. Sky Flower prayed to every Earth Goddess she ever knew. A regular computer screen was wired into the alien craft and was pointed at outer space. There a smooth, moon-like body appeared dead ahead. Seconds rolled by like hours but they made it into the upper atmosphere.

"We didn't die." Sky whispered.

Everyone was quiet as Dad struggled to fly for the moon while dodging debris. Each one was tense and focused except Po-boy who couldn't stop laughing.

FORTY-THREE

Aggie in Control

Aggie didn't have time to fart around. She stormed onto the bridge and straight into her Captain Kirk chair with Ben on her heels. She wasn't acting like a captain before and everyone knew it but it was time to step up.

"Hey, chair engage." Nothing happened. "Come on, wake up already."

She felt it kick on. Mother didn't have direct access into her thoughts. The chair was a buffer. That's what Aggie thought the belt was really for: Mother's conduit into Aggie's deeper self and not the other way around. *That's a big fat intrusion.*

She had a minute to think while people boarded. The first time she took the chair she became one with the ship. It was exciting and weirdly exhilarating and scary all in one. Afterwards, once she thought about it, she wasn't OK with it. Since then, over time the more she thought about letting spaceship Mother inside her head the less she liked it.

"But it's necessary." Aggie whispered. *It's for survival.*

She was a low-tech girl. Old stuff was cool. Like the outfit she wore to the Winter Dance that now seems like years ago. *OK, maybe I'm not ready.* Still, like it or not, she was the captain and responsible thus obligated to use whatever tools were necessary.

"Chair full access. Mel, what's going on with Earth?" Aggie asked that question a million times in her two weeks orbiting Mars. Holo screens popped up in response. The chair said it was all there, but it was way too much information.

"You'd know," Ben said stealing into his station, "If you'd put the belt on. Oh damn."

"Daddy, don't curse," Sarah said looking up from her coloring book as if nothing was happening.

"You're right, Honey, I'll try and remember that." Sanderson was into his security station screens doing whatever it was he did. More holos materialized around him.

Aggie's mind shifted into overdrive. Sarah's info streamed in on the thought. She was the physical age of four when Aggie left for the moon. Now Sanderson's daughter was six. Near death and too sick for a quick fix, Sarah was made young to regrow unredeemable body parts. Like Mother did to save Ben's life. She'll get adult memories back when her body's bigger. All this and more came to mind like a lightning flash. Aggie shivered. *No way, not letting Mother control my memories like that.* A machine deciding when you can know your stuff. No way.

"Crews on, we're detaching." Mel said.

Aggie saw it on the relative positioning holo screen. The chair helped her zero in on the right one. A giant cigar moved away from a ball surrounded by bubbles. Mother's thrusters pushed away from Moon City slowly. Aggie's long starship teetered in and out as thrusters worked to balance detachment. Aggie felt Mother's nervousness. *One wrong move and we'll bash our hull.* Two minutes ticked by before Mother cut thrusters reaching a buffer of ten miles apart. Mother fired her big motors.

Ben called out "Earthside MACs incoming. Tactical says the lead two are Moon's hardware and targeting us. Why skip Moon? Is it a weapon? I got no readings. Navy is chasing. These assholes really want your head, Aggie. If you're going back, you better do it now."

Ben checked another screen. "Security AI says Navy has a new workaround. Moon's long distant scanners blocked. Navy got a tactical AI. What a shit storm."

"What if the Navy is pretending to chase them, yeah, makes them look like good guys." Mel said.

"What's our long-range scan say ... about the incoming?" Aggie asked. She didn't have time to look at every screen. The chair was set too high, she couldn't keep up.

"Three to five people onboard, no robot pilot." Mel replied. "Human people. One's a shuttle with one passenger ... I don't understand the other. It's not Navy, it's not a shuttle, but it's after us."

Sanderson put his hand to an ear. "It's one of the ships the NRO shot down. Branford used it for tests. I know that ship."

"Do you trust it?" Aggie said.

"Hell no."

Aggie heard via the control chair the non-vocalized instructions Sanderson sent to the security AI. He armed the solid projectile cannon Mother made while Aggie was away. She had a vision of the projectiles, huge iron balls bigger than Buddy. The cannon was more powerful than a railgun. Sanderson was aimed and counting down to fire. He didn't say he was doing it, he just reacted.

"No, stop," Aggie said. "It's out real far, we'll outrun it. Don't kill them."

"What if they have a nuke, range doesn't matter!" Sanderson snapped. "We're too close."

Aggie was about to go with Sanderson's logic but a deeper thought came. First, scan for a bomb. *Can any bomb even penetrate force skin?* In a flash she understood Ben's first answer will always be reactionary. He's a hammer no matter the nail. She needed to temper him. Teams were a balance. Aggie opened her mouth but Mel raised his hand.

"Moon's tractor beams," Mel said, "shooting rocks at the Navy but not the others. I don't get it."

"That won't hold long. Come on Praytis." Sanderson was waiting to hear that crew was secured.

"Wow, you actually did what I want, that's novel." Aggie knew via the chair that he stopped the projectile launch.

Was the ship overriding him on her word? But Ben was right, this is dangerous. Logically, shoot first was the way to go but Aggie felt something wasn't right. Like Mom always did, Aggie errored on the side of life. She slapped her forehead. Maybe that was a bad idea.

"Moon City is tractor-pulling the first shuttle in." Mel said. "The one from her system. One passenger."

"Ags, crank the chair up, talk with Mother." Ben said. "Main engines ready. We got to skedaddle pronto. More Navy's coming. Whoever's going back, now's the time."

"I got it already!" Aggie said. "Told Mother to ready the escape shuttle."

"If you're leaving do it!" Ben cried.

Mel turned from the com desk and said, "He's right, get going."

"It's for you, dumbass." Aggie said to Mel. "I'm staying."

"You're staying? I'm staying." Mel said.

"Fine, fine, now shut up we got work to do." Sanderson yelled.

Ben's old job as a kickass admiral was all over his voice. Aggie and Mel got busy. There was stuff to do. They had to wait until they were at a safe distance from Moon before Mother's main engine could engage, and there were a lot of little details that Mother missed that needed attention before exiting. One was an info-dump exchange that Mel was handling. Mother and Moon were swapping parting downloads.

"Dude this is gonna take years to review." Mel said about the download.

Mel wanted to go back home, right? What changed? Maybe the ship knew, but Mel didn't say. There wasn't time for conversations. *I can't fault Mel.* It was still a big surprise. But Aggie was glad.

She needed Mel's technical support and a lot more. Mel was the resident computer wizard. How he electronically covered up his absence on Earth was pure genius. Nobody knew Mel wasn't on Earth. *That'll drive the butthead military guys bug-nuts. Nobody ran computers like Mel.* But still she had to admit, Aggie's need wasn't practical only.

Mel dressed like an office wonk. She missed Mel's old clothes. No more black, heavy metal T-shirts and giant pants. Getting used to Admiral Ben Sanderson as a young, long-haired man, who was on Aggie's side, was challenging. Mel in a boy haircut, brown slacks and striped button-down shirt was harder. *You can't even tell Mel has boobs.*

"OK, Praytis is good." Mel said. "Hold on for acceleration. Cool, Moon City's tractor has the other MAC. Dude, we're safe."

"Where's Praytis?" Aggie said.

"Hydroponics. On his way to residence quarters with a group. You'd know if you weren't so thick headed." Ben said. "What're you going to do with sixty crew members running around and three hundred civilians? How the hell you going to keep track? Aggie, wear the goddamn control belt. Jesus!"

"Daddy, you cursed!"

"Sorry, Honey."

"Mother's far enough away." Mel reported. "She's hauling ass outbound, full power any second."

"I wonder who made it to the moon. I bet Mark … do we have — "

"The belt, Aggie." Ben said.

Aggie bolted upright. "I promised Mother I'd never wear a control belt. She's a free being, right, am I right? She's not a dog on a leash. I promised!"

"Dog! Can we get a dog?" Sarah said, holding up the picture of the Saint Bernard she was coloring.

"That's not the point." Ben said sharply. "Tell her Mel. Acceleration. Here we go."

The entire ship started vibrating. Aggie ignored it.

"Dude, it's not like that." Mel said. "Belt isn't a shock collar. That dick Karnack modified one to make Mother do what she didn't like, but that is not this. Mother's mind is so big it's in parts and ya got to give it direction. Subroutines need basic commands so the whole can work as a unit, yeah. Like a team, see? Mother allows it, more she needs it, needs someone to tell her what to do, understand?"

"That's bull." Aggie said retaking her chair. It was hard to stand with vibrations making her feet tingle. "That's forced labor, like convicts working a chaingang, they got no choice. Mother can decide her own stuff."

Sanderson came over with something in his hand. A thin, silver belt.

"What's that?"

"Your belt, you'll need it. Me and Mel can't do everything and Praytis is tits on a bull when it comes to command issues. That guy is a four-legged indecision machine. Grow up, put the belt on," Ben said.

She checked the positioning holo, Mother was well clear of the moon and still accelerating. "OK fine, give it. Mother, back off, I'll get used to it later. Just the basics, OK." Aggie stood and unwrapped the ship's coveralls that were still around her waist after three days. She put the belt on over her ratty cutoff shorts without threading belt loops. She only had one left anyway. Nothing happed.

Ben was wired. He opened and shut doors on the thought. His control belt was made of ordinary brown leather. It fit right in with his jeans and flannel shirt. Why'd Mother make a silver one for her? Aggie didn't like belts. She wore sundresses all the time. Sundress and a belt? Really, that looks stupid.

Mel didn't have one. The com station didn't need one or was it because Mel wasn't officially permanent yet. Everyone was tired of Aggie's stupid questions and they were still in survival mode, but Aggie asked anyway. It was too late but she had to know.

"Mel, got anything on my parents, what about Mark?"

Mel didn't respond. He had three computer screens going. He could have used holographic screens which floated on air, but Mel loved solid hardware. Mother made everything user friendly. Even Sarah's coloring books were made to order. The database had copies of everything ever printed on Earth. Praytis said such info was a commodity for trade.

"Hello, Mel anybody home?" Aggie called more forcefully. "What's happening with that?"

"Dude, you're getting butch, don't have to yell. You got space nits in your V-jay or what? Not on the roster, OK. Moon or ours … it's incomplete. Moon has a lot of people not registered yet."

"Incoming." Ben said. "One heading for the moon. Navy MACs. Moon's accelerating too slow."

"Not Navy," Mel said. "Moon's shuttle, not ours. Latecomers."

"Moon City got it on tractor. She's accelerating," Ben called. "Moon's pulling them inside. That was close. Whoever they were, Moon's got them."

"What if the Navy sends more fighters, we're a neon light?" Aggie said looking at the outside screen.

Mother's hull was glowing like Moon did over the last few days. The answer was reported inside her mind. The Navy didn't have anything close enough to catch them before achieving greater velocity. Sanderson's cannon was on standby and operational. Mother could send projectiles at crazy speed but didn't need to. She had a hold full of iron balls. Sanderson's modified anti-impact device was for repelling space junk but he made it into a weapon. Thankfully, they didn't need it. Aggie felt in her bones: Mother didn't like it either. *We both hate guns, go figure.*

"So, do you think one of the late ones might be … maybe my parents?" Aggie said.

Mel rolled eyes. Yeah, Mel's tired of her endless questions. An idea came to mind. *We are finally safe.* She almost collapsed from the release of tension.

"I don't know." Mel said. "Moon and us aren't going the same way, we won't get her final roster before we jump … wait … that last one. Got something on scanners.

"I wonder who it is?" Aggie said hoping in the back of her mind it was family. "Hey, were out of range, call. Navy can't get us now."

"Good point." Mel said. He dialed up the craft in transit and struggled to get a fix. Under acceleration tight beam was tricky. "Can't get audio, here comes a picture." A grainy image came up on a display and quickly lost. Mel captured the picture. "I don't believe it, it's Jimmy Brown."

If Jimmy made it my parents must have, Jimmy's always late.

"Stop the presses, we have to go back, it's Jimmy!" Aggie cried.

The deck lit. A hologram appeared; it was a woman dressed like a Greek war goddess. *It's the AI Sanderson communes with.* Sanderson talked to it all the time. Aggie didn't know how he and the ship worked together until that moment. Everyone saw it even Sarah. Impressed into her, Aggie knew this was rare. It was a real time manifestation of Mother's full attention on her human counterparts. Mother didn't pull herself into one entity unless she had something important to say. Aggie felt humbled.

It said. "No Aggie Piper, we are not safe. We cannot go back. Moreover, the universe is not safe from Earth. The genetic virus that activates the sociopath gene remains. Earth will venture forth and cause harm to others. If she survives this childhood. The GTO failed to understand or arrest Earth's disease. There is a cure, a protection. I cannot send it. You must decide for Earth."

Inside her, Aggie was flooded with a river of information. But she saw a path just under the surface, she followed and moved around things that did not matter. There it was. Inhumanity worked into the genetics of everyone. It gave Earth innovation and light and intelligence but also evil. A small number of people were ruled by it and as a result they ruled. The worst of humankind were perpetually in control. If it continued Earth cannot survive. Earth will destroy itself like Praytis' world and countless others did. Earth will suffer that end unless a paradigm shift occurs. A universal change was required. Aggie had sparked that change and the process began. *Should I finish it?* Mother will not play god. Starships won't control sentient beings. Aggie's biggest fear washed away. But a new one came and she had to decide. Earth hung in the balance.

All that and more happened in a flash. Aggie went on a trip of a million years and came back in an instant.

"What do I need to do?"

The goddess answered. "Send the entity." And Mother's image was gone.

Aggie knew what it was. Mel had taken it from the surface of Phobos. It was the seed of a billion-year-old intelligence. How could it save Earth? She didn't know but it was a hope. She saw it true. But there was a problem. As seconds ticked by, they traveled an incredible distance. Too far out for a shuttle to fly inbound and return. Magnetic fields were weak and getting weaker by the millisecond. Once away from planetary bodies, magnetic drive ships can't work. At this rate of acceleration there was no time. A small probe was the only way. A one-way trip.

"Mel, ask Buddy to the bridge."

"Are you sure?"

"No, but I'm doing it anyway. He's the best we have."

Buddy rolled onto the bridge and did his happy dog dance for Aggie. Mel got up from the com desk. He wore a control belt. *I should have known.* Mel hooked Buddy up to a black case with a wire and uploaded. It didn't take long.

"Ben, you're sure Buddy fits the air cannon?" Aggie said. "It won't hurt him, will it?"

"He'll be fine. I'll walk him down and see him off myself." Ben took Buddy and left the bridge with Sarah trailing.

"I need a shower," Aggie said after a few minutes passed and Buddy had launched. The last drops of her adrenalin were spent.

"Me too," Mel said. "Mind if I join you?"

"I hoped you'd ask. Come on, we'll talk in the shower. Let's make up, OK?"

"You're the Captain."

Aggie and Mel left the bridge together. They walked to Aggie's apartment quietly, each with their own thoughts. *Crew shouldn't fight. We have to work together. We need each other.* Aggie was thinking practical but there was more to it. Mel changing gender was unexpected but he was the same person inside. It's not that weird compared to all the other weirdness passed and more ahead yet to be discovered. Right then all Aggie wanted was to discover a way back into the friendship she almost rejected. This wasn't just a friend with benefits thing, it was more and it wasn't ending. Aggie felt it was expanding.

They got into the shower together. For once Mel didn't cover up. They tried to avoid it but they embraced anyway. Inside Mel's kiss was a whole new universe that Aggie was ready to explore.

FORTY-FOUR

Shanghaied

All hell broke loose last night and there was nothing Jon could do about it. He stood there in the compound drinking beer, waiting for his assignment while Navy MACs raced around and that big spaceship parked in the marina he heard tell of, up and took off like a spurred bull.

Sanderson did him right and wrong at the same time. When Jon went to the CO with his "found letter" the commander reactivated him. The CO didn't know Jon was holed up at the jail complex. Hell, he didn't know a cream pie from a cow pie. But what the CO did know was, he was short on bodies. Jon was passed his hitch and he might have re-upped on principle, for America, but the CO didn't give him no option. There was that dang standing stop loss order. Jon couldn't leave if he wanted. He was fixin' to have a little vacation; he had enough time in for it.

He rolled all last night thinking about it, felt like a caged badger. Sanchez, like a lot of others, went AWOL. People said the Navy was in on the coup. The damn military was taking over the government and that was about all he could stand. *Should have gone with Aggie.* He was trying to figure a way off the island. Wasn't going to let the Navy Shanghai him no how.

Dog tired, and half drunk, he crashed on the dayroom's couch early afternoon. He didn't have but a few hours hard rest when woken out of a fitful sleep.

Gunfire rattled him off the couch. He ran to the window. A man all blue strode toward him, skin, clothes everything was blue. Smith at the gate was drilling fire into him but rounds just up and bounced off. Ricochets kicking dust was the proof. The blue man didn't flinch marching for the Officer's Club. Smith emptied his clip, dropped the gun and ran off. He didn't get far. Smith bounced off something and went down. Jon backed away from the window.

"I gotta git outta here."

He had one leg in his jeans when the blue man busted the door in.

"Where is Aggie Piper, Earthman? Which way did she go?"

"What, what y'all want?!" Jon spit out.

Blue man spoke into a small device on his wrist. "Andy, you sure this is the one?"

"Ask his name," a voice replied over the device, sounded British. "Said she was coming here for Colbert."

"Who are you?"

"I'm not giving you squat — "

The blue man pointed a thing what looked like an electric razor at Jon and he plumb froze. He balanced there like a one-legged statue. He couldn't move. The blue man took Jon's wallet out of the jeans he was trying to put on and checked the license.

"It's him. He's the one Piper was after. She's not here. Bio-scan reads she left days ago. She's gone."

"We should have given her a tracker. I can't believe — Bloody hell, get back here."

"What about the contract? Without Piper we're in breach."

"Oh Christ … wait … take him. Piper's looking for him. She bought a round trip. We bring him up instead. That satisfies the agreement — "

"What about Moon City?"

"Get back here or Moon won't matter. She's lifting off!"

"Roger! Coming now."

The blue man pointed his handheld device at Jon again and held it there. Jon floated off the floor. Blue had a problem getting Jon out the door. He was bent over. The man rotated him so his face was upward. Jon faced the sky but straining at the bottom of his eyelids he saw what was directly in front.

The moon was split apart worse than yesterday. Dead ahead a spaceship blinked into existence. Two guys were at the gangway's door. A short fat white man and a tall skinny black man came down the ramp.

Jon was hustled up the gangplank and leaned against a wall like a piece of barn siding. The cabin was small. Just enough room for three people and a robot pilot. Jon in this weird position took up too much space and the black man had to straddle over him. Blue took the driver's seat. The moment the gangway closed the saucer took off.

"Goddamn it Blue," the white man said, "She's accelerating. Navy's closing."

"Full power, best direct course." The black man said. "Shoot for Piper's boat first."

Jon could not follow what all was said or what all they did, but the aliens got past the Navy and followed in Moon City's wake. They mighta tried for Aggie's ship but it was too far along, one of them said. Once free of pursuit they seemed to relax.

Jon was a lot of things but relaxed wasn't one of them. He was fit to be tied. Given how much space was there, he didn't have any way to fight them. No point starting up and getting them and himself killed.

"ETA?"

Blue put a hand on his ear. "We dock before jump. Two hours. She'll wait. We're too far out for Earth ships."

Jon didn't see a lot. The guy named Andy mostly had his ass in Jon's face. Jon knew about holo screens and such and his curiosity got the better of him. He wanted to see what was happening. He gave it a try and spoke.

"Y'all might want to unfreeze me." Jon was surprised to hear himself talk. "I won't be no trouble."

"Right, of course." Andy said. "Sorry mate. I was a bit preoccupied."

Jon was used to being on hold at Gitmo. He wasn't locked in although he was a prisoner. This wasn't no different. Andy pointed that thing what looked like an old electric razor and he was free. It took some unscrambling to get settled onto the central bench seat.

"Y'all don't mind a question? Does prisoners have rights. Just sayin' I need food is all. Before y'll hand me over … I can't wait that long."

Andy laughed. "No mate, you aren't that, just another refugee."

"Thought you was taking me to Aggie?"

Did he hear right, wasn't the blue man set on getting him to Aggie? Hand him over to Aggie was what Jon understood and he was thinking he didn't mind. The three looked at each other. Blue put a cupped hand to his ear. These three was passing notes, Jon figured. Some kind of internal com system betwixt them.

"Sorry Gov, Starline Mother's gone. Andy said. "She's pushed off; we'll never catch her. Don't worry mate sooner or later we'll cross paths, yeah … Seems there are refugees named Piper in Moon City."

"We aren't chasing Mother, not possible." The fat white man said.

"What'll I do between then and now?" Jon asked. "Can't you call them?"

"No, too late. Mother jumped. She can't receive. Once we settle accounts, if Moon doesn't have a job for you, we do need another with us." Blue said. "Know anything about cows at all?"

"Besides they taste darn good? Not much." Jon lied.

The three aliens cringed. The pilot turned and blinked its big black eyes. It was like asking PETA activists how they liked their cats cooked. Jon zipped his lips. No sense in giving away anything. He started out life on Daddy's ranch, learned to fly to get off it, never expected to wind up herding cows again. But then again, life on the ranch was just fine.

They say you can't go home again, but wasn't home where you hung your hat? The phrase "space cowboy," what Melisa called him once, ran through his mind and, somehow, it fit just fine. Jon kicked back and lowered his cowboy hat over his eyes. He didn't remember putting it on, hell, he must have slept with his hat on, but no matter how it got there, there it was. *And here I am.* Jon considered his hat a good omen.

POSTSCRIPT

Starship Mother had come to the Ishtar quadrant for an off-business side venture. Mother and most of the crew were not happy about it. There was no profit in it. Captain Piper's habit of tracking down old Earth refugees was getting old. If the crew knew who she was looking for they'd flip. *Get over it, Aggie, your parents must have died a thousand years ago.* Earth people had spread far and wide in known space but they were still a tiny minority. Former Earth people were locatable, the ones living in AI colonies at least. The mixed alien settlement below was a rouge state rarity. No central AI keeping the peace.

Many Earth settlements were clannish like this one. Mother's people were so far removed from Earth, few of those spaceborne gave a hoot about that old degenerate planet. Sarah felt the same. This wasn't a good place to stop, the facilities were primitive as was the planet's flora, and without a city AI, trade was too much a rigmarole. It wasn't worth spending one's off-ship R&R allotment there either. At least the air was good. The planet below was named after the legendary pirate Jon Colbert like so many others. Maybe that's why Aggie decided to drop in.

Sarah Sanderson, this year's first mate, was on the bridge when her father called. Ben had gone out seeking contracts, and was many light years away. Quantum communicators made the distance irrelevant.

I wish we could travel that fast. It will take weeks to get there.

"Sarah, glad you're on deck," Ben Sanderson said. His image appeared on holo. *He'll need another regen soon.* "Me and Praytis set up the deal of a lifetime. Problem is you have to get here pronto, best speed. They won't wait long."

Mel turned from his station. "I have the data. We need to lift out within twenty-four hours or we'll miss the boat. I'm recalling planetside crew."

"Yes, please do," Sarah said. She checked the away roster and eleven of the twelve affirmed the recall. "One's not responding, who is it? I can't find him or her."

"Who do you think?" Mel said. He spun his chair and pointed at the command seat with his goatee.

Aggie's belt was left there. "Oh no, not again. We'll never find her in time. How we going to do this?"

"It's a big settlement." Mel said. "Have the search party check the bars first. Ship's scanners can't pick her out of that biomass. Too many Earth people, besides."

He was right. The planet was covered with huge flowering plants. Flowering vines crawled up the walls of the city's force enclosure and were interfering with non-quantum sensors.

"That'll take too long. Wait, I've got it." Sarah pressed the ship's com device on her chair. It was one of the throwbacks Aggie instigated. "To make this feel more human," so she says. "Argolis, find Buddy and meet me at Bay Two." She released the button. "Mel, I'll be back in two hours. Order all hands to make ready for departure."

Mel sent the all hands call and Sarah's belt picked it up before she reached the bridge's door.

Sarah landed in the only spaceport and she was surprised to see so many local MACs. Then again, they do mine the moons for minerals. The second the hatch opened Buddy took off. Argolis tried to stop him but Buddy eluded expertly. Argolis was a strapping athletic young man, athletic much like his mother, and on his first life cycle. Youth doesn't think fast. Buddy was quicker.

"It's fine, Argo, he has a collar. Come, let us proceed."

Argolis slapped himself in the forehead. "Duh OK I'm an idiot."

They walked the city far behind Buddy. There wasn't much to see. It was like most non-AI towns, that is to say a dirty mess. The streets were made of local cements with a pink hue as were most of the stucco buildings. Dwellings were low and smooth and the tallest buildings only six stories. Metals were costly here and little used. There was trash in the streets, mostly paper. On a world where plants dominated paper was common while plastics were not. She was amazed they extracted sufficient plant based LF to run town systems and manufacture paper as well.

Sarah picked up a piece of trash. It was a handbill for a rock concert written in English. It said, Grateful Dead cover band, whatever that was. *That's unusual.* She expected German or Chinese. *Maybe Aggie was on to something here.* In the distance Buddy entered a bar. It was one of the few with a neon light. *Is it Earth vintage?* There was a large nonhuman population here but where there are sluggos, there is neon. They love it.

Sarah and Argo entered. It was dark inside and Buddy being black was hard to find. The room was fairly large and crowded with a lot of people. Earth types and otherwise were drinking. When her eyes adjusted Sarah noticed the blue man at the window table. *Their kind is always ready for a quick exit.* She wished Aggie would adopt that practice.

"Biddy you'ol buddy, buddy. Hahahahah."

Sarah and Argolis found her in the corner with a standing lamp behind her. Buddy's big Labrador's tongue was licking Aggie's face. Aggie's hanging jowls lifted and flopped down with each big slurp.

"Thash my ol biddy boo boo hahahahahah."

Argo pulled an injector out of his medical kit. "Mom's pretty drunk."

"Hold on," Sarah said. Aggie was way past due for regen. She said she wanted to grow old and die. Sarah knew what that was like. In regen Sarah had Mother keep her memories of when she was that old and she reinstalled them each time. It was horrible but she wanted to remember what not to do. But Aggie was stubborn about it. She liked old age. Didn't want to deal with hormones and the other youth related problems.

"I'm first mate, isn't that so?" Sarah said.

"So, what's the big deal?" Argo looked confused.

"The Captain's incapacitated and I have command."

"This'll sober her up," Argolis held up the injector. "She'll never make it to the shuttle on her own two feet in that condition."

"That's exactly right. Have Mother send a medical chair."

"What, why, how's that make sense?" Argo fumbled with his radio. It was an award device.

Sarah activated her radio. It was the only way they could contact Mother from there. "Medical, prep a tank for regen. Aggie's going in."

"Oh Jesus, she's not going to like it. When she comes out, holy crap."

"That's fine. I'm acting captain. I'll take responsibility. In my judgment her condition threatens ship's safety." Sarah winked at Argo.

"You got brass ones." Argo said as he finally figured out how to turn the walkie-talkie's power on.

After the call Argo traded injectors and jabbed Aggie with a medical stasis pen knocking her out. A few minutes later a medical chair arrived with Dr. One Love. Aggie was loaded and they made it back to ship with time to spare. Launch window was open and they left immediately. By the time Aggie was out of regen, they'd be long away. Goddess knows they need the money.

With the ship underway, Sarah handed bridge duty over to a pair of sluggos, Jerry and Phil. She never could tell which was which between them. She then retired to her favorite watering hole for a well deserved drink. She was going to have a big headache when Aggie came out of regeneration so why not compound two headaches into one?

****

Back at the bar, the Earth woman owner sat in her office smoking a joint. The barroom was on screen, she was checking to make sure no one welshed. This wasn't an AI town, people had to pay. Somebody just paid the tab for table nine and with a big tip. Sky Flower was surprised. That old lady was drunk as a skunk. She had hoped to suck more LF out of that one before she stumbled out the door.

"What's doing Honey Peach?" Po-boy said, entering the office. People in uniforms were loading the drunk lady into a medical chair on the barroom's screen.

"Look at that, must be starship's leaving." Sky said.

"Doggone, Jon was hoping to buy some cows off 'em." Po-boy said.

"You mean steal."

Po-boy laughed and wandered off to go find Colbert to tell him the raid was off. Sky Flower leaned back in her chair. She wasn't worried. Sooner or later another one would come by. Cows didn't grow on trees, everything else's on Colbert's World did, but at least they now had feed developed from the local flora that cows can eat. *Thanks starship whoever you are.*

With luck maybe the Ishtar ship will sell a few cows so they didn't have to rustle them. The pot they got from that departing starship was pretty good anyway. Trade wasn't a total loss. Nice to smoke something different for a change. Sky Flower snuffed out the joint, thinking she never did get the name of that starship. Checking the pot's package, the label read, "Mother's Finest." No clues there.

"Boy, that's cliché."

Sky tossed the wrapper aside and went about her usual business.

THE END.

ACKNOWLEDGEMENTS

Many people went into making this fictional series. I'd like to thank my beta readers, Lisa Cross, Thornton Blease, James Gallahan, and Emily Thompson (No relations to me). Thank you Gayle F. Hendricks my formatting and book design guru. Thank you, Pattie Giordani, for your excellent proofreading and line editing. My thanks go to the many writers I've associated with over the years especially the Greater Lehigh Valley Writers Group (GLVWG.org). Many unnamed here have gifted me with constructive criticism and supportive encouragement. Dear to me is Angel Ackerman a longtime friend, mentor, and editor on many of my early writing projects. She taught me much. My greatest thanks are for Lisa Cross, my partner in life, who tolerates my writer's life and is instrumental as a story critic and proofreader. Without Lisa's support, I could not write.

ABOUT THE AUTHOR

Rachel Thompson, writing as R.C. Thom, began her writing career after surviving a devastating motorcycle accident in 2003. She has since published nonfiction pieces in newspapers and magazines, a handful of short stories and political cartoons. *Soul Harvest* is the first book of this series. The sequel and second book, *Aggie in Orbit*, is also available along with her anthology, *Stalking Kilgore Trout*, and the novel, *Dragon Fire. Book of Answers* is due for release later this year.

www.ingramcontent.com/pod-product-compliance
Lightning Source LLC
Chambersburg PA
CBHW071518110726
47908CB00003B/874